T0090288

The Incense Coast
Piracy—Around the Horn of Africa

A Novel by Brooks Tenney

Order this book online at www.trafford.com
or email orders@trafford.com

Most Trafford titles are also available at major online book retailers.

Printed in the United States of America.

ISBN: 978-1-4269-3823-8 (sc)
ISBN: 978-1-4269-3824-5 (dj)
ISBN: 978-1-4269-3822-1 (e)

Library of Congress Control Number: 2010910904

*Our mission is to efficiently provide the world's finest, most comprehensive book publishing
service, enabling every author to experience success. To find out how to publish your book,
your way, and have it available worldwide, visit us online at www.trafford.com*

Trafford rev. 8/09/2010

 www.trafford.com

North America & international
toll-free: 1 888 232 4444 (USA & Canada)
phone: 250 383 6864 ♦ fax: 812 355 4082

THE INCENSE COAST

Also by Brooks Tenney

Killing Mauritius (A Novel about Terrorism)
New Silk Road (A Novel of Central Asia)
The Ten Thousand Things (Adventures and Misadventures on China's
Silk Road)

Note To Readers

On a wall of the sun room off my kitchen, an old Red Sea maritime chart, Hydrographic Office No. 3627, is captioned *Plans in the Red Sea*. It shows details of Mersa Fijab, Mersa Wi Ai, Mersa Darur, and Suakin Harbor. This latter one, the twisted channel to the old slaving port of Suakin, has captured my imagination for years. The chart came from my son, a merchant ship's officer for his working life.

It's easy to dream about sailing a dhow up the river to this fortress-like city, surrounded by its Red Sea moat. I wrote *The Incense Coast* with charts and maps of the Red Sea, the Gulf of Aden and the Horn of Africa constantly before me.

This book is a work of fiction. While I hope that the characters succeed in reminding readers of real people—that was my express intent—no character is intended to represent an actual person. Every character is a creature from my imagination; as are the details of the story.

On the other hand, the events described in the epigraphs—most of them—are taken from media and reflect things that have happened—are happening—in the world today. A few, taken from works of fiction, are so noted, but most are from recent newspapers, news magazines or the internet. The story of piracy is a long and violent saga whose final chapters are unlikely ever to be written.

As a confession to the audience for my book, I acknowledge that the story turned out to be darker and grimmer than I had intended. It just happened. One thing led to another, Characters began to behave in ways I had not anticipated, and there isn't much I can say about it. Hopefully, this statement will make sense as you turn the pages.

For background, I relied upon both fiction and non-fiction, primarily about pirates, piracy and the countries and cultures of Somalia, Kenya, Eritrea, Ethiopia, Sudan and Yemen. None of these countries score highly in terms of stability, human rights, and other measures of democratic societies. Hardly news.

Since this is not a scholarly book, and I'm not a scholar, I will forego the inclusion of a list of references, but several works stand out and deserve to be mentioned.

Somalia, by Salome C. Nnoromele is brief and easily read but it provides a comprehensive, introductory overview of the nation and its people.

Infidel, by Ayaan Hirsi Ali is the story of one woman's struggle against Somalia's repressive culture. Hirsi Ali won world attention when she defied her family, fled Somalia for Holland and eventually became a member of the Dutch Parliament. Currently she lives in the U.S.

Prisoners of the Ritual, by Hanny Lightfoot-Klein, is subtitled *An Odyssey in Female Genital Circumcision in Africa*. *Prisoners'* contents are as chilling as its title. It's hardly recommended reading but it was an important aid for the story.

On a more esoteric note, Somali Poetry, An Introduction, by B.W. Andrzejewski and I.M. Lewis is exactly what it claims to be. It's interesting to note that despite the harsh, primitive nature of many aspects of Somali culture, most observers concur that they are a nation of bards, highly dependent on the oral transmission of a large body of literature.

I borrowed a short paragraph describing 'orphan ghosts' from Jonathan D. Spence's history of the Taiping Rebellion. Its title is "God's Chinese Son, the Taiping Heavenly Kingdom of Hong Xiuquan."

Excellent articles on various aspects of piracy and efforts to suppress appear regularly in *Foreign Affairs* and in *Proceedings of the U.S. Naval Institute*. Useful articles on the cultures of nations previously mentioned appear from time to time in *National Geographic Magazine*. In recent months they have written authoritatively about piracy in the Straits of Malacca, the role of *qat* in Yemen, and lawlessness in Somalia.

The second revision of my manuscript stood at 105 K words when I read Joseph Conrad's *Lord Jim*, and concluded that Jim shared several characteristics with Vance Morrisette. And, like Jim's ship, *Patna*, Vance's vessel never made it to *Perim* as planned. I hope readers will forgive me for invoking the spirit of Conrad's Tuan Jim. It was interesting to note that when Conrad wrote *Lord Jim* in 1899, he was constrained to use d——d (sic) little profanity. My characters—hard men, some of them—invoke the *f-bomb* with reckless abandon that I hope readers will recognize as characteristic of some males, and not simply gratuitous profanity by the author. Be warned.

Many other sources provided helpful details for my story and my debt to others is large.

Rather than explain each foreign word (or have other voices do it for me) I have included a brief glossary of foreign words at the end. Most are Somali, but a few come from other languages. Hopefully, in most cases, context will do the job, but the glossary is for special cases.

For those who might be offended by some of the material in this novel, I can only remind them of what they ignore at their peril; that on a planet where ignorance is cultivated, and faith is valued as a more desired condition than knowledge or the pursuit of truth, situations will frequently arise that transcend the bounds of any fiction. As is, in fact, the case.

I am grateful to my constant proofreader, reliable critic and coffeemaker, my wife, Hope. Thanks also to several early readers with special appreciation to Bob Fischer, Library Director Cheryl Gravelle, and Dr. G. William Whitehurst, Kaufman Lecturer in Public Affairs at Old Dominion University (after serving Virginia for eighteen years in the U.S. House of Representatives.) Dr. Michael Henderson steered me to the book on female circumcision. Their comments and suggestions were invaluable. Surviving errors are, of course, chargeable to me.

Maps and charts of the area were constantly before me. You might find a map handy to help navigate your way around the Horn of Africa.

"The Incense Coast or Land of Myrrh of ancient Egypt offered several commodities including ivory but it was frankincense and myrrh that brought the ancients to the two coasts of the Gulf of Aden. As early as 1500 BC fleets of small ships carried many tons of these resins to Egypt. Frankincense is obtained by tapping the bark of Boswellia species; the resulting resin provides an aromatic smoke, a scented oil known as Oliben, a sort of chewing gum called Siri and another form which was the old Balm of Gilead. In ancient Egypt and Rome these were regarded as perfumes of the Gods."

Island Africa
(The Evolution of Africa's Rare Animals and Plants)
Jonathan Kingdom

Prologue

October 8, 2007. Tarik Saadawi led his herd of thirty-seven camels into the coastal town of Boosaaso on the north coast of Somalia. He had been out for twenty-one days subsisting for much of the time on camel milk and edible plants foraged from the countryside. The rice and dried meat he carried in his bag was gone at the end of the sixth day. He was hungry and bone weary; and to make matters more uncomfortable he had stuck a thorn in his foot three days ago, and although he laughed at first—unconcerned by blood and pain—it was throbbing continually and nothing to laugh about. He called to his brother.

"Ya, Tarik, you have returned," his brother replied. "Alhamdulillah. Come and take food with me. After you have watered your camels."

It angered eighteen-year old Tarik when his younger brother teased him about his fondness for the camels. Even more infuriating, his brother invited him to watch the new television set, a Sony, that had been purchased following a distribution of money from the last successful pirate raid. He had come to a decision during his walk home.

"How hard can it be to capture a vessel manned by infidels, Ya my little brother? Perhaps I should just leave my camels and try the sea where the money is much better. Take me to your leader. When we have finished the *qat*."

On October 12, 2008, the Turkish freighter *Gelibolu* was steaming southbound around the Horn of Africa after transiting the Suez Canal, descending the Red Sea and leaving the Gulf of Aden. *Gelibolu* was carrying a load of bagged wheat, loaded at the Ukrainian port of Odessa and bound for the Somali port of Mogadishu. The wheat was from Ukraine; the best wheat in the world. Not Russian wheat or Kazakh wheat. Ukrainian wheat. The best. Talk to your wheat dealer if you have doubts. It was also the most expensive. It had been purchased with money from the UN.

Gelibolu was sailing under contract to a United Nations food agency concerned with addressing a shortage of food in Somalia. It was widely believed by the ship's owners, Istanbul Shipping Ltd., that widespread advance knowledge of the ship's mission would prevent any possibility of attacks by pirates who were known to be active along the ship's path.

On the evening of October twelfth, the weather was mild and wind from the east was just wrinkling the darkening surface of the Indian Ocean. All ship's officers had been alerted to possible danger from a pirate attack, but shipping managers had advised the captain that the probability was estimated to be low. Consequently, Captain Nazim Kesbiner had turned in shortly after dinner, and the bridge was under the command of Second Officer, Osman Yildirim. Captain Kesbiner had access to the only firearms on board, a Glock automatic pistol and a shotgun, both of which were securely locked in a gun safe in his compartment, the key to which was on a string around his neck.

Second officer Yildirim was an experienced seaman with more than fifteen years of sea time under his belt, and he recognized—based on radio reports—that when the ship changed course after rounding the Horn of Africa, the possibility of a pirate attack was real and vigilance was essential. But, he wondered, what did it mean to be vigilant?

There were only three men on deck duty at one time; himself, the helmsman and an ordinary seaman standing a four-hour watch on the bow. What were the chances that they would see any approach by a small, unlit, wooden-hulled craft overtaking from astern? Periodically, because of the pre-trip briefings, he walked to the wings of the bridge on either side and looked astern for signs of lights or the telltale indications from a wake, but these actions, he knew, were perfunctory and any success he might have in alerting the crew prior to an attack would be simply a matter of luck.

Second officer Yildirim was—as many sailors are—an interesting individual who had seen a great deal of the world and had become a true, blue water sailor. His trips had taken him to many parts of the world but he had never failed to return to his home in Trabzon, where he had a wife and two children, a boy and a girl.

Coastal Trabzon with its long history, dating back to the days before Jason and the Golden Fleece—or Xenophon—had lured him to follow the sea; and he had never looked back after his first coastwise voyage down to Istanbul. But he had always returned to Trabzon.

Second officer Yildirim never saw the attack coming. In fact, nobody aboard *Gelibolu* saw the attack coming. The chronometer on the bridge showed Yildirim that he had an hour to go before being relieved when the explosion occurred.

It was never clear to Yildirim exactly where the pirates came aboard. True enough, it would have been a relatively easy matter to board *Gelibolu*. Hull down, her stern rail would only have been about twenty feet above the sea. But Yildirim had been watching the radar intently and he had, periodically— conscientiously— walked on the wings from time-to-time looking for any signs that they might be intercepted.

Whatever precautions he might have thought he was taking, they were— clearly—insufficient. Their inadequacy was attested to when a loud explosion carried away part of the port wing of the bridge and caused the helmsman to fall to the floor.

Yildirim and the helmsman were stunned by the blast, which blew out windows and showered the bridge with shards of flying glass. Both men escaped serious injury and Yildirim quickly helped the frightened seaman to his feet and placed him back at the wheel. Then he called for the captain to come to the bridge in response to a pirate attack.

Captain Kesbiner had been awakened immediately by the blast, and he sensed at once that his ship was under attack. *Those arrogant dogs at Istanbul. They will hear from me on this.* It never—not even for a moment—occurred to him that he might conceivably not return to Istanbul. Kesbiner quickly opened his safe and withdrew both weapons. A holster for the Glock pistol was on a web belt that he snapped around his waist. He removed the magazine from the Glock, pulled back the slide, and snapped the trigger to confirm that it was empty. Then he replaced the magazine, chambered a round and put on the weapon's safety.

The shotgun, he remembered, was already loaded with slugs. He checked to insure that the safety was on before stepping into his comfortable Adidases that never slipped on deck. Then he headed for the bridge. Very little time had passed.

In the scant minutes that had elapsed, eight Somali pirates had boarded *Gelibolu*, using a boarding ladder. The ladder had been pulled up and secured by the first two Somali pirates who had scaled the knotted ropes that had been flung over the railing by the boarding crew in the rubber boat.

The process was relatively simple and straightforward. The first boat, an Italian-made Pirelli, had come alongside with seven men aboard. A boarding hook had been thrown and it had caught on the second attempt. An agile pirate had climbed the rope and come aboard unseen and undetected. The second man had followed quickly while the first man stood guard with his AK-47. Once the second man had come aboard, the two men hoisted up a proper boarding ladder and another four men came on board. They all carried AK-47s and two of them had RPGs. It was one of the RPGs that carried away much of the port wing of *Gelibolu's* bridge.

The purpose of the RPG shot had been, simply put, to intimidate *Gelibolu's* crew. It had been triggered when a nervous pirate was startled by a Turkish crewman emerging, unexpectedly, from an outside doorway. No one had been on the wing when the trigger-happy shooter had fired. Seconds later, armed pirates had gained access to the bridge and were leveling weapons at the occupants.

By this time, the bridge defenders were Captain Kesbiner and his Second, to whom Kesbiner had tossed the loaded shotgun as he entered. "It's loaded," he said. "Just take off the safety." As a consequence of these seven fateful little words, Second Officer Yildirim had, in fact snapped off the safety, and—being a man of action—he had fired at the first pirate to come bounding in from the starboard wing of the bridge. Unfortunately, it was a hip shot and even sadder, it missed its intended target, Tarik, the camel-herder turned pirate. Now invincible.

It did, however, come close enough to frighten and anger Tarik who resisted the urge to squeeze the trigger of his weapon, but instead, used the barrel as a stick to hit Yildirim in the head. The blow glanced off his left cheekbone and struck his left collar bone, fracturing it painfully. The shotgun hit the floor. Captain Kesbiner did not fire his Glock but simply handed it over.

In the immediate aftermath of the boarding, *Gelibolu's* crew was assembled on the bridge and made to sit on the floor with their backs against the chart tables. *Gelibolu's* bridge signaled for her engines to be stopped and the engine room crew was summoned to the bridge to take their place beside their mates. The ordeal was just beginning for Turkish sailors.

A month after the attack on *Gelibolu*, Tarik was back leading camels into the scrub desert wastes of Somalia. His recently impregnated wife now had a television set and he was happy to be out of a job that had made him seasick.

It's curious to learn that six weeks after he left piracy to return to the desert, he fell from a camel while pushing the animal too fast in rocky terrain, and broke his collarbone. On the right side. Call it a coincidence.

"On Monday, Yemen's Interior Ministry says Somali pirates have hijacked a Yemeni cargo ship in the Arabian Sea. It said communication with the vessel was lost last Tuesday after it had been out to sea for a week.

The ship is called Adina, and it was not immediately clear what cargo it was carrying. The U.S. 5th Fleet based in Bahrain could not confirm the hijacking.

A blockade along Somalia's 2,400-mile coastline would not be easy. "But some intervention there may be effective," Swift (managing director of the International Association of Independent Tanker Owners) told reporters on the sidelines of a shipping conference in Malaysia."

"Shipping officials seek military help."
The Associated Press, Tuesday, Nov. 25, 2008

—1—London Meeting

Windows of the twenty-third floor conference room in the Lloyd's Insurance Building faced south, with a great view of the Tower Bridge, and HMS Belfast tied up on the south bank of the Thames. The view, however, was lost on the thirteen executives who had gathered promptly at eight a.m. to discuss the piracy situation in the Arabian Sea and to consider possible solutions.

Five of the attendees were insurance executives, with backgrounds in Risk Assessment. Another five were executives of shipping companies, having special interests in security matters, which until recent months had focused primarily on port security, with particular reference to anti-terrorist measures.

The final three represented various government ministries. The Admiralty was represented by the oldest man in the room, Nigel Harringdon. Harold Crofton, the Lloyd's vice-president who had called this meeting expected little from Harringdon; but his boss had agreed that the Admiralty must be represented and the invitation had been tendered and accepted. Harringdon was, essentially, what is known as "a place holder."

Considering the relatively early start of this meeting, a variety of breakfast beverages was arrayed on a long sideboard, together with a selection of rolls and pastries. *Where else might they set out guava juice with the pineapple and OJ?* There were few takers, and within minutes following the introductions around the table, Crofton got down to business.

1

"My thanks to you gentlemen for your support with this activity. Now that we've all been introduced, I would like to go around the table and have each person describe his position and any special interests or background that might be relevant to the matters we'll be discussing. Please be brief. Following this expanded introduction we will immediately state the problem as it appears to insurers and shippers. Then we will open the floor for a round table discussion of possible solutions."

Sound boring?

"Our plan is to continue this discussion until mid-morning when we will take a short recess before resuming. It's planned to continue the discussion until approximately eleven when we'll try to wrap up with conclusions and recommendations for the next steps. This outline should have been covered in the information packages you were all provided; and, in any event, a copy of today's remarks are in the folders in front of you. Fair enough? Any questions?"

There were murmurs and shufflings around the table, but no questions.

"I will go first," Crofton began, and he followed up with half a dozen sentences describing his background in applied mathematics and his career up to his appointment to a special task force dealing with solutions to piracy on the high seas as it applied to insurance rates. This procedure was quickly repeated around the table. A female clerk who had been introduced by name only adjusted the blinds to block out the Thames view, and, room darkened, Crofton began his graphic presentation.

Piracy; 2008, A Global Problem. The second image depicted the Horn of Africa including the Red Sea, Gulf of Aden and Indian Ocean. Dots indicated the location of all piracy events since careful records were kept— from the beginning of 2007.

Most of the attacks occurred in the Gulf of Aden, between Somalia and Yemen, but the numbers from the Indian Ocean to the south of the Horn were increasing.

Crofton's charts summarized the types of ships that were being targeted. Most were small freighters and tankers. The presenter warmed to his topic. Only in recent months in 2008 had pirates begun targeting larger tankers.

"This table show the breakdown by tonnages. So far there has been relatively little loss of life. By all appearances the pirates, most or all of whom appear to be Somalis, are after ransom money; either for the ship and its cargo, or the crew, or both. Most killings, so far, seem to be accidental."

"This next table depicts the money known to have been paid out as ransoms, by month. As you can see, the amount paid by shippers—and insurers—is climbing rapidly. By the end of calendar 2008 we expect more than thirty million in ransom will have been paid. Actually losses are of course, much greater, reflecting lost time, increased costs of fuel and labor due to delays and—in some cases—to cargo damage from spoilage in transit. The dotted lines above show estimated true costs based on all factors including ransom payments."

"You can see in this next chart the breakdown of nations involved based on ship registries. To date, the ships of more than twenty nations have been attacked at sea. As a consequence, many nations, and several coalitions of nations, are considering appropriate responses. These activities are in progress in many locations even as we speak here. This is particularly appropriate since eleven attacks have taken place within the past calendar week. Piracy seems to be paying off for the pirates. Some shipping companies are considering rerouting their vessels to avoid the Suez Canal. The impact on shipping costs will be crippling for many firms, especially in today's straightened economic climate."

Crofton's presentation continued in this thoughtful, scholarly manner for nearly ninety minutes, concluding with a summary list of all international groups and agencies known to be concerning themselves with potential solutions.

The lights came up and Crofton took a seat at the end of the table. "Does anyone have any questions concerning the material that was presented?"

Theo Athanase, the representative from Hellenic Shipping, grunted and Crofton encouraged him to speak up. "In your opinion, as a foremost insurer, who do you feel owns this problem?" Athanase asked. "To whom should the world look for a solution? Is this a problem for NATO? The European Union? African Union? OPEC? The United Nations? The U.S.? From what quarter should shippers expect actions to be taken? Or...is it a case of every man for himself? What should we be doing?"

Crofton smiled. "A good question, indeed. Precisely. This is at the nub of why we are here today. Perhaps at the end of a few hours of participatory thinking we may have some tentative clues concerning the answer to your question. Well put. Thank you sir."

At ten the group took a break for about twenty minutes. Cell phones came out and, for the first time, members of the group took advantage of the great views of ever-changing traffic on the Thames as they made their calls to check in with offices, brokers, homes. After the meeting resumed, Crofton got the discussion going with a proposal.

"Rather than just go free form around the table, I propose that we take advantage of some prior work that has been done by considering various categories of solutions. We have already engaged two strategic planning firms to assess possible approaches. Consider this menu of options."

More boring charts flashed on the screen.

A. Responsibility for protection
    —Individual skippers crews
    —Shipping firms
    —Private security contractors
    —Individual nations (Armed Forces, Naval, Air, Coastal, etc.)
    —Multinational coalitions (UN, NATO, Arab Union, etc.)
    —Mode of Attacking Pirates

B. During attacks; repelling boarders
    —At sea; intercepting attacking vessels, from sea
    —At sea, from the air
    —Attacking coastal bases
    —Destroying all involved infrastructure
    —Any combination of the above

C. Criteria for declaring success
    etc., etc.

Crofton was on a roll. His staff had been working on his slide presentation for two weeks. Nevertheless, nothing seemed to hang together. Nothing seemed logical. Or particularly imaginative.

In the back of the room, Harringdon, the Admiralty representative, was snoring quietly. Of course, *quietly* is a relative term. From mid-morning until the catered lunch, the meeting was very boring. After lunch, it was even worse.

It was nearly six p.m. when the meeting came to a close. Everyone was requested to be back at 8:30 the following morning.

Boring. Boring. Boring.

"Because bomb-sniffing dogs don't work well underwater..."
(accompanying a picture showing a marine robot) "It locates and
destroys underwater mines at the command of an operator who's
nowhere in the vicinity. And it's just one example of the cutting edge
technology you'll be able to get your hands on when you become a
proud part of the U.S. Navy."

—2—Pentagon Discussion Group

A group of six career naval officers were meeting in a second-ring Pentagon
conference room for an all-day discussion session. Two of the officers were
rear admirals, two were captains and two were commanders; but rank was
not a factor in this free-form discussion meeting and all participants were
wearing civilian clothes.

The topics for the day included but were not limited to, the coming
opportunities for unsymmetrical warfare in the worlds navies, the roles for
various unmanned vehicles, surface, subsurface, and aerial, and possible
applicability for dealing with the pirate attacks currently occurring in the
Indian Ocean region.

The six officers sprawling around the conference table all had reputations
as "out-of-the box" problem solvers and they had been summoned together
by a request out of the Office of the Undersecretary. For now, their names
are unimportant to us, although we may encounter them again in the future.
The senior officer was acting as discussion leader and he had been briefed
by a staffer from the Secretary's office concerning expectations from the
meeting.

The first couple of hours were consumed in discussions of unmanned
surface vehicles. Four participants represented the surface and subsurface
navy. The other two were naval aviators. They began by looking at some
budget figures for classified programs of prototypes for unmanned submarines
that could be used initially in surveillance or intelligence gathering—later for
possible roles in ASW, minesweeping, or blockade chores. Later in their
discussion, they were constrained to consider the role of unmanned aerial
vehicles—UAVs— against surface ships—blue water and littoral operations.

After a midmorning coffee break, they kicked around the notion of drones—unmanned aerial vehicles or UAVs—operating from carriers. The discussion quickly expanded to include possible roles for drone helicopters operating from...what? Anything big enough to carry the proposed birds.

At one point Captain—let's call him Bligh for now— slammed down his pen and pushed away from the table to refill his coffee cup. "Is it just me?" he asked, rhetorically, "or does anyone else get the feeling that Pandora's box has had its lid stolen and it couldn't be closed even if we wanted to?"

The topic of appropriate responses to piracy didn't come up until after lunch. The noon meal was light, brought in by several enlisted yeomen. After lunch the room was secured and each man had a chance to visit his own office, return calls, check mail and perform any other routine chores before they resumed work at half past one.

Admiral—let's call him Perry—got things back on track.

"Piracy. We've been asked to brainstorm this topic and to recommend possible solutions, both conventional and unconventional. Nothing to be off the table. You've all been getting regular briefing papers on our programs today. So I'm sure you know what we've been doing. And in addition, you know what others have been doing. The French have ships in the area. China is there. Britain. Germany. And India. It's the Tower of Babel. But the pirates are still managing to succeed. So where shall we start?"

They were almost as boring and ineffectual as insurers and ship owners.

"Let's talk about what steps commercial shipping lines are doing on their own. Everyone seems to be hiring civilian security guards whose sole purpose would appear to be repelling boarders. But so far, from what I've read, these people are generally unarmed. They're using water cannons. High frequency noise. And often they succeed."

Captain Bligh laughed. "Whatever became of cutlasses?"

"That seems to be the problem," his neighbor offered. "No one seems to want to harm the pirates. They are simply being released after their weapons are confiscated and their small craft destroyed. They can be back at sea the next day."

The conversation began to skip around the table.

"Concern for legal ramifications. That's what making shippers hesitant. No one wants to confront the world court over deaths or injuries to a bunch of Somalis."

"And not all these pirates are Somalis. Some, we know, are Yemenis. I'm guessing that we're going to learn that there are some Saudis involved as well. Possibly some Sudanese. Maybe not in the attack boats. But Saudis as grubstakers—backing the Somali groups with financial support to get started."

"OK. Let's stay focused on some solutions. We know that our ships are not currently authorized to destroy pirates at sea."

Captain Bligh: "Yeah, but the UN has just authorized attacks on pirate installations on shore. We can't blow a fiberglass boatload of armed Somalis to hell, but we can put a JDAMs in a shore installation? That we suspect to be a pirate base? That doesn't make sense to me."

Commander A: "Especially if it turns out to house a Somali kindergarten."

Captain Midnight: "Not in Somalia. Maybe a hospital, but not a kindergarten."

Admiral Perry: "We're wandering, gentlemen. Let's stay focussed. Perhaps it would help if we reminded ourselves of the configuration of Somalia's coast." He pressed a button on his phone line to the administrative aide outside the room and requested the sequence of graphics he had prepared in advance.

This meeting stumbled and staggered along with breaks as needed until slightly after six p.m. By the time they called it quits their ideas had included aerial surveillance from carriers to locate and track pirate support ships, use of fighters, helicopters, or possibly UAVs to interdict, and a gamut of weapons from conventional munitions to advanced systems such as JDAMs to destroy approved targets. They discussed the formation of naval coalitions involving cooperative roles for various navies representing the U.S., NATO and the EU. They emphasized the need for division of Somali's coast to assign areas of responsibility to various navies—or possibly to various classes of ships, the formation of an integrated data base of information to be supported by—and accessible to—all participants, etc., etc. Their ideas—all captured on laptops by several techniques—filled sixteen pages of closely spaced text.

Admiral Perry offered to take them all to dinner, but it was a spontaneous offer no one had been expecting. Consequently, all of his juniors had other engagements. So he invited his long time friend and colleague, Admiral... Yamamoto?...to go back to his office for a drink before they headed out together.

Yamamoto: "Did this go about the way you expected?"

Perry: "Christ, I don't know Ted. What was I expecting? What did you think of it? We certainly hoovered up a lot of ideas. These egg-heads upstairs will have some new ideas to consider."

Yamamoto: "What did you think about the notion to strengthen our ties or connections to all of the civilian contractors that are serving as guards and security personnel? About possibly training them?"

Perry: "We captured all the suggestions. That one, frankly, sounds like bullshit to me. The Navy doesn't need to get involved with a whole phone book of opportunistic contractors hiring a bunch of ex-military or borderline sociopaths in a training role or an advisory role. No. I couldn't get enthusiastic about that approach. But maybe something...." His voice trailed off as he filled Yamamoto's glass with three fingers of good Scotch and tried to get his mind around the new idea that had just formed.

"Y'know Ted, today we spent a fair amount of time talking about the roles being performed by private security firms. There are a lot of these outfits in every country, but some of our biggest civilian security contractors expanded greatly as a result of Iraq. None bigger than UBSA, United Brothers."

"The organization they call Uncle Bob's," Ted—*Admiral Yamamoto*—interrupted.

"Uncle Bob's?"

"Yeah. That what they call them. How much do we really know about these people? Their goals, their training, the details of their contracts?"

"I'm guessing the NSA knows quite a bit. But us? Not so much. We don't have much work for them as far as I know. None that I know of. But Ted, if they're putting armed guards on ships going through the Bab el Mandeb—through the Gulf of Aden—maybe we need some insight into how they're planning to stop the pirates."

"Private firms? Think they're gonna share much information with us? Not too likely."

"But Ted, what if we had someone on the inside? Come on, finish that and let's get some dinner. I'm buying. We can talk about this later."

"'When coalition warships board pirate ships, they dispose of the weapons, but have to let the suspects go,' Vice Adm. Bill Gortney, commander of the 5th Fleet, told USA Today on Wednesday. 'That is the biggest shortfall that we have. We could have a huge effect if we could solve that problem.'"

Off Africa's Coast, pirates 'out of control'
Tom Vanden Brook, Jim Michaels and Peter Eisler
USA Today, November 20, 2008

—3—Vance Morrisette

As Lt. Commander Vance Morrisette, USN, tooled his PT Cruiser through DC's nasty afternoon traffic heading for his three-bedroom apartment in Georgetown, he was already dreading the evening he was likely to be facing.

His wife, Rhonda, had been bugging him to go out for an evening of dancing and—in her case—drinking. To avoid a protracted argument, he had agreed. It was Friday evening and she wanted to go out. The years he had been stationed at Little Creek in Norfolk had been much more to her liking. They had a bigger apartment, traffic was more manageable and, best of all from her point of view, they were only twenty minutes drive away from Officer's Clubs at Little Creek, Fort Story, or the Norfolk Naval Air Station. And there were other interesting military OCs only slightly further away. There, the drinks were cheap, the atmosphere was pleasant—not to mention safe, and the music was usually pretty good. And there were always good-looking officers around who would ask her to dance. Their military situation ensured that they were usually respectful and polite when they approached her in the clubs, but not infrequently some of the things they would say to her on the floor—especially later in the evening—were definitely not by the book, and these proposals did not make it back to Vance. Some of them, however, did sound very appealing and in several cases she spent considerable time weighing the possibilities.

Vance had met pretty, blonde Rhonda at a private club in Norfolk where she was working as a hostess. He went out with her for a year before he decided to go the distance. She was a good cook, southern style; which frequently meant tossing a ham hock into the turnip greens or collards. She knew how to pick crabs, and she could cook oysters. He liked everything she fixed him, and during that first year her cooking included a lot of breakfasts.

Born and raised in Utah where most of the people he grew up with were

9

LDS, Vance had never even heard of a hush puppy. After a night of serious, major league sex, the hush puppies seemed to be made in heaven, just to go down with scrambled eggs. Rhonda, who grew up in eastern North Carolina, had been taught to cook by a grandmother who knew that she was dying from leukemia and had neither wherewithal nor will to deal with her condition. In other words, she was ready to go—and she wanted Rhonda to be capable and self-reliant. Her grandfather had died before Rhonda's mother dumped her on Gramma and headed west with a con man. Gramma knew that life for Rhonda was likely to be better if she had the ability to provide food for hungry men. At twelve, the girl's blouses were already spiking in a way that suggested she wouldn't lack for admirers. But men also had to be fed.

When Vance met Rhonda, he was fascinated by the rose tattoo at the base of her spine. Which he discovered for himself, without any clues from her. She had never told him the true story of its origin. She never will. But she did tell him enough to keep him happy. *OK. To keep him from unhappiness. It's close enough.*

Vance knew that Rhonda was working as a hostess at a club when he met her, but he did not know that she had begun as a dancer before an opportunity presented itself to move up. He met her when he was an officer with a SEAL Team operating out of Little Creek. Back in Utah, he had attended BYU, joined the Navy's ROTC program, been torn between track and wrestling and majored in history. He still enjoyed reading history and had vague notions that he might someday return to a university; possibly as a teacher. To this end he still read purposefully, but little encouragement came from Rhonda. After nine years of a childless marriage (recall that Rhonda had essentially been abandoned by her mom) Vance had come to the conclusion that his wife was flighty. That was a generous assessment. Her southern Gramma might have concluded that her granddaughter was "trashy." Not bad, mind you, but just trashy. Trashy women can—at least for a time—be very appealing to men. She was, in fact, uncommonly pretty. And she was, beyond doubt, stacked. "Easy" might have been a better term than trashy. And so, as Gilbert and Sullivan have reminded us, "joy incessant palls the sense, and love unchanged will cloy." It was slow to sink in, and he hated to admit it, but the former SEAL knew that they would never grow old together.

In Norfolk, Vance had spent several years with his SEAL Team, and they had been involved in series of "exercises" in the Indian Ocean in which his performance had resulted in several awards. His role in clandestine operations on the island nation of Mauritius following the disastrous tsunami of 2005 had resulted in several letters of commendation. Later, he had been wounded in action against terrorists in waters off Pakistan, resulting in a

Purple Heart and several more letters of commendation. At one time he had been up for the Navy Cross but the board who reviewed recommendations never understood the significance of what his team was doing, and so the recommendations were rejected.

The sad fact of which he was also not aware was that while he was at sea, Rhonda screwed three junior officers at Little Creek, and two of them knew Vance.

But Vance's name had made it to Washington. By this time he was a Lieutenant Commander, and, in consequence, someone requested him for an assignment at the Pentagon. When he broached it to Rhonda, she jumped. Moving up. But it turned out to be considerably different than she thought, and stuffy Georgetown wasn't to her liking. She missed the softer, southern nights of Norfolk, and the steamy advances of horny young naval officers who were smart enough to say it when they liked what they saw, and clever enough to say it carefully.

Now, he was poking his way across the bridge, homeward bound, to a wife who would be all dolled up for an evening under the lights. He would have preferred to stay home, run a few miles, read or listen to music, then maybe go at it.

Just now he had been reading about the Barbary pirates and their role in the birth of the U.S. Marine Corps. *Four years of college and I never heard a word about any of this shit... Plenty about Brigham Young. And Joseph Smith. Nothing about Pericardis. Tripoli.*

He thought about the events that had landed him the desk assignment at the Pentagon. It was, he felt sure, just a stepping stone to somewhere else. But would the next move be something that would make things better or worse with Rhonda? He was loath to initiate the split, not wanting to have to accuse her. Since being in Georgetown she had never made hush puppies a single time. And she had laughed when he asked her about grits. Which he had loved. "Are you kiddin'," she laughed. "Grits? They didn't even know about grits in Virginia. You're in the north now, sailor boy. I cain't buy 'em up here."

He was across the bridge, past the Treasury Building, and traffic was beginning to ease.

It was going to be a crappy evening for him. She would expect him to have eaten. It was after six. In any case, she wouldn't be cooking and she would look like...well...goddammit, she would look very sexy. And she would be wound tight.

The Pentagon assignment wasn't working out like he had expected. But, as some of his men had said, "In for a dime, in for a dollar." He had picked up the hand and now he had to play it.

The question uppermost in his mind was, *when* can I get out of Washington, when can I get back in an assignment that I can love and where I can be challenged? *And, oh yeah, where my wife can manage to get interested in something that will keep her from being a pain in the ass.* He couldn't bring himself to say the words out loud; that he wanted to dump her.

The world—including his own personal universe—was in turmoil. *Surely... surely, something will turn up.* One thing he was sure of. The first chance he had to get out of Washington? He intended to take it. He thought about some of the highlights of his naval career to date. Some of his most challenging experiences had occurred in the Indian Ocean when he was heading a team that had operated for a time out of Djibouti. For several years his swimmers had been involved in the testing of some advanced diving gear that had since been accepted for Special Ops use. *I'd go back with the SEALs in a heartbeat.* He was working hard to stay in shape. *Just in case.*

In his first assignment with a Piracy Task Force at the Pentagon, he had been thoroughly briefed on the situation in Somalia by members of the East Africa desk at NSA. Their briefing took two days and would have to be, by almost any measure, considered thorough. But how—in two days—can one learn about a country that is as old as the oldest places anywhere on the planet; that was a destination for trade when the boats of ancient Egypt and Greece plied the Red Sea and Gulf of Aden, seeking cargoes of frankincense, myrrh, spices, ivory and other exotic cargoes?

Vance was exposed to salient details of the region's sad history since the 19th and 20th centuries when it was, for a time, colonized by British, French and Italian occupiers, all with different motives and methods of establishing their governments. He knew that in the first decade of the 21st century the region occupying the Horn of Africa was ungoverned and apparently ungovernable.

On the evening of his first day he had taken home a copy of *Black Hawk Down*, a film he had watched before but had not studied carefully. Like a good student, he watched it carefully this time and—despite the ferocity of combat scenes—he found it difficult to reconcile the U.S. withdrawal after the death of eighteen soldiers. To him it represented a clear failure on the part of senior decision-makers to define the mission's objectives before sending armed men into Mogadishu. Either we should have gone in with some clear objectives to win or achieve—in which case we would have followed up with a massive retaliation—or we should have shrugged off the chaos as an internal problem for a failed state.

In the late morning of the second day, the NSA intelligence officer doing the briefing, a sharp featured woman of about forty, asked if everyone in the class was familiar with the writing of Ayaan Hirsi Ali. Of the ten navy and three marine officers present, only two raised their hands.

Agent Sutherland filled them in on the courageous Somali woman who left Somalia as a child, lived for a time in Saudi Arabia, Ethiopia and Kenya, before fleeing to the Netherlands. She had not yet turned twenty. She fled to avoid an arranged marriage with a Somali man living in Canada. She had actually been in route to Canada when her plane landed in Germany, providing her with a chance to jump ship.

After making her way to The Netherlands, Hirsi Ali, now estranged from her family, found a way to learn Dutch, attend college, manage to get herself elected to the Dutch legislature and earn the enmity of Holland's large Muslim population for her rejection of many aspects of Islamic culture. Although she entered Europe as a sincere Muslim, her repeated exposure to non-Islamic ways and her willingness to accept many elements of Dutch culture made her recognizable to other Muslims as an infidel. After Islamic extremists announced their intentions to kill her—and demonstrated their capability by assassinating a prominent Dutch film producer, Hirsi Ali emigrated to the U.S. where she is currently a member of a conservative think tank.

The big Marine major was having trouble hiding his feeling of disgust at the way this session was going. As Agent Sutherland spoke briefly about some of Hirsi Ali's activities since coming to America USMC Major Mike McGregor muttered "Jesus H. Christ," in a voice loud enough to be heard at the front of the room.

"Excuse me. Is something wrong, major?"

"Maybe it's just me," McGregor said in a sarcastic tone, "but I can't see how knowing about this lady is gonna help us understand Somalia."

"My point—and perhaps it was too subtle—was that Somali people are highly intelligent even though poor and lacking in opportunities for formal education. Try learning Dutch sometime and then running for their parliament. It won't be all that easy, even for a marine."

There were a few snickers that were quickly suppressed as McGregor glowered.

"But perhaps I should get back to a few more pertinent elements of Somali ways and culture. Oh, but wait a moment. I'll digress briefly. Maybe leave Somali culture for tomorrow. How many of you gentlemen have daughters, one or more?" Of the thirteen men in the room, six raised their hands.

"OK, Who would like to tell the group what is meant by the term, 'infibulation?' "

No one spoke up.

"OK, well, perhaps someone *knows* the meaning of the term, but just may be a bit squeamish about describing it to the group. Is this the case?"

Thirteen career military officers were looking puzzled by a term they had never heard before.

"That, gentlemen, will be your homework assignment on this waning afternoon of our little discussion. I'm sure you all will have a computer at home. Tonight just Google a term you should know in order to better understand Somalia and Islam as it's practiced in the Horn of Africa. Spell it correctly. I-n-f-i-b-u-l-a-t-i-o-n. Infibulation. Check it out. I'll ask one of you to report to your colleagues. You'll probably be hearing more about it when you get over there. Oh yeah, don't ask your daughters."

Coughing all around.

"Now, let's review a bit and then we can call it a day. You know that in Somalia genealogy and lineage is of paramount importance."

Vance was starting to regret that he left his SEAL unit in Norfolk to take this assignment.

"Pirates already are driving up the cost of shipping and insurance. Some shipping lines have already begun avoiding the shipping corridors near Somalia and their shortcut to the West through the Red Sea and Suez Canal, which can add five and ten days to a trip from Asia to Europe, says David Ellis, president of Odfjell USA, a Norwegian-owned shipping company. Each extra day at sea, he says, costs about $30,000.

> Off Africa's Coast, pirates 'out of control'
> Tom Vanden Brook, Jim Michaels and Peter Eisler
> USA Today, November 20, 2008

—4—A New Assignment

Several minutes after Vance Morrisette arrived at his Pentagon desk on a Monday morning, a uniformed clerk delivered a printed message. He had been scheduled for a ten a.m. meeting with the admiral in his office. No preparation required. Subject: Discussion of possible future assignments. Vance had been looking at possible roles for various naval personnel in Afghanistan. The pending meeting didn't cause him to lose much productive time. He notified his secretary to alert him ten minutes in advance, and then he swung into the morning's tasks, which included a review of the Navy's past roles in Kuwait and Iraq. When the time came to leave, he locked his papers away and put on his uniform cap and headed for the admiral's office. He had no idea what to expect, but with his record, how could it be anything but good?

Ushered into the admiral's office without delay, he found the grizzled veteran just completing dictation to a smartly uniformed young officer. The admiral offered coffee which Vance considered declining. He had consumed three cups already, but then he considered the possibility that the lieutenant might be the one to bring it in. The admiral came from behind his desk and sat in an easy chair across the sofa where Vance had been directed.

"I've been looking at your file," the admiral said, "and it's impressive."

"Thank you sir," Vance responded.

"I was particularly impressed by the account of your swim ashore at Mauritius. Following that tsunami in 2005. Then later, your role in the exercises off the coast of Pakistan. Very dangerous. And that assignment with the marines in California. Challenging."

"I've been fortunate to have interesting assignments."

15

"Yes. I can see that. But I also gather that you have the ability to operate independent of formal command, and to make good decisions in the field. Not every commander can do that. It's easier, sometimes, to follow orders narrowly, rather than to think through the situation."

"I always follow my orders, sir. I would never attempt to outguess my superiors."

"Yes, I can see that, Morrisette," the admiral said. "But sometimes, in the absence of formal orders, you seem to have had the ability to decide the proper course."

Vance held his tongue. The admiral didn't seem like he was being critical. *Where the heck is this going?* There were several moments of silence while the admiral played with a teabag.

"Let me change the subject for a moment. Are you familiar with the roles that have been played by civilian security firms in the past decade? In the jobs that civilians, under contract to DOD are performing in many places in the world?"

"I have a general familiarity, sir. But specific details, no sir. I haven't been tracking."

"Are you familiar with the organization known as UBSA? They're one of the biggest, and recently they've been in the news."

"I have been following that part of it, sir. Yes, I do know a bit about UBSA. In fact, when I was operating with the SEALs out of Norfolk, we lost two good swimmers, who got out and doubled their salaries after they joined up with UBSA. My people used to refer to those guys as Uncle Bob's. Their new recruits were sometimes referred to as 'swamp rabbits.' Yes sir, I have a bit of familiarity."

"Did you ever think of the possibility of joining them, Commander?"

Vance sat up straight on the edge of the sofa. "No sir. The Navy is my career. It never crossed my mind. When those guys left I..."

The admiral cut him off with a wave of his hand. "You don't need to explain anything, son. I know that you are unlikely to have any idea where I'm headed with this discussion. So let's shift gears for a moment. Take a moment and tell me what you know about the activities of the Somali pirates operating in the Gulf of Aden and the Indian Ocean."

This was one of the key areas that Vance had been assigned to track, and he was part of a ten-man task force that had been meeting three afternoons a week for the past year. The admiral had to be up on everything that had been recommended by this group.

"Sir, you are aware that I'm...." Again, his senior officer waved him to silence.

"Yes, of course, Commander. But we're having a conversation. Just tell me, conversationally, off the record, what you think we should be doing."

Vance found this off-the-record approach to be very annoying, but it was also disconcerting. Was the admiral looking for disconnects? What?

"Sir, nothing I might say to you privately would conflict with anything published in any of our assessment papers."

"Look, Commander, just go along with me here. I have a purpose in the way I'm asking you questions. Your performance isn't being threatened. Quite the contrary. You are held in high regard. But go along with me for the moment."

What the hell, Vance thought. "Admiral, since you've read our assessments, you know that the Task Force believes that it's a mistake to apprehend pirates and then release them back on shore. Most of the men we've captured at sea have been under thirty. The oldest, to date, I believe has been under forty. In Somalia, you know, the average life span is under fifty. These pirates have already received more money than their entire nation's GNP. They are the biggest industry in their whole country. Why would they cease operations just because we have huge aircraft carriers and guided missile cruisers at sea in the area? Especially since they know they'll be set ashore if apprehended. The Indian Navy and even the Malayans are being more effective than we are. And when the Chinese get involved...as they inevitably will...."

"Our politicians are concerned about world opinion."

"Certainly. But sir, you have been in the Gulf of Aden and you know that COSCO sends a lot of container traffic through the Bab El Mandeb. Wait until Somalis try moving a COSCO ship bound for Romania down to Eyl to wait for ransom payment from the Chinese. Our group was unanimous on this one. We expect fireworks."

"Commander, you're aware that many ships transiting these waters are engaging civilian security personnel?"

This question pissed Vance off. It sounded too legalistic. But he bit his tongue. "Certainly sir. And they're equipped with the latest thing in high pressure hoses." This, he regretted as soon as it was out of his mouth, but the admiral smiled, realizing that he had brought on the sarcasm with his question. He pressed on with his agenda.

"The civilian security firms for American flagged ships usually come from English-speaking firms, such as UBSA in the U.S. or Roundheads, operating out of Liverpool."

"About 85 percent of security personnel hired by American-flagged or American-owned ships come from UBSA, and Roundheads doesn't have all of the balance," Vance replied.

The admiral smiled. Perfect answer. "So you understand that, since UBSA conducts most of the shipboard security for our flags, that if we understand their approach to security, we understand most of what's likely to happen."

"But American-flags are only a tiny portion of the traffic in that region."

"True, But it's the portion over which we have the most control. Legally. Morally. Politically."

Vance was stymied by the admiral's words. So far, he could form no clear picture of why he had been summoned. Nor where his interrogator was going with this line of questioning. He finished the coffee in his cup and looked at the thermos as if he wanted more. "Do you think it would be possible, sir...." he said. It was the only thing he could think of to say. Conversation was put on hold for several minutes as a fresh coffee was brought in, and this time is was the tight-assed lieutenant who looked almost edible in her uniform.

With his cup on the table, Vance was perched on the first six inches of the leather sofa, wondering how long it was going to take before he could understand what this was all about.

The admiral got things back on track. "We were discussing UBSA's dominant role in on-board security for American-flag ships." The admiral paused to tamp his pipe.

"Which, as you well know, makes up only a small fraction of the total traffic in that region."

"Yes, but, as I mentioned, the segment over which we exercise some degree of...what, not control, maybe not authority, but certainly national self-interest. Wouldn't you agree, Commander?"

"Agree," Vance responded, still mystified. American-flagged ships were almost irrelevant to pirate success.

"Suppose, commander— just suppose—that we had an insider placed within UBSA and privy to their strategies. This would allow us to fill in the gaps. To pick up the slack. To understand how far they were prepared to go. If necessary to bias, restrict or possibly redirect their efforts and to meld their strategy with our own. Wouldn't that be a desirable situation? If it could be attained?"

Stated like that, phrased in that fashion, it might make sense. He had to agree "Yes sir." He was surprised to hear the hesitation in his own voice. "But..."

"What if we had an operative placed inside UBSA? On their payroll? Operating in some type of position of responsibility with regard to security from pirate attacks? Someone who could keep us informed on plans and strategies?"

"It sounds like a worthwhile activity. But...." The light bulb flashed.

What the hell? Is that what all this has been about? "But I have no intention of leaving the Navy, sir. Why would I be considered for a job like this? It sounds like a job for...maybe NSA. It doesn't even sound Navy to me." He hesitated. "But..."

"And who, Vance, better qualified than you, to be privy to the decisions and strategies being formulated at UBSA?"

"But...." He was starting to sound—to himself—like a goat.

"Consider, Vance. You're a veteran of combat missions in Iraq and Afghanistan, as well as your exemplary work in the Indian Ocean and off Pakistan. You've been tracking pirate actions closely and within a narrow community, you are recognized. UBSA is, beyond doubt, familiar with your name and background. Their directors would give their left nuts to bring you on board."

This was, to Vance's mind, old guy hyperbole but he treated the suggestion as if it had been serious.

"I've never entertained the least thought of leaving the Navy, sir. And it's not likely that..."

"Vance, bear with me here. These are extraordinary times and they require extraordinary methods. What if we created a special category of operative, still solidly in the U.S. Navy, but appearing to have been discharged and with papers to attest? This individual could be hired by anyone. For any purpose. Based on his special knowledge and qualifications. My guess is that UBSA might try to get their hands on you within seventy-two hours."

"You are seriously considering that I might...."

"Careerwise, it's a chance to jump ahead of your cohort, Vance."

The talk lasted for another hour and the admiral's closing sentence lingered. "I want you to think about this carefully over the next few weeks, Commander. Then we'll talk again."

"Young or old, men are apt to become Merlins when they encounter Viviens."

From: Chapter 11, Tribute
The Eustace Diamonds
Anthony Trollope

—5—Meet Jitka Malecek

The dark-haired girl descending into the Swiss Cottage tube station for the Bakerloo line to Piccadilly Circus, was carrying a boxy briefcase filled with photographs and press clippings of some of her work. From Piccadilly Circus she was planning to walk to nearby BBC offices for a meeting with a producer with whom she had worked in the past. Rocketing along in the tube, she let her mind drift back.

Jitka Malecek's biggest assignment with the BBC in the past had required her to fly to Khartoum in the Sudan and from there to proceed by air to Port Sudan. From Port Sudan on the Red Sea she had made arrangements to travel overland to Suakin, a crumbling but picturesque port with an ancient history that included some interesting British connections.

The BBC had been pleased with her work and the compensation had been sufficiently adequate to encourage her to remain in Suakin for an additional two weeks after the assignment had been completed. During that time, the young woman had hired a former Ethiopian soldier who spoke English to act as a guide. It goes without saying that without male accompaniment it would have been difficult for a single woman—particularly one who looked like Jitka Malecek—to get around the twisted streets of Suakin without problems. Her guide's name was Dourgan and he had lost his right forearm to the elbow in the long wars between Ethiopia and Eritrea. How he came to be in Suakin, Jitka never learned, nor did she have any curiosity to learn. She hired him because she had gotten his name from a Sheila at the BBC's office in Khartoum, but she had stuck with him because he knew his way around the town and its outlying features, spoke passable English, had a family including two children, and she felt his disability might deter him from attacking her; at least from attacking her without help from other assailants.

It was a risk, she knew; but Suakin—despite its dust and squalor—had a certain element of —what? Antique history, nostalgia for a lost past, the presence of ghosts? Romance? It had once been a slaving port. Jitka couldn't quite articulate the elements that drew her to want to capture images of the crumbling town, but she knew that she did so wish, and she had learned to trust her instincts.

As it turned out, the young photojournalist had made a good call. During her stay in Suakin, she was often very tired, frequently hungry, thirsty or both, and usually filthy. But when she finally returned to London she had nearly 1500 digital images. Three months later her work—carefully edited, cropped, blown up, and only slightly enhanced—was on display in the Africa Centre and individual photos were being shown in three London galleries.

Now, as the girl strode out of the station at Piccadilly Circus into London Street traffic, she was contemplating a repeat of the feat she had accomplished at Suakin. This time she was thinking about photographing pirates on the coast of Somalia. On their home grounds. Like the photo essay she once did on Welsh miners.

In the BBC office, Jitka found that she was talking with not one executive, but three. All of them were very familiar with the work she had done for the network and in addition, they had all seen her Suakin photos on display at the Africa Centre.

After introductions around the room senior production executive Phyllis Kendall-Smith got down to business.

"Well Jitka, everyone here has some familiarity with your work and we're confident that you can deliver something that our viewers will find interesting. But your letter seemed to us to be—how can I put this?—insufficiently precise as to what you might photograph; what we might expect to see. Take a few moments and try to help us visualize what you expect to contain in—what did you call it?—a photo essay on piracy."

"Certainly, Phyllis. First off, let me say how gratifying I find it that all of you have taken the trouble to view my show at the Africa Centre. In that group of images I have tried to capture the feel of Suakin. Now, in the case of the Somali pirates, I would like to do the same thing. I would like to—assuming, of course that it is possible—to show the pirates in their daily lives. Such images as are coming back fail to give an accurate impression of how these men live. How they go about their daily lives, what, in fact, they were doing to make a living before piracy attracted them."

The tall, young man in the pin-striped suit—Douglas something she couldn't remember—cut in.

"Much riskier, I should say. Much riskier. I shouldn't think that it would have much resemblance to photographing coal miners in their homes and in the mines."

"No, of course not. And honestly, I don't exactly know the best way to go about it. But I have lived for a time in East Africa before, and I'm willing to chance it."

"You speak Arabic, then?" Douglas Effingham persisted.

"No. Unfortunately not," she replied.

"Or any other East African languages, perhaps? Somali? I'm told they also speak some Italian."

"No," she admitted. "Although I can survive in Italian. And I have my French."

Douglas seemed to have a twist in his knickers. "And Somalia was influenced by the Italians." Supercilious ass hole.

"Just so," Jitka replied with a smile, determining that she would not let this young man get under her skin. "But my intention would be to launch my efforts from Djibouti, where French will do quite nicely, thank you very much. In fact, Djibouti is home to the largest overseas contingent of French military personnel in the world. The U.S. also operates a military base in Djibouti. I would hope that your letters of accreditation would succeed in getting me into the facilities of both nations. From there on, I would just have to figure out the best technique for working my way out onto the Horn of Africa.

"It sounds to me as if many—or perhaps I should even say most—of the details of contacting the pirates have yet to be worked out," Phyllis offered.

"Indeed, yes." Jitka said, with as much jauntiness as she could muster. "But I have faced similar situations in the past and it's always surprising how things work out when one is confident and able to respond quickly." She could tell they were intrigued by the photos circulating around the table. "And flexible," she added. "It helps to be flexible."

The meeting lasted just slightly under two hours and the upshot was that Jitka was promised a marginally adequate contractual relationship with the BBC, which would provide her with all appropriate letters of introduction, and sufficient funds to hire necessary guides, drivers and translators appropriate to the assignment. The broadcasting company would have the first rights of publication for all photographic or written material from the trip, but ultimate copyright ownership would remain with Jitka.

Shortly before the meeting ended, Jitka tossed in another notion. "So far, it appears that the pirates have refrained from any attacks on passenger ships. But that could change in the near future. In fact, I'm told that some experts believe that it will change; possibly soon. In that case, it might seem appropriate at some point to book passage on a liner of some type, maybe even going as far south as Mombasa in Kenya. But I want the latitude to move around the east coast from, say, Port Sudan to Mombasa. To go where

I'm certain to come in contact with pirates to shoot." Effingham's eyebrows went up. "Photograph," she corrected.

Since she had stood up to him boldly, but without any show of temper, Douglas Effingham had looked at her very carefully. Despite her plain, businesslike mode of dress, she was actually quite attractive.

"Remarkable," he thought. "The scar under her right eye in no way detracts from her appeal. I feel quite certain that a good plastics man could eradicate that scar completely. And yet...why bother? I rather like it. Somehow it seems to adds to her authority as a photojournalist. Plucky girl. I'll wager there is a damn good yarn connected to that scar."

Yes, Douglas, there is indeed. But it's unlikely that you will ever hear it.

"With their capture of a colossal Saudi oil tanker on Novenber 15, Somali pirates seized their largest vessel yet amid a torrent of other high-jacking in the Gulf of Aden, where there have been at least eight attacks in just the past two weeks. Pirates currently hold an estimated 17 vessels and some 300 crew for ransom. Some shipping firms are resorting to the long, costly route around Africa to avoid the gulf's dangerous waters."

Pirates Aim Higher
Briefing,
Time Magazine, December 1, 2008

—6—Around the World

In the fall of 2008, piracy in the Gulf of Aden had impacted most of the world's major seafaring nations and was threatening to become worse. In the first nine months of that year, Somali pirates had attacked 92 ships flying the flags of a dozen nations. No particular class of vessel seemed to be immune, since the Somalis were interested primarily in obtaining ransom money for returning ships, cargoes or crews.

Pirate crews, operating from small, high-speed boats, would use boarding ladders to get aboard any vessel where they could land grappling hooks. Then, brandishing automatic weapons and RPGs, they would concentrate on capturing the ship's bridge, while additional pirates boarded. The unarmed crews usually capitulated, not unreasonably, with little or no resistance.

As a result of these attacks, many shipping companies were hiring security personnel whose job requirements—curious in the twenty-first century—was to repel boarders. Unfortunately, these personnel were frequently prohibited—by standing rules of ship owners, the U.S. Coast Guard or other national and international regulations—from taking weapons on board. In the initial attempts to turn pirates away, shippers leaned toward non-lethal methods; high-pressure water hoses or high decibel noise.

Shipping companies had several alternatives to consider, all of them expensive. Insurance could be purchased against the probability of a successful attack. Ships in transit could be rerouted to avoid the Gulf of Aden, Red Sea and the Suez Canal in favor of the longer southern route around the Cape of Good Hope. Security guards could be hired. Each of these approaches carried substantial cost penalties, and the probabilities of successful outcomes furnished plenty of work for actuaries. Often the cheapest alternative was to simply pay the ransom.

Navies of the world obviously faced a challenge that was part of the reason for which some of them had come into existence. By the beginning of the 21st century, anti-piracy techniques had evolved into a kinder, gentler type of activity, in which captured offenders were simply relieved of their weapons and dropped off at the nearest friendly coast. Often this happened after the pirates had received a meal and medical attention. The days of walking the plank, or swinging from the yardarm, were gone. And, said many, including the pirates...'Good riddance!'

In 2008 more than $30 million was paid to Somali pirates. Men operating from open boats had succeeded in hijacking the largest vessel ever taken by pirates, the 318,000 dwt Saudi-flagged oil tanker, *Sirius Star*, carrying crude oil valued at $100 million. As the year slouched to a close, *Sirius Star* with crew aboard was anchored in the Indian Ocean offshore from the Somali port city of Harardhere.

In troubled Somalia, conditions had gone from worse to absolute worst. President, Abdullahi Yusuf resigned at the end of the year, after his government, with nominal but obviously inadequate support from the west, failed utterly in its attempt to stabilize the country. The country was under the ineffective governance of a Transitional Federal Government, TFG, whose Islamist leaders supported a return to sharia law.

Among the country's young men, Islamic extremists were encouraging pirate gangs to pass up Saudi-flagged ships in favor of attacks against ships of non-Islamic nations. Thus, crimes at sea, heretofore motivated by simple greed and lust for plunder would become acts of terrorism, with religious motivation. This entire development carried with it the notion of increased violence, since danger to passengers and crew would increase significantly if armed, Islamic fundamentalists might gain favor with Allah simply by tossing captives over the side.

Then, an attempted attack on a passenger cruise liner made the danger from these new developments apparent to the world. Insurance rates soared. Passenger bookings through Suez declined. In a score of naval facilities around the world, new meetings were convened to consider appropriate methods for combating the menace at sea.

Meanwhile—ashore in Somalia—money from ransoms paid for ships, cargoes and passengers was enabling new lines of work to emerge. Media personnel attempting to cover the situation were encouraged to believe that pirates were simply frustrated fishermen, disgruntled because more sophisticated fishing vessels from other nations had plundered their traditional fishing waters in the Gulf of Aden and the Indian Ocean. But the facts showed that Somalia, despite its more than 2400 miles of coastline, was never much of a seafaring or fishing nation. Instead, the majority of Somalis were herders, managing flocks of sheep, goats and camels.

As money was collected by agents and middlemen representing pirate bands, businesses were expanding in Somalia. Traditional wooden boats, such as dhows and large skiffs, have always been fashioned slowly from appropriate wood—always an expensive commodity along Somalia's arid northern coast. With an influx of cash, it was easier to purchase hulls made of fiberglass or—even better—large inflatables, of the type employed by maritime assault teams of the world's navies. These craft could run at high speeds in relatively calm seas, and—unless completely perforated—they were hard to sink. Large outboard motors were imported from makers in Japan. Global positioning equipment enabled crews to position themselves appropriately along established shipping lanes leading in and out of Bab el Mandeb, the strait linking the Red Sea with the Gulf of Aden.

With money from successful raids, pirates could buy or lease buildings to serve as headquarters where men could live, eat and chew qat; or receive instruction. Classes could be held in chart reading, GPS techniques, marine radio use—including the ability to intercept and interpret messages from vessels underway—as well as messages from warships sent to protect. And, of course, weapons training.

Although the amounts of money collected to date were insufficient to limit maritime traffic, other concerns were arising, stemming from the possibility of expensive environmental disasters, such as oil spills or a release of toxic industrial chemicals. Then, there was the possibility of disasters involving major loss of life—crews and passengers—either due to deliberate action or to accidents. Finally, the capture of a large passenger vessel—with hundreds of innocent civilians being held for an indeterminate time—was a possibility that could not be ruled out. And these potential disasters were not mutually exclusive.

Late in 2008, shipping representatives of major seafaring nations gathered in Kuala Lumpur, Malaysia, to develop recommendations for appropriate responses. Kuala Lumpur was chosen because it is the headquarters for the Piracy Reporting Center of the ad hoc International Bureau. The Reporting Center was maintaining records of attacks around the world. When representatives of major shippers met earlier, one of their key recommendations had been the establishment of a blockade closing the Somali Coast. But, attendees now concluded that although the existing United Nations Convention on the Law of the Sea would permit a robust response to pirate attacks, legal scholars were correct in stating that "There is a certain political hesitation to forcefully engage in anti-pirate acts."

Perhaps attendees at the conference had seen too many pirate movies to get a burn on against a bunch of opportunistic thugs who claimed to be protecting their fishing grounds, because their call for action was basically— let's hope this isn't too strong a word—lame. No nation wanted to host a pirate Guantanamo. In any event, a blockade was rejected as impractical. And no one wanted pirates in their prisons.

No country has more to lose from piracy than Germany whose fleet of container ships is the largest in the world. German shipping firms own and control 36 percent of container capacity on the planet, and from the outset, Germany's navy has been a strong presence in the Indian Ocean. But German naval commanders have been reluctant to take strong action against the pirates. For one thing, their government, and indeed all the world's governments, were at a loss with regard to the treatment of captives, the ground rules for prosecutions, and the protocols for extradition. As a result, piracy continued and the Somali seamen were well aware that, for a time, they had free rein to act.

While the rest of the world was scratching its head relative to a course of action, Somali pirates were still putting out to sea. Typically, their cruises would last less than a week unless they were successful. In the late spring, Abdallah and his crew were successful in boarding a freighter flying the flag of Liberia. The owners were quick to negotiate a buy-back and the ship was consequently released after Abdallah had taken her down to Eyl. The settlement, which was kept out of the news, was for 1.5 million dollars, U.S., and the transaction occurred in Switzerland. Saudis were involved.

When the pirates returned to Boosaaso, they took a couple of weeks off to celebrate. Abdallah bought two television sets and a DVD player for his family, and an Italian hunting rifle for himself. He took a week off and went south into the mountains of the Warsengeli to hunt the Beira, small antelope that he had frequently watched during his years as a camel boy. Equipped with a scoped rifle, he intended to kill and eat one of these beautiful, elusive creatures. And, *Inshallah*, he knew where to find them.

"Most of the houses stand on a small barren island which is connected with the mainland by a narrow causeway. At a distance the tall buildings of white coral, often five stories high, present an imposing appearance, and the prominent chimneys of the condensing machinery—for there is scarcely any fresh water—seem to suggest manufacturing activity. But a nearer view reveals the melancholy squalor of the scene. A large part of the town is deserted. The narrow streets wind among tumbled-down and neglected houses. The quaintly carved projecting windows of the facades are boarded up. The soil exhales an odor of stagnation and decay. The atmosphere is rank with memories of waste and failure. The scenes that meet the eye intensify these impressions. The traveler who lands on Quarantine Island is first confronted with the debris of the projected Suakin-Berber Railway. Two or three locomotives that have neither felt the pressure of steam not tasted oil for a decade lie rusting in the ruined workshops. Huge piles of railway material rot, unguarded and neglected, on the shore."

"Suakin"
From "The River War"
Winston S. Churchill

—7— A Bit More about Jitka

She came to France from the Czech Republic when she was just five. Although she spoke Czech as a small child, all of her schooling took place in France. Jitka Malecek grew up in Paris, the only daughter of Czech immigrants. Her father and mother were both musicians and her father, during the years when she was growing up in the City of Light, taught composition at the University of Paris. In addition he composed music and worked, from time-to-time, as a guest conductor for various orchestras in Europe. His works, with a strongly nationalistic Czech flavor, were well-received particularly in eastern European countries.

Jitka's mother, Eva, was a soprano who had just started on a career of her own before she married Jitka's father. A child appeared on the scene shortly afterward, and the new family moved from Prague, where she had been born, to Paris where the girl attended school. Her mom tried for a time to resume her career, but she lacked the contacts she had enjoyed in Prague, and she had the misfortune not to be a good Francophone. As the years passed, Madame Malecek gradually came to accept the loss of what had once appeared to

28

be a promising career. She still sang on occasion, but it fell far short of providing the satisfaction she had expected from music. For a time in Jitka's early teen years, Madame M. attempted to encourage Jitka musically, and for almost three years there had been voice lessons. But Jitka hated singing, even though she enjoyed playing the piano and listening to music. By the time her mother was ready to throw in the towel on ever having a daughter-accompanist, both females had altered their long-term relationship in ways that would take years to recover.

The dark-haired girl with a camera attended public schools where she made friendships with several girls from Africa, among whom were a few Muslims. But these were not intimate friendships because Muslim girls were admonished not to become friendly with western girls.

Jitka grew up speaking French; very little Czech was spoken in the Malecek household. M. Malecek was anxious to encourage his wife's fluency in French. To Jitka it was the language she grew up with. Through Ecole Superieur, she also studied English, and when it came time to go to school, her father thought he might use his influence to get her into St. Catherine's College at Oxford University.

When she had been just fifteen, a twig of a girl with an inexpensive Japanese camera, she had been captivated by the story of French photographer Hippolyte Bayard, who had developed a process for producing positive images on paper almost in parallel with Louis Jacques Daguerre. But Bayard was reluctant to push his claims, while Daguerre had influential friends in government. It was the age-old story, one that often appeals to the young. A good man got screwed because he lacked friends, influence, pull, connections. It was exactly the type of story that can inspire a fifteen-year old and Jitka, neglected by her talented family and frequently on her own, was looking for a field to make her own.

When a gallery in Paris held a retrospective on the works of Bayard, Jitka went every day and soaked up his black and white images until they were etched into her memory. Bayard's depictions of mills, silhouetted against the sky near Montmartre, were fixed in the girl's consciousness like paintings by old masters in the museums of Amsterdam.

For a long time her attempts at photography were limited to black and white. She played, for a spell, with tray processing, but her real interest lay in looking through the lens of an SLR camera, and—even though it was an awkward transition—she eventually switched to digital photography and began the slow process of absorbing the tricks and anomalies of that flexible method of capturing the world.

Bayard wasn't the only Frenchman to inspire the French teen. When the

Louvre held an exhibition of the works of Maxime Du Camp, Jitka went several times and made notes on what she saw. Du Camp, in 1849, had convinced the French government to send him on a photographic tour of the Middle East. Moreover he had managed to finagle a job for the reporter friend who would accompany him. This friend just happened to be Gustave Flaubert.

Departing in 1847, Du Camp spent twenty-one months in the Middle East, returning with over 200 calotypes that he used to produce an album of photographic prints titled, "Egypt, Nubia, Palestine and Syria."

Du Camp's album was published in installments and depicted—for those wealthy enough to afford his album—a glimpse of the exotic civilizations of the mid-east that had never been seen in Europe.

For a fifteen-sixteen year old girl with a vivid imagination, Du Camp's images lit a fire that would take decades to burn out.

When it was time to send Jitka to university, her parents both agreed that England was the preferred choice. Mostly, they agreed, it was the demands of total immersion in a second language, coupled with the change in culture.

"This girl is French, and nothing can change that," her father said. "If she would live for the remainder of her life among the Esquimaux, she would still be French." Her mother agreed. "C'est vrai," she laughed. "She is cast in concrete. You must find a place for her. Perhaps Oxford? Let's see what they might do to broaden her." And so...Oxford it was.

One of Jitka's memorable accomplishments during university years was to walk approximately eighty percent of Hadrian's Wall carrying her camera. By this time she was experienced at looking through the lens of a digital SLR camera and, on occasion, playing with the images, using commercial software to enhance, fade, crop, or otherwise improve the images consistent with her vision or imagination. Her photos were displayed in the library at St. Catherine's and once she received a strong positive review in the Oxford town newspaper.

The young woman had been out of university, earning a precarious living in London as a free-lance photographer, when she conceived the notion of visiting Suakin with her digital camera and an ample supply of batteries and memory cards. In her experience to date as a free lancer she had estimated that the ratio of images captured to images sold was somewhere in the range of one-in-seventy to one-in-a-hundred. This didn't mean that you could ever get sloppy and let your mind drift. Every shot had to be a keeper, whether of not it found a buyer.

She stayed in touch with her parents in France, and visited from time-to-time; at least once a year, but sometimes more. In recent years, as she moved into an age when they considered her to be marriageable, they seem to have less interest in her visits. They loved their daughter, but she had failed to meet their expectations. Now, later in life, it wasn't clear that she would give them grandchildren. It was true, she had to admit, she had never brought a male friend along, much less a fiancée.

But that didn't mean she wasn't interested in men. For the pretty, dark-eyed girl, admirers and lovers were easy to find. She just hadn't met any that she considered would be worth it for the long pull. And her parents, she considered, had signed on for the long pull. They would be a tough act to follow. It had never crossed her mind that her parents might separate. They seemed as constant and as fixed in place...as stars in the firmament. So far, she had not met a man she felt could measure up.

Jitka Malecek, the photographer, had heard of Suakin before she read Winston Churchill's description of the place. But nothing she had seen or read captured her imagination as strongly as Churchill's paragraphs describing this Red Sea coastal slaving town. Even before she visited Suakin she could visualize the fading blue paint on the old Arabic doors.

Three years after she graduated, Jitka had run across an essay on Winston Churchill that led her to seek out a copy of "The River War." Reading Churchill's description of the Red Sea port of Suakin, led her to do additional research. As a consequence she conceived the idea of a photo essay on the decayed slave terminus, depicting its ruins, cemeteries, antique fortifications and the population that had elected to linger. Suakin was undoubtedly dying, had been dying for decades, but it hadn't died; therefore some inhabitants had obviously chosen to return and stay. This meant that some elements of social organization still remained.

Jitka went to work, contacting several London papers, promising to provide them with interesting images in return for a measure of support. It took six months before she was able to put a program together that seemed to promise a measure of financial support, coupled with freedom to move around. With persistence and her interesting portfolio, she won a modest commitment from the BBC.

The BBC maintained a bureau in Khartoum in the Sudan and they would provide an initial contact point for Jitka's foray into Africa. Khartoum, famed as the place where the White Nile and the Blue Nile come together, is about 500 miles from Suakin, from whence thousands of Sudanese were shipped to labor for Arab slave owners on the other side of the Red Sea.

In Khartoum, her contacts put her in touch with a driver and a sound man who would accompany her on the drive. She didn't want a sound man, but BBC insisted. The staff at Khartoum recommended that she take a local puddle jumper and fly into Port Sudan. "You could pick up a driver and a sound man there," they had advised her. But she wanted the experience of driving beside the Nile and seeing temples and tombs in the vicinity of Shendi. It wasn't clear that she might ever come this way again, and Jitka wanted to see what could be seen.

The drive to Haiya across the desert after leaving Atbara on the Nile, was an eye-opener for her. For the first time in her life she entertained thoughts of what it might be like to die of thirst in the desert. Fortunately, the ride to Haiya took less than four hours. After that, the road was a lot better and, besides, there was plenty of traffic. The discomfort of getting to Suakin was soon forgotten. During her college years, Jitka had frequently hitched rides in out-of-the-way places in Britain's hinterlands. She had usually been picked up by the first or second vehicle after she gave a sign. Naively, she had never reflected too long on the possible reasons behind her successes in this arena.

Actually, during the days when Jitka was photographing in Suakin, she stayed overnight at accommodations in Port Sudan, located about thirty-five miles to the north. Port Sudan had comfortable guesthouses and there were several hotels with decent food and even after-dinner entertainment. Her driver and sound man dropped her at her hotel in Port Sudan and went off to find cheaper digs, and, although she wasn't completely comfortable with this arrangement, she realized that this was the way things were done.

Her minions were there bright and early on the next morning and by eight-thirty, they were bouncing south on the road to the coast.

Jitka photographed at Suakin for a week—actually nine days— and each day passed in a flash. She could have stayed for two more weeks and been perfectly happy. Everything wanted to be photographed; everything was crying to be captured with images. The ruined buildings, the cemeteries, crumbling docks, rusting rolling stock; everything begged to have its story told...or at least acknowledged.

After Suakin, many Londoners came to share Jitka's vision. She was, in every sense, a photographer.

"Mogadishu, Somalia—A radical Islamic group in Somalia said Friday it will fight the pirates holding a Saudi supertanker loaded with $100 million worth of crude oil.

Abdelghafar Musa, a fighter with Al-Shabab who claims to speak on behalf of all Islamic fighters in Somalia, said ships belonging to Muslim countries should not be seized.

In the past two weeks, Somalia's pirates have seized eight vessels including the supertanker. They continue to hold hundreds of crew members on the ships off the Somali coast."

Somali Islamists say they'll fight pirates
Mohamed Sheik Nor, for AP
Rochester Democrat & Chronicle, Nov. 22, 2008

—8—Abdallah's Anger

Pirate commander Abdallah was in a white-hot fury as he called his extended pirate family into a meeting. This family had now grown to include four trained boarding groups operating from a well-equipped mother ship, a small trawler captured from Mauritius. Everyone in his crew was a member of the Issaq clan of the Samaale family group. Everyone, that is, except Mahmood, one of Abdallah's best boat steerers and mechanics. Mahmood was from Sudan, a Dinka, but he had been to sea for several years with a small Greek line operating in the Mediterranean. Mahmood attended all meetings, although unlike Somali men, he rarely spoke.

The offense that had enraged Abdallah was a visit by eight members of Al-Shabab who had journeyed from Mogadishu to rebuke him for the recent capture of a small Turkish-flagged freighter taken northeast of Bender Beyla. The Turkish shipping line had employed tough negotiators, but in the end a settlement figure had been reached and his men had been well satisfied with the outcome.

The young Islamists from Al-Shabab argued that the Turkish ship, as all ships flying flags of the Ummah, should have been exempted. Their meeting with Abdallah and his closest lieutenants had been confrontational. The session began badly and quickly degenerated. Neither side had any interest in hearing the arguments from the other.

Somehow, Abdallah had been under the misconception that the men from Al-Shabab were of the Darood clan, which—though they live in the south—were also related through the Samaale line. But when he learned that they were Rahanwins, from the Saab family, he exploded.

The meeting ended just short of violence. But it was far from over.

"I will have to kill that young man—Dajaal," Abdallah told Tarik, one of his lieutenants.

"*Inshallah.* He was insufferably rude."

"I cannot tolerate it. He will have to die. I cannot accept *dallill* at his hands. *Diya* cannot sway me. *Goon* will not satisfy me now. And if I exact *dil* as I plan, his kinsmen are likely to require *diya* themselves. "

"*Inshallah.* But he was not alone." Tarik wondered if there might be a role for him.

""That is true, brother. However it was Dajaal who was completely offensive."

"Will you speak to the Imam first?"

"Under consideration. I do not think it would be *haram* after the words that came out of Dajaal's mouth. We had many men present who heard the insulting way in which he addressed all of us."

"Will you call a meeting of the *Heer* to determine how you would pay the blood compensation?"

"It will be unavoidable. I am considering to call them before the deed, so that I might know their assessment of the penalty I might face."

"By now, you must know, they are likely to be halfway back to Mogadishu."

"I know that city, and he will not be too hard to find. But I may need help to track him down while avoiding detection."

"If I can assist...."

Gradually, Abdallah was cooling down.

Eight men were chewing *qat* in Tarik's apartment two blocks from Boosaaso's waterfront. They were sprawled across three leather sofas, cheeks stuffed with leaves just in from Yemen. They sat in silence for several moments before Tarik said, "When do you plan on going south?"

"Soon. Soon."

"You will take the new rifle?"

"Not necessary. I think I must kill him with a spear."

Tarik smiled, remembering the poet's words. "*The iron-shafted spear...*"

"Just so. The iron shafted spear."

"And drive it through their ribs."

"So that their lungs spew out." The men were alternating familiar lines from noted Somali poet, Faarah Nuur.

"Let's say the lines together," Abdallah proposed.

"Begin."

Abdallah started at the beginning of the last stanzas of Nuur's famous poem, *The Limits of Submission.*

"If they are still not satisfied.
A beautiful girl
And her bridal house I offer them."

Tarik picked up the next lines.

"If they are still not satisfied,
I select livestock also
And add them to the tribute."

And then, the two Issaq clansmen were reciting together as the others listened intently to words that were familiar to them all.. In perfect synchrony, they recited...

"If they are still not satisfied,
'O brother-in-law, oh Sultan, oh King!'
These salutations I lavish upon them."

Now they were warming into the home stretch.

"If they are still not satisfied,
At the time of early morning prayers I prepare
The dark gray horse with black tendons,
And with the words 'Praise to the Prophet' I take
The iron-shafted spear,
And drive it through their ribs
So that their lungs spew out.
Then they are satisfied!"

They were laughing together as everyone shouted that memorable last line several times.
Markaasuu sellimaa!
Markaasuu sellimaa!
Markaasuu sellimaa!

"You will come with me to Mogadishu?" Abdallah whispered to his lieutenant.

"Of course," Tarik replied. "You have but to tell me when you will leave."

"First, I will speak to the Diya-paying group to see what this bloodshed must cost me."

"The piracy industry started about ten to fifteen years ago, Somali officials said, as a response to illegal fishing. Somalia's central government imploded in 1991, casting the country into chaos. With no patrols along the shoreline, Somalia's tuna-rich waters were soon plundered by commercial fishing fleets from around the world. Somali fishermen armed themselves and turned into vigilantes by confronting illegal fishing boats and demanding that they pay a tax.

"From there, they got greedy," said Mohamed Osman Aden, a Somali diplomat in Kenya. "They started attacking everyone."

By the early 2000s, many of the fishermen had traded in their nets for machine guns and were hijacking any vessel they could catch; sailboat, oil tanker, United Nations chartered food ships."

> "Somali pirates tell their side—they want only money."
> www.nytimes.com
> November 24, 2008

—9—Somalia's Coastline; and a Bit More

The ancient land that wraps around the Horn of Africa hardly deserves to be called a nation; this assessment at the end of the first decade in the Twenty-first century. This is unfortunate, since it is occupied by people who share a common—and very ancient—ancestry and are united by both a common language and a common religious faith. Although many Somalis speak Arabic, Italian or English, their Somali language, written (today) in Roman characters, is universal, despite the absence of a formal system of universal education.

Somalia's coastline extends for more than 2,400 miles to encompass some of the oldest and most stable geography on the African continent. In ancient geologic times, it is now believed that the tear in the earth's crust known as the Red Sea Rift extended far beyond today's Bab el Mandeb, the southern gateway to the sea created by the rift. This extended rent in the crustal surface once continued south to slice off the tip of Africa's horn as cleanly as if it had been a dead rhino under a chainsaw.

In subsequent eons other geological shifts allowed the tip of the horn to be rejoined, but the evidence remains in the form of the Nugaal Depression, a broad, low-lying strip of desert that effectively isolates the Horn's rocky, mountainous tip. Geologists sometimes refer to the projecting end of Somalia's horn as "an incipient island."

The northern coast of Somalia borders the Gulf of Aden and faces to the north, toward the mountainous Republic of Yemen, a country with which it has cultural and economic ties. After rounding Africa's horn southbound, Somalia's coast angles to the southwest facing the Indian Ocean. The northern third of this littoral consists primarily of arid scrubland extending to the sea. The lower two-thirds of this coast are bordered by a narrow strip of land whose climate is regulated by the bordering ocean or by Somalia's two major rivers, the Shabela and the Guiba. This sliver of coast is reasonably well watered and supports the cultivation of sugar cane, sesame seeds, bananas and coconuts.

To the north, desert meets the ocean. In the south, there are mangrove swamps and tropical beaches.

Despite its extensive coastline, Somalia lacks great natural harbors. Nevertheless, those that it has have been noted for maritime commerce since antiquity. Together with Yemen, its neighbor to the north, Somalia was known to the ancient civilizations of Egypt, Greece and Rome as a principal source of highly valued commodities, such as frankincense and myrrh. Somalia's coastline was known to ancient Egyptians as the *Incense Coast* or *The Land of Myrrh*.

Exposed coasts facing the Gulf of Aden and Indian Ocean make it easy to launch the small craft favored by pirates. But they quickly learned that operating from the beach is inefficient and impractical. It is easier to operate from a mother ship; from a larger craft such as a large dhow, tug or utility boat, preferably with a hull form that belies its purpose, from which assault teams can launch their craft.

Conventional wooden fishing boats, whose designs developed over centuries, were used initially. These boats, long and narrow, were fast when propelled by powerful outboard engines, and they had reasonably good sea-keeping properties. When these were in short supply, pirates tried other configurations; fiberglass hulls were fast and light. But inevitably the pirates, connected to the larger world by the Internet and wireless phones, began migrating to more optimal small boats for speed, toughness, and versatility, the same type of vessel used by U.S. Navy SEALs and their counterparts around the world; inflatable rubber boats.

Inflatables are easily launched from anything that floats. They can be landed on almost any beach, and carried inland for concealment.

By 2008, more than two hundred pirate groups, organized along clan lines, existed in the lawless territories known as Somalia, Somaliland and Puntland. Some banded together along clan lines but, so far, the plunder from the sea had been sufficiently abundant that internecine warfare between rival clans had not erupted. Piracy is the single largest contributor to the Somali economy.

In recent decades, Somalia has been so violent, dangerous and lawless that most international aid organizations shun missions there. At least, one might say, the violence today is no worse than usual.

Lt. Commander Vance Morrisette was grabbing a fast lunch in a small corner cafeteria in the Pentagon. He was eating alone when a sharp-looking female officer approached.

"Hi. Expecting anyone? OK if I join you?"

He recognized Lt. Sheila McKendrick, an Annapolis grad who had spoken to him a couple of times in the past. She worked, he remembered, in some kind of cryptography job, and he had never seen her except in situations like this. Since she had approached him more than once, his antennas were out and he suspected that she had sized him up.

She did look very appealing and it wasn't just the uniform. If she looked as good out of it, as in it, she would be impressive. But...there were consequences; she might be a ticking bomb. He was suspicious of pushy females.

"Sure. Have a seat. But I'm almost done. And I'll have to get back for a meeting in a few minutes."

"I haven't seen you around for a while. They're keeping you busy?"

"Pirates never sleep."

"You're looking at those attacks off the Horn of Africa?" He was intrigued by the way she lifted her pinky as she dipped a fry into the little ketchup cup. And the way she put it in her mouth? Oh, boy. This woman looked like trouble.

"Where are they from? Somalia?"

"Yeah. Somalia. Know much about it?"

"Take a minute and brief me." *Yep. This is a hit. Girl alert!* But it had been a while since a woman hit on him. *What the hell...*

"OK. Let's try free association for a moment. I say—Eggs? You say bacon. Salt? Pepper. OK?"

"Go ahead."

"Black?"

"White."

"Somalia?"

"I quit." She laughed and ohmigod! *Dimples. And all that other. What is she doing in the Navy?*

"Most Americans never heard of Somalia, and couldn't find it on a map.

We'll just ignore those folks. But for the ones who know about Somalia, the response you might expect to hear is 'Failed state.' "

"Somalia?"

"Failed state. Somalia. Failed state."

He started to pull the clipping out of his shirt pocket. He had just cut it out of *The Economist* for October, 2009. The radical youth were beginning to kill Christians in the country, wherever they were found.

"The shaky transitional government led by Sheik Sharif Ahmed, whose writ runs weakly across the territory the Shabab does not yet run, is unlikely to speak up for any of its citizens caught with a bible. Though professing moderation, he promotes a version of sharia law whereby every citizen of Somalia is born a Muslim and anyone who converts to another religion is guilty of apostasy, which is punishable by death."

But, drawn in by the magnetism of this stunning female, he ended up giving her a fairly complete rundown on some key facts he had picked up. She gave him her full and undivided attention, something which most men would respond to, and he talked much more than he intended. Here are the highlights of what Vance told Sheila.

The interesting "nation" that wraps itself around the Horn of Africa has a long, fascinating history. And prehistory. Geologically, it is ancient, linked to the world's great deserts that sweep across the expanse of Asia only to be separated from the arid wastes of Africa by the Great Rift that became the Red Sea, separating the Dark Continent from the Middle East.

Anthropologically, it is also ancient. The ancient Egyptians once sailed down the Red Sea to bring back frankincense and myrrh. Somalia was on the receiving end of invasions by Arabs from the east and by Europeans from the surrounding sea, British, French, Italians.

Italians came in the 1800's to establish banana plantations in the well-watered regions of the south. British came later in the 1800's to occupy British Somaliland along the northern coast, bordering the Gulf of Aden. Their objectives were linked to visions of an empire where the sun never set, and in particular they wished to protect their installations at Aden, across the gulf.

Not to be outdone, the French came to occupy the northwest corner, eventually causing it to be split off to form today's independent nation of Djibouti.

Since prehistoric times the Somalis have been nomadic herdsmen, following their flocks of goats, sheep, cattle and the versatile and adaptive camel. Camels can eat almost any plant, including those with thorns.

40

The camel, able to survive and thrive where other mammals fail, has been a mainstay of the Somali's ability to inhabit arid northern regions that are principally harsh, sweltering deserts for much of the year.

Italian presence in what was called Italian Somaliland lasted until the years of WW II, when they were ousted by Britain. The independent state of Somalia wasn't formed until 1969 and that first government was overthrown almost immediately by a military coup. Since then this unfortunate country has been beset by famine, drought, war with neighboring Ethiopia, civil war, cold war rivalries between the east and west (in which Somalia's strategic location made them an unwilling pawn,) and the inherent intransigent nature of Somali people.

An early British visitor, Colonel James Outram, once tried to dissuade explorer Richard Burton who visited Somalia in 1854. Outram cautioned that, "...the country was so extremely dangerous for any foreigner to travel in and the Somalis were of such a wild and inhospitable nature that no stranger could possibly live among them."

Today, more than a century and a half later, Outram's assessment still holds for non-Muslims. For despite the differences that separate Somalia's several clan groups, they are united by their Islamic faith, a common language, and unique cultural traditions. They are united in their Sunni faith just as they are divided by clan loyalties.

Somalia, despite attempts once made by Italian, French and British to effect cultural changes, is still, in 2009, not a country where non-Muslims are likely to thrive, or even survive. Today, the Islamic fundamentalist group known as Al-Shabab, *the Youth*, search the countryside looking for Christians or for evidence of Christian influence—such as the possession of a Bible. Such offenses are punishable by death.

Since the Shabab are heavily armed, it's easy for infidels to be shot and dumped by the roadside. Taking a chapter from the books of their Saudi teachers to the east, some offenders against Islam are beheaded.

These are not stories that find their way into the western press with any frequency because...well, take a guess. Statistics describing most nations of the world are particularly dismal for Somalia. Life expectancy for males is 47.1 years. For females it's 50. Literacy rate is 37.8 percent, skewed toward males because females don't attend school. There are 14 TVs per thousand people, and about 60 radios per thousand. Somalia has no court system and no army. One doctor serves 20,000 people. Female circumcision is an established cultural practice, with the consequent impact on public health.

Life in cheap in Somalia and some lives are cheaper than others. One factor in Somalia's lawlessness and failure to thrive is the increasing prevalence of *qat* as a recreational drug. Although it has long been present in Somali society, the changes in recent decades have made it more easily available and more easily affordable to ordinary people. This has led to increased usage as a social lubricant. Across the Gulf of Aden in Yemen, an estimated eighty percent of the population use *qat* on a daily basis, and their entire society is impacted by the plant. Improvements in agricultural practices—irrigation, pesticides, herbicides—coupled with improved methods of getting the product to markets have resulted in widespread use and acceptance. *Qat* is not prohibited by sharia law; at least not as this law is interpreted in Yemen. This acceptance has been transmitted to Somalia where *qat* use is rising sharply. It is an escapist drug, well suited to Somalia's miserable living conditions, and the best *qat* in the world comes from just across the gulf in Yemen.

As in other parts of the Arab word, *qat* use requires separation by gender, and women are less likely to be frequent or regular users. But among both sexes, usage is on the rise.

It's a dismal picture and the outlook for the future is grim. Somalia can't feed itself and food shipments from other nations only delay inevitable episodes of famine. Shipments are routinely hijacked by Somalia warlords and used to increase their grip on power. Piracy is the only "industry" that sustains this broken region.

"Absent that, Somalia is literally hell on earth," Vance concluded. The young officer was clearly impressed by his command of the material. *He's smart, too.*

At the end of twenty minutes, Sheila had eaten her lunch, pushed the tray aside and had both elbows on the table like a high school girl. Vance knew he was behaving badly, but damn, it felt good. Lt. McKendrick was a killer. He could have bedded her that afternoon; but it just didn't feel right. He was tempted, but she seemed to be too hungry. He had lied about having to get back for a meeting but she figured it out immediately and was optimistic for the future. She already knew he was a SEAL.

"Maritime terrorism is not a serious threat. Acts of terrorism at sea or from the sea, that is to say acts of violence committed by politically motivated groups to inspire their supporters or induce feelings of fear among their enemies, have been rare and are likely to remain so."

The Unwanted Challenge
Dr. Martin N. Murphy, Senior Fellow
Center for Strategic and Budgetary Assessments
In 'Proceedings, U.S. Naval Institute,' December 2008

—10—How the World Sees Pirates and Piracy

At the same time Jitka Malecek was looking for a way to get an assignment from the BBC, groups of shippers, insurers, investment brokers and maritime organizations were continuing to meet in half-a-dozen venues around the world. NATO headquarters in Brussels was having one continuous week of all-day sessions by a working group with representatives from England, France, Netherlands, Germany, Italy and Greece. In Malaysia, similar meetings were being held but at wider intervals. Shippers in that region had been dealing with pirates for a longer time, and they periodically sentenced captured pirates to prison terms. Typically, these terms were short, willingly served, and the well-fed pirates frequently returned to their vocation shortly after release.

In the U.S., working group meetings were conducted at the UN, and these particular get-togethers deserved acknowledgement as the least effective of any of the multitude of ineffective meetings held around the world.

The Pentagon had a team of military men augmented by several civilians from such diverse agencies as the NSA, CIA and ONR, the Office of Naval Research. Their interest in problems relating to piracy were as unclear as their charter to participate in activities to counter piracy, barring perhaps, the utilization of some hitherto unrevealed death ray.

In Athens, a consortium of Greek shippers met at an elegant waterfront hotel in Pireus and discussed possible solutions that usually involved a degree of violence that they knew they would be unable to sell, either to the world community or to their own government.

Istanbul was home to gatherings of Turkish shippers and insurers. A Turkish ship was being held for ransom at Eyl even as the group met. Much of the wheat that was being shipped to Somalia—usually by way of Mogadishu—came from Black Sea ports supporting Ukraine or wheat growers in other Central Asian countries.

Arab countries too, had meetings to discuss their response. Since Arab moneyed interests routinely funneled quantities of money into Somalia—for the purchase of weapons and, in some instances, food—they felt ill-used by Somalis, when any Arab ship was taken. They were especially incensed when a Saudi-flagged vessel was captured. The recent capture of the Sirius Star, a Saudi tanker with two million barrels of oil with an estimated value of $100 million, was a bitter pill. The heartening news from a Saudi perspective, was recent information from Al-Shabab, a radicalized Somali youth organization, that in subsequent raids pirates would consider avoiding all-Arab flagged vessels. This division, based on religious belief, had major advantages for the beneficiaries of this exclusion, but it tended to change completely the nature of the act of piracy for money.

These are only a fraction of the meetings that were being held in the centers of the world's maritime trade. Insurers were scrambling, weak-kneed and concerned.

Piracy, of course, is not a new crime. It's as old as commerce on the sea, but pirates of yesterday did not have GPS systems to help pinpoint destinations on featureless oceans; or details of departure times and planned routes. Neither did they carry automatic weapons, grenade launchers and other twentieth century weapons. There was a time when pirates carried cutlasses and pikes and other simple weapons, and in those days the seamen faced with repelling them carried similar weapons and knew how to employ them equally well.

Back in the days of wooden ships and iron men, the method of dealing with pirates was "no quarter" and captives were dangled from a yardarm before being fed to sharks.

As the amount of piracy increased around the world, various attempts were made to present the pirate world to the public, and bold journalists frequently traveled far and slept hard in order to speak directly to these men; whenever possible to their leaders.

In 2007 a bold journalist on the *National Geographic* staff, Peter Gwin, traveled to Malaysia to speak with, and photograph, pirates in the dangerous waters of the Straits of Malacca. Accompanied by a photographer who lives in Malaysia, Gwin managed to speak with several individuals who had been successful pirates for years and had no intention of giving up their chosen way of life. The account provided in Geographic's article made it clear that the lifestyle of pirates was essentially unchanged in 2007 from the way it was practiced in 1607. The big difference seemed to be that today's hijackings on the high seas are less dangerous, more highly rewarding and less severely punished than in former days.

One of the lessons learned from examining the record of pirate depredations in the Straits of Malacca is that the authoritarian governments in places like Singapore and Malaysia's capital Kuala Lumpur, insure that pirates are dealt with by an established police force, judiciary, and penal system that are capable of capturing, judging, sentencing and punishing marauders. In contrast, when ships from the world's great maritime nations confront Somali pirates, capturing them only begins the headaches that follow.

What is to be done today? There is no government in Somalia with the capability or the will, to take the necessary steps to deal with captives. To the contrary, citizens in pirate towns in Somalia now depend on the revenue brought in by pirates. A whole range of services catering to pirates is now prospering.

Data from Malacca Strait indicate that between 2002 and 2007, 258 attacks occurred. Considering this interval to span six years, it's clear that the rate of attacks was approximately 3.6 attacks per month for the entire period. For shippers in the region, a cruise down the Strait was—still is— essentially a dice roll.

At the Pentagon, Lt. Commander Vance Morrisette attempted to gather, analyze, digest, collate, interpret and summarize every shred of factual information he could gather from a wide range of sources. And while most of the best sources came from the military, it became clear that while the Navy knows a lot, they don't know everything. Sometimes information comes from unsuspected sources. Some of them more credible and useful than others.

As a former SEAL, Vance was aware of the difficulties in boarding a ship underway from a small craft alongside. This explains why one of his favorite accounts came from Geographic's report from a Malayan pirate or *lanun*, of the type called "jumping squirrels."

When asked by Geographic's staff writer how *lanun* boarded ships undetected, a pirate known as *Beach Boy* provided an answer that Vance typed out on his computer and carried in his pocket for a week.

"We use magic," *Beach Boy* had answered. "We cast a spell to make the crew stay asleep. We can be invisible, bulletproof. It's a power you learn." Then, his interrogator asked *Beach Boy* why, if magic, he had been wounded after boarding

"They fired twice," *Beach Boy* answered.

"I resisted the first bullet but wasn't strong enough for the second."

Vance read the entire article several times, but Beach Boy's words lingered. As a former SEAL leader he wasn't buying into the magic answer. Growing up in Utah, he had heard stories of Native American Ghost Dancers, but that was absurdity.

These bastards are wired on something before they board. What it is probably varies. Alcohol, qat, marijuana, cocaine, heroin. Maybe methamphetamines? Like some of our military in the past. Gotta be something that doesn't make you drowsy. Some kind of upper. I'll bet some kind of drugs are involved in most of these attacks.

In Somalia, that drug was qat.

"Nairobi, Kenya—The U.N., African Union and Arab nations struggled to respond Thursday to a surge of pirate attacks, authorizing more sanctions and calling for international peacekeepers to stop Somali sea bandits who appear undeterred by nonviolent tactics. The economic reverberations of the attacks widened as A.P Moller-Maersk A/S, the world's largest container-shipping company said it would begin sending some slower vessels thousands of miles around southern Africa to avoid the perilous waters on the shorter Suez Canal route."

African Union, Arabs try to fight piracy
The Associated Press, Friday, November 21, 2008

—11—The U.N. Condemns Piracy

Unexpectedly, Lt. Commander Vance Morrisette, USN, was ordered to fly out to Djibouti following a request from the SEAL Commander at the U.S. Naval installation in that country. That unit wanted to hear from someone who had experience using the Hammerhead Helmet in an actual field mission, and Vance came highly recommended.

The request came up suddenly and it was not expected to take more than two weeks at most. Meanwhile, the possible assignment to UBSA would be on hold.

To tell the truth, things at home with Rhonda were so miserable and unpleasant that the thought of a month's respite away from the constant bickering was appealing. And Vance had some good memories about past experiences in Djibouti, even though it had been a few years.

Rhonda watched him pack, taking potshots from the doorway of the spare bedroom of their small apartment. "When can I expect you back?" she asked, in a tone that suggested that it really didn't matter.

"Honestly, I don't know, myself, the way these orders were cut. It could take as long as a month. If I'm right about what they want to know, it shouldn't take more than three days." He had already told her this once. "Nominally, two weeks. But it's impossible for me to know what else may be going on."

"So I'm just supposed to put my life on hold until...."

"Jesus, Rhonda. Cut the act. This assignment won't make a bit of difference in the way you're living your life. Don't try to make me feel bad.... or guilty."

"I was just trying to..."

47

"Because it won't work. How about just getting me a cup of coffee instead of trying to bust my balls."

He didn't want to let her make him angry, but he knew if they kept at this for twenty minutes, he would be likely to lose his temper and she was certain to lose hers.

When the details of his travel orders were clear, he was a bit surprised to learn his outbound trip was not on a military transport, but on a chartered executive jet, leaving out of Dulles. That promised to be interesting, and it turned out to be even more interesting than he expected.

There were twelve or thirteen passengers aboard the twin engine jet. A couple of nurses were headed for a new assignment and several high-level civilian defense contractors were going out to monitor some construction projects that were underway. There were three officers from nuclear submarines and three or four more whose specialties he couldn't make out. And there was one admiral. The admiral seemed to know who he was which was a surprise to Vance; but he didn't want to ask any questions. It was possible that the admiral had requested a copy of the flight manifest.

In any case, the admiral let it be known that Vance should occupy the adjacent seat. After Vance moved his seat—in response to the steward's request—the officer introduced himself. Rear Admiral Julius Fantone, Naval Intelligence. That was all. It didn't ring a bell with Vance and he wondered if this might be some sort of test.

Admiral Fantone seemed anxious to engage Vance in conversation, and it was quickly apparent he was aware that Vance had been tracking African pirates. This had the effect of making the commander very guarded in his comments. When the steward came through with snacks, the admiral asked for a can of cashews and a scotch "drizzled over one ice cube."

Vance, raised in Mormon country, wasn't much of a drinker but in his excursions with Rhonda he had come to prefer good rum, straight. His selection made the admiral smile. "An appropriate choice for a man who deals with pirates," he said, chuckling at his own wit.

As the second rum settled and his inhibitions lowered, Vance decided to turn the tables and ask a few questions of his own.

"Admiral, I spend a lot of time studying what pirates have done in the past, and trying to use that information to predict what they are likely to do in the future. But, although I can and do make recommendations, I don't make policy. That's done by men like you. I would be interested to learn—insofar as you're able to talk about it—what commanders like yourself think should be done to stop the pirates."

His initial answer nearly made Vance laugh.

"You are aware, I'm sure, Commander, that the UN has issued a resolution condemning piracy."

"Yes..."

"Well, that's the first important step."

Some rum went down the wrong way—into his airway, and Vance coughed. It was a bad place to cough.

"Excuse me," he said. "I think I got a piece of peanut in my throat."

"UN Resolution 1816 condemns piracy in the strongest possible terms. Now, we'll wait and see how the world responds." The admiral was trying to sound stern.

"But—pardon me if I seem slow, admiral—how long will we wait, and what do we expect to happen?"

"Sanctions. Economic pressures. Barriers to trade and commerce. There are a vast array of actions that will follow as a logical consequence. Trust me, on this, son. This isn't a situation where we send in the marines." The admiral sipped on his scotch and looked comfortably smug.

This gent seems to be hidebound and maybe constipated. It was becoming obvious to Vance that the admiral wasn't likely to be sharing any useful ideas. He had heard the same old 'cover your ass' approach from top brass fifty times before and it was boring. His mind wandered. *Anyway, about Rhonda. Why did I ever marry that woman? Just because of the way she looks?* Vance was asking himself. *It not like I didn't know what she was...or at least what she was capable of. Was I that needy, myself? Was I that lonely?*

"But the pirates are from Somalia, sir. Where there is no government and no legal system. Fundamentalists are trying to reinstate Sharia law. You probably saw 'Black Hawk Down,' just like everyone else. We won't even send in our marines because they wouldn't know what to do. Because we don't know who to fight. So what do we expect a UN resolution to accomplish?"

Vance could see that the admiral really would have preferred for him to simply agree and fall into line. But what the hell. The reality was that regardless of whether or not the Somali pirates captured a thousand ships or quit tomorrow, the odds were long that he was going to have to divorce Rhonda and the idea was far from pleasant. Most of the men he knew who were divorced were living somewhat squalid lives in shabby apartments with different women—married or unmarried—and usually raising somebody else's kids. He felt he was stuck with her. Just like he was stuck with this knucklehead who thought a bunch of eggheads living like lords in NYC and DC were really going to have any sort of impact on Somalia where we had already pulled out our armed forces. We simply lacked the will to do what needed to be done. For a brief instant while the admiral was talking about the navy's determination to increase its presence, he thought about the experiences of the first Mormons to settle in today's Utah. Then, suddenly, he was back in the conversation, listening to the admiral.

"When we apprehend these criminals at sea—which we can easily do with our superior technology—we are constrained by international law to turn them over to the appropriate jurisdiction for prosecution."

"So pardon me if I keep asking questions that betray my ignorance, Admiral, but what usually happens when we do that?"

"A good question—revealing your understanding of Somalia's court system dilemma. So...as you are also well aware, they often end up in Kenya where the court system is able to deal with them."

"To date, Admiral, what has been the result? How many prosecutions? Or convictions?"

"I don't track these things personally, Commander. I would expect this to fall within your province."

"Based on what I know, admiral, no prosecutions, no convictions. In a lot of cases some other navies are just setting the pirates back on the beach. That what the Danes are doing. Nobody knows what to do with these bastards." Vance was thinking of harsh punishment. Something like he would like to dole out to Rhonda, that selfish bitch, always thinking about gratifying her own wants and needs.

"Well, Commander," the admiral said—now it was his turn to be amused— what would you propose be done with the pirates we capture at sea?"

What the hell, Vance thought, *he asked me, so apparently he wants to know. And he seems to be listening. Why not tell him what he needs to hear?*

"Well admiral, as your comments indicate, we have no legal evidence at the time of capture, that these seamen, armed with AKs and rocket launchers, are actually pirates. There has been no trial and no conviction; therefore, you seem to assume, no punishment can be exacted."

"You're putting words in my mouth, Commander."

"Beg pardon, sir. But are they guilty of anything when captured? You don't have to answer. It was rhetorical." *Yes, and also sarcastic.*

The steward interrupted with a list of sandwiches that were available and Vance chose a tuna salad on white bread. He couldn't see what the admiral chose.

"Look," Vance continued, "You and I are in the U.S. Navy and this means that we know what it means to go to sea. Fishermen don't use AKs. They don't use rocket-propelled grenades. They may use harpoons and spears and explosive lances if they're whaling. But, let's not kid ourselves, there isn't any whaling off the coast of Somalia, and you can't fish with an AK. So all of this talk is just legalistic....legalistic...."

"Bullshit?"

"Thank you," Vance said, smiling. "I was groping for 'persiflage' but bullshit does nicely. Armed men with scaling ladders who board ships uninvited—in my judgement—convict themselves. Back in olden days, there was a term for pirates, a legal term—damn, I can't remember the Latin words, but they meant something like "a common enemy of mankind"—and with this designation, they were headed for the gallows anywhere they were encountered."

"So would you have us regress, commander? To those unenlightened times."

"Compared with what, Admiral? Today's enlightenment? We seem to be paralyzed by inaction. Most Navy men I know—including my cohorts who graduated Annapolis—seem to be embarrassed by the lassitude and torpor prevalent today."

"Don't rant at me, Commander," the admiral said. Vance could see that he might have pushed a senior officer too far, and that was not his intention. He was, however, quite willing to push Rhonda far past her comfort zone, and he had no intention of leaving her well off to screw her way through the Atlantic fleet at his expense. *She'll be back outside Little Creek within a month—I'm willing to bet on it.*

"Beg pardon again, Admiral. But you did ask. In the past, we strung pirates from the yardarm."

"That's what you would propose as today's solution, Commander? I'm surprised."

"No sir. Not at all. We don't even have a lot of yardarms around. No. I'd propose something much different. Something easily within our capability."

"So? Don't keep me in suspense, Commander."

"We're dealing with poor men working from wooden boats with a curious mix of equipment that varies from sophisticated to crude. Their crimes are largely economic—based on money—contrasted with the ideological attacks by Islamic fundamentalists. Of course, this could change. But right now, piracy is based on the desire for money and wealth. It's an easy crime because the risk is low."

"Help me here, son. How do you figure the risk is low?"

"If you board and capture a ship, the ransom money will be in millions. But if you fail, you get set back on the beach. Shit, Admiral, pardon me, we feed them breakfast and put bandaids on scratches before they get beached. Where's their risk?"

"So? What's your solution, Commander? Imagine yourself as Lord Admiral of the Planet."

"Thank you, sir. I accept. OK. Here it is. A ship leaves with men carrying AKs and RPGs. We spot them. They are—*prima facie*—pirates. 'We' meaning our ships. Our swimmers. Our UAVs. Our carrier-based planes. Anyone who sees them. Our snipers. Their configuration, their weaponry, identifies their intention. That vessel and all its occupants and contents never returns to its home port. Nothing washes up one the beach. No ship. No men. No bodies. No survivors. No nothing. The key notion I want to stress is thoroughness. Nothing washes up on Somali beaches."

"My God, Commander. You would have us actually..."

"Deal with a real problem realistically, sir."

"You wouldn't propose that we reopen Guantanamo?"

"Nothing even close."

"Then what?"

"For the common enemy of mankind? The same regard we give to disease germs. In other words, open season. We kill germs."

"You would engage in a fire fight?"

"That wouldn't be my solution."

"What then? Get on with it, Commander."

"We have weapons that can make small craft vanish. My solution would be to have pirates simply disappear. Boat, weapons, engines, safety gear, all crew, simply vanishes. They are going further and further offshore every month. Who knows what can happen on the Indian Ocean? My proposal would be to create a mystery. The pirates leave home. They lose radio contact. And are never heard from again. Nothing. Nada. Not a trace."

"A tall order. Bodies float ashore."

"Not with my plan, sir."

"Some nuclear weapon? You can't be serious."

"Sir, the drones we have now can carry JDAMs-type weapons. I just want some weapons that will chop up a wooden boat and crew into small pieces. Or fiberglas. Or rubber. The sea can do the rest."

"This is not something we have in our arsenal. Off-the-shelf."

"Off-the-shelf? Probably not. But flechettes have been around for a long time."

"I don't know, son. You're starting to make me a bit nervous with this wild talk."

The admiral was starting to be bored with this young upstart who was challenging everything he had been saying. Of a sudden he felt the need to try to snooze a bit. *Then too, there had been three whiskeys.*

"Well, Commander, it has been interesting to hear your views on a somewhat complex and controversial topic. I'm sure your superiors have been paying close attention to your ideas. Thanks for sharing them with me. Now, if you don't mind, I going to try..."

Vance had seen it coming for some minutes. He had known that he was saying far too much. But what the hell...

"Certainly, sir. I think I'll just move back a row. Thanks for the conversation."

As Vance got up to leave, the admiral stuck the paperback he had been holding in his lap into the seat pocket behind Vance's seat. Vance noticed the title. *Lord Jim.*

"Is that any good, Admiral? I've never read it."

"Take it, son. I've never figured out its perennial appeal and I've read it three times trying to understand. Since college. A good yarn but its too wordy. But it's supposed to be a masterpiece. Take it. It has some pirates in it. Maybe you'll get some ideas."

"'If you're finished."

"Take it. Otherwise I'll just leave it here for the next guy."

Now he would be alone in the seat with just thoughts of Rhonda to keep him company. He didn't want to support her. Fortunately, they hadn't had kids. *To hell with this Pentagon crap,* he thought. *When I get back I'm taking the assignment with UBSA and starting on papers with Rhonda. I'll use adultery if I have to.*

"The Republic of Djibouti is committed to protecting its vital interests... ...which are in large part dependent on maritime trade.

To this end, the main lines of Djibouti's maritime defense strategy can be summarized as: To organize a system of surveillance and permanent watch/lookout including gathering information about maritime activities; to have available active means of defense; and to rely on the cooperation of different national departments and institutions responsible for maritime affairs and on bilateral cooperative agreements."

Colonel Abdourhahman Aden Cher
Commandant, Djibouti Navy
in "Proceedings, U.S. Naval Institute", March, 2009

—12 —Djibouti

The Republic of Djibouti is located on Africa's side of the Red Sea opening at its southern entrance into the Gulf of Aden. This small country—just under 9000 square miles, faces across the Bab el Mandeb toward Yemen. Its population is about half a million. Like Panama, Djibouti is important to seafaring nations of the world because of its strategic location.

For much of the 20th century Djibouti was a territory of France while Aden, for the same reasons, was a colony of Great Britain. Djibouti became an independent republic in 1977 but it still retains close ties to France and it is home to that nation's largest overseas contingent. About 3000 French military personnel—mixed services—are stationed in Djibouti. The relationship between Djibouti and France is somewhat tortured and French presence dates from the time of America's Civil War. It was originally known as French Somaliland and it did not become a French territory until 1945. Then, in 1967 it was awkwardly renamed for the tribes living there—French Territory of the Afars and the Issas. Just inland from Djibouti the Afars region of landlocked Ethiopia lies astride the Danakil Desert and the Danakil Depression, some of the hottest and least hospitable real estate on the planet.

During early years of French presence, the French Foreign Legion maintained an outpost and was the dominant military presence. For much of its early history both Ethiopia to the north and Somalia to the south attempted to gain control of Djibouti, but in recent years these nations have both renounced their claims. Ethiopia's desire for Djibouti is somewhat more understandable than Somalia's, since landlocked Ethiopia—lacking access to the sea—relies on rail lines from Djibouti for much of its foreign trade.

The U.S. Navy has long been interested in Djibouti as a fueling station for its fleets in the Indian Ocean and adjacent waters. During the years of the Cold War, the entire region was a hot bed of plot and counter-plot, where James Bond would have stuck out like a sore thumb. Today the U.S. maintains a military presence of approximately 2000 personnel, nominally about two thirds that of the French. Our navy occupies the site of a former French Foreign Legion station rebuilt after being abandoned for a time. Camp Lemonnier was named for the French officer who once commanded Legionnaires but today the base commander is an American naval officer. A naval fueling station—Defense Fueling Supply Point— is maintained at Doraleh.

In the days since 9-11 and the rising prevalence of piracy off Africa's Horn, naval forces from seafaring nations have showed up in the region where the two chief naval stations are at Djibouti in the east and Aden in the west. Neither region could be considered optimal, but Djibouti seems to have won the toss. It is, at present, the headquarters for the CJTF-HOA, Combined Joint Task Force-Horn of Africa. Their force is effective in reducing piracy to the same degree that the United Nations is effective in enforcing world peace.

Officially, the CJTF has a mission that consists of de-mining, humanitarian aid, and counter-terrorism. It is certainly true that the presence of a large warship makes pirates think carefully before boarding a targeted victim. But it doesn't necessarily deter them.

In any case, the military force at the disposal of the CJTF commander is a mixed bag, consisting of elements of the 5th Fleet, U.S. Navy SEALS, Seabees, Marines, U.S. Army Engineers, Artillery, and elements of fleets from participating nations; a coalition of the willing.

Civilians? The half million people who occupy Djibouti speak French and Arabic, both languages being the official languages of government, but both Somali and Afar (an Ethiopian language) are also spoken.

Islam is the dominant religion. Much of the country's interior, like that of its neighbors, Eritrea, Ethiopia and Somalia, is desolate, sandy waste land, a continuation of the great swath of desert that extends across much of Africa. Fishing is an important occupation in Djibouti, as is livestock husbandry; in order of importance—goats, sheep, cattle.

Life expectancy is one of the more depressing statistics from Djibouti. For men it's 41.9 years; for women, 44.7 years. It's not clear if war has played a significant part in these numbers since the three-year uprising of Afars rebels was only ended in late 1994.

To the average person, Djibouti is not a particularly appealing travel destination. Despite the fact that it has some nice beaches, it doesn't give much competition to the French Riviera or even the snug little topless beaches of Greece, or rocky picturesque harbors of southern Turkey. But to the people who operate and manage firms known as security contractors, Djibouti can get the juices flowing.

In the late summer of a recent year such people gathered for a meeting with the express intent of targeting Djibouti as a business opportunity. Interestingly, the gathering was initiated by the American government who seemed to be anxious to spend a large sum of taxpayer's money.

Djibouti is also a topic for discussion at several locations in the U.S. At a secure facility in Virginia just a short drive past Quantico, a meeting was in progress between four members of an unnamed government security agency and three representatives of a privately owned firm known as UBSA, United Brothers Security Associates. To those who know something of the exploits of UBSA they were sometimes called the *Unregulated Bastards*, but among those who paid for the services of this firm they were known simply as UB. Among themselves, employees of this clandestine firm—largely drawn from former military men with specialized skills—they were simply Uncle Bob's.

A group of seven were seated around a circular table, whose selection was probably a bad idea since the room was rectangular and the projection screen was against one wall. Consequently, almost everyone needed to shift their chairs to get a good view of the images being projected. The meeting had been called by representatives of a government agency, whose specific links to the Pentagon were unclear but it was apparent that agency checks were issued from the Department of Defense.

Uncle Bob's headquarters were located in a comfortable facility near Honey Hill, South Carolina, where it was rumored that they had exclusive access to a considerable tract inside the Francis Marion National Forest bordering the Santee River. They had other training facilities on South Carolina's beaches and in the mountains of North Carolina.

The meeting was called to discuss problems related to piracy by groups operating out of Somalia. The unstated—but obvious—purpose was to determine whether the government felt there was a role for UBSA to play, to make a preliminary estimate of what would be involved and to set the stage for subsequent contract negotiations. The two dogs were sniffing one another.

Of the government men it is not necessary to know names except for that of speaker, Martin Hemingway, who was coordinating the pace of the meeting. It had been scheduled to last two days and the visitors from South Carolina had been booked into comfortable overnight accommodations for three days—just in case things ran over. No briefing notes had been prepared and there was no agenda preceding the meeting.

The three men from UBSA included Michael Sullivan, president and principal owner, Bill Prichard, his executive officer and CEO, and Vance Morrisette, a former officer with the U.S. Navy SEALs who had experience in the Indian Ocean and Gulf of Aden. Morrisette was a relatively new addition to UBSA but a computer search of their personnel had listed him near the top three times. Even after they expanded their search to include consultants they had employed in the past, Morrisette's name still showed up near the top. His background history, physical conditioning, weapons training and test scores made him an ideal candidate.

Introductions had occurred the evening before when the whole group got together for drinks and socializing before dinner. Hemingway had made it clear that no business was to be discussed at this get-together.

"I want to make sure that everyone here is on a first name basis with everyone else. No business. We'll have all the time we need later. Tonight, just sports, women, even a few war stories—especially if they're good ones. No bullshit."

In just a few well-intentioned sentences, Hemingway managed to piss off all of his guests from South Carolina and the group broke up shortly after dinner. On the way back to their rooms Morrisette asked his UBSA bosses, "Is it apparent to either of you exactly what these government people are after? What they're looking for?"

"We've got a few ideas, but let's just wait. We'll know better tomorrow this time. Don't worry, Vance. We'll make out OK out of this. Sit tight."

Vance went back to the bar. He ordered rum and sat alone, thinking about his failed marriage and wondering why he had made such a bad choice. *No. Actually, I know exactly why I made it. Damn!* He went straight to his room and had a good night's sleep. Morning came fast.

"Good morning, gents. I hope everyone slept well. Here's how I envision the day going."

The first slide for the day's agenda came on the screen.

"By the way, before we begin, I would like to request your permission to tape today's session in its totality. We would like to make a transcript of the entire discussion, including your initial responses, so that both we—and you—can review them and consider them in more detail than the continuous progress of the discussion may permit. Do we have the permission of each of you? If so, I would appreciate if you could signify your approval on this waiver form." He passed out three forms to the seated guests and quickly returned the signed forms to a folder, then walked to the conference room door and made a signal to recording technicians stationed in an adjacent room to start the presentation slides. *What the hell was all that about?* Vance wondered.

"The subject for today's discussion is piracy. Piracy off the coast of Somalia, a subject that I'm certain will be familiar to each of you. As you know, this situation is getting a great deal of consideration at the United Nations, as well as in DOD."

"To a large extent, the world community is frustrated by the fact that Somalia is so lawless and fragmented that appeals to its provisional government are useless. Even when pirates are apprehended no one knows what to do with them. These gangs of—I hope none of you will be offended by the political incorrectness of this description—these gangs of *sand niggers* are being captured and released after their weapons are confiscated. This means they may have to borrow their children's AK-47's for their next raids."

The chart on the screen showed a large scale map of the Somalia coast, extending north past the Bab el Mandeb to include that portion of the Red Sea where attacks had occurred, and south past Somalia's border with Kenya. Different symbols distinguished between those attacks that had been successful and those that were repelled.

The next chart identified the names and locations of just under thirty security firms known to be participating in, or interested in, anti-piracy activities. UBSA was on the list, which included firms in Germany, Holland, England, India and Turkey.

Next, there were charts listing all of the vessels that had been boarded and captured by pirates. A series of charts provided specific details of each capture. Characteristics of the ship; its owner, registry, crew size and composition, cargo and other details including the outcome of the capture when it was known.

After the break, Hemingway began with a new header called *Possible Solutions*, followed by a chart of the firms known to be involved in anti-piracy. Some of the names on the list were in red.

"Red indicates companies that have active programs with security personnel on board ships. At this stage the data you see is about three days old and things are changing very rapidly. To date, concerns over international maritime laws have kept most companies from arming their security personnel. Typically they're using high pressure water hoses or water cannons, and high decibel noise guns. Based on data, most of the successful efforts to repel boarders have been accomplished by the simple expedient of cutting ropes or simply dropping the grappling hooks back overboard. But shots are being fired by boarders and it's just a matter of time until security personnel are killed. So far as we know, only seven people have been killed by pirates in all the time this has been going on."

Details of the fatalities were tabulated in his next chart.

Three days of rehashing all this familiar crap would make anyone's head spin and Vance wondered if the senior commanders who had tagged him for this assignment had any idea how the military establishment was chasing its tail. If they did, they'd probably ask for reassignment to a weather station at Point Barrow. But the upshot of the session was a contract for Phase I which was worth forty-seven million dollars to UBSA. Vance was numbed speechless. He ran three miles when he heard the details. He would be going to Djibouti.

"French aid is the mainstay of the economy, as well as assistance from Arab countries. A peace accord December1994 ended a 3-year-long uprising by Afar rebels. An estimated 3,000 French and 1,800 U.S. troops are based in Djibouti."

Djibouti
The World Almanac and Book of Facts, 2008

—13—Jitka Heads East

Somehow, in Khartoum, things began to come unglued; at least that's how it seemed from Jitka's perspective. The flight in and the taxi ride to the hotel where she had been booked by the BBC were uneventful and she was excited about the prospects of being in Djibouti within a day or two.

The bosses in London had led her to believe that, once in Djibouti, she would be provided with a vehicle and driver, and an interpreter who could speak Somali as well as English and French. For a time they had suggested that she might carry a video camera and that it might be appropriate to send along a sound technician to get an audio record of her experiences. But no specific details were ever discussed, and the idea of a video camera was not exactly what our photographer had envisioned. She didn't push, and no one at BBC pushed, so the idea was essentially stillborn before she left Heathrow.

The London headquarters had offered a car, driver and translator with the understanding that details would be arranged by the bureau office in Khartoum. On the morning after arrival Jitka was at the BBC office at nine a.m. where she had a warm welcome from the local staff, before sitting down to work out the details of her program with her key contact, Katherine, "Kitty" Murchison.

Kitty was a bit older than Jitka, a career BBC field agent who had spent the last four years in and out of Khartoum, and—most recently—had done a stint in Cairo. Kitty could speak and write Arabic, which made her valuable. Secure in her position and confident of her abilities, Kitty, who had never married or had the least desire for a domestic life, had developed a hard edge to her persona, which endeared her to the 'old boy' network in London, but which also made her something of a prickly character in personal dealings. Especially with subordinates. She wasted no time in letting Jitka know who was top dog.

"Welcome to Khartoum, Ms. Malecek. I trust your accommodations were adequate. May I call you Jitka?"

"Good morning. Yes, thank you. Everything was nice. I'm happy to be here."

"I'm afraid you won't be able to enjoy Khartoum for long. You're booked on a morning flight out day after tomorrow. And we have your entry visa in hand."

"Fine with me. I'm anxious to make contacts and start shooting. I'm looking forward to meeting my driver and interpreter."

Kitty Murchison sat up straight and adjusted her eyeglasses. "Driver and interpreter? I'm sorry. Has there been some mistake? I received no instructions concerning a driver and interpreter."

"They assured me in London that these would be provided for my trip into Somalia. And they said that arrangements would be made out of this office." *Oh fine,* she thought. *First day out of London and already a cock up.*

"Well, righty oh, as regards the arrangements coming from this office, but none of the messages I received concerning your visit said anything about drivers and interpreters. Or vehicles. I'm afraid you may have misunderstood the London office, Miss Malecek. Jitka."

"Jitka. Please call me Jitka. No. There was no misunderstanding between me and the home office. Maybe the message hasn't reached you yet."

"Not much chance of that Ms. Male...Jitka. None at all. We communicate regularly and thoroughly."

At the end of forty-five rather unpleasant minutes, Jitka had been given permission to address Ms. Murchison as Kitty. Kitty had made it clear that— even in the face of proof that commitments had been made by the London office—recently received budget guidelines mandated by prevailing economic conditions made it impossible to provide Jitka with funds for a vehicle, driver and interpreter. *And, Jitka—whatever kind of name that might be—what you tell me doesn't even come close to qualifying as compelling evidence.*

Kitty did agree however that she could provide information on dependable drivers, interpreters and rental agents who might be contacted in Djibouti.

Jitka was caught off guard by this development. When the BBC decision-makers had met with her she had been encouraged by their offer of logistical support and that offer had been a key factor in her decision to take the assignment. Actually, if her own financial situation had been stronger, she might have considered making the trip on her own money, as a freelancer with the expectation that if her stuff was good enough it could be sold to the highest bidder.

Now, facing the somewhat formidable Kitty Murchison, Jitka had to quickly reassess her situation and make some important decisions. Should she turn around and abandon her project to return to London and renegotiate, or to press on and improvise? It was in her nature to press on. Pirate photos might be sold to many news agencies, both in Europe and in the U.S.

For the next two hours she explored some of her possible alternatives with the assistance of Kitty Murchison. It was true that Kitty had not received specific instructions from the home office, but it was also true that she had considerable latitude to act and decide on her own initiative, and it was well within her prerogatives to approve expenditures that would have given Jitka the support she had been expecting. But in fact, Kitty did not like the idea of a young, attractive female setting off for Somalia without one or more male accomplices with ties to the home office. She would have rejected the idea that this was a sexist concept, and that Jitka was just as capable as any man of visiting a remote region and coming back with a solid picture story. Kitty had already decided to deny this support to the photographer, expecting it might dissuade her from making the trip; and once she had formulated her plan, she was too rigid to change.

The fact was that Kitty Murchison had covered too many rape stories—some of them gorier than others—and she had processed too many photographs, that were filed but not run because they were considered too grisly for BBC viewers. If she made things sufficiently difficult, there was a good chance this young woman would turn around. *Somalia? Absurd, my girl!*

"The best dance is the dance of the eastern clans.
The best people are ourselves,
Of this I have always been sure,
The best wealth is camels.
The duur grass is the best fresh grazing.
The dareemo grass is the best hay,
Of this I have always been sure."

> The Best Dance
> (Somali poem by an unidentified poet)
> quoted in "Somalia"
> by Salome C. Nnoromele

—14—Abdallah Ahmad

The Yamaha-powered Pirelli motored toward Boosaaso's gently shoaling beach until the outboard's skeg gently tapped into the rippled sandy bottom. The boat driver cut the big engine and hoisted it up, out, clear. Immediately, the eight men aboard stepped out into the knee deep water and began to pull their craft the last thirty or forty yards to the beach.

Only their leader, Abdallah Ahmad, did not help to pull the rubber boat onto the beach. With his AK 47 slung over his shoulder, he lifted a Chinese-made RPG out of the Pirelli and stalked ashore. For anyone who knew the thirty-five year old Somali male, it was easy to see that he was angry.

Abdallah was a member of the Isaaq clan of the Samaale family, who for most of Somali history have been identified as pastoral nomads, who lived by moving their herds of sheep, goats and camels across the arid north of the troubled region known as Somalia. Like most of his clan members, Abdallah had spent much of his youth as a camel boy but sometime during his sixteenth year his life took a dramatic turn that sent him in a different direction from most of his clansmen now hauling their new Pirelli up the beach.

Years ago when he was fourteen, together with three male members of his clan, he had taken a herd of camels into the Indian Ocean port city of Eyl. There he had been impressed by the size and complexity of cargo operations at the harbor front. Dockside cranes were lifting loaded lighters onto the shore where they discharged cargoes that included several large machines he had never seen before. He was astonished and impressed by a dock filled with yellow payloaders, crated and compressed for shipment by sea, and he asked a lot of questions. A year later when he returned at the same season, he was eager to return to Eyl's waterfront with new questions he had been formulating for a whole year.

The third year that he visited Eyl, a man on the dock watched him for twenty minutes before asking him if he had ever considered going to sea. Of course, the answer was "No." But when the man explained what the job would pay and assured him that the ship would return in a year, he made an instant decision without consulting any of his elders or clansmen. Instant... and fateful.

By the time the sun had set, Abdallah was signed on as a messman aboard the Liberian-flagged *Monrovia Queen*, a small container ship that had been unloading at a nearby pier. A month later, the young ex-camel driver, just barely eighteen, watched in awe as *Monrovia Queen*, carrying a mixed cargo—including nutmeg, guar gum, black pepper, baseball caps, tee shirts and scores of other items—slipped under the Verrazano Narrows Bridge. For a young man who had never seen a city larger than Eyl, the Big Apple was a sight that was indescribable—*magalo*—and it was probably well that Abdallah did not have an opportunity to go ashore during that first visit.

Another year passed and he found himself—now an ordinary seaman—back in New York. This time he had made friends among the older sailors and he had proven himself to be a capable shipmate who was not afraid of hard work or bad weather. This time he had the opportunity to go ashore with his companions and, visiting Harlem, they took him to restaurants where they could get a reasonable version of Somali food while speaking to American citizens who had emigrated from Somalia.

Abdallah had been surprised to learn that there were American communities where Somalis could live, work and pray as they did at home while driving automobiles, watching movies and television and enjoying lives that only the very wealthiest could afford in a few Somali cities.

On his third trip to the United States—this time docked at Baltimore—his ship was tied up for several days to make some essential repairs to on-board cargo handling machinery. In Washington, he again met Somalis who had obtained citizenship and this time he met with several who were also members of the Isaaq clan. From them he learned that several U.S. cities had substantial communities of Somalis. Two of the strongest were in Raleigh, North Carolina and Milwaukee, Wisconsin.

After five years, Abdallah, now age 21 and an able-bodied seaman with enough money saved to return to Somalia and start some type of business, found himself again in NYC with sufficient contacts and money to visit one of these cities where Somalis lived alongside Amercans. He chose Raleigh.

Settled at North Carolina, the tough, young seaman was forcefully reminded of his skin-color, and the reminder was reinforced regularly in many different ways. After a year in the city, he married an American-born Somali woman he met through a Carolina mosque and moved into her small apartment. For the next two years he worked at a succession of menial jobs and learned—with considerable help from his wife who had been born in North Carolina—to speak acceptable English. After two unsatisfying years during which he barely escaped going to prison for violent behavior, the Somali couple attempted to relocate to the coast near employment opportunities at Morehead City. Their plan was based on the availability of work in the tourist industry; in hotel and motel laundries and housekeeping jobs. During off-season they could work at fast food places. But eastern North Carolina was a tough nut for the Somali couple to crack, and 9/11 took place shortly after they arrived. Abdallah learned to recognize the term "sand nigger," and it made him long to do violence.

By willpower and tenacity the couple managed to hang on in Morehead City for nearly a year but before twelve months were up they had packed their bags, piled into a battered Datsun, and headed for Milwaukee.

There, despite the tense post 9/11 climate, they found a Muslim community with many Somali immigrants and they welcomed the opportunity to attend a mosque, find Somali food and occasionally speak their language with older Somalis. The big drawback with Milwaukee was the weather. But the straw that broke the camel's back was the profound difference between a man who grew up as a Somali camel boy, unschooled, and a woman who attended school in the United States and grew up with partially-Americanized expectations. His wife, Aisha—who was two years older—had learned to speak Somali from her parents and the two young adults could communicate reasonably well in two languages, but emotionally and psychologically, they were miles apart.

Abdallah had never gotten over the fact that Aisha did not bleed on their wedding night, a fact that would have led to an immediate divorce and possible bloodletting between families if they had been back in Boosaaso. He would have been shamed before his entire clan. In Carolina, he had simply had to swallow his pride and keep going. From her however, he did learn to speak passable English.

At Milwaukee, they both had worked hard to earn a living, and when they were not at work they had access to other members of the Somali community, but winter weather often limited what they could do outside their small apartment. It angered Abdallah that his wife had failed thus far to become pregnant and this did not make things easier between them. When Abdallah found a group of men his same age with comparable experiences, he began to meet with them at their local mosque. The atmosphere of hostility in weeks and months following September 11th was oppressive. The perceived inability of these young Muslim males to speak freely about their concerns for the world caused a buildup of smoldering resentment that was frequently difficult to conceal. This created a destructive spiral which over the next several years resulting in the return of several young men to Somalia, and the abandonment of their wives by several more.

Abdallah was guilty on both counts. Telling his wife that he was going to New York to look for a better job—either there or somewhere with a warmer climate—he headed back to some of the haunts he had frequented in earlier seafaring visits. Once back, he immediately began looking for shipboard jobs that would take him back to the east coast of Africa.

For those seeking to reenter Somalia, the simplest route led first to Kenya. From there Somalia could be entered by a variety of means. Most of them, illegal.

After a few weeks of diligent searching around the New Jersey waterfronts he found a job on a container ship of Panamanian registry that shuttled between New Jersey and Amsterdam.

The Dutch port supported a large Islamic community, and although the Somalis were not the dominant group, there were enough of them for him to find some reasonably good advisors along the waterfront. Dutch was incomprehensible to him, and he had little interest in remaining there, so, at the first opportunity he shipped out again, this time ending up in Marseilles. From Marseilles he learned that shipments of food were being sent to Somalia by EU nations, Canada and the U.S. Within a few days he had found a spot on an old Greek-flagged freighter bound for Mogadishu with a cargo of grain. This was perfect. When his ship arrived in Mogadishu's harbor, the captain attempted to hold on to his Somali sailors by refusing them permission to go ashore. The skipper even had the agent for the shipping company hire armed guards at the gangway, but this failed to stop the determined former camel boy, who literally jumped ship.

He was back in his home territory—northern Somalia—within a week. He had not been home for ten years. When he returned he spoke passable English, was married to a Somali-American woman and thus was eligible for American citizenship, which for a time he had considered. He had seen a good bit of the world. The eligibility for citizenship was an option he preferred to keep open. Additionally he was a competent seaman and a good boat handler. Among a group of former camel boys of the same age, there were very few whose experience could compare with his. He told no one of his American wife, Aisha, and she had no personal contacts in Somalia. The fact of his American marriage was unknown to his Somali associates, and he was happy to simply forget it.

Now, striding up Boosaaso's sandy beach, thoughts of his seafaring days and his American wife, now abandoned, were far behind. He rarely thought of her these days, occupied as he was with the three Somali wives he had taken during the years that he had been back,

Piracy had been a development which had not originated with him. Actually, it had originated further to the south—the area around Mogadishu—and even further south, at Chisimayu. But he took to it like a duck to water. Within his first year, he had a small team, a new wife, a substantial income and a promising future.

"For Somali pirates, 2008 was a bumper year. In more than 100 major documented attacks, pirates seized approximately 40 large commercial vessels in the Indian Ocean and the Gulf of Aden.

Several merchant ships and their crews are still being held in pirate enclaves, but others have been ransomed back to their owners for an average price of $1 million. In January, the owners of the MV Sirius Star, a brand-new tanker with a load of crude oil valued at $100 million, paid $3 million to secure the release of the tanker and her 25 crew members."

Defeating Somali Pirates on Land: The Kenya Connection
David Axe
in Proceedings, U.S. Naval Institute, March 2009

—15—The Pirate Agenda

More than a decade ago, while living in Boosaaso on Somalia's northern coast, Abdallah Ahmad learned about the success of pirate activities from radio broadcasts by the BBC coming out of Sudan. During the years when he went to sea for a London-based shipping firm he had learned a thing or two about piracy. This was because he had made three trips to Singapore, and pirate activity has long been a serious business in the Straits of Malacca. Although none of his ships had ever been attacked, several of his shipmates on voyages to the east had told stories about Malayan pirates coming aboard and taking command of their ships.

Abdallah was intrigued by the idea of Malayan pirates, lightly armed and operating from small craft, boarding and taking over ships that were thousands of times bigger. Oftentimes, he learned, the successful pirates did not even wear shoes.

They were bold and daring, and when their attempts failed there were consequences. But the risk was worth the gamble. For men with no work and no prospects for the future, the idea of an adventurous gamble capable of providing great wealth presented an opportunity that almost anyone might consider.

On one trip, Abdallah had a Filipino steward as a roommate and after they had gotten to know each other, José told him that he had once—several years ago—joined a pirate band operating out of Palawan on Sumatra. José described how they trained in practice for boarding at sea, one of the most difficult steps in the process. They practiced in jungle hideouts until they were as agile as monkeys. They could climb the boarding ropes with weapons slung over their backs before most ship's crews could respond to repel them.

Abdallah listened—fascinated—as José described several raids made from a pirate base on Sumatra's eastern coast. Abdallah remembered his early years as a camel boy in the harsh country of the Guban. There had been weeks at a time when he subsisted almost entirely on camel milk. It had not seemed harsh at the time, but having seen a bit of the world he felt that he, in common with many of his Somali friends, had endured hardships beyond the capacity of many people. For young men who were strong, adventurous and self reliant, piracy had a great deal of appeal. So he had thought at the time; but it did not occur to him to put his thoughts into action.

It was only after he had been ashore for several weeks, living back at coastal Boosaaso, that he began listening to BBC broadcasts from Khartoum from whose broadcasts he learned that warlords from Mogadishu had begun sponsoring bands of pirates, crewed initially by disgruntled fishermen.

The warlords had amassed their fortunes by every conceivable crime in the book. If it would produce money, it would be practiced by the heavily-armed gangs who operated with impunity over most of the country. With money at their disposal, warlords could use it to expand their fiefdoms in any direction that would help to consolidate their holdings in money and territory.

Piracy held out the prospect of solid rewards for ransom of officers, crew and the ship itself, Often the value of the cargo, or its nature—possibly as a danger to humans or the environment—gave it high value in negotiations.

In a few cases the cargoes in large, modern carrier ships, made high-value goods easy to steal. This was particularly true of container ships, roll-on, roll-off (Ro-Ro) vessels and LASH ships. (Lighters Aboard) When these ships were occasionally taken, it was highly desirable to examine the ship's manifest to determine which of the high-value containers was worth taking.

For this, they would need someone who would know how to read; preferably in several languages. An American, perhaps. Or someone educated in the UK. That shouldn't be too difficult.

"While Navy leadership engages in finger-pointing with the shipping companies, a golden opportunity is passing us by. Let's be honest: The Navy looks stupid in its most recent actions vis-a-vis the piracy occurring off Somalia."

"We Look Stupid"
Commander John T. Kuehn, USN (Ret.)
In: "Proceedings," The U. S. Naval Institute, Jan. 2009

—16—Why Pirates Target Certain Ships

What is the rationale for container ships and Ro-Ro ships as desirable targets?

Before container ships became the queens of the commercial seas, Ro-Ro ships were popular for a time. Roll on, roll off. Freight haulers operating at certain ports found that it was easier to drive on with loaded trailer-trucks, then park the trailer, tie it down, and drive the truck to pick up another trailer. It was an economic trade off. If it made no sense—economically—to leave the truck (let's call it a tractor), on board when the trailer was left aboard. When the ship reached its destination, a new 'tractor' came aboard, and took the trailer off. The cargo was loaded by the seller, and unloaded by the buyer. Or their brokers. It was a cruder, earlier version of what ultimately became the container ship.

In the opening stages of Somali piracy, small freighters were preferred. Low freeboard, small unsuspecting crews and ease of boarding were key factors. Concerns over armed resistance or fear of international retaliation never played much of a role. From the beginning, captured pirates were simply released back on shore. The lure of money was irresistible. With Ro-Ro ships, unloading cargo was a snap, given the right dock configurations.

Other considerations requiring outside help had to do with money transfers. Pirate leaders had to think about practical details, equitable distribution of ransom payments, or the relative ease of moving small ships into areas where they could be protected or defended with minimal effort. Pirates correctly assumed that naval vessels would not be involved in serious attempts to recover the pirated vessels and their crews. The fear of damage or destruction of ships and cargo, coupled with possible death of crews or passengers, assured that pirates who boarded successfully were unlikely to be hindered by the mightiest warships.

Later, in the evolving practice, small container ships were picked in preference to Ro-Ros despite being slightly more difficult to board. Valuable cargo could be sold ashore while negotiating the return of ships and crews. Electronic items; television sets, cell phones, clothing and a wide array of consumer items, could fill and swamp the small markets and trading centers of poor Somali ports. Typically, container ships are big; bigger than Ro-Ros. Their containers are multi-modal, that is, they can be carried on land or sea; by ships, tractor-trucks or trains. But they require sophisticated port facilities to be unloaded quickly. Not every Somali port has the necessary equipment; but this is changing.

On some routes, the Ro-Ro ship is still a viable option. Ro-Ros still ply the seas over selected routes; but their numbers are substantially fewer than container ships.

When Ro-Ros transit the Gulf of Aden, they can expect trouble. They can expect trouble because the pirates that operate in that region find it easy, convenient and lucrative to dock a Ro-Ro ship in a harbor with marginal off-loading facilities and drag out the cargo.

Ro-Ros are intentionally easy to unload. For pirates, this means that the cargo can be confiscated and distributed; given that they have the trucks (tractors) to haul them away. The ship and its crew continues to have value. But the value of the cargo doesn't have to be negotiated. It can be sold at whatever price the local market will bear. Additionally, the return is immediate. No tedious negotiations required if the cargo can be easily sold inside the country.

Abdallah Ahmad's band peaked, for several months, at forty-three men, all but a handful from the same clan. They have been together now for several years and during that time they have been successful more than a dozen times. They have collected approximately twenty-one million dollars, split about sixty-forty between dollars and euros

At an early stage, Abdallah realized the advantages of good global positioning systems. He had already singled out Jimale as a bright young man who had been educated as an electrical engineer in France. He gave Jimale the assignment of identifying reliable equipment, purchasing the necessary hardware, and training key members of the boat crews in its use.

There were a few problems to be resolved but by the end of the second year most of the startup wrinkles had been ironed out and his mother ships had good systems installed and operational. Shortly afterward, the attack boats had smaller sets that were linked.

Operators in several Red Sea locations provided information on ships passing through Bab el Mandeb into the Gulf of Aden. With operators reporting from Kenya, Yemen, Aden and Djibouti, Abdallah's contacts in Boosaaso, Eyl and Mogadishu were well provided with information on ships, cargoes and schedules. Internet connections provided a steady flow of information. By the end of the third year, Abdallah had found that it was beneficial to have a committee of five of the most experienced mother ship operators weigh information on a case-by-case basis before selecting a target and a recommended location for a boarding attempt.

Abdallah had three command centers that operated much like war rooms, with data coming in continuously and decisions being made in real time.

Over time, the information arriving from various sources included data on warships of various nations patrolling in the region.

Warships? Abdallah had to laugh. In the past he had five crews captured by four different nations. India, Denmark, Germany and the U.S. (two captures). In every case the weapons and attack boats were confiscated and the crew were put ashore on Somalia's beaches. In three of these instances the men were placed back in their attack boats and told to go home. Lacking jurisdiction, the naval officers responsible for these captures had no inclination to hold the captured men on board their ships.

"The United States and its allies should also increase the number of warships stationed off the Horn of Africa. Naval forces from the United States and more than 20 other countries operate under the aegis of Combined Task Force 151, currently commanded by a Turkish admiral. But although there are as many as 30 warships in the region, most are devoted to antiterrorist missions or other tasks, often leaving no more than 14 warships available for combating pirates."

Pirates, Then and Now
(How Piracy Was Defeated in the Past and Can Be Again)
Max Boot
Foreign Affairs, July/August 2009

—17—A Port in Eritrea

The independent nation of Eritrea is located to the north of Djibouti. Its east coast faces the Red Sea; the western border, Ethiopia. It was until 1993 part of Ethiopia, but in that year it won independence after a struggle of more than three decades. When Eritrea became a separate nation, Ethiopia lost its access to the Red Sea and became landlocked. One might expect friction to exist between these two countries and this is, in fact, the case.

As far as we are concerned, Eritrea is not a base for pirates and few of the crimes at sea occur in the Red Sea. Most of the offenses take place in the busy shipping lanes of the Gulf of Aden, leaving or approaching the Bab el Mandeb from the east. In more recent weeks, an increasing number of attacks are taking place far at sea in the Indian Ocean, where detection and response is more difficult. But Eritrea factors in because it has several harbors on the Red Sea, where ships of all nations engage in commerce with that country and its landlocked neighbor. Thus, ports in Eritrea—Mersa, Massawa, Aseb—can harbor maritime informants who provide information on ships, sailing times, destinations, cargoes and other details essential to pirate operations. It helps to know what the pirates know and when they know it.

Aseb, near the southern border with Djibouti, is conveniently placed to observe not only commercial vessels, but warships traveling the Red Sea to engage in anti-piracy surveillance.

Marty Kinsella was one of the CIA's reliable, deep cover agents in the Middle East. He was sitting on a bench facing Aseb's waterfront reading a paper when a man in a white pin-striped Arab *jellaba* took a seat at the opposite end of the bench. Kinsella had been there for forty minutes and he had eaten his breakfast there. The paper wrappers were at his feet.

"Assalamu alaikum," the newcomer said.

"Alaikum assalum," Kinsella replied, coughing. *"Inshallah."*

"SubhanAllah, this is a great day to be alive."

"We are here in the sunshine. *MashaAllah."*

"May you live ten thousand years, my friend."

This was the line that completed the handshake.

"Be brief," Kinsella said.

"Four container ships will pass today. Southbound. And six bulk carriers. Five tankers. The containers ships are all for Mogadishu. Expected in by Wednesday. Bulk carriers are heading east. Only two for Somalia. One to Berbera. Tuesday. One to Eyl. Wednesday. Others on to Pakis."

"OK. Got it. Bye."

"One more bit of news. New pirate capture. They have a Spanish ship and took five crew members for hostages. To show they mean business, they delivered two corpses by dropping the bodies outside the base in Djibouti. The ransom money is expected tomorrow."

Kinsella smiled and grunted. *What the hell is wrong with these people? They like to kill or to just cause pain? What the fuck kind of god are they worshipping? It seems like they are just trying to create hell, right here on earth.*

"Bye."

"Bye."

You may wonder about the nature of the job performed by Kinsella. His dangerous and largely unappreciated task is to find out what the pirates know and how they know it. It's not a job you'd wish on your worst enemy. You, gentle reader, might also have trouble comprehending why any sane person would want a job like the one that must be satisfying to Kinsella. He has been doing it for seven years, and he's married to a very attractive woman. She is an Irish citizen and prefers to live in Dublin. You might more easily understand why they have elected not to have children.

Vance, in civilian khakis and a contractor's badge, had been invited for a drink at the Chief's Club on the naval base at Djibouti. The chief who invited him was an artificer with the SEALs, and he had heard of Vance from one of his pals. When he learned that Vance had left the Navy for more money with UBSA it did not surprise him because he had been approached in the past and had considered making a similar move. But he was within eight years of retirement and the pension and benefits seemed too good. He and Patricia had already made plans to get a place in the Pensacola area.

The chief, Dan Grimes, was now pulling a tour on a new fast frigate deployed to help with the pirate situation. The ship carried a small detachment of SEALs, but they had no duties in connection with running the ship, so all their time was spent exercising and training. For Dan it was probably one of the most boring assignments of his career. Almost as bad as the tour at Guam. Everyone, everything, was primed and ready...but ready for what?

They sat outside the club in the sunshine and a cool breeze off the Gulf was pleasant. Whitecaps were just beginning to kick up on the water. They were each nursing a beer when they were joined by two of Grimes's friends from his ship. After introductions all around, the talk turned to recent news from the pirate front.

An Italian bulk carrier had just been captured, and several crewmen, reportedly five, had been taken ashore in Mogadishu as hostages. They were being held and threatened in an effort for the Somalis to recover two of their crewmen who had been taken recently by the French. Apparently the negotiations were not proceeding smoothly—news reports were confusing—and the Somalis were threatening to kill their hostages unless action was immediate.

Ben Foreman, a ship's engineer with a tattoo on his forearm—*Louisiana*—was incensed.

"Goddam these sonsabitches, anaway. Nobody is less prejudiced than me. I don't have a prejudiced bone in my fuckin' body. But these motherfuckin' sand niggers need to be wiped off the face of the earth."

Grimes and the other chief, Harvey Donaldson laughed. "So what will you guys do about it when you see them at sea, scouting for targets?'

"We'll keep doin' what we been doin'. Basically nothin'."

After twenty minutes of conversation along these lines it was clear to Vance that the level of frustration among active duty personnel was high. He said little, hoping to encourage all three men—more than half a century of service between them—to keep talking. But he could feel their anger and annoyance at the orders they were getting from the top. He had no doubt that ship commanders were feeling the same frustrations, although they were trained to conceal their displeasure.

Forty minutes went by and almost everything Vance had believed to be true was confirmed by these veterans. After a while Grimes's two shipmates got up, handshaking all around, and went off to walk back to their ship.

"Those dudes are both really pissed," Grimes said.

"So it seems. Understandable."

"So where do you think this is going, Commander? What's the long term outlook?"

"If I knew that, I could be your boss. I don't know Dan. But you know the old saying. If you do what you did, you get what you got. I don't know what the final answer will be, but it's clear that our present approach—do we even have a present approach?—isn't working. And will never work."

"So what does UBSA expect you to do out here? What can you possibly do for them that you couldn't do for the navy?"

"I can take home more of their money. C'mon, Dan, I don't know any more than you do."

"Sure, I understand that. But you know what I mean. In the navy you had access to armed men, armed ships. With Uncle Bob, you got squat. Unless you guys are doing something I don't know about."

"I can't give a hard answer, Dan. 'Cause I don't have one. Part of this first trip out is to understand the situation a little better."

"See, fuck it. This is what I can't understand. What part is so hard for all these people outside to understand? Don't they get what happens? A bunch of young boys mostly, get in boats and board merchant ships. They hold the ship, cargo and crew for ransom. The shippers usually pay all or most of what's demanded. If we—our navy—capture them, we let 'em go. Put 'em ashore. We don't have jurisdiction. We turn 'em ashore in Somalia. Which has no court system. No police. They are back at sea after they eat supper. Why is this hard to understand? I don't fucking get it."

"You're right, Dan. I'm frustrated too. That's mostly why I left the navy. You think I quit for better money, but that's actually not the case."

Dan Grimes sat up straighter and took a big swallow from his Heinikens.

"Then why *did* you make the change?"

"Because they threw out my ideas. Without a hearing. I'd been working the pirate desk for three years. I thought I had a good answer that deserved a fair hearing."

"Which was...?"

"Which was to treat pirates like pirates."

"Spell it out for me."

"OK. We know they are working further and further off shore.

76

Sometimes hundreds of miles at sea. They're hard to find but we can find 'em if we just keep looking. So..."

"So. That part ain't hard."

"So. The pirate ship goes out. It's easy to confirm that a ship on the open sea contains pirates. You don't fish with AKs or RPGs. You see one, you know you have pirates."

"So?"

"So...that ship just suddenly disappears. Dis. Appears. Like in gone. Vanished. Sayonara."

"Until the bodies wash ashore. Life jackets. The empty vessel. Wood floats."

"No. No bodies, No flotsam. No nothing."

"Something always floats."

"Nothing recognizable."

"Bodies, you can recognize. Even after a long time, they don't look like dead turtles."

"Nothing comes ashore."

"Pardon me for seeming obtuse, commander. But how you gonna make that happen?"

"Flechettes."

"Flechettes?"

"Flechettes. You know what flechettes are? Yes?"

"Fuck yes, I know what flechettes are, but..."

"And I know you know what JDAMs are?"

"Sure, but..."

"Stick with me, Chief. Picture a JDAMs weapon. It could be launched from anything. Let's say, for discussion purposes, from a drone. Picture a special JDAMs that can drop right down the pirate helmsman's jock strap. And the flechettes mince up everything a fraction before the big bang. There's nothing. Metal sinks. What's left of the pirates is all fish food. Maybe somebody's flip flop would float ashore, but I would expect the foot to be gone. Metal sinks, wood and fiberglass should break up pretty well. Hopefully, that flip-flop would be in pieces."

Dan Grimes was trying to picture the event. He had seen half a dozen pirate boats so he could form a good mental picture. He was silent, thinking it over.

"That's my plan. But the heavies considered it far too radical. No trial, no jury. I think of it as justice at the yardarm. These Somalis, in my opinion, convict themselves when they leave shore with the AKs and RPGs. They are their own crime, trial and conviction. They leave shore with AK and RPGs? Game over. Case closed. All this other stuff is just legalistic bullshit."

Dan had been thinking. He knew quite a bit about sophisticated weapons and what could be done with them. Damn! This could work.

"Know what, Commander? I like it."

That's how things started to take shape in Vance's head.

"A number of brave ex-Muslims have been warning us for many years that Islamist demands are not to be interpreted as some kind of 'civil rights' claim. Even within the frontiers of Europe and North America, there are now 'honor' killings, the mutilation of female genitalia, the imposition of veilings and beatings on wives and daughters and sisters, and calls for censorship and repression backed by serious threats of violence. Several European capital cities, from London to Madrid, have shared the fate of New York and Washington in becoming the scene of random bombings. "

From the Foreword to "Infidel"
(Ayaan Hirsi Ali, author)
By Christopher Hitchens

—18—A Mosque in Minneapolis

There is a substantial Islamic community in Minneapolis and many of them are from Somalia. The Haad family were regular mosque attendees each week, even though the imam knew that they didn't pray five times a day. Actually, Mohamuud Samataar was not completely clear about the long-term consequences of failure to pray five times daily. And, based on what he knew of the hadiths, it was not clear how the Prophet himself (xyzzyx) would punish offenders regarding this requirement.

Imam Mohamuud made half a dozen trips to Detroit each year. Usually he would be passed a detailed letter in a sealed envelope handed over by a different member of his congregation after the mosque had cleared of worshippers. Never any contact by telephone.

The envelope would include a prepaid round trip ticket from a travel agency in Detroit, and instructions on how to reach a particular hotel in that city. At the hotel, there was usually a message for him at the front desk directing him to a restaurant where good lamb dishes could be ordered.

The first time he responded to one of these unsolicited invitations, it was nerve-wracking because he had no clear idea what to expect. But after the first couple of times, he understood. The men who contacted him never gave names. He was being recruited by moneyed interests on the Arabian peninsula—*not exactly clear where this money was coming from*—to select and condition American Muslim youth for jihad. Their participation, it was felt, would have a propaganda value far in excess of their actual contributions.

Mohamuud agreed. He was thrilled to be a part of something this big, even though the ultimate objectives of his sponsors were unclear.

After the third meeting, he was given a substantial quantity of cash and he was taken to a small storefront grocery where two men with dark glasses explained that he was expected to send some of his young Somalis to Somalia or to Afghanistan. Maybe to other places as well. He would receive instructions.

The instructions were from an imam in Yemen whose name Mohamuud had never heard before.

Such details were of little consequence. He had made his initial connections years ago, in Saudi Arabia. There, he had sworn his oaths and chosen the path from which he could not swerve. Allah had spoken to him directly on three occasions and he knew that he had been chosen. He had a mission and he intended to keep his vows.

"For after all, philosophy—that is, the best wisdom that has ever in any way been revealed to our man-of-war world—is but a slough and a mire, with a few tufts of good footing here and there."

From "White Jacket"
Herman Melville

—19—Rhonda

Vance had met Rhonda in Norfolk while he was an officer with a SEAL unit at Little Creek. Being an officer with SEALs is no picnic, because one must endure everything the men go through while continuing to be responsible for all the related administrative details they are spared. The work is hard. Consequently, the play is hard.

There is no shortage of bars, joints, dives and similar establishments within a short distance of Little Creek's gates; and there is no lack of female companionship within these places. Vance met Rhonda in the Officer's Club at Little Creek but he had seen her before.

It would not be an exaggeration to say that Rhonda was very attractive. It would also be accurate to describe her as "loose." Actually, that might sound a bit judgmental. Perhaps "easy" would be more accurate and less harsh. The young woman had a warm heart—and she liked men.

She had been raised by her grandmother—from an early age—after her mother ran off with an Oklahoma rigger who worked the oil fields, and her unknown father had disappeared into the drug world; possibly into Mexico.

The girl grew up with one parent, a frail old woman, who could barely see to read her Bible and whose arthritis was so bad she could hardly turn the pages. They lived on social security, food stamps and what the local Baptist church could provide from its food kitchen. Rhonda quit school in her junior year when she became pregnant by a football player, and in desperation she aborted herself with a clothes hanger. It was done under the bleachers at the football field on a drizzly overcast afternoon and she was alone. After she recovered, she refused to attend school. A year later she ran away to Norfolk where she found work as a waitress in a strip club. After getting to know some of the stripper girls she concluded that she was just as good-looking as any of them and was built better than most so she asked if she could strip. The money was a lot better, the hours were easier and you got to talk with more people between sets.

But there was a problem. She was a lousy dancer and stripping wasn't an act she could perform gracefully. Think *klutzy*. Her first attempts were embarrassing and she was slow to improve. Some males could actually appreciate her awkwardness but most could not, and the club owner told her she had to go back to waitressing. It hurt her feelings and three weeks later she found a better club paying more money.

She had a very pretty face with fluffy blond hair she wore short and one of her best attributes was her voice, which was soft and feminine with an eastern North Carolina accent. Growing up without a father and never having a brother, she was inordinately interested in men and responsive to their attention. Because she was young, her judgement about men was not good, so it was hard for her to tell good ones from bad ones. After she was in the new club for a little over a year, a man came in and spoke to her about a job at a club inside the Amphibious Base at Little Creek. She agreed to visit the club and check it out. At first she was hired on a trial basis. But she worked hard, was pleasant and her looks helped. The result of that happy encounter was that she soon found permanent work at the Officer's Club. She had been there for over two years and was able to live in a small apartment—alone—when she caught the eye of Lieutenant Vance Morrisette, an officer with a SEAL Unit training on the base.

"Hi."

"Hi hon. Are you expecting someone? What can I getcha?"

"Nope. I'm alone. Yeah, a rum and tonic would be good. Barbados rum. I know they have it."

"Your wife out of town? You were alone last night too. You want a menu?"

"No wife. I'm a lone wolf. Didn't you hear me howling? No thanks, no menu."

"Lemme get that drink, hon. Maybe I can hear you from the bar. Can I bring you anything else?"

"Anything?"

"I'm leavin' hon. Be right back."

Their first encounters could have been scripted. As he put it, *intial contact was prosaic.*

After a few dates to movies, he took her dancing one night at the O.C. in Fort Story. The night was warm and she wore a sleeveless dress. They danced some, then walked outside onto the terrace to look at the moon. Back inside they danced some more. He watched as perspiration formed and slowly trickled down between her breasts. Beads were forming on her forehead, just below her hairline, and a little later he noticed that she was actually sweaty all over. When a drop ran down the side of her face, she made no effort to wipe it away. As it ran down her cheek and came near the corner of her mouth, her tongue flicked out to lick it away. *Oh, man!* That was when he saw that her upper arms were damp. She was damp all over.

"All this time, and you never asked me inside where you live."

"Because you told me at the very beginning you were a lone wolf."

"You never even offered."

"You never even asked."

"C'mon. Let's dance. I like this tune. Let's keep you warmed up." Now, he had watched three droplets snake down languidly to disappear between her breasts. He had seen this before, but somehow that night it was different.

He took her to Virginia Beach a couple of times to swim and he was impressed at the way she looked in a bikini. She didn't have much of a tan and so she lacked what he called the California Look he had been accustomed to in San Diego, but pale on her really looked good. *Really.* She, in turn, was impressed by the way he looked in trunks. SEALs are unusually well conditioned, and he was a SEAL. On the beach, they were a couple who turned heads. But she burned easily. *Just cover it up.*

Then he took her to the beaches of Carolina on two successive weekends. That clinched it.

They got married in a civil ceremony performed in North Carolina at a little town Vance had never heard of. No one else attended. Her grandmother had passed away and she had no close friends. Vance's living relatives were in Utah and he had very little contact. His SEAL Team were mostly enlisted men, and the other SEAL Officers were all married and living off base with their families. They were each living lonely lives and they came together like two starved animals, trying to eat each other alive. Both, in fact, were lone wolves. For the first six months, sparks flew. But then he was called away for a secret assignment in a place where he could discuss nothing with her.

After so much closeness and attention, the abrupt change was hard for her to take and she began to drink when she was alone in their off-base apartment. He was gone for four months.

A year later, after returning to Little Creek, he was offered a position at the Pentagon. It was an eighteen-month assignment after which he could, if he desired, go back with his SEALs; probably with increased administrative duties.

Rhonda was eager for an opportunity to live somewhere else. She had never been west of Richmond, or north of Norfolk. They found a place in Georgetown. It was expensive but the commute for Vance was easy. For Rhonda, unemployed, childless, with few internal resources, the charm of

Georgetown wore off in a few weeks. Vance could see trouble on the horizon, but there wasn't a lot he could do about it. They were keeping him busy at the Pentagon. The promotion to Lt. Commander meant more money, but he would have been happier to be back with his SEAL unit. The officer and his wife were headed for trouble. This scenario will probably sound so familiar that many readers will think they could have written it—possibly experienced it—themselves.

All these tapes had played endlessly through Vance's mind as he reached his decision. They could not stay married. Despite all her appealing attributes he could not tolerate what he now knew she had done in Norfolk while he was gone. The photographs were hard to contemplate. She had made it too easy. The lawyer was confident it would be uncontested.

"Piracy off the coast of East Africa is growing at an alarming rate, with 41 ships attacked in 2007, 122 in 2008, and 102 as of mid-May 2009. The more high-profile captures include a Saudi supertanker full of oil and a Ukrainian freighter loaded with tanks and other weapons. An estimated 19 ships and more than 300 crew members are still being held by pirates who are awaiting ransom payments from ship owners or insurers. Such fees have been estimated to total more than $100 million in recent years, making piracy one of the most lucrative industries and pirates one of the biggest employers in Somalia, a country with a per capita GDP of $600."

Pirates, Then and Now
(How Piracy Was Defeated in the Past and Can Be Again)
Max Boot
Foreign Affairs, July/August 2009

—20—The Insurers Gather

London was again the scene of a meeting of executives from the world's great insurers. Representatives attended from Indonesia, China, Germany, France, Singapore, The Netherlands, Spain and the U.S. Members of the Arab bloc were conspicuously absent, even though Saudi ships had been attacked and captured by pirates.

As in previous meetings, the Insurers Council who had called the assemblage together, presented a statistical compilation of events to date, in which summaries were made showing tonnage captured, value of cargoes lost, sunk, missing, destroyed or ransomed, crewmen ransomed, injured, killed, missing or unaccounted for, and the estimated total cost of increased fuel consumed, man hours compensated, time lost, cargo lost due to excess shipping times, etc. etc. The statistics alone took half a day to review. All morning.

There was never any mention of pirate ships sunk, pirates killed, captured, hanged, decapitated, branded, or imprisoned. Pirates were conspicuous by their absence. It was eerie. At the end of the first day, a gentleman from Indonesia made mention of this odd discrepancy.

The cost of providing armed guards was calculated using several different measures, one of the most interesting of which was in dollars per thousand ton-miles. Nautical miles, of course. Considering the costs of fuel to evade known pirate hot spots, costs to arm guards, insurance expenses to protect against loss, and other cost elements attributed to piracy, it was easy to conclude that it was cheaper to pay up. This did not bode well for the future because it almost guaranteed that pirate ranks would swell. It was Somalia's only growth industry. From an economic perspective, piracy should increase until the amount of ransom payments or theft losses exceeded the cost of the cheapest effective preventive method.

Nobody liked the answer, but the arithmetic was irrefutable. The men went to dinner, ate roast beef, drank good wine and went home late, often with indigestion, to ponder the sad facts they had heard pounded home.

This conference lasted three days. Nothing came of it.

Piracy did not stop while the London Conference was in progress. In that regard, the impact of the insurers conference was much like the deliberations of the UN Security Council. News reports kept trickling in.

Bender Beyla, Somalia: UN relief workers in Bender Beyla managed to get a mobile phone message to a U.S. naval warship patrolling off the east coast of Somalia near the Horn of Africa. They reported that a crew of Somalia pirates had just entered the protected harbor with a Liberian-flagged container ship, *Monrovia Queen*. The crew was put ashore and transported to an undisclosed location in the vicinity of Mogadishu.

In a recorded meeting with negotiators the pirate captain, who gave his name only as Ahmed, said that they had harmed no one during the boarding and that the officers and crew had complied fully with their demands. Ahmed boasted that the entire process went smoothly and no shots were fired. The capture, he claimed, was necessary because Somalia's territorial waters had been invaded by fishing boats from other nations and as a consequence, Somali seamen had no other means of livelihood. When asked why the ransoms demanded were so high, Ahmed replied, "The insurance pays the cost of ransom. No people actually lose money and no children go hungry as a result of our actions. Somali fishermen and seamen need piracy if we are to feed our families."

It sounded almost logical.

"Since the Golden Age of pirates in the 17th and 18th centuries, bands of thieves have scoured the seas. The same factors that triggered piracy then—extreme poverty, looters with nothing to lose, weak governments that didn't intervene—have prompted a recent surge in piracy off the coast of Somalia."

Captain Crooks
Samantha Henig and Marc Bain
In *Periscope*, Newsweek, December 1, 2008

—21—Vance Has an Interview

Vance Morrisette had completed four weeks of training at Uncle Bob's Honey Hill facility and his instructors had realized from the beginning that they were dealing with a seasoned professional. It wasn't possible to say that he breezed through the physical challenges they threw at him because no one on the planet could breeze through some of these ordeals; but he had been through everything the SEAL Teams could throw at him and it wasn't likely he was going to let Uncle Bob get him to say "Uncle."

After four weeks the big guns at UBSA called him in for what was described as "a placement interview." There were five management types at a long table. A single chair had been placed in front of the table in the center of the room. It was hardly a conventional interview. More like an interrogation. The five gentlemen lined up at the table had been well briefed the previous day and they had a game plan. The big man in the center of the table seemed friendly.

"Thanks for coming in, Vance. We've all heard a lot about your performance during training. Let's make sure that you know everyone here."

He introduced Vance to each man at the table and then, after the last handshake, he said in a tone that was still friendly, "Would you care for some coffee, Vance?" And he indicated a thermos and some cups at a nearby credenza.

The whole set-up of the room was irritating to Vance, and it was such an apparent and pathetic attempt at intimidation. If he took coffee to the seat obviously placed for him in this situation, there would be no place to set his cup.

He filled a cup from the thermos and slowly stirred in cream and two packets of sugar. Then he stirred the coffee for almost a full minute. Walking back to the chair, he took a sip of the coffee while standing and then placed the cup in the center of the chair seat. Standing beside the chair he faced his interrogators. "Very good coffee," he said, smiling. "Shall we begin?"

The big man in the center shifted uncomfortably. "Why don't you just take a seat?" he said. "Make yourself comfortable."

"Ah," Vance said, "Thank you very much." Retrieving the coffee and hooking his right foot under a chair leg, he slid it across the floor to abut the table, at a point obviously not opposite the big man. Then he sat down and placed his cup on the long table. He was still smiling.

If the big man was annoyed he didn't show it. Lifting the folder on the table in front of him, he got down to business.

"As I expect you know, Vance, we have been able to get access to your service record. Or, I would guess, most of it. It seems as if you had an impressive record while you were with the SEAL Teams. Before you moved to Washington. What made you want to leave the Navy?"

"I'd guess my motives weren't much different than those of most of the guys who get out. Money. A clearer sense of objectives and mission. Avoidance of a lot of political bullshit. Although when you boil it all down, it usually comes out...money. I hope I haven't given you the wrong answer. But there it is. My wife was tired of living in government housing. Or in the kind of places that we could afford. But it wasn't just a case of wanting to please my wife. It was a case of what they call in private industry, "pay for performance." I felt like I was worth more on the outside."

"That's an answer I think most of us here can understand. And how would you rate the training you've just received here?"

"On the whole, it was OK. Some parts were better than others. It if would help anyone, I'd be happy to critique the whole training program step-by-step. I think that would be more helpful in trying to strengthen your program."

"Fair enough. But what was your take on our weapons training?"

"It was OK for the limited arsenal we used. Some of the weapons used in training could be replaced by stuff that is better. In general, the firepower is adequate for the type of missions expected; but there is other equipment that is more reliable when you get into dust and grit and heavy use. Or salt water. It doesn't matter what the rate of fire or the caliber if it's jammed. Pardon me. I realize you know this. Your training program is generally adequate."

The broken-nosed chap next to the big man laughed. "Damned with faint praise."

"My bad," Vance said with a grin. "Unintended. I'm not trying to sound critical."

"Not a problem, Vance," the big man said. "We asked. All of us here are on the same team." He hesitated, then pushed his folder to one side and leaned closer to Vance. "Let me speed things up a bit, Vance. Tell us what you think about the pirate situation in East Africa. Off Somalia."

Vance smiled and looked around the table slowly, looking each man directly in the eyes. When he had their undivided attention, he spoke slowly.

"I am now in your employ, correct?"

The big man answered. "Of course."

"And you all know that I have been in the Navy for more than a decade."

"Go ahead."

"So you don't want any bullshit. This is straight talk time. Right?"

"Get on with it, Vance."

"The Navy has its thumb up its ass with regard to pirates."

"That much seems clear, but...."

"Let me run on for a minute. The Navy actually has people who are recommending that we find alternative employment for pirates, that we break up the clan and tribal units that have enabled them to flourish. Relationships that date back to the Stone Age. This is bullshit. You know it. I know it. Actually, they know it too."

"Then what..."

"Hold up. You asked me. So listen. Here is the answer. And it's the only answer. Every time a pirate vessel pushes off a Somali beach anywhere, it should get well off the beach and simply disappear. Just disappear. This can happen relatively easily if anyone really gave a big shit about dealing with the problem. But we are likely to pussyfoot around and try a dozen stupid things before the problem gets fixed. The last thing we want to do is to attack the pirate bases and kill a lot of Somali women and children. We want to focus on the pirates. Only the pirates. They're easy to recognize. Fishermen don't use AK-47s or RPGs to catch fish. So if you can see either of these items, you're looking at a pirate."

"So, Vance, how do you propose to get a look at these..."

"UAVs. They're out there and they're affordable. We could do it now, but we don't want to tip our hand about how effective they are. Because the rest of the world will catch on quickly and it's easy to duplicate this technology. Right now, we could use them for many other applications, but we want to keep an advantage for later use. But our lead time will always be very short once these weapons come on the scene. By the time they come into widespread use, some other weapon will have emerged. So, right now they're perfect for use against pirates."

"What are we missing here? UAVs have been widely used for reconnaissance."

"And for taking out isolated targets. Get up to date on the Reaper. We might want to use some new type of weapon on a Reaper-type UAV."

At this stage, each man was leaning forward, listening intently and two of them were making notes.

"Listen to my scenario. A pirate vessel leaves port. Let's say on the Gulf of Aden. Let's say, for discussion purposes, from Berbera...but you pick. The mother ship leaves and let's say they're taking four large Pirellis and let's say a total crew of 30 or 35 pirates. The four boats leave, each with a crew of six. Four boats on the water. UAV spots five vessels. Four small, one large. The bigger vessel lags back. UAV approaches each of the smaller vessels. Four explosions in sequence. The mother ship will be unable to see exactly what happens and there won't be enough time to send a lot of messages back and forth. The idea of the weapon to be used by the UAV against the pirate attackers is to leave nothing that will drift ashore. No whole bodies, no whole rubber boat, no gasoline containers. Nothing. Nada. Nil."

"So how do you envis..."

"Some type of flechette weapon perhaps. Right now, I don't know. But we need to make those vessels, and their crews, simply—and totally—disappear. No bodies to wash up on the beach. Just fish food. No bodies for washing, for shrouds and for burials. Nothing to reach heaven."

"You realize—of course you must—that all this would be highly illegal. That we could possibly all be indicted as war criminals. Probably. Hauled before some frigging international court. How *practical* is that?"

"You asked me how to get rid of pirates. Not how to run for elective office. The right choice of weapons would probably not leave a lot of incriminating evidence floating around. In any case, all this is just hypothetical. I can't see much evidence that anyone in this country gives much of a flying fuck if the pirates are stopped or not."

"Well, we might disagree with you there, Vance. Shippers and insurers seem to be willing to put up considerable funds to stop the pirates."

"We must be looking at different sets of data. When the cost of ransom payment begins to approach the security payments and route changes, it will become a simple business tradeoff and will eventually be looked at by some people as the cost of doing business. People have been paying ransom as far back as...well...for a long time. Perhaps some of you have..."

The man who Walt suspected was the CFO for UBSA cut in.. "Major shippers and international insurers are not likely to accept payoffs to pirates as part of the cost of doing business."

"Yes? Well, that's another area where we can disagree. They're paying off the pirates today, and they have been paying them for years. You don't have to join the CIA or NSA to see what's been going on."

The finance guy was persistent.

"We make business decisions based on hard data. Until you have something to back up...."

Vance recognized this behavior. The bean-counter was trying to show off in front of the boss. He didn't know squat, maybe could have cared less, but he wanted to trip Vance up in front of the Big Boss as a way of making himself look sharp and insightful.

Vance thought about the assignment he had been given. He would either put himself in a position where he could gain useful information about UBSA's strategy, or his utility to the Navy was dramatically reduced. He decided to go for it. He would have to make an enemy of this bean counter. He cut his critic off at the knees.

"Look, gents. Let's cut the bullshit. Let me tell you what is known. Since 2002, over 300 carefully documented acts of piracy have occurred in one of the ocean's major choke-points, the Straits of Malacca. Ever been through there, gentlemen? I have. It's the funnel of ocean that passes Singapore to link the Indian Ocean with the South China Sea. It's a pirate haven. For decades. Actually, centuries. And this, despite the best efforts of the Malaysian police force to suppress it.

"Goddammit, gentlemen, don't play games with me. Christ sakes, the *National Geographic* magazine ran a piece on Malaysian pirates in 2007 and they showed the locations where 258 attacks occurred. Don't talk to me about hard data. Look at what's under your nose.

"Specific details—or at least some of the details—are available from the Piracy Reporting Center of the IMB in Singapore. This agency estimates that fifty percent of all pirate attacks go unreported."

The finance man had slunk back into his seat and was quiet, but Vance was reasonably certain that their paths would cross again.

"Look gents, I'm reasonably certain that you all have done your homework on me and my background before I was hired in. You know my Navy background. And you probably know that I left the Navy because of disagreement between their policies and my own personal beliefs. I won't say that I'm correct and that they're wrong. But I will say to you that my own personal beliefs are that the proper strategy for dealing with pirates can be expressed in two words." Here he stopped. It was a sophomoric technique he would have admitted, but he didn't believe he was dealing with a tableful of heavyweights.

The big man bit.

"And?"

It was too easy. Vance couldn't resist. "And what?"

"And what two words?"

"NO QUARTER!"

Actually, he felt that he had been somewhat manipulative, but as things turned out, he had played it correctly.

The second hour of Walt's interview, discussion, planning session, whatever you want to call it, went considerably smoother than the first hour. The group quizzed him on the techniques he would employ against Somalia's pirates.

"My strategy is simple," he said. "The pirates leave shore and they do not return. Period. They go out to sea. Something must have happened to them, because they never returned. We just didn't hear from them again. No bodies washed up. No empty boats drifted ashore. No flotsam and jetsam. No interrupted radio messages. They leave shore. They disappear over the horizon. And that's it."

"So tell us, Vance. How do you propose to carry out this vanishing act?"

Vance leaned across the table made a point to look each of his interrogators in the eye. "Are these conversations being recorded?" The big man started to speak. "Vance..." But Vance cut him off. "Because if I learn subsequently that they are, I will consider that any of our contractual arrangements have been voided."

"You can talk freely," the big man said.

Vance was thinking it over. His boss at the Pentagon had told him to work with his superiors at UBSA unless and until they gave him an assignment that was clearly illegal. At this point the admiral had stopped talking. He didn't tell him *not* to obey an illegal order. The implication to Vance was that he was being told to use his own judgement. OK. This was it. He had been working on these problems for almost three years; just two months shy. And most of what he had heard at the Pentagon sounded like bullshit. OK. This was the time to go. He stood up.

"OK, gentlemen. I will share what I have learned about pirates, and what the U.S. Navy can be expected to do in the near future."

His audience adjusted their chairs in anticipation of what might follow. He reminded himself that these were not members of the local Kiwanis Club—or the Boy Scout council. All were former military.

"Let me tell you what some of the Navy's top thinkers believe to be the key factors in creating a pirate threat. They have identified five factors. I've written them down so I can remember them exactly as they were given."

He removed a frayed and folded index card from his wallet.

"Viable pirate organizations, including our current batch in Somalia, need five factors to make it.

"*First*, an available population of potential recruits.

"*Second*, a secure base of operations.

"*Third*, a sophisticated organization. The infantry, for example, couldn't make it for long with the Quartermasters or the Ordnance department.

"*Fourth*, Some degree of outside support...and...

"*Fifth*—this one is my favorite—cultural bonds that result in group solidarity. Somalis all speak the same language. They're all Sunni Moslems, and they all value their genealogy.

"That's it. That's what our leaders think it takes, gentlemen. What do you think?"

A few heads at the table were nodding slightly in agreement.

"What I like—personally—about this list is that it is soooo...universal. This could apply to McDonald's chain of burger joints. Or to the Boy Scouts. Or right here, to UBSA. These are the factors that enable any organization to operate effectively.

"A chain of pirate operators is not substantially different from any franchise operation. But if you satisfied all these conditions for a cohesive group of mariners living in Tierra del Fuego, its highly unlikely that they would become wealthy. Even if every raid they made was successful. On the other hand...operations in the Straits of Malacca have been very successful. Just as they have in the Gulf of Aden." He paused again, for effect. "I think out experts have overlooked two of the most important elements."

Now his listeners were really paying attention.

"Don't keep us waiting, Vance. Keep going."

"To be effective, you need a steady parade of potential victims. Such as the Bab el Mandeb provides. Or the Straits of Malacca. Plot the data of past successes by the pirates." There was a murmur of agreement.

"Gentlemen, forgive me, did any of you ever have a girl friend who was in real estate?" They looked puzzled, but Vance didn't wait for any response. "Because if you did, you have heard the three most important words in real estate. Location, location, location."

"There are no pirates in the waters off South Georgia Island." But he stopped himself because he didn't want to sound like he was insulting their intelligence. He had started to say that pirates have to go where the ships are.

There was a moment of silence as his audience considered their responses. He continued.

"The other factor our experts left out—you might have guessed it

93

already—is the role of *qat*. This stuff is kin to amphetamines. It makes them feel smart, strong, invincible. Actually it works in reverse, but they don't know that. The use of *qat* is on the rise all across Somalia, and pirates depend on it. The most potent varieties grown come from right across the gulf. From Yemen. Half of our active commanders never even heard of it."

Vance could tell he had made an impression, but he had a feeling that it might not have been a good one.

"Today, much of the pirate plague is emanating from Somalia. STRATFOR, an intelligence clearinghouse, notes that "there may be some limited business transactions" between al-Qaeda and the pirates but adds that "the clan politics of Somalia simply do not allow for broader strategic cooperation.

Of course, the two problems can be traced to the same source: anarchy in Somalia. To bolster the fragile Somali government, the Obama administration began shipping weapons and ammunition in 2009. Washington is also supporting efforts by Somalia's neighbors to train the Somali army.""

> Forgotten Fronts—Somali
> Alan W. Dowd
> In "The American Legion, Magazine for a Strong America"

—22—Military Planners Consider Options

Inside the Pentagon, and outside—at the Naval War College—and half a dozen places you might or might not expect, teams of planners, logisticians, and warfighters were meeting to consume gallons of coffee as they struggled to come up with ways to deal with modern piracy.

Believe it or not, there were—there are—substantial numbers of military planners who—like their civilian counterparts—view piracy as the lesser of two evils.

The logic runs something like this. In the case of a failed state like Somalia, famine and extreme poverty could predictably be expected to carry off a substantial fraction of the population. Humanitarian concerns dictate that nations of the west find some way to provide food aid.

Experts in climatic behavior were predicting the drought cycles characterizing the Horn of Africa were becoming more frequent, making a harsh environment even harsher.

The inability of rural communities to drive bore holes through rock layers meant that changes in water tables sometimes had the effect of cutting whole communities off from any water at all.

Military planners, unused to considering this category of causal factors usually relegated to Civil Affairs personnel, found it hard to accept that deforestation from charcoal production, changes in water tables, inability to dig bore holes, animal die off, and increased levels of infant mortality were driving many able-bodied men, once employed as animal herders or agriculturists, to take up piracy as a way of life.

It was easier for them to muse on the unpleasant fact that, despite overwhelming U.S., NATO and EU Naval superiority in military equipment and weaponry, they were unable to deter pirates, because there were few consequences following their apprehension.

Pirates who were captured at sea could expect their weapons, and possibly their small craft to be confiscated. But as a matter of course they could count on being set ashore, unharmed and usually well fed. Their wounded, and often their sick, would be treated prior to release. For many of the Somali pirates and their occasional shipmates from Yemen or Sudan, the treatment they received on military warships of several nations would be the first encounter with a doctor in their lives.

In the crenellated towers they occupy, hundreds of military specialists are considering how best to deal with Somali pirates. While you are reading this, they are still pondering.

"My mother had her clan's love of words. She insisted that we speak perfect Somali at home, mocking us mercilessly for the slightest slip. She began teaching us to memorize poetry, old chants of war and death, raids, herding green pastures, herds of many camels.

There is little romance in Somali poetry. Even the lesser, women's poems do not mention love. Love is considered synonymous with desire, and sexual desire is seen as low—literally unspeakable."

Infidel
Ayaan Hirsi Ali

—23—Said Haad; Studies in the Heartland

From Said's home in Minneapolis, it was only about ten blocks to Riverside Park, a good place for kids to hang out for most of the year. It was as easy for him to walk to the park as it was to walk to the mosque. Most days he preferred to walk to the park because that's where a lot of his friends hung out, and usually someone would share a joint.

During the school years when he was a freshman and a sophomore, he usually had pocket money based on what he earned in the summer. He had found a job working for a nurseryman who started a greenhouse full of annuals for sale in the spring. There was a lot of lifting and carrying involved—and watering. It was interesting working with the plants and flowers and even though it was dirty work, Said didn't mind it. After school started, his job had to end, and just as well, because there wasn't much to do in winter and they would have had to let him go anyway.

When he started working he didn't go to mosque as often and the imam got on his case, eventually complaining to his father who told him that he would have to go at least once a day. He had a choice, either get up early for the morning prayers, or make a trip at sunset.

His pals at the park included half a dozen Somali boys whose parents had told them the same thing. During the year Said was a junior, the imam began to target these boys for extra training, and for a time a group of seven—occasionally as many as nine—were targeted for special attention. There was even a proposal from the men who managed the mosque to start a class in Arabic for these boys. But nothing came of it.

Most of them had learned some Somali at home and at the mosque, and it was fun in some ways because they could talk among themselves at school without their teachers or classmates knowing what they were saying. That was cool.

The Somali boys—of whom there were quite a few in his school—formed a gang that Said considered joining. But they had some secret marks tattooed on their bodies and he didn't know if he was up for that.

School was basically shit. They covered stuff about English grammar. Some American history. Math and Science. The math was a drag but science wasn't too bad. Said liked electronics. He had an old computer that someone had put on the sidewalk. He took it home and plugged it in and it still worked. It took him a couple of days to figure out how all the wiring went together, and then he had to buy a cable to connect an old printer. That little piece of crap cost him twenty dollars. But after he got it running he could play a few games that he got from his pals. His success in getting that "piece of shit machine" running made him think that he might become a computer repairman. He felt that he must have learned something, because he had managed to make the old machine work. But when he applied to a couple of computer shops regarding an after-school job, the reaction from shop owners was humiliating. It made him want to punish the people who worked there. Somalis were always being insulted.

It made him angry and sometimes he felt ashamed. The imam asked him about it once, after the evening prayers were over.

"Stay around for a while," the imam said. "Some of your friends are going to be here later."

Said stayed and four other boys came about twenty minutes later. The imam took them back into his office.

"In Somalia, you would have much more respect than you will ever have here in America. There, you would be treated as men. Not just men, either, but Muslim men. There, every female would show you respect."

It occurred to Said to wonder why, if it was so crappy in America, the imam was still here. But this was something he didn't want to say.

"Your families are ancient," the imam continued. "Somalia is an ancient land, and your ancestors have lived there since days long before this godless nation came into existence. To your generation has been given the opportunity to reunite the people of Somalia with the community of Islam that struggles against our oppressors."

Oppressors? It wasn't immediately clear to Said how he was being oppressed. But he was being disrespected. He did agree that because he was a man he should have respect. He was unhappy at school. Girls paid no attention to him, and his grades were bad. He had prayed to Allah for help in getting a girl friend, but nothing had happened. Then the imam told him about the rewards that come to martyrs. But of course, martyrs are very special individuals. They must earn their rewards in paradise by the sacrifices they make here on earth.

"Americans were appalled. The military fiasco and sudden hostage crisis brought the war home; the event clearly ranked among the nation's worst disasters since the founding of the country.

Wasting no time, President Jefferson on Tuesday March 20, addressed Congress with a call to arms, asking them to "increase our force and enlarge our expenses in the Mediterranean: *The National Intelligencer*, which everyone knew acted as the house organ for Jefferson, ran a prominent item, headlined, "Millions for Defense, but not a Cent for Tribute.""

The Pirate Coast
(Thomas Jefferson, the First Marines
and the Secret Mission of 1805)
Richard Zacks (2009)

—24—International Coalitions; Strategies; Tactics

As the number of pirate attacks increased, international bodies were compelled to pay attention. At the United Nations, the UN Security Council urged nations to employ military forces as needed to fight against piracy. Only one nation, France, specifically used the word "force" in describing how resources might be employed to fight the pirates.

UN Resolution 1838 called upon "all states interested in the security of maritime activities to take part actively in the fight against piracy on the high seas off the coast of Somalia, in particular by deploying naval vessels and military aircraft."

To anyone paying close attention to the exact wording of the resolution it was apparent that no approval was given to ground forces, for example, marines or similar forces who might be able to destroy operational bases in coastal towns harboring pirates.

As jawboning continued in the UN, member nations with capable naval forces began deploying ships. Formidably-armed ships of all sizes began to ply the waters of the Indian Ocean and the Gulf of Aden bordering Somalia's 2300-mile coastline.

The problem was they were all operating under the same fuzzy guidelines. They could fight "by deploying naval vessels and military aircraft." *OK. We did that. We're deployed. Here we are. But military presence doesn't seem to faze the pirates. They still keep coming. Sometimes they have even tried to board naval vessels that could have swatted them like flies. But still they come.*

Nothing in the mandates provided by the UN or by interpretations from the Combined Joint Task Force resulted in any guidelines that included effective deterrents.

Vance had followed all of the UN directives and debates from his desk in the Pentagon. Now, on an assignment that had him working for a civilian security agency, he was better informed on the nature of the problem than his bosses at the agency.

Assigned to the naval installation in Djibouti, he was discussing the state of affairs with his mission chief, Dick Emery—*a former marine.*

"The UN Resolution is worthless. It's just a bunch of diplomats sitting in Manhattan, stroking themselves."

"You seem to know what's wrong with it." Emery wanted his people to think he was on top of everything.

"Have you read it?"

There was hesitation. "Not all of it."

"I'll take that as a no. It really doesn't matter. It's useless."

"We can't all be geniuses, Vance. What would you have said?"

"First of all, we've got to agree on what we want to accomplish. Do we want to stop piracy? Or do we want to have a friendly discussion about the pros and cons of wealth distribution?"

"Let's go with stopping piracy."

"And I'm the person you're giving the job to?"

"You're doing the talking. Just get on with it!"

"All pirates captured at sea, to be destroyed on sight, vessels and weapons sunk, and everything committed to a watery grave. No one returns home. No message. No signs. No trace. After action reports to be secret and collected in a central info repository at the UN."

"Jesus, man. No trials, no due process? You didn't tell them this at the Pentagon? No wonder they kicked you out."

"I left on my own. You know that."

"But you can't just go around killing people. Because you think they might commit a crime."

"Of course you can. It's done every day. You know that, too."

"You see a boat load of dusky seamen approaching a commercial vessel and you're gonna terminate 'em? Just like that?"

"Yep. When I see AKs. But it has to be thorough. That's key to the solution."

"I don't believe this. What if they were fishermen?"

"Out trolling with AK's? And RPGs? No doubt they were looking for whales and they wanted to board to ask directions."

"Would you wait 'til they had tossed the grappling hook?"

"Nope. They're fair game once their craft is afloat and the men aboard are armed."

"It'll never fly. Your idea."

"Yeah, I know. That's why I'm out here with Uncle Bob. If no one is gonna listen to you, you might as well go where they pay you more to reject your ideas."

"Damn, Vance. You're *dangerous*. Is this how the navy trained you? You were a SEAL?"

"And you were a marine? They trained you to read armed towel-heads their Miranda-rights before taking them in for questioning? We may have taken this about as far as we can go, Dick. I'm kinda disappointed that you don't get it. I talk to some marines who pick up right away."

Dick Emery picked up a letter opener that was shaped like a Yemeni dagger and it looked as if he might be thinking about using it. But then he laughed. Vance couldn't see anything funny.

"Before I go, Dick, have you ever read much about piracy in the past?"

"A little. Not a lot. Just the usual stuff. Blackbeard and all."

"You know what navies used to do with pirates? Back in pre-colonial and colonial days?"

"That was a different time. Lawless. Today we have the rule of law."

"Well, you got me there. We do, indeed. But why are the Dutch and Canadians and Brits putting Somali pirates back on the beach. Why don't they take them home to be tried? Why give them back to Somalia? There's no law enforcement. There are no courts or judges in Somalia. The pirates are back at sea after supper."

"But maybe after they're captured once, they'll rethink their actions."

Vance started laughing. Emery was being serious. *Good grief!*

"Why would they rethink anything? They'll get laid, eat dinner and next day spend three hours chewing *qat* with their pals. And then they will actually start to think they may be bulletproof."

"Why would they think they're bulletproof?"

"Hold up a minute, Dick. What state are you from?"

"Ohio. What's that got to..."

"I wanted to know if you were from out west. Do you know much about American Indians?"

"Sure. A bit."

"Do you know anything about ghost dancers?"

"Ghost dancers?"

"OK. Forget it. My mistake. Back to the pirates. Where the hell was I? I forget."

"Bulletproof."

"Oh yeah. It's the *qat*. It makes them feel they're superior, invincible, bulletproof. Like we used to do with amphetamines at various times in our past.

"You navy, maybe. Not marines."

Vance bit his tongue. *Fuck you, jarhead. You can't provoke me.* Then he smiled.

"OK. As you say. Anyway...one more factoid before we quit. One of the things that stuck in my mind was a statement by the South African guy at the UN who addressed the council regarding piracy. He said, and this may not be letter perfect, *'The problem in Somalia is the civil conflict, and until you fix this, you will always have piracy.'* So if you think this jiboney was in any way correct, what do you think of the chance we can impact the pirates by patrolling at sea?"

The conversation was going nowhere and both men recognized it could easily develop into an argument both might regret.

"Why don't we continue this tomorrow?"

Vance laughed, but there was no hostility. Just frustration. *How about next month?*

"OK."

"You can tell me about the ghost dancers."

Vance laughed. *Fat chance.*

"Nah! You can look 'em up on Google. Right after UN Resolution 1838."

Doonnidii ma arag
War, machaad durduradiyo
Hadal aan dawo lahayn
Dakhalkiyo shiraaciyo badda

dacwad baan ka leeyahay
dilacanta ugu diman?
sow ka ma diiqootaan?
yaa ka dawli yah?

As to your statement, 'We have not seen the sailing ship' I also have a complaint.

Why are you tiring yourself out, working your wiles?

Do you not get weary of pointless talk?

Who rules the sea, and controls the sails and holds of ships?

From "The Sayyid's Reply"
(lines 22-25)
Mahammed 'Abdille Hasan
(in Somali Poetry, an Introduction)
B. W. Andrzejewski and I. M. Lewis

—25—Pirates and Poets

In common with most Somalis, Abdallah Ahmad loved poetry and he felt that he could do a good job of reciting lines that were popular with his clansmen. This was particularly true on long, lazy afternoons when his crew was seated comfortably in his complex, with air conditioners taking the worst of the edge off the day's heat and bales of *qat* smoothing off the edges of any internal jags.

His last three attempts to board had been failures, and another one of his boarding crew had been careless and managed to break a finger in returning to the skiff.

Now, thirteen men were seated around the wall on the second floor apartment in Abdallah's building that served as pirate headquarters and his family's residence. Raajiv's hand was bandaged and the finger had been straightened—painfully—by his wife but it was unsplinted.

His mates had teased him mercilessly for being so clumsy. The accident had happened after he was back in the skiff.

Abdallah did not want his men to become discouraged and he been thinking for several days about a poem that he would compose to give them heart . He thought of the lines when he first woke in the morning, and on one of his hunting trips into the Warsengeli he had thought of the poem intensely as he waited patiently for the Beira to appear.

Now, he felt that he had spent enough time shaping the words, and he wanted to share them with his men. Siraad, one of his trusted lieutenants, clapped his hands for attention, and the roomful of *qat*-chewing pirates sat up straighter. "Our commander wishes to share a poem."

Abdallah stood up, having previously discarded his wad of wet leaves, cleared his throat, and began. He had been practicing privately for several days.

"A Message to Mariners

Seamen—with your big ships and your valued cargoes, and your bright flags
Listen well. You ply the waters of the Somalis, and build wealth steadily, from our seas.
But we watched from the shore and considered why our families went hungry
We are, it must be told, men of the Issaq clan
We have lived along this shore forever; our roots are deep,
And we can sail to Yemen as easily as we can saddle a camel.
A trip to Aden, laden down with frankincense, was nothing to our fathers.
We do not fear the sea, and we hurl defiance as you pass our shores
Never stopping to share your treasures.
But we are Somali men, as you will learn.
Come to our shores, and take your chances.
We will teach you things
You never saw at sea, 'til now.
For we are Issaq men.
Somalis.
Respect us,
Or fear us."

Abdallah's crew loved his poem and there was applause around the room. A few of the older men had already picked up his opening lines.

"Seamen with your big ships and your valued cargoes and your bright flags. Listen well.
You ply the waters of the Somalis....."

The room hummed with the buzz of individual conversations as men, wits honed to a sharp edge by cheeks stuffed with *qat*, began quoting snatches of poetry that had caught their imagination.

Many of the popular favorites were only four lines long, written years ago by anonymous poets. One of the most popular had only three lines. But each man could recite those lines, bringing some personal interpretation or inflection that could make the others laugh. For example; *Dance Hunger.*

I don't take any of the best meat,
I don't drink from a big vessel.
But I have a great appetite for dancing.

Even Raajiv with his broken finger rose to recite; the fifth man to interpret these lines. His version, with the first two lines rendered slowly with a somber expression, came alive, with a flourish of his injured hand when he expressed his desire to appease his hunger for dancing.

No one had a poem that could compare with Abdallah's and, in fact, no one had anything original for this gathering. But several men left with a determination to work on lines to match with Abdallah's; inspired both by the recitation and by the admiring responses of their companions.

"Events in the Gulf of Aden took an unexpected turn this weekend when the German Naval Tanker FGS SPESSART, that is currently attached to EU NAVFOR from NATO, was attacked 85 miles north of Boosaaso yesterday afternoon. The attacking skiff fled after the warship returned small arms fire and then gave chase with helicopter support from the nearby Dutch NATO warship HNLMS DE ZEVEN PROVINCIEN, the EU NAVFOR Spanish frigate SPS VICTORIA, and the CTF 151 American flagship, USS BOXER.

Once the skiff was stopped, the Greek Operation Atalanta Flagship PSARA was soon at the scene and detained the vessel until the seven suspected pirates were taken into German custody onboard the frigate FGS RHEINLAND-PFALZ early this morning.

A decision concerning the venue of their trial will be taken later today."

Seven Pirates in Custody after attacking EU Vessel
EU NAVFOR Public Affairs Office
March 30, 2009
From the Internet

—26—At Sea

The large, flat-bottomed fishing boat had been at sea for four days and they were low on drinking water. During the days at sea, Abdallah had followed Somalia's north coast heading east, keeping the shoreline just out of sight. Assuming they were unsuccessful in boarding a ship, he intended to put in at *'Abd al Kura*, an island about a hundred kilometers offshore from Ras Casseyr—Cape Guardafui on some charts—the tip of Africa's Horn.

'Abd al Kura was a place he had never visited himself, although he had frequently heard it described by some of the other pirate leaders working from bigger vessels out of harbors on the east coast.

Eight men were in the boat and their plans called for six, possibly seven, of them to board the selected vessel. Based on radio messages originating from Mogadishu, there were three container ships and one bulk carrier that should have been in the vicinity within the next twelve-hour interval.

Abdallah was working with four new crewmen. Jamal who spent most of his time with the big Yamaha engine, was experienced as were Ibrahim and Jiijo, the two who were first to board. But Abdallah knew that he would need more experienced boarders if he was to expand his organization. It was his intent to use two new men as the first boarders, and he had made a point to explain this to his veterans before they left Boosaaso.

Now, as his vessel wallowed in a greasy swell, the two that he had chosen were looking queasy again. Usually, once a green hand got over the initial seasickness, it didn't come back, but now, the rhythmic rocking seemed to be inducing a second bout. Abdallah hoped the warm northeast wind might pick up just a little; just enough to change the pattern or timing of these swells that kept rolling down from Yemen.

None of the four ships he was expecting put in an appearance, but several military vessels from as many nations could be seen from a distance.

The fishing boat was well made, but in short chop she pounded mercilessly. Abdallah continued to the east, motivated in part by curiosity.

Hopefully they would make a landfall at *'Abd al Kura* in the next hours and they should be able to refill their water carboys and pick up some fresh fruit within a few hours. Then, they would continue their search for the three container ships—small ones—flying the flags of Pakistan, South Africa and Spain. The bulk carrier, which had probably been carrying wheat, was reported to be Greek and she had probably passed already.

On board, Abdallah was carrying eight rocket-propelled grenades, but he hoped that none would be used. He had only used them in the past on three occasions, and in every case he later concluded that it was a mistake. Their primary utility was for intimidation, but he had to be prepared to use them when and if necessary. Sooner or later they were almost certain to encounter armed resistance and the time would come when they would be essential. Other than that, each man carried his own personal AK-47 and four to six additional clips. An equal amount would remain on board their boat in case of any unanticipated emergencies.

Abdallah had the only sidearm, a weapon that made every Isaaq clansman in Boosaaso envious. He had a nine-millimeter Glock. Brand new. What's more, he was a good shot and everyone knew it. So far, he had never shot anyone with it.

The island of *'Abd al Kura* was about halfway to Socotra. When he had a larger vessel, suitable to act as a proper mother ship for several smaller vessels. Abdallah intended to visit Socotra, an island famed for its spices. He had seen it from sea during his years as a sailor, but had never set foot on the island, and now that he was a pirate—recognized as such around the world—he intended to satisfy his curiosity. *Inshallah.*

'Abd al Kura was something of a disappointment to Abdallah, although he couldn't pin it on any one thing. Food and fuel cost more, and *qat* was nearly twice as expensive. Water was expensive as well. He let the crew stay ashore

overnight, and two of his men got sick, *possibly from local beer.* In general the people seemed poorer. The harbor was nice enough, but small, and there was little to recommend the place. There wasn't much in the way of commerce or trade. He was glad to be back at sea, and this time—disgusted and impatient with his lack of success—he made straight for home.

His trip did have one major consequence. As a result of the difficulties and discomfort of an extended cruise in a cramped, flat-bottomed vessel, Abdallah decided to head south into warmer waters to capture a trawler with a vee bottom. A bigger vessel would make extended trips safer and more convenient and they would carry two or three fast rubber boats. This task was going to take high priority before their next boarding attempts. *"I'm not going on a cruise like this in a flat bottom—ever again."*

"...police charged 12 men and five youths with planning a wave of attacks, ranging from blowing up the Toronto Stock Exchange to storming the national public broadcaster and the Parliament buildings in Ottawa—and beheading the prime minister.

All of the suspects were Canadian Muslims from the Toronto area, most of them of South Asian origin and two from Somalia. That prompted comparisons with the made-in-Britain London bombings of last July."

"The plan to behead the prime minister"
The Economist
June 10, 2006

—27—Said Haad; A Big Decision

He was born in Somalia and came to the U.S. from Kenya shortly before his fifth birthday. His parents had fled Somalia for Kenya around the time he was three, bringing his three older sisters with them. They came as immigrants from Kenya, using documentation that had been obtained by a combination of techniques including, bribes, threats, intimidation, and a modest amount of physical violence. And, of course, U.S. money; cash provided from sources that are still murky. Although they came into the U.S. as citizens of Kenya—they almost immediately settled in neighborhoods of Minneapolis where there were significant concentrations of Somalis; primarily of the Hawiye clan.

Despite what you might have heard from Garrison Keillor, Minneapolis and that corner of the country is neither all Lutheran—nor heavily populated by Norwegian bachelor farmers.

Said grew up speaking Somali at home, but he attended public school in his neighborhood, and by the time he finished elementary school, he spoke conventional, unaccented English with a slight Minnesota accent. But he also spoke moderately decent Somali, because that was the language that was spoken at home. His mother, a conventional Somali woman who rarely left home, never learned—or cared to learn—more than a score of words in English. His father, who worked as a cleaner in a local factory, was often on the second shift and mostly worked alone, as so his English was rudimentary. On weekends, the father sometimes helped out a local Somali grocer, where he could rely on Somali for most of his interchanges.

The three older sisters were in school ahead of Said, and after two or

110

three years they were able to become somewhat integrated and the youngest tended to be the most rebellious, resisting Somali strictures about clothing, headscarves and integration with *gaalo*.

Saadia, the oldest, had several *gaalo* friends at school, and she occasionally visited with them in their homes, but none of them ever visited the Haad household. Saadia would have been embarrassed to bring them home. Looking into the Haad kitchen cabinets it might have been difficult to distinguish the family from any typical American household, but listening to breakfast conversation would have been a whole different story.

Like most Somali families, they were not scrupulous about observing all the rules laid down by the prophet. Prayer, for example, was seldom conducted five times daily. But, for the most part, family members visited the mosque daily where they sometimes prayed and sometimes listened to their imam.

Imam Mohamuud Samataar had been in the U.S. for more than a decade, and he didn't like it one whit better after the first decade than he had in his first ten days....still remembered with bitterness.

Mohamuud lived in quarters adjoining the neighborhood mosque, and unlike most of his flock, he did pray five times daily. At night he sometimes had vivid dreams of hell, with all its torments, but, for him, these were never fearful dreams because he felt that Allah spoke to him and blessed him and encouraged him to work toward the establishment of the worldwide *ummah*, a condition in which *sharia* law would prevail and Allah's peace would become universal. Hell was for other people; infidels, *gaalo*.

The imam felt that he had been given a mission. He was resigned to the acceptance of the fact that he would be unlikely to see the establishment of God's kingdom on earth, but, nevertheless, he had been shown his role in making this happen.

Imam Mohamuud was forty-seven years old; unmarried and with the exception of his rape of five underage girls in Somalia, years ago, he had no sexual experience. From an almanac, he learned that the average longevity of a Somali citizen, living in Somalia, was 48.5 years; and for this reason he felt that he was nearing the end of his life. It was necessary, he felt, for him to complete some good work to win Allah's special blessing.

Earlier in life, shortly after arriving in the U.S., he had given considerable thought to the advantages of martyrdom, the rewards of paradise, the access to his allocation of virgins, the glory of sharing the presence of Allah, and of meeting—*inshallah*—the Prophet (xyzzyx), himself. He had considered the reward connected with the destruction of a large number of infidels, and for a time he had been associated with some mullahs from Saudi Arabia who had been encouraging him in this direction. But then, he had seen them consuming alcohol together and it had turned him against their teachings and he had left that group. That had been in another city. On another continent. Before 9-11. Now, physically comfortable in Minneapolis, with his own mosque and his own flock of mostly Somalis, he had come to believe that his secret destiny was as a teacher of martyrs. He had contemplated it for so long, it almost felt as if he had done it. Now, he was prepared to teach.

From the time Said Haad was old enough to become a cub scout (this didn't happen), he had been exposed to Mohamuud Samataar, and from the time he could have been a boy scout (he wasn't one) he had received weekly instructions from the imam. By age eighteen, when he was a senior in high school, Said had listened to six years of weekly instruction from Mohamuud.

For the past three years, Mohamuud had been using the Internet to stay abreast of events in Somalia. Apprehensive about U.S. anti-terrorism surveillance, he avoided e-mail correspondence with most Somalis, but he followed developments concerning piracy with enthusiastic admiration. *And I have been contacted.*

Pirates, he knew, had initially been supported by money from Saudis, the Arab Emirates and from Yemen. The Somalis—penniless—provided manpower. He was aware that Somali willingness to run high risks at sea, in the face on frequently overwhelming odds, was based on the consumption of quantities of *qat*. About this aspect, he was ambivalent. There was no explicit mention of *qat* in the Quran, nor in the *Hadiths*. It was an easy matter for him to push this out of his mind; or to attribute *qat* chewing to "the will of Allah." To Mohamuud, the important thing about pirates was their willingness to attack *gaalo*, despite the odds. If the *ummah* was to prevail— ultimately—this was the correct route to follow. *MashaAllah.*

As a high school senior in Minneapolis, all that Said Haad knew about pirates was what he learned from watching Johnny Depp in "Pirates of the Caribbean." The imam had spoken approvingly of Somali pirates, but all Said could picture was Johnny Depp, and that slender girl who reminded him of some of the *gaalo* girls in his class. When he had tried to approach one of them, one of the prettiest, Janifa, a transfer from somewhere in the south, had later overheard her describing him to a girl friend as "a sand nigger."

This had made him angry and he had wished to punish her. He had, at the time, racked his brain to think of a way to harm her that would escape detection, but which would let her know that he had been responsible without being able to prove anything. After a bit of thought he settled for the unsatisfactory expedient of shaking up a bottle of Coke and shooting most of its contents into the vent openings of her locker, leaving her with a sticky mess to clean up. This he did. But he was never aware of her response.

Still, he remained curious about the imam's apparent fascination with the pirates and the recurrent stories of their successes.

After one of his Saturday classes, Said stayed behind to question his teacher.

"Why do you tell us that the Somali pirates have the blessings of Allah, and that they will reach paradise?"

"Said, did you listen carefully to everything that was said? The pirates are Muslims, All of them. Most of their captives are *gaalo*. Non-Muslims. Infidels. Most. Nearly all. They have only taken a few Muslim vessels and there is a movement underway to discontinue all attacks against Muslim vessels. Al-Shabab are formulating new rules. You know who these Al-Shabab men are. Soon, the only attacks will be made against the *gaalo*, most of whom are likely to be *Kiristaan*."

"The newspapers say that the pirates are only seeking money. I read this."

"You read it in papers published by *gaalo*. But you are not talking to people in Somalia."

"That is true, but..."

"And you do not understand what is really happening. You understand only what the *gaalo* papers report."

"Explain it to me, *ma'alim.*"

"Then you must pay attention. The pirates are doing Allah's work by weakening the *gaalo* economy. Already, the captured *gaalo* ships must either pay tribute to the faithful, or they must incur the high costs of longer routes, or increased insurance to offset the cost of piracy. Soon, when jihadists join our Somali pirates; or when our pirates adopt jihad, we will begin to slaughter the *gaalo* at sea."

"Our pirates do not command warships. Their craft are made of wood. Sometimes perhaps of rubber." Said didn't want to remind the imam of what he had learned from the papers; that pirates sometimes captured ships flying the flags of Dubai, the Emirates; even the Saudis.

"Yes, but with Allah's help they are keeping warships from around the world at bay. And when the pirates are captured, the *gaalo* navies do not know what to do with them. In the eyes of the world, the navies have no jurisdiction. They take our Somali fighters back to shore; deposit them safely on the beach. Trust me, Said."

After his session with the imam, Said met in the River Park with his Somali pals. The Somali boys had formed a club and they gathered informally at any of several park shelters near the riverside. In cold weather they had three or four abandoned residences where they could enter without attracting much attention, and where they used a Coleman lantern and flashlights in the cellars, after checking carefully to see that no lights were visible from outside. In this place, his friends seemed to be like children to him. They understood nothing.

"So, Said. Do you think you will go?" The imam was pushing to close the deal.

"I don't know, *ma'alim* ."

"Has Allah spoken to your heart?"

"I don't know. Not for certain. But my parents have spoken to me."

"What have they told you?"

"They say I must listen to you.

"And I say you must listen to Allah. Or to the words of his prophet, Muhammad (may God exalt his mention and protect him from imperfection).

The conversations with his Imam had wakened Said to the revered role of martyrs. More to the point, it intensified his understanding of the benefits that could accrue to dead martyrs. He could picture Janifa's dark nipples, showing clearly through her bra and t-shirt, and they helped him to come to a decision. When pirates reach heaven, their virgins will be waiting. For Said, Heaven had much to do with Janifa, and those dark nipples.

"The U.S. Navy has led Combined Joint Task Force humanitarian and training efforts in the Horn of Africa for more than six years. Now it's time to return to mission number one: maintaining freedom of the seas."

"Bring the Navy back to Sea"
Lieutenant David S. Coles, U.S. Navy
In: Proceedings,U.S. Naval Institute, August 2009

—28—Vance Considers Some Options

The U.S. Naval Facility at Djibouti may not be ultramodern in all respects, but with regard to electronic equipment, weaponry and comfortable facilities for the men and women who operate this gear, it's not a bad place to be. Especially if the tour is short—which is usually the case.

As an important civilian contract employee, Vance was initially put up in a BOQ especially designated for contract personnel. He quickly learned that he had several former shipmates on shore assignments in the facility and he spent a whole day visiting old mates and renewing acquaintances. He did a bit of checking in the personnel section and learned that several of his closest friends were at sea, operating in the Indian Ocean and he made note of the ones he would try to see when their ships returned.

Among the SEALs at the base, there were—at the moment—none he knew personally, but several he knew by reputation and SEALs—like Marines—become part of a brotherhood in which ties are quickly established or reestablished. He decided to save the SEALs for last.

His civilian status, and the identity card he carried, enabled him to have access to any of the clubs where alcohol could be consumed and food obtained. After the third day, Vance developed a preference for the CPO Club. Unlike the Enlisted Club, the bar for Petty Officers could serve hard whiskey. Many—perhaps most—of the important jobs at the base were handled by Chiefs, and these veterans were the 'can do' guys when there were difficult assignments to be handled.

Vance had made up his mind to sound out as many Master Chiefs as possible, to learn their take on the pirate situation in the Gulf of Aden. He was anxious to listen to some of the senior chiefs to see how they would tackle the problem. Naturally, this meant that some alcohol would necessarily be consumed.

On the third night after his arrival in Djibouti, Vance was seated with three Chiefs at a table on the terrace at the CPO Club. The sun was low but the western horizon obscured by the skyline of Djibouti City. Still, the view of the Gulf was pleasant and there was still a perceptible bit of sea breeze from the east.

All three of the chiefs at Vance's table worked with logistics. Only one, Tony Antonucci, had worked directly with SEALs in the past, and he had been responsible for almost everything except the weaponry used by SEALs. It was easy for Vance to strike a rapport with Tony. He knew diving gear. The other two, one a burly Irish type named McGonigle and the other, an LDS named Cartwright, from Utah, had spent years with logistics including fuel and fuel storage, and other consumables that held little interest for Vance.

The LDS guy seemed to have the most interest in asking about details of Vance's background in Utah, but the other two were singularly uninterested. They asked him a lot of questions of a political nature; about the response of folks back home to the Obama presidency, about the response to the economic situation.

News had just reached Djibouti about the movement to question the legitimacy of the last election, based on weird claims by some that the new president was born outside the United States. It wasn't something that Vance knew anything about and it had just come up suddenly around the time he was putting his affairs in order to fly out. So he didn't have much information to add, but their shared interest in the topic made him decide to hold off introducing the topic of piracy until they knew each other a bit.

The had been talking together for just over an hour and—though they knew he was a civilian—no one had asked him his role in Djibouti. It made him wonder. Was it a form of courtesy? Or was it that they were totally lacking interest?

They did ask questions about the economy, the shriveling job market, and the details of life in South Carolina, where they knew Uncle Bob was headquartered. Cartwright and Mac would be eligible to retire in a few years and they were giving some thought to settling in the south.

Everyone drank slowly with the deliberation of men who are really tired after a long day at the grindstone, and none of these old pros seemed in a hurry to get back to anywhere else.

Sometime, into the second hour, Vance asked his question. "What's the scuttlebutt on this pirate situation that's getting so much press? Your sources are close to everything that goes on. What's really happening?"

Earlier in the day, in Dick Emery's office, he had read the news from the

Internet. From the EU NAVFOR Public Affairs Office for June 7th, the headline said "Castaways safely brought back to Somalia." It read:

"Early today four sailors from Somalia, who had been rescued during a distress at sea incident, were safely brought back to their home country by a French EU NAVFOR warship. Ten days ago, on Thursday, 28 May 2009, eight Somali sailors were found in a small boat with a malfunctioning engine in the Gulf of Aden. Two were found dead, four others were injured and two remained unhurt. They were found by the French EU NAVFOR Atalanta ship, COMMANDANT BOUAN, investigating a distress call from a merchant vessel under pirate attack. The attack had been thwarted by an Indian warship escorting a convoy, however no further information could be gleaned. No evidence was discovered concerning the question whether the Somali sailors were involved in the attempted piracy incident. Subsequently, they were rescued by the French warship in accordance with the International Convention for the Safety of Life at Sea (SOLAS) obligating masters of all vessels to provide help to those in distress.

The castaways explained to the BOUAN's crew that they were citizens from Puntland in the north of Somalia. The two unhurt sailors and the two dead sailors were transferred to Boosaaso and handed over to the Puntland Coast Guard last Monday."

Vance was interested to know the reaction from the half century of U.S. Naval experience gathered at his table. "What's really happening?"

McGonigle belched. Tony Martucci laughed and Cartwright set down his glass of lemonade. They looked at one another as if trying to decide who would answer first. Tony Martucci started first.

"It's just a bunch of bullshit if you ask me. Most of the people here would agree with that. The people who make all the decisions have their thumbs up their asses and no one wants to be the first to do something that might piss off someone anywhere else in the world."

"Nobody has any balls," McGonigle added.

"Best I can tell, just about every sailor and marine on this base would like to see pirates be hung up from yardarms. If we still had any. They usta dip 'em in tar and just leave 'em hanging on shore for a while. Most people I talk to are disgusted with the notion that until this last thing with the snipers, we were catching them at sea and taking them back to shore,"

Martucci nodded his agreement.

"That's the general opinion from almost everyone I talk to," Jim Cartwright added.

"But, to be fair, our big guns pretty much have their hands tied. They're told when they go to sea that they can't kill 'em where they find 'em. Instead, they're told to take 'em into custody and release 'em to authorities in their country of origin. Which is usually fucking Somalia. It's disgusting."

"Where there's no functioning government and no law enforcement," Martucci added. "The pirates are back at sea as soon as they can find ships." Martucci's expression was one of total disgust.

"The word for incense, 'ntyw,' appears early in Egyptian writing and would have included a variety of aromatic woods and resins. Two of the best-known incense resins were *frankincense (Boswellia papyrifera)* and myrrh *(Commiphora myrrha)*, members of the balsam family. They were transported to Egypt from the land of Punt, or Pwenet, an area that is believed to be in what is now Somalia and northern Ethiopia."

Scents of Time
Perfume from Ancient Egypt to the 21ˢᵗ Century
Edwin T. Morris

—29—A Chance Encounter

Of all the interesting characters in Djibouti, few could compare with silver-maned Silvio DiPaolo. Silvio is an Italian university professor who had done no classroom teaching for the last six years, after reaching his sixtieth birthday. Occasionally he would participate in graduate seminars, but his interests now focussed on collecting and cataloging plant specimens from the Horn of Africa.

In the world of academia, Silvio was considered an expert on all species of *Boswellia*, the tree whose resin is famous as *frankincense*. But the hundreds of papers and monographs he had published over his long career had also qualified him as an authority on most of the families of succulents found along Africa's Incense Coast. He had also published scholarly works connecting the botany of the Horn with the geologically-linked island of Socotra to the east.

With a long established reputation, Silvio spent most of his time shuttling between Africa's East Coast and Italy, but he made occasional visits to London, where he sometimes gave talks at Kew Gardens. These appearances were dependably well attended and Silvio had many friends in England, both within and outside the academic community.

In recent years Silvio had established a base of operations in Africa within Djibouti, whose government was substantially more stable than that of surrounding nations; Sudan, Eritrea and Somalia, The presence of America military together with a substantial French and European Union military, allowed this polished scholar to move in many different circles. Additionally, over the years he had developed a base of African contacts allowing him to live and work with relative ease within Djibouti.

Silvio had constructed an interesting residence in Djibouti, and to this home away from home he frequently invited a variety of guests, who could always be assured of an evening of good conversation and memorable food. His wife had died years ago, but he was assisted by the slender Eritrean woman—twenty years younger— who was—nominally—his housekeeper, but had in actuality been his mistress for more than a decade.

On evenings when Silvio conducted his soirees, one could expect to find a few American and French naval officers, several soldiers of fortune or arms dealers, doctors and nurses, and merchants from Djibouti's active port who might be French or American; or Greek, Turkish, Indian or Italian. And, of course, East African. His various guests from the academic community could be from anywhere in the world. Botanists from Japan had visited with some regularity in the past, and for a time, Silvio, who conversed readily in five different languages, had considered adding Japanese.

Jitka Malecek had met Silvio on previous visits to Djibouti in the past. After their initial meeting, by a quirk of fate Silvio happened to be in London while Jitka's photo exhibition was on display in London. He had visited the gallery where her photos were being shown and been entranced by her work, but unfortunately she was not there when he visited. He had contented himself with writing her a note of congratulations. The following year they met at an event in London. They had been friends for several years. It was natural that Silvio would be one of the first people Jitka contacted on reaching Djibouti.

Vance was introduced to Silvio indirectly by Dick Emery, his UBSA chief. Emery also had known Silvio for several years. The dinner invitation from Silvio suggested that Emery should bring another guest and Emery chose Vance. But on the evening of the event, Emery was down with a bout of diarrhea. He passed the invitation to Vance, gave him the keys to his Honda and told him not to miss a good dinner.

"Bring it back in the morning. I won't be going out. Maybe you'll meet a nice woman from some place interesting; over from Oxfam maybe. Or MSF—Doctors Without Borders. WHO, UNESCO. Who knows? Maybe a navy nurse if you're lucky. Silvio has a good eye for females. Even the older ones he invites are good looking. I'll draw you a map. It's easy to find."

Vance introduced himself at the gate and showed the invitation. He liked Silvio immediately. The older man asked him how long he had been in Djibouti; if he was enjoying his visit and similar questions but refrained from inquiring about his occupation. The room was filled with people and conversations, which were being carried on in at least half a dozen languages, and the naval officer raised in Utah and trained as a warrior felt himself at a disadvantage. There were several U.S. naval officers present, in summer khakis, as contrasted with their French counterparts who were wearing whites.

Somewhat uncomfortable with the babble of talk and laughter in French, Italian and other languages he couldn't even name, Vance circulated awkwardly nursing his glass of wine and trying to figure out how Silvio had managed to build this curious structure. It made him think of a Rubik's cube. Puzzling. The complex was actually an intriguing place with plenty of nooks and corners. Most spaces opened out on a courtyard that was enclosed on three sides. Trees and shrubs in the partially covered court were strung with white Christmas-type lights giving the residence a festive, party appearance. It was, he had to admit, a great place to throw a party. Too bad he didn't know anyone.

He was determined not to migrate immediately to the uniformed U.S. Naval officers, none of whom he recognized, but lacking even a few words of French he also avoided the men in white as well. In the whole group, he had only noticed six women and only two of these appeared to be unattached. After the two apparently unescorted females became engaged in an animated conversation, Vance drifted past to overhear part of their conversation, but they were speaking in French. Damn. *They're both knockouts and the little one is really put together.* He moved away in the direction of a small bar where a young man in a white jacket was making drinks, and he took a refill on his wine before wandering out into the court.

The open end of the yard faced away from the city. Overhead, Djibouti's summer night sky was always much clearer than in DC, due in part to the sea breeze that carried away smoke, but primarily because there was less light pollution. He looked up at the sky trying to find some convenient constellations and he was reminded of the role that low latitudes play in changing the appearance of the summer sky.

He was gazing up, trying to recognize some familiar constellations, when someone spoke to him in words that were incomprehensible. Turning, he saw that it was the pretty girl he had admired earlier.

"Sorry," he said. "I didn't understand what you said," Actually, he hadn't even been sure what language it was. It had sounded like French but he wasn't sure.

"Ah," the girl said. "American."

"When frankincense and myrrh were valued highly they sustained thriving communities, their towns, ports, ships and camels. The trade also sustained large tracts of woodland in places where all vegetation has a rather tenuous grip on existence. The trees were protected because local people derived wealth and influence from them but ultimately it was the rituals, pleasures and value systems of distant peoples that maintained the incense trade for so many centuries. Now that the trade had become the victim of changing values the question arises—will the goats and fuel needs of impoverished countryfolk eliminate the rare endemics before the value of these plants and animals has been adequately recognized? There is an even bigger threat; commercial charcoal."

"The Incense Coast, Horn of Africa"
in "Island Africa"
Jonathan Kingdom

—30—Silvio DiPaolo

Silvio DiPaolo was a professor of botany at the University of Milan. He had been on the faculty there for thirty years. But although he hasn't taught any classes in the last six years, he's likely to remain on the faculty—with all its rewards and privileges—for the remainder of his life. This has to do with an endowment by his father who was a wealthy food manufacturer and wanted to encourage his son in academia. Another story.

Silvio's interest in botany stemmed from early childhood trips to distant lands where he was constantly exposed to flora and fauna of the most exotic types. His parents always encouraged his interests, supporting him with books, microscopes, cameras, tools; virtually anything he felt he needed to better understand what he was looking at.

During the years of travel, his father, who had earlier business connections in East Africa, took Silvio on extended trips to Egypt, Sudan, Ethiopia, Eritrea and Somalia; to seaports along the Red Sea, Gulf of Aden and the Indian Ocean. Something about the geography of this region was fascinating to young Silvio.

In Somalia, prevailing winds from the west bring ocean moisture to a coastal strip bordering one of the world's most arid regions. It was terrain designed for a curious naturalist. Plants and animals need toughness and adaptability to survive here. The youth had always been fascinated by the ability of plant roots to seek water. Even as a boy in high school, he had made careful studies of the rates at which plant roots could grow, relentlessly seeking water.

By the time he was in college, he had already published two papers in botanical journals. Some of his professors were not pleased to have a student whose questions were so logical, yet so difficult to answer.

Predictably, he migrated into teaching soon after graduation, seduced many of his female students and caused at least three scandals, married late, had two children, a son and daughter before losing his wife in a car accident. She was driving a sports car, alone, on a mountain road.

By this time, his daughter had married and was living with her husband, an automotive engineer, in Uzbekistan, and his son, estranged, was addicted to heroin, living somewhere in Sicily.

Silvio, himself, at this stage, had published widely, knew botanists on several continents, and could travel anywhere and be accepted as a welcome, urbane houseguest. Deeply tanned, with a thatch of silver hair, he looked the way an Italian botanist is supposed to look when he posed in his study.

He chose instead—at the time when we encounter him—to spend the greater portion of each year in Djibouti, an independent republic, primarily Muslim, with strong ties to France. The government was more stable than any of the others in the region, and both France and the U.S. had a strong military presence. From Djibouti, it was possible to make brief excursions into other regions, more dangerous places, to gather specimens, examine soils, measure rainfall and do the myriad tasks that occupy field botanists. Actually, he would have preferred to be in Somalia, but for the last decade that country had been too dangerous.

Entering his sixties, Silvio had maintained a quirky, youthful streak that was reflected in the residence he chose to have constructed for himself. Back at the University he challenged friends in the School of Architecture to create a comfortable, relatively inexpensive dwelling using standard shipping containers as building modules.

At first, the architects had laughed, but after some consideration they concluded the idea had merit and they set it up a student project. Numerous designs were submitted and judged. Some were very bad. Others even worse. But, then some very imaginative concepts began to appear and the teachers became interested.

One day some months later they invited Silvio to their department and showed him two promising designs that had evolved. By treating the containers as if they were cardboard boxes, they could be cut apart to make modular panels that could be reassembled in many different ways.

He had already given them requirements for his master bedroom, three guest rooms, and a servant's or housekeeper's room, large living-dining area and a kitchen capable of preparing meals for twenty or so guests. And, of course, a library-study. Open, airy. A raised roof spanning the boxes could provide a clerestory for light and ventilation. It was a tall order to be fashioned from a heap of steel boxes. But the final designs seemed to have every attribute that Silvio had been looking for. "They should stack easily," he had told them, laughing. "Guest rooms." Djibouti was full of unused shipping containers.

For some minutes as he examined the sketches closely, his friends stood by, anxiously awaiting his verdict. When he finally turned to face them, his face deliberately non-committal, they were holding their breath. He didn't speak for a long moment. After the tense pause, Nicholas, the Austrian could wait no longer. "Well," he said. "What do you think?"

"I am thinking that one of you—or perhaps both?—will have to come out to Djibouti with me and help to get this thing built. What are your plans for the summer? How long do you think this might take?"

The building site in Djibouti had a view of the Gulf of Aden. It was located in the southeast corner, close to the border with Somalia, and the neighborhood was semi-industrial, but his property was bordered on two sides by industrial areas that were fenced. On the other two sides, the highway and the sea. Along the fences there were heavy growths of local endemics that he planned to utilize and incorporate into the garden he envisioned. Actually, his property had almost one hundred yards of beachfront access.

One of the neighboring industrial yards was a storage area for empty containers. Silvio's team of Italian builders had no trouble getting the containers they needed, and labor was cheap.

As soon as his compound was complete, Silvio threw a party for friends and associates. His creation was open and airy. The number of guest rooms had increased to six, all on the second level with views of the gulf, and each with its own bath and shower. Small but cozy. It was like a small, upscale motel. Comfortable. Unique.

In Djibouti, Silvio DiPaolo was a man worth knowing.

"The Somali are cattle-raising people who have lived in the inland country of the Horn of Africa since very ancient times, and belong to the ancient Cushitic language group. Their distant ancestors were known to the Egyptians who visited them in ships going down the Red Sea, in the second millennium BC, to a country the Egyptians called Punt."

"A History of East and Central Africa—
(to the Late Nineteenth Century)"
Basil Davidson

—31—A Memorable Weekend in Djibouti

Silvio had offered Jitka the use of his dwelling while he was away on business. "I secure everything with four heavy padlocks, and a fifth one locks the gate," he said. "It is foolish, I realize, but at least it will deter curious children. For serious thieves it will delay them for only a few moments. When I am not in residence, there is little to steal. And when I am there, my housekeeper—who is formidable—lives on the premises.

"But those who know me will know I keep nothing of value to them in these boxes. If you decide to use the place I will give you the keys. As you choose. But I will be leaving day after tomorrow. Early in the morning."

Jitka thanked him for the offer and promised to get back to him. "A generous offer, Silvio." *If this handsome gentleman was thirty years younger,* she thought, *I could think of a good way to pay him back.* She was driving a privately-owned Renault that had been loaned to her by a black American naval officer she thought was probably a lieutenant commander. The light in the OC had been poor and she hadn't been able to see his rank clearly.

It was an interesting fact about Jitka, that men of every age seemed to be eager to please her. True, she was pretty and a lot of people, women included, found that the scar under her right eye didn't take anything away from the attractiveness of her face. But it was something more than good looks. Jitka was intelligent, and one of the ways she demonstrated this intelligence was by being a good listener and by asking questions at the right moment.

The naval officer had only known her for three days when he asked her if she needed to borrow his personal vehicle to get where she was staying. Jitka had asked him if he had gone to Annapolis because his father had been an admiral and her question had kept him awake for half the night. Maybe it wasn't *just* her question.

He might not have been concerned for her if he had known that her driver, Jamal, was waiting, sleeping outside in the battered Nissan pickup.

Jitka accepted the offer in something of a prankish mood, simply because she wanted to create some type of change from looking at Jamal behind the wheel—looking so self-important. When the young naval officer had walked her to the vehicle, telling her he would look forward to meeting her tomorrow for dinner, she pretended to drive away until he had walked back into the club. Then she doubled back to the parking area where Jamal was sleeping in the open back of the truck and told him he was released for the rest of the day. She told him he could pick her up at ten the next morning, at this same place.

Instead of driving directly back to Silvio's complex, Jitka took a rambling excursion through the streets of Djibouti. It felt good to be behind the wheel.

The old city still reflected its ties to Europe, but signs of the American and French military presence gave the place the time-warped look and feel of scenes from some World War II movie. Jitka had parked, locked up and was just starting to prowl with her camera, looking for anything that took her fancy, when she was stopped by the horn from a jeep. Vance Morrisette was smiling and waving her to climb in beside him.

"Want to head back to the base and grab some lunch at the O Club? Unless you already have other plans."

"Let me think for a moment," she said. She wasn't in any particular hurry to tell him that she was planning on staying at Silvio's place for a few days, and she hadn't given any thought to inviting someone out, even though she was certain that Silvio wouldn't have any objections.

Even though she had jumped at Silvio's offer, just for the change it offered, she still had her room at the Djibouti Sheraton. And their restaurant also served a decent lunch beside the pool. That might be a more interesting afternoon than going on the naval base.

"I have a better proposal," she said. " I have a vehicle parked across the street. Follow me back to my place at the Sheraton and we can have lunch by the pool. We can go swimming first if you'd like. That is, if we can find you a suit. Probably a manageable task for two people like us."

Vance wondered how she might define *two people like us*, but it had a good sound to it and he didn't object to the notion that they both might share some of the same characteristics.

He bought a set of trunks on the drive to her hotel and they changed in her room. She came out in a two piece bikini that gave him a woody. He had never seen her with so little clothing and usually she was loosely wrapped in garments that looked like they came from military surplus—although in a tee shirt, she had shown promise of things to come.

"Oh, wow!" he said. Actually, as bathing suits go, it was somewhat modest, but she fitted it nicely.

"What?" she lied. "This suit? You like? Not too much?"

She was graceful in the water, like a child and when she came out of the water, with a few shakes of her short hair, Vance found her to be irresistible. Despite the warmth of the day, there was a strong breeze from the water and she shivered with goose bumps over much of her body.

"You look as if you're freezing."

She slipped on the light matching jacket that went with her suit. "I get like this when I am the least chilled. You Americans have a funny name for it. I can't remember. We call it *chair de poule*. Goose flesh."

"Goose bumps. Or goose pimples. Take your pick."

"That's it. I must remember. I hope they do not offend you. It is one of my several defects."

Vance laughed. "Yeah, something must have gone wrong at the factory. Here, stick your legs over here and put them on this chair."

He took his towel and scrubbed the tops and bottoms of both her legs to get the circulation going and in a minute she was temporarily restored to perfection.

After lunch they sat at a poolside table on the sunny side, away from most of the other diners. They still had half a bottle of white wine, and they were sipping it slowly.

"You had your camera with you when I picked you up," he said.

"Looking for targets of opportunity," she answered. "You never know what you'll find. Shopkeepers, displays of fruit, cripples and beggars, kids playing the streets. But you can't get the images if you don't have the camera. I try to find themes."

"I'm sorry that you didn't bring a copy of your coffee table book from the London exhibit. Your photo collection from Port Suakin. I would like to have seen some of your work that got all the attention."

Jitka had learned that Silvio had bought a copy of her book when he visited the exhibition in London. For a moment she toyed with the idea of inviting him out, but then...if....

"Well...maybe before I leave I can find some way to get access to a book. Perhaps. We will see." She looked at him directly and smiled, and Vance knew that he would see her again.

"Tell me about your name," he said. "I never heard it before. What does it mean? It seems—if you don't mind my saying it—to be perfect for you, even though I don't know what I mean by that. You've got me talking nonsense."

She smiled. "Very few people know where my name comes from. It's Slovak. It was the name of a girl in a heroic opera by Czech composer, Bedrich Smetana. The opera was titled *Dalibor*, about a tragic hero. Jitka, was the young girl who helped rescue him. But I know this must be boring for you."

"No, no! Keep going. I've never heard of *Dalibor*, but then I know very little about opera. Actually, nothing. I once saw Madame Butterfly when I visited the Naval Academy. That's about the extent of my opera. Please. Keep going."

"My father is—was—a conductor-composer. He was conducting *Dalibor* when he met my mother who was a singer. She was in the role of Jitka when he conducted, and that was the beginning of their relationship. It's a straightforward story. And I have always liked my name. Some children grow up with names they despise. I learned this when I went to school in England."

"Thanks for telling me your story. With musicians for parents, you must know quite a lot about music. Are you a performer? How did you come to pursue another profession?"

Jitka laughed and stood up. She was beginning to goose pimple again. "Vance, if I tell you everything about me all at once, my mystery will be all gone, and you might not want to see me again. Anyway, I must get out of this wet suit that is making me cold, as I'm sure you can see." It was true. He could tell.

She was thinking, *What is the best way to get the Renault back to its owner? My book of photographs is in Silvio's study.*

"Nairobi, Kenya—Somali pirates seized a Chinese cargo ship Monday with 25 people on board, according to a naval spokesman for the European Union's anti-piracy force, which is tracking the ship from the air.

It was the first successful attack on a Chinese vessel since the country deployed three warships to the region."

Somali pirates capture Chinese ship, crew of 25
The Associated Press
USA Today, 10/20/09

—32—Said Goes to Mogadishu

When Said Haad, who grew up in Milwaukee, was encouraged to return to Somalia and join Al-Shabab, with a possible view to killing infidels and perhaps martyring himself in the process, it was true that the thought of all those virgins played a significant part in nudging him into the decision. Once he told his imam that he was ready and willing to go, things took on a life of their own.

At home, some of the rules imposed by his parents suddenly seemed stupid and irrelevant. School too, became totally irrelevant. What good would any of this information about government, American history and geometry do him in Somalia? The main draw at school was the girls, many of whom were now wearing clothing that would allow him a glimpse of their underwear.

Some of his companions were beginning to speak openly about the things they did with girls and these things, to him, seemed too astonishing to be true. Yet he wanted to believe.

In Somalia, things would be different. He would be respected. He would be with people of his same clan; people who would understand him and they would find things for him to do. And one of these things would be to hunt down infidels—*gaalo*—to be killed or to be chased out of the country. For this, he would be rewarded, on earth, and after ascension, by Allah. *Inshallah*. The imam had made it all clear. Not completely clear, but clear enough.

All Said had to do was make the decision. The mechanics were out of his hands. He helped the imam fill out some forms. He signed some papers, and two months later, when the weather began to cool, he had a passport and a visa to enter—not Somalia?—no, his visa was for Kenya. And he had tickets from JFK to London; London to Nairobi.

"Why am I going to Nairobi?"

"It was either Nairobi in Kenya or Khartoum," the imam replied. "In Sudan."

"But why not Mogadishu? That's where I want to go."

"And that is where you will be taken," was the reply. "But not by plane. At least not by commercial air. Where tickets are easily traced and where passports and visas are checked."

"What will I do in Nairobi?" he repeated.

"Someone will meet you at the airport. Do not worry, Said. From this point, people will be watching out for you. Brothers. You will find many brothers waiting to welcome you in Nairobi and they will know the best way to enter Somalia."

"I thought I would be flying into Mogadishu."

"There are few commercial flights into Mogadishu. And passenger lists are carefully scrutinized. Anyway, you would not have entry papers for Somalia. Don't talk foolish, Said. Here you are a Kenyan. Sadly."

"How will I travel in the country?"

"Said. Said. You are beginning to worry too much. You must trust me. Trust others. Before, you were a lone person. Now, you are something more, part of something bigger. You know you are, of course, Issaq. You will be welcomed because of your blood. Many people will help you. Inshallah."

Although it was hot outside on the streets of Milwaukee, inside the imam's tiny office it was cold and clammy. Muhammad kept his window AC unit running on high from the time he entered until the time he left, and sometimes it felt like a meat locker inside. Said shivered.

"I have to go. Some friends are waiting for me. I have not told them I'm going away."

"Good. There is no reason why anyone should know. Not even your parents. I hope you have kept your word to be silent. If it becomes known—the details of your arrangements—lives could be imperiled. Allah's work could be compromised. You have not spoken to anyone?"

"No. As we agreed."

"Good. That is important. There are only two weeks to go before you will be on your way. To a new and rewarding existence." The imam was looking at Said's face carefully.

"Do not worry. Allah is protecting you. You can call home from Kenya."

Two weeks later, just as the imam had said, Said Haad, with a checked duffel bag containing clothing, and a small carry on, with a Quran, Sony Walkman and four tapes of the Grateful Dead and ZZTop, and a couple of clean tee shirts, boarded a Northwest flight for JFK. The next day after watching two in-flight movies, he landed in Nairobi where he was met by two young Somali men in a battered Toyota pickup. His parents had not been overly alarmed when he had not come home and they waited for three days before notifying police that he was missing.

By then he was in Mogadishu. When authorities began tracking him, it was easy to follow his tracks to Nairobi, but from there he disappeared.

He had entered Mogadishu in the cargo hold of an old C-47 transport plane flying out of Garissa with a load of Kenya-grown *qat* ordered by two Somali warlords. It was uncomfortable, but it was exciting.

When Said, stiff and hungry, finally climbed down the steps to Somali soil, he did not know whether he should be elated, or simply admit that he was bone-tired. No one came to pick him up for three hours, and he waited outside a hangar in the shade, until a truck came and three men asked him his name and the name and mosque of his imam. They told him to get in the back of the truck and he was too tired to protest.

Welcome to Mogadishu.

The first week in strife-torn Mogadishu was much harder for Said than he had imagined. He was taken to a strong house occupied by youth of Al-Shabab. The house had been a small hotel before the war when it was gutted and all internal furnishings removed. It sat empty for nearly two years before being taken over by a warlord and used to house fighters. When they abandoned it for better quarters, Al-Shabab moved in. The original group numbered in the twenties, but young men came and went, and occasionally one would be killed in an encounter with other fighters, who might be armed with better weapons.

The youth of Al-Shabab were funded and encouraged by the imams at mosques across the city. Funding sources were unclear, but it was generally believed that money came from Saudi Arabia and was channeled through programs sponsored by Saudis. Since Somalis were Sunnis their clerics were closely allied with the most powerful and influential Saudi religious leaders.

Most of the youth in Al-Shabab were either orphans or lacked any knowledge of the whereabouts of their parents. Almost without exception, however, they knew their clan ties back several generations. Even though memories of their parents may have dimmed, their awareness of clan connections was still strong. Most of the young males in the abandoned hotel were under twenty. Their nominal leader was only twenty-eight, and he had studied at a madrassa in Yemen, where he had become a regular user of *qat*.

Some of the youth in Al-Shabab were only twelve, and the very youngest were not allowed to chew with the group. These boys usually found ways to get their hands on leaves and they had places near the beach where they would gather by twos and threes while the older boys were enjoying their regular daily sessions, which began shortly after the noon meal.

Said was not included with the older boys at first, and his initial introduction came with younger boys who wanted to ask him about America. The older boys seemed to have no interest in Said, his background, or what he was doing in Somalia. Where was the respect the imam had mentioned?

It was at the beach with younger boys that Said became aware of the activities of pirates operating in open boats launched from the beach front. By the end of his first two weeks he had spoken to several members of the pirate crews, and though they made fun of his speech, he had not been rebuffed and soon he felt more at ease talking to pirates than to his hosts in Al-Shabab. So far, nobody had given him an assignment. He had a dirty mattress and a light cover with a bloodstain in one corner, and he was fed every day, but so far he had no idea what he was expected to do, and he had not seen any *gaalo* needing to be dispatched.

Praying five times a day was a total pain in the ass, but most of these boys were regular and there were several imams who came regularly with minders who drove the flock to the neighborhood mosque. This was a lot worse than Minneapolis,

"Pirate cash washed ashore; the body of a Somali pirate who drowned just after receiving a huge ransom washed ashore with $153,000 in cash Sunday. Five pirates drowned Friday when their small boat capsized after they received a reported $ 3 million ransom for releasing a Saudi oil tanker."

The Associated Press
Monday, January 12, 2009

—33—Plans Solidify, And Sometimes They Melt

At the U.S. Naval Station in Djibouti, Vance Morrisette met up with three old friends from SEAL Team days. His pals invited him to join them for a few drinks at the O.C. They all knew that he had left the Navy and the SEALs to work as a private contractor. *News travels fast.* But Vance hoped they were not going to press him too hard for details of his employment.

No such luck. Billy Cowkiller—*aka Indian*—went straight to the heart of the matter.

"So, Vance? The lure of big bucks finally pulled you from behind the desk at the Pentagon? What happened? That pretty little squaw of yours got tired of living on navy pay?" The guys at the table laughed.

"Yeah, Billy. I'm already working on my second million. If you boys are tired of being stimulated by violence, and would like to experience a life of boredom in return for fabulous wealth, you should consider making the move."

He hoped to redirect this conversation. There was no way he wanted to give the impression that he was recruiting for Uncle Bob. The last thing he wanted to do was to suggest that he liked his new job.

Fred Kaiser laughed. "I'll bet you already traded in that piece of shit you used to drive at Little Creek for a big, new Lexus. What was that heap? A Pontiac?"

"Nah, Freddie. No Lexus for me. *Dot's a girly cahr!* I got myself an armored Hummer," he lied. "The squaw has the Lexus." Actually, he hoped his ex-squaw was taking the bus.

The misdirection worked, and Leon leaned forward, elbows on the table, to ask, "Actually what does bring you out here, Vance? It can't be that you came to audit the PX."

"Well, boys, I could tell you. But then I'd have to you know what."

133

Laughter around the table.

"As if."

"Don't even think about it."

"Oh, fuck me!"

"You boys can guess why I'm here. Same reason that your detachment has just doubled in size. We've been asked to take a look and see if we have any new ideas. *We* being Uncle Bob"

"Well, Jesus, I hope you do," said Billy. "I been out four times now, and we've made contact with pirates three out of four. In two of the three cases we just watched. Nobody wants to see a tanker explode. They had boarded foreign-flagged ships and we had no orders to act. In the one case where we captured a wooden fishing boat, we took all seven aboard the frigate and sunk their boat. I sure hated to see two brand new Honda engines go to the bottom."

"Then what did you do to the mother ship?" Vance asked.

"Never bothered to approach it."

"What about the seven pirates?"

"Took 'em to Mogadishu and set them ashore in the harbor. Them skinny sand niggers had all gained a pound or two on the chow."

"And did you give 'em back their weapons?"

"C'mon, Commander. Don't be a wise ass. People won't like you."

"Seriously, gentlemen, do you think this is the way the problem is gonna be solved?"

Billy signed to the bartender for another round of drinks. His expression looked as if he was really struggling to find a good answer, but there was none.

"You know that we follow orders, Commander. We don't make the calls. If I had my way those cocksuckers woulda been fish food at the scene. But our leaders tell us the military has no jurisdiction. *These aren't terrorist acts. They're merely crimes for money.*' That's what we got to listen to. No shit. It's disgusting."

The drinks came and the table fell silent for a few moments.

"'Seriously, Commander. If you're looking at this from another angle, give us a squint at what you think would work."

"Look, guys, you all know me; that I'm no genius. The first two words that pop into my head are 'yardarm' and 'plank.' But that wasn't popular at the Pentagon. The big brass got tired of hearing my theories which they considered 'totally unmilitary.'"

"So now that you're a civilian you've modified your stance?"

Vance paused thoughtfully before he replied. He had known these capable men—in fair weather and foul—for more than a decade. Cowkiller was a

Choctaw from Mississippi who had graduated from the Academy near the bottom of his class, but he had been a superb athlete in three sports and it didn't take long for him become a highly regarded SEAL Team leader. These guys were all his friends. This was his third drink. What the hell.

"OK, gentlemen. Here's my approach. All this is just between us, right?" They all nodded agreement. "Mind you now, this is just a theory. It hasn't been tested and proven. Yet." His audience was paying attention.

"It's not hard to recognize pirates at sea. Right? Even without a skull and crossbones flag, if it's a small, fast boat with armed men—AK's and RPGs—they're pirates. Coming, going or in action." It was inflected as a question. All nodded agreement.

"These pirates are using radios and GPS equipment to navigate and communicate. They're in touch with the mother craft and with their shore base. Plus they can communicate their position at any time.

"If they're approached by a naval frigate, you think anyone else is aware of it? Of course. Our hand is an open book. It one of you had taken a notion to shoot one of these bastards, chances are that footage of his four wives and fifteen orphan kids would be on the evening news within 48 hours. The shooter would be facing Leavenworth. So—in one sense—we are as the old Scotsman put it—*fooked.*"

There was shuffling at the table, but everyone knew that more was coming.

"Imagine if communication from the attacking boat just ceased abruptly. Permanently. In mid sentence. If anyone was watching on radar, the blip was there one moment, gone the next. No wrecked hull ever washed ashore. No bodies on the beach. No identifiable wreckage. No nothing. The pirates went out, but they didn't come back. Period. End of discussion. As Forrest Gump would have put it, 'And that's all I have to say about that.' "

It was an unsatisfactory ending and Vance's audience wasn't swayed.

"So where do we find this transporter beam, Mr. Spock?" Leon said, as chairs shuffled and positions shifted.

"Stick with me on this, guys. You know that we could pinpoint a small craft with JDAMs. It would terminate the mission and sink the vessel. That's good. But bodies float, and wreckage on the beach—jetsam—can often be identified. That's bad. We need a different weapon. Something with the accuracy and power of JDAMs, but with the ability to shred everything to bits. Shreds. Bits. Fish food. Metal stuff sinks; everything else—minced."

"So how do you create this sausage grinder?" Leon asked.

"That's the right question. Flechettes. Suppose you had an explosive weapon completely packed with flechettes? Don't you think that would do the job?"

The audience was silent. Thinking it over. Then it came clear.

"Oh yeah! Proximity fuse."

"Goes off about twenty feet or so overhead," Leon said. "Far enough got get some dispersion. The whole idea is that nothing very big remains."

"Unless, of course, it's metal; and that'll sink."

For the next half-hour the four old comrades discussed the feasibility of Vance's proposed weapon. Then the conversation morphed into a discussion of some of the weapons that the SEAL teams were currently using.

At the end of the evening, Vance had consumed five drinks, something he had planned to avoid doing. On the way back to his quarters, he was gloomy and somewhat disappointed with himself because he had not intended to be so forthright about his ideas. Even though he was talking to friends, he had made a mistake for which there was no excuse.

"Gotta tighten up," he told himself. "No slips, if I want to succeed." For a time he had been trying to think out of the box as a UBSA contractor while trying to understand exactly what made them worth what the government was paying them, but now he was beginning to think like a SEAL.

Three days later, Vance was at his desk when Leon Dombrowski strode in. Vance stood to shake hands. Leon was the armorer-artificer with one of the transient SEAL teams.

"Yo, Commander. A bit of information for you to process. I've been thinking about what you said to us the other evening. My brother-in-law is the Deputy Chief of Research at Pickatinny Arsenal and I mentioned the idea of a flechette weapon to him. It didn't seem to faze him. He only asked some technical questions about the size of flechettes and the height above target for detonation. Stuff like that. He gave me the impression that it would be a no-brainer. I never mentioned your name, or our conversation, but I get the impression that it would be easy to do. Maybe you ought to talk to him sometime."

"Well, thanks Leon. I wasn't expecting this, so I've got to process it. But I appreciate your efforts. Can I get a name and phone number?" Leon already had everything written out.

"Keep me posted, Commander," he said.

Vance knew that he was treading on dangerous ground. His work with the Uncle Bob's didn't give his the authority to pursue this idea, and back at the Pentagon this task would have been far removed from his bailiwick. But out here—in this alternate reality—one was tempted to see how far the envelope could be pushed.

The commander was feeling pretty good. Wary, but good. That night he had talked Jitka into having dinner with him and she had promised to bring along the book with her photos of Suakin. Last time she took down her book, they hadn't gotten very far.

Every day or so, Vance checked in with Dick Emery, the head of mission for UBSA operatives in Djibouti and the theater of operations covered by the Combined Joint Task Force. Emery had been a colonel in the Marines, but he had taken early retirement to join UBSA. Vance liked him well enough, but he didn't strike the former SEAL leader as an ideal companion for a tight spot. Nevertheless, he had an office inside the base, and it had air conditioning and a secretary who could help with paper work, so Vance tried to stay on his good side with regular visits. So he was surprised when a courier brought a summons for him to come at once.

"What's up, Chief?" Vance said.

"Hi, Vance. Grab a chair. Things are starting to happen. I just received a long message from HQ. You want some coffee?" He motioned to the Indian girl who was waiting in the doorway and she was back in moment with a fresh pot.

"So, what's the big news?"

"OK. Sit back. We have a bulk carrier that just transited Suez and is headed down the Red Sea. On board Uncle Bob has a team of six security guards. They're all either former marines or ex-airborne. But they're unarmed. Trained in the non-lethal techniques that are currently endorsed by the CJTF. Yeah, I know. I see that look. It's bullshit. But the CJTF is the controlling authority. Not the U.S. Navy. And last time I looked the commander of the Combined Joint Task Force was a Turkish Admiral. No telling who the hell is in charge now. So. Six security guards. OK. But UBSA also has another man on board. Like you, he was a field grade naval officer, and his job is to observe everything. Everything pertaining to our team. The team thinks he's a big shot from DOD. They don't know he's from Uncle Bob. Only the skipper knows. And he's been sworn."

"And this ship is headed where?"

"Couldn't be worse. Mogadishu. With grain. A food ship. Corn. And wheat. Name of the ship is *American Farmer* and the deck officers are American. All the deck officers. Engineers are European; Scots, a Dutchman, two Brits. The *Farmer* is registered, flagged, Panamanian, but she's American owned."

"They're certain to be vulnerable. Especially as they discharge."

"Yeah. Or before. So here's the drill. Uncle Bob wants to swap out the observer. His wife is ill and they want to take him off and fly him out of

Djibouti. But they don't want him to be visible leaving the ship at Djibouti because they know that the waterfront is being watched. They don't want him ID'ed coming ashore."

"OK."

"They want to swap you officer types in the Bab el Mandeb." There's a fast pilot boat available for the job immediately...in the harbor. Navy operated. They want us to take the guy off and put you on. Out in the strait. Just beyond the island."

"Perim?"

"Yeah."

"OK. The mechanics of the transfer should be straightforward. But I need some guidelines for my role."

"I thought so, too. But the communication said you were an expert at knowing what to look for and that I should provide you with whatever tools you'll need. Laptop, mobile, camera, shit like that. The note said just to ask you. Then do whatever you asked."

"Can we get that AC out of your window?"

"I knew you wouldn't be able to resist being a wise-ass. Take an hour and think about it. You gotta leave tomorrow afternoon in order to make the rendezvous."

"How long do you figure? And how do I get back here?"

"I make it at ten days, outside. One duffle bag. It should be cooler at sea. The rest? Getting back? Later."

"Yeah, OK. Say Dick, did you ever read *Lord Jim*? Joseph Conrad?"

"Naw. Why are you asking me that?"

Vance laughed."Just curious. I just remembered that's where Jim was headed in the *Patna*."

"What the hell is the *Patna*? What are we talkin' about?"

"Perim. The ship was somewhere off the coast of Somalia. Plotting a course for Perim."

"You've got me completely confused here, amigo."

"Not important. Some other time."

Vance didn't need Emery to provide anything. He was ready to go that same afternoon. But on the afternoon of the day of departure he had a nasty surprise about an hour before he planned to be on dock. Emery rang him to come to the office.

"What's up, Dick? I should be on the dock in twenty minutes."

"Goat fuck," said the ex-marine, disgustedly. "You won't believe what's happened."

"Go on."

"You've heard of Admiral Fosbenner? Rear Admiral?"

"Heard of him, yes. I never met him personally. But I know some people who worked for him. So I've got an idea."

"Well, this asshole is on the base. And he has his wife with him. They came in on a military flight. They have the Admiral's college-age daughter and her room-mate from school."

"And?"

"And the room-mate's dad went to Annapolis."

"And? I'm still not getting it."

"The admiral had promised his ladies a cruise around the Red Sea coastline of Djibouti because the girls had spent thirty minutes on Google Earth. So he has commandeered the pilot boat and crew for the next two days. *American Farmer* will be well into Gulf of Aden by the time your boat is available. Our UB guy is shit out of luck."

"Well, Dick, situations like this make me wonder."

"Wonder about what?"

"About whether or not you keep anything containing alcohol in your desk."

An hour later, Vance left Dick Emery's office with a duffel bag over his shoulder and had a military driver take him back to the BOQ where he had been assigned a transient room, along with half a dozen other UBSA operators.

He was not particularly annoyed by the false start, because he had never actually boarded the ship and gone into high gear. But he was much more than annoyed four days later when he learned, with everyone else, that *American Farmer* had been attacked and boarded by pirates just after rounding Cape Guardafui.

The pirates took the ship to Eyl where the entire crew was herded into two trucks and driven to Mogadishu where they were held for ransom. No one was killed and the crew was ransomed for an undisclosed sum, paid within two weeks. A skeleton crew of Somalis took *Farmer* down to Mogadishu where she eventually went back into the hands of owners after her cargo was unloaded and stolen by warlords.

The lone misfortune befell the ship's third officer who happened to be female. The young third, a tough, blond graduate of Mass Maritime Academy, was also aggressive and she swore at her captors using terms which insulted them and their parents, along with Allah and his prophet; and unfortunately one of the pirates understood pretty much everything she said.

As a consequence of her intemperate response to a simple act of financial opportunism, she was singled out of the crew, isolated and gang raped by five

Somalis. In a way she was lucky. In the hands of Al-Shabab she probably would have been killed. When Vance learned this, he was sorry that he had not been aboard. Not for the first time, he felt anger and disappointment at the actions and responses from some of his senior officers. He also felt anger that he had not been aboard for the trip down the coast.

Pirates had faked the security guards by attacking on the port side with two boarding craft and actually boarding from the starboard quarter with a third smaller vessel following at a distance. How the hell had the guards fallen for that fake?

For a week after learning about *American Farmer*, Vance was in a bad frame of mind. The only highlight of that gloomy period occurred during a couple of visits to Silvio's place where he enjoyed the Italian's hospitality and food, enhanced significantly by the presence of the little French photographer. He was surprised to notice that being around her made him smile. Something that was rare for him.

"You looked so gloom...what?...glooming?..when you first came in," she told him.

"Sorry. Yeah, I've been disappointed. I was supposed to take a sightseeing trip."

"To where?"

"To Bab el Mandeb. I wanted to see that island in the strait," he said. "Don't you speak a bit of Arabic?"

Jitka laughed. "I know a few words only. I can't really speak a whole sentence. But I can buy water. Some food. And count to ten. I find it hard to pronounce."

"Do you know the meaning of Bab el Mandeb?"

"Bab, I know means door, or gate. That much I'm pretty sure of."

"An old pal just told me that it means 'Gate of tears.' But I know that he can't speak it at all. So I'm skeptical. It doesn't sound right."

Silvio walked up at the tail end their exchange. "Bab el Mandeb? Yes. It means 'gate of lamentations.' Probably named by early sailors in flat-bottomed dhows who got into trouble out in the Gulf. Gate of tears, gate of lamentations; that's the meaning. Can I get you children some more wine?"

The day after Silvio's, Vance made a phone call to his SEAL acquaintance, Leon Dombrowski, the armorer. He hadn't called Leon's brother-in-law because he knew the call might be traced or monitored.

"Spain was working to secure the release of a Spanish tuna trawler hijacked Friday in the Indian Ocean with a crew of thirty-six. Pirates seized this ship about 375 nautical miles off the east coast of Somalia. All thirty-six crewmembers are in good condition and unharmed, Defense Minister Carme Chacon told Spanish National Television."

"Pirates release ship after ransom paid"
The Associated Press
In USA Today, 10/6/09

—34—Paths That Cross

Said Haad had been in Mogadishu for nearly a month and he was learning a great deal about Somali culture and ways of which he had been totally ignorant. But, on the whole, he was beginning to regret his decision. The music wasn't bad but Somali girls did not talk to him, except in rare cases where he was buying water, or fruit. He had hardly seen anything of the girls and women except for street vendors and girls in shops. And they were generally covered head to toe. He had made no close friends, and the food was mostly miserable, except the *angello*.

It was much better in Milwaukee, in school, and in the shopping malls, or the public parks. And the swimming pools! Ya! Ya! Nothing like that in Somalia. At least, not that he had seen.

One morning after he was somewhat settled-in and less uncomfortable, he wandered down Mogadishu's waterfront and engaged in a conversation with two men standing guard beside a small trawler. He learned that the fishing vessel had been captured earlier in an attack made from an open boat. It had originally been manned by six Mauritian fisherman who had been set adrift in a raft, near shipping lanes where they were likely to be picked up. The trawler had been modified to serve as a mother ship for four rubber Pirellis each equipped with a large Yamaha and a second smaller outboard used for loitering.

The trawler, renamed *Sea Camel-3*, had recently come down from Eyl where it had first put in after its most recent capture of a Malaysian tuna boat. The Malaysian crew of twelve had been held until recently, when their ransom details had been completed. It was felt that it would be easier to negotiate from Mogadishu than from Eyl. So both ships had moved south to the capital as middlemen worked out details of transferring men, money and the captured ship. The transactions had just been completed and other members of the pirate crew were engaged in a shopping spree before returning to their home base in Boosaaso.

When the pirates learned that Said could converse marginally in Somali, but that he was also able to speak, read and write fluent English, they encouraged him to stay around until their leader returned.

This was how Said met Jiijo, one of Abdallah's chief lieutenants. Three hours after their initial conversation, Said was back at the dock with his duffel bag, and the Sea Camel was fueled and ready to head north for home. Despite the calm weather that prevailed on this trip, Said became violently seasick in the long, slow swell, but by trip's end he was fully recovered.

When the trawler reached Boosaaso, Abdallah was not immediately available to speak with Said, so four days elapsed before the meeting took place. But Abdallah was interested to have a crewman who could read and write English. A few days later, the Milwaukee teen who wanted to kill *gaalo* to earn his quota of virgins found himself among a bunch of *qat*-chewing pirates operating out of Boosaaso.

"The late seventeenth and early eighteenth centuries were known as the golden age of piracy, when the likes of Blackbeard and Captain Kidd preyed on merchant shipping. But compared with today, that era was a mere Bronze Age; modern pirates surpass their predecessors in numbers, riches and violence. Since the end of the cold war, piracy has become far more prevalent than at any other time in history, developing into a business with multinational impact, multibillion-dollar cost, and a deadly human toll."

> From the prologue to...Terror on the Seas
> (True Tales of Modern-day Pirates)
> Daniel Sekulich

—35— Jitka Contemplates Eyl

Dry, sandy Djibouti was an amazingly comfortable base of operations for Jitka Malecek, due, in part, to the fact that there is a large military presence of French and American soldiers in the country. Many young men are starving for the companionship of women, especially pretty ones, and Jitka is uncommonly attractive. Ensconced in a comfortable hotel where she could usually be confident in getting a tolerable meal and coffee, tea, safe potable water and hot showers, she could have remained for a long time without complaining about accommodations.

In truth, Jitka was fairly undemanding about the basics of daily living. It's conceivable she could have lived among the Beduins. While in the city she looked up the names recommended by her BBC contacts in Khartoum. Her BBC contacts had tried to convince her to take a video camera and a sound man, and they had given her a couple of recommendations in each area. Jitka quickly connected with the recommended driver who made a good impression but she decided to hold off. The first sound man couldn't be located, and the second was non-committal. She decided to forget about sound. After meeting Vance, she decided to relax for a few days and put her plans on hold for another day or two. He was different.

Silvio was a good host. Leela, his Ethiopian housekeeper and mistress, had prepared dinner for them. Two young Djiboutis, actually Ethiopians, were hired as waiters and stewards for this dinner which was intended as an acknowledgement of his friendship for Jitka, whose artistry he had first admired in London.

The dinner was elegant. Silvio had succeeded is obtaining several large lobsters of a type found in the Gulf, and he had been demanding in his instructions for their preparation. Sensing the chemistry, he asked Jitka to invite "a guest."

After dinner, they lingered at table with white wine and conversation. The Soave was very good—especially chosen by Silvio for private occasions—and the conversation shuffled back and forth between English and French, with occasional exchanges in Somali between Silvio and Leela who did not understand English at all and whose French was limited.

When Silvio beckoned, she joined them at the table. Despite her limited understanding of everything being said, the Ethiopian woman appeared attentive and interested, even when uncomprehending, and in this manner she made herself into an acceptable dinner companion for the other three. This ability to accommodate was not lost on Jitka.

At dinner, Silvio queried Jitka about her plans for the coming weeks. He was astonished to learn she making plans to visit Eyl and to photograph and possibly videotape pirates operating from Somalia's beaches.

"Have your employers approved this activity?" he asked.

"Of course," she replied. "With some reservations—naturally. But they believe that any footage or images obtained will be valuable in the world of information...news."

"That is probably true. If, that is, you survive to bring it back. This is always a problem with news personnel who work on the front lines."

Vance was taking in every fragment of the conversation between Jitka and Silvio and it made him think of a conversation that might occur between a father and his daughter. Silvio had spent a lot of time in Somalia, and clearly he did not feel that it was a safe place for Jitka to visit. But then, he was neither father nor big brother, nor lover nor anything but an acquaintance and a hospitable friend with no real say.

"I plan to leave in three days," she said, as if to close off any further discussion.

Vance wanted to help her put a stop to Silvio's hectoring questions and he decided to change the subject.

"Jitka?"

"Vance?"

"Do you mind if I change direction, here?"

"Try me."

'Maybe our host will be interested as well And his handsome companion." He nodded at Leela and Silvio translated into Somali. Leela smiled.

"I've been wondering if Silvio knows the origin for your name. Have you ever heard it before, Silvio? Would you like to know?"

She smiled and the frown that had accompanied Silvio's badgering interrogations disappeared.

Silvio nodded and lifted his glass. *Yes.*

"Avec plaisir. Do you mind this, Silvio? It will not be too boring for you? And Leela?" Silvio nodded and spoke a few words to Leela. And Jitka began.

"My name comes from an opera. Jitka is the character in an opera in which my mother had a role when she first encountered my father. She was a singer and he was the director of a big opera company."

"Opera. I love opera," Silvio said. "Aida, Rigoletto, La Gioconda. But I don't recall hearing of an opera called Jitka."

"That because all operas weren't written in Italian," she laughed. "The title of the opera was *Dalibor*." She tried to make it pleasant, but it had come out with a harder edge than she intended, and she blushed at her rudeness.

"It was written in Czech, and it was, at one time, directed by my father when it was performed in Paris. One of the important roles—not the lead—was for a heroic female called Jitka and my mother sang this role when she first encountered my father. Except for that role, the role of Jitka, I might not exist today.

"There are many operas," Silvio said. "I cannot know them all, But *Dalibor*...this is a new title for me.

"Not surprising," she said. "It is little performed today. Nevertheless..." She hesitated, wondering whether they wanted the complete, boring lecture.

"Don' t leave us hanging," Vance prompted. "What about the opera?"

Jitka laughed, realizing what he had done. "As I said, it's a Czech opera. By Bedrich Smetana. You might know him from other works, like Ma Vlast—My County— or the Moldau, but he also wrote opera; this one called *Dalibor*. One of the characters in the opera was named Jitka and this role was sung by my mother when my father was directing. They were both musicians. Both disappointed that I didn't take up music as a career. But they still love me, even if I have chosen to follow a different path. So. Now I have told everything...twice."

"But getting back to your question...this Jitka role was apparently quite a—how you say it?—*a turn-on* for *mon pere, et ma mere*, and shortly after the performance of the opera they were wed."

"And the name again?"

"Of the opera? It was *Dalibor*. By Smetana. I grew up with it in a way." She was conscious of talking too much, of repeating herself, but Vance had successfully changed the subject.

"*Dalibor?* H'mmm." said Silvio. "I must remember. This is an opera and I have never heard of it."

Jitka just laughed. "And you an opera fan? Well, now you know. Try it. You might like it. My parents did, and that's how I got my name. How I came to be born."

But Vance was still not satisfied.

"Tell us about Jitka. What does she do in the opera?"

"What does she do? Wait. Let me think. It's a complex story. She tries to help free *Dalibor*, the knight who has been falsely charged and condemned to die. Jitka makes plans to help free him from imprisonment."

On the way back to the hotel where Jitka was staying, Vance asked her if she felt secure there, and if she slept peacefully through the night.

"It is not so bad," she said. "They have a night watchman at the entrance to their lobby. All night—and he is supposed to provide warning if anything nasty is afoot. Not much, but it's what they provide. Who really knows? No one in this world is really safe at every moment. I sleep well."

That wasn't the response Vance was hoping to hear, but he didn't want to come on too strong. She was, he felt, worth a long wait.

Back at Silvio's place, the old scholar was thinking their conversation, but it wasn't about opera. He was thinking about Jitka's ill-conceived plan for entering Somalia.

Hijacked M/V ASIAN GLORY Arrives Off Somalia

Hijacked M/V PRAMONI Arrives Off Somalia

Pakistan Flagged Fishing Vessel SHAHBAIG Released

UK Flagged Vehicle Carrier Hijacked

Hijacked MV ST JAMES PARK Arrives Off Somalia

> EU NAVFOR Press Releases
> January 9, 2010

—36—Frustrated in Djibouti

Despite the distraction Jitka provided, in the welter of news concerning AMERICAN FARMER, Vance was depressed and moody for several days. The pirate attacks were not decreasing despite the presence of a fleet of European Union warships, and thousands of highly trained seamen.

It seemed to be a form of madness. The pirates could attack anyone with the certain knowledge that if they turned back at the last moment, there would be no consequences. No repercussions. They would not be pursued back to their home base.

If they were successful in boarding, the strongest navies in the world would not attempt to retake the vessel. It was considered too much of a risk to life.

If a pirate attempt failed and there was an injury to some of the pirate crew, the injured man could, if he desired, be medevac'ed by helicopter and carried to the French Military Hospital in Djibouti. There he would be treated and cared for at no expense until his injuries healed, after which he would be returned to Somalia.

Why would any camel boy, who lived within walking distance of the sea, not aspire to become a pirate?

When he was alone in his room Vance thought about the moral dilemma of dealing with piracy. There had been instances in which a disabled pirate vessel would be hailed by a warship and subsequently towed safely into home waters. After all, the reasoning seemed to go, they haven't actually been convicted of anything. *Sure, they look like pirates, walk like pirates, quack like pirates. Whatever happened to the Duck Test?* he wondered.

147

In many ways, the presence of the EU armada was providing protection and cover for the pirates. This could almost be proved to critics by looking at the statistics of attempts since the fleet's arrival. Piracy was a growth industry. On the coast of Somalia, half a dozen cities were enjoying a boom town economy. The whole country was benefiting.

Before he left the Pentagon, to take this current assignment with a private security contractor, Vance had decided to educate himself regarding the complex way in which money—for ransoms or for the return of vessels and cargoes—was transferred. How did these large sums of money change hands? Who else profited? Bankers? Brokers? Middle men? In what way did these transactions resemble those of illegal arms brokers? Would a clearer understanding of the money flow help in disrupting this illegal, but highly profitable, activity? But he had not proceeded very far before his superiors had redirected him to North Carolina and Uncle Bob's.

Now, UBSA had a total of fourteen people in Djibouti. Probably this contingent was raking in between five and six million dollars for Uncle Bob every year. Minimally. And what was the end result? Nada. Zip.

Of course, this cost paled into insignificance when compared to the cost of the naval force provided by England, France, Germany, Spain, Denmark, Greece, Turkey and a few others he couldn't remember offhand.

The other people from Uncle Bob were frequently deployed at sea. They traveled as unarmed supernumeraries on merchant ships who had room for them and requested their presence. Vance did not know whether or not the shipping companies also paid Uncle Bob, and Dick Emery, his local UBSA consigliere, had not seemed willing to discuss this topic. So Vance was still in the dark. Not that it mattered.

But what the heck did they expect him to do out here? The home office seemed to think he would know what they wanted when the right situation arose. Just use your own judgement, they had told him.

In a way, it was a vote of confidence. But in another way, it suggested that they were simply using him to jack up the fees they charged the U.S. government, the DOD. Everybody was making money. The Navy, Uncle Bob, French and Dutch sailors, Somali Pirates, their Arab sponsors. Everyone was riding the gravy train. Those who were footing the bill were clueless.

Fucking—pardon my French—clueless. And he was supposed to be on the side of the white hats.

In Djibouti as a civilian contractor for UBSA, Vance was hard pressed to know where to begin. His organization had a Chief of Mission who seemed to be a competent administrator, but after their first meeting both men decided that they would probably never be friends, even though they knew they must work together. Dick Emery also had a convenient office inside the fence at the U.S. Naval facility.

Vance was directed to follow any instructions from Emery closely, and his boss was told that Vance was a go-to guy with valuable experience and many contacts in the military establishment. Still....the chemistry was bad.

It happens.

Within the first several days, Vance had been introduced around, briefed on the nature of contracts with shipping firms and told—retold actually, for he knew it by heart—about the techniques that had been approved for repelling pirate boarding teams.

His boss had provided him with a desk in the room where UBSA agents occasionally worked. Most were at sea on assignments. He met the young Eritrean woman who would provide secretarial support, and he was given a phone directory for the US naval installation whose main gate was within a short walking distance.

In the directory he found several familiar names and he spent one morning on half-a-dozen phone calls. On the first page he noted the name of a former member of his SEAL team; Leon Dombrowski, the weapons specialist. He had already met Leon and had spent some time considering his suggestion for contacting his brother-in-law to discuss some of his weapons ideas. But, on reflection, Vance had considered it too risky.

He had been sent to learn what actions a contractor was planning, only to learn that the contractor expected him to come up with the plans? He was beginning to suspect his bosses in the Navy might have hung him out to dry.

No shit? What the hell am I doing here?

"The United States' efforts since 9/11 to prevent Somalia from becoming a safe haven for al Qaeda have alienated large parts of the Somali population, polarized the country's diverse Islamist reform movement into moderate and extremist camps and propelled indigenous Salafi jihadist groups to power. One of these groups, a radical youth militia known as Al-Shabab, now controls most of Somalia's southern half and has established links with al Qaeda."

"In the Quicksands of Somalia"
Bronwyn Bruton
in Foreign Affairs, Vol. 88 No. 6

—37—Inside a Pirate's Den

Time out! Have you ever wondered where pirates congregate? If you have or had teenagers, a pirate's den will probably seem much like the fort they used to hide in when boys and girls got together to play doctor or learn to smoke. Perhaps their parents were enjoying a nap, cocktail hour, maybe doing volunteer work at the senior living center, or any other adult activity. In other words—*neglecting their offspring*. Pirate dens don't get high marks for cleanliness, decor or adult supervision.

A pirate's den, these days, whether found along the Straits of Malacca, the Dark Continent's west coast or the beachfront around the Horn of Africa—anywhere—is going to have certain basics. These might possibly include...several old rump-sprung sofas that appear to have survived curbside rescue, possibly facing a big screen TV, a bar, and a place to hang hats, coats, jackets, turbans, djellabas or anything else in order to leave hands free for other activities. Maybe they'll just use cushions on the floor. Or even better, just a pile of rugs against the wall.

Somalia isn't much different respecting its pirate dens. Except....maybe there is one big difference. That would be...*qat*. And hashish. Mostly qat.

Qat. The chewable leaves and twigs from a small tree. A narcotic plant. Its effects are not unlike marijuana. Chewers become lethargic. *But much, much more intelligent. Also braver. More fearless.* It is not an upper. But you also reach a stage where...how can one say this so that it becomes understandable?... where *you just do not give a damn.* This means that if you have a boat with half a dozen teen-age boys—about to make a dangerous attempt to climb aboard a moving ship in a distant ocean where there are many men on board who don't care if boys live or die—it helps if the boys have been chewing a wad of *qat* before they toss that hook and shinny up the side.

When Somali pirates come ashore, like most males, they need a place to hang out. Thus, the case for a "pirate's den." There will be no skull and crossbones on the wall, but there may be a reminder that "God is great.". It may just look like an ordinary room. If, however, you look inside it will begin to look much like the place just described. Look—and smell.

Why would we even care what a pirate's den looks like? One reason is that if we could be given access to listen in on pirate conversations, we just might gain some insight into the minds and thought processes of pirates, and thereby come up with strategies to defeat them.

But, you may counter, we have been talking about *Somali* pirates. And they will be speaking in Somali. Which we don't understand.

Ah, but this is fiction, and anything might happen. Out in Seattle, Bill Gates's software engineers might come up with something to stick in your ear that converts spoken Somali into English. Don't laugh. It could happen. Let's just try it. We will enter a den.

Hey, this is not so bad. Rugs on the floor. Lots of pillows. Spaced-out Somali males just lounging around. They seem to be in their zone. Most of these guys seem to have something in their cheeks; a big wad of something. Huge wads, actually. Gosh, it smells funny in here. It's probably that stuff they're chewing. Plus B.O.

This place would smell a lot better if these pirates took an occasional shower and changed those sheets they're wearing instead of dousing themselves in pine scent. Or whatever the heck that is. Conversation? It sounds like everyone is talking at once. Talking....or just buzzing.

Otherwise, this place is not much different than your basement used to be after the kids took over the rec room and put in that drum set. Actually, a couple of neighbors down the street had a garage that looked a lot like this. Especially after those experiments with homemade beer.

Best guess is—after this brief peek—is that the odds *against* learning anything helpful from examining dens are overwhelming. Let's get outside before we start coughing again.

The dependable element in a Somali den will usually be...qat.

"The draft would give a six-month mandate to states cooperating with Somalia's transitional government (TFG) in fighting piracy to "enter the territorial waters of Somalia for the purposes of repressing acts of piracy and armed robbery at sea."

UN resolution to combat Somalia piracy set for approval
June 2, 2008
From the Internet: Http://afp.google.com/article

—38—World Powers Look at Piracy

While Vance was in Djibouti, there were warships for seven different nations in the harbor, and on active patrol assignments in the region. During the first four weeks of his assignment, several pirate groups were turned away by the physical intrusion of heavily armed frigates, inserting themselves between pirate skiffs and potential victims. But if the frigates failed to intervene physically, the pirates attempted to board anyway, even when the warships were in sight.

The United Nations, the European Union and the U.S. Navy had armed men present, took prisoners, heard testimony, collected information, listened to recommendations and drafted a resolution. But, as one unnamed observer put it, "They're gumming their Rice Krispies." *He must have been trying to convey the notion of toothlessness. We get it, Fredo. We're smart.*

"What the hell are these guys thinking when they see a fuckin' frigate coming their way? Are they insane?" It was Geronimo speaking.

Vance laughed. "Saner than us. They know that all that firepower is unlikely to be trained on them. And anyway, most of them—possibly all of them—are half stoned, half in the bag— however you want to describe it—from *qat*. They think they're invincible."

The two men were sitting on the terrace of the Chief's Club on the U.S. Naval Base. Vance was the guest of Master Chief Vincente Torres, a.k.a. Geronimo to those who had served with him.

"I don't want to bore you, Vincent, because I know that you've been out or at sea in these waters for more than six months, and this isn't your first tour. But I, too, have spent a couple of years looking at this problem from every conceivable angle. And there are only a few options that are likely to succeed in stopping piracy."

152

"Then why the hell aren't we doing it, Commander? Why didn't you make it plain to the Pentagon crew?"

"Why do you think I'm out here instead of back there? I made the case. Made it so plain and obvious that my listeners could find nothing wrong, nothing to improve. But it was politically unacceptable. So, since they couldn't find anything to correct, change or improve, and at the same time they couldn't adopt the techniques I proposed, they only had one option."

"Kill the messenger?"

"Nothing quite so drastic. Just move him somewhere else where he be out of sight and hearing."

"And that's the reason you're out here? As a civilian contractor?"

"That's one of the reasons. Not the only one. I had to get away. Personal things."

"Uh huh. Like that, eh?"

"And maybe the money," he lied.

The truth was that Vance had done almost exactly what he was describing to Master Chief Torres. He had identified ways to attack and destroy pirates from the air, by land, and on the sea. For every approach he had considered the pros and cons, likely countermeasures and possible casualties on our side. To help make his analyses rigorous and unassailable he had enlisted the services of a systems analysis group within the Pentagon and they had helped with organizing much of the information he had collected into formats that were comprehensible, even by non-technical audiences.

Vance's preferred approach, which he had spelled out to his superiors, would have been to employ expert snipers, operating as shipboard teams and taking out two pirates simultaneously, as they came within range. Typical targets would have included the RPG man and the helmsman, but outboard motors also made good targets. While none of these approaches was free from some element of risk, Vance felt that they merited a trial.

In discussing the details of some of his many ideas with Geronimo, and others whose talents he appreciated, Vance was probing delicately to find a kindred spirit, someone whose zeal would make them willing to walk over the edge. Geronimo Torres was a good man, but he was not such a one.

I'll just keep looking.

"Nairobi, Kenya—Crews on oil tankers aren't allowed to smoke above deck, much less carry guns, for fear of igniting the ship's payload. That's one of the main reasons Somali pirates met little resistance when they hijacked a U.S.-bound supertanker carrying $20 million in crude. The Greek-flagged tanker—traveling from Saudi Arabia to New Orleans—had no escort when it was hijacked Sunday because naval warships are stretched too thin."

> Somali pirates hijack ship carrying $20 M of oil"
> Katharine Houreld
> The Associated Press
> December 1, 2009

—39—Every Attempt Doesn't Succeed

Within the community of pirate commanders, news of successful captures and speedy payoffs by western shippers and insurers was quickly passed around and used to spur unsuccessful leaders into action. It had been several months since Abdallah's group had been successful in boarding anything with payoffs in excess of a million U.S. dollars. Their last two successful boardings had been of fishing boats; one Spanish and one from the Indian Ocean island of Reunion. In both cases the final payout that ended up for distribution by Abdallah's band was less than a quarter-million. True, the full settlement was substantially higher, but the negotiators, London-based, were demanding increasingly higher fees. Abdallah's Yemeni contacts were telling him that he should complain and switch to negotiators in Dubai.

Complain? Where should he direct these complaints? He had been looking at the literature for new navigational systems made by an Italian firm and he believed that this equipment installed in two of his captured trawlers would give him the ability to extend his range of activities far beyond the area he was currently covering.

To date, all of his big successes had been in the busy shipping lanes off the south coast of Yemen. His crews rarely lingered offshore for more than a week.

In the weeks after Ramadan, Abdallah determined to step up his activities. With a hand-picked crew of twelve, he set out in the early morning at the beginning of December, the season of *dayr*, the brief rainy season that precedes the droughts of *jiilaal*.

A light misting rain was falling as they pulled away from the Boosaaso dock shortly after dawn. His men's spirits were high and they had spent most of the preceding day chewing *qat*, telling stories and competing with poems from their past experiences.

As the modified trawler set a course to the north—easing into a low swell—the men congregated in the cramped living space and spent time checking their weapons and discussing alternate strategies for boarding.

Abdallah had stored food and water for eight days. Information he had received from personnel in Djibouti indicated that at least nine European-flagged bulk carriers would be passing south of Aden within the next 48 hours. They were bound for ports in Saudi Arabia, Dubai and Pakistan.

The pirate commander planned to intercept these ships somewhere to the south of the Yemeni coastal city of Balhaf. This was sufficiently distant from Aden and Djibouti to be fairly confident that the ships would not have naval escorts. In case they did, Abdallah's crew—simple Somali fishermen—would simply fall off and wait for the next carrier.

Six days later, he turned and ran for home. They still had ample food and water and their fuel was only half gone, but four successive attempts to board had failed and one of his men, Dajaal, had crushed two fingers in the next to last attempt. It wasn't likely that the fingers could be saved. Anyway, Abdallah reasoned, Dajaal didn't strike him as a good Muslim. Allah was punishing him. But other crew members prevailed on Abdallah to head for home and medical attention.

"It is tempting to be jaunty about piracy. So what if a few Robin Hoods in skiffs nick the odd tanker off the Horn of Africa? Often enough, the owners pay ransom and nobody gets hurt. Everyone needs a living in these hard times. And if the worst comes to worst, gunboats can always be dispatched to clean the problem up, just as the British and Americans did off North Africa's Barbary coast at the turn of the 19ᵗʰ century.

It is tempting, but it is wrong."

The Lawless Horn, Anarchy in Somalia
The Economist, November 22-28, 2008

—40—Some Deaths at Sea

From his home port on the north coast of Puntland, Abdallah and his handpicked group of eight had attempted piracy fourteen times in the last two months and they had been successful in five attempts. Their last three attacks had succeeded and in the next to last, they had taken captives and succeeded in obtaining a ransom payment from a Danish shipping company of over a million dollars. The money was transferred from Denmark to Switzerland to a legitimate bank in Kenya. This was the easiest and fastest money transfer to date.

When the money eventually reached Abdallah and his marauders, the windfall allowed them to purchase a supply of RPGs from Yemen and they augmented their armory of Kalashnikovs with a dozen new automatic weapons that were shorter, lighter and more effective at close range. They also purchased four new Zodiacs and two new GPS systems for their mother ship, a small fishing trawler, which originally had flown the flag of Mauritius. Actually, this ship had been their first big prize since their visit to 'Abd al Kura. It was captured offshore in what the Somalis considered were their territorial waters. His crew, at that time, considered that the Mauritian fishermen were poaching in Somali fishing waters and they were angry, from the moment they boarded. When the Mauritian skipper wanted to argue, they discovered that they could communicate in French, and argue they did.

It was a lopsided argument, since the Somalis had weapons and the Mauritians had none. Insults were exchanged and the skipper was struck. Things got out of hand quickly; one thing followed another, and the six -man crew of the old trawler were shot and dumped into the Indian Ocean.

The circumstances had infuriated Abdallah, because this was the first time that there had been killings when there had been no resistance. And they were precipitated by the American youth he had picked up for his English language skills. Said Haad, a boy from a northern part of the U.S., had been eager to fire his weapon and he had been the shooter, killing three men with his initial burst, despite instructions never to fire unless ordered by Abdallah.

Subsequent to the death of the initial three, Said told Abdallah that the Indian skipper, a Hindu, had made an intolerably offensive comment about Allah speaking in English, thinking it would not be understood. Said, acting in defense of Allah and all Islam, had fired a burst at the offending skipper, but the men were clustered together and Said was inexperienced. His burst killed three men.

Contemplating three dead bodies and three terrified Mauritian crewmen—all witnesses to the crime—Abdallah took Said's weapon and signaled his men to execute the remaining three as a way to cover up the crime. But he remained angry with Said who had been working primarily as a cook's helper.

The Somalis took the precaution of removing clothing and other potentially identifying objects. To ensure the bodies would not float ashore, they were systematically opened up to make any possibility of floating unlikely.

As a consequence, this crime on the high seas received no attention in the world press. Even in Mauritius, no information was ever available. A ship went out. It never returned. A few widows, a few orphans; end of story.

But for Abdallah and his gang, the Mauritian vessel, repainted and renamed, was well suited for its new role as a mother ship. They carried three Zodiacs on board and they towed a dory-like Somali fishing vessel that rode easily in moderate seas.

At first the Somalis launched their Zodiacs by hand, but they quickly found that a little experimenting with alternate rigging techniques, allowed them to place the Zodiacs on either side with greater ease. The first three times Abdallah's band made attacks on targeted vessel from their new mother ship, they were unsuccessful, but their experiences provided invaluable training. His six best climbers gained a lot of confidence in their ability to get up the ropes quickly and take command on the bridge.

Some Somali pirates were having even better luck.

Nairobi, Kenya. News reports from sources in Kenya stated that Somali pirates operating out of Baraawe south of Mogadishu on the Indian Ocean, had attacked a private yacht belonging to an unidentified Greek millionaire and were holding twelve passengers and crewmen for ransom. The hostages were being held at an undisclosed location in Mogadishu and the Greek government reported that they had been given a thirty-day timetable to come up with ten million dollars ransom. One of the passengers was reported to be ill from undisclosed causes, but the pirates said no exceptions would be made.

The U.S. Navy had a frigate patrolling off the coast of Baraawe and the commanding officer said that any attempts by pirates to move the yacht to another location would be met by force.

The Internet carried a constant tally of pirate successes. Regular news reports from the European Union's Naval Task Force PAO was slowly making Vance Morrisette—languishing in Djibouti—grind his teeth.

EU NAVFOR Public Affairs Office, May 5, 2009, German bulk carrier hijacked in the Gulf of Aden "A German owned and German managed bulk carrier this afternoon was hijacked in the Gulf of Aden in a position approximately 120 nautical miles north of Boosaaso in Somalia. The vessel, carrying a load of 10,000 tons of rice, was sailing in the transit corridor and was picked out of a group transit within only a few minutes. A helicopter from the closest warship was too late to prevent the ship from being hijacked. The crew of 11 sailors is believed to be unhurt."

Fortitude
Like a she-camel with a large bell
Come from the plateau and upper Haud,
My heat is great....
One of my she-camels falls on the road
And I protect its meat,
At night I cannot sleep,
And in the daytime I can find no shade.
I have broken my nose on a stick,
I have broken my right hip,
I have something in my eye,
And yet I go on.

Somali poem, from "A World Treasury of Oral Poetry."
Ruth Finnegan, Editor,
Indiana University Press, 1978
(quoted in Somalia, by Salome C. Nnorormele)

—41—Jitka Revises Her Plans

For nearly two weeks, Jitka had been stalled in Djibouti, trying to make arrangements for crossing into Somalia. Much of her time had been spent on the telephone; speaking with the BBC in Khartoum, trying to reach the Somali UN Mission Headquarters in New York. She had also—good French girl that she is—been in touch with *Medicins Sans Frontieres*—in France and Switzerland, to see whether they had hospitals in Somalia (they did not) or if they could provide any advice on how she might enter the country (they could not.) She had spoken with their bureau chiefs in France and in Switzerland. Everyone advised her to forget Somalia.

None of the French military personnel had been able to help regarding entry into Somalia; nor had she been encouraged by any U.S. or EU military people.

The entire time in Djibouti would have been pretty boring, shading toward miserable, if not for her friendship with Silvio. His home, as curious and bizarre as many people find it, had been a refuge for the girl with a camera. They met occasionally in the city; and every three or four days she visited at his home. Silvio held an open house on most weekends, which he defined as Saturday and Sunday nights. And his list of invitees was wide and flexible.

A few years ago, when the Italian professor first began to hold his open house events, there had been an episode in which three sides of a love triangle showed up as "guests" and there was a nasty scene, followed by a shooting. Silvio was saddened to have been involved, even though, in this case, all three individuals had been previously unknown to him. The victim, who did not survive, was the husband, and the shooter was a French senior enlisted man. It was a sad mess. Best forgotten. *Friends of friends.*

In subsequent months, Silvio had looked into the possibility of hiring an off-duty policeman for weekend security. This proved to be easily affordable and shortly afterward the entrance gate into Silvio's compound was manned by a big, tough, off-duty policeman, a Kenyan, whose credentials had been vetted by Silvio's friends on Djibouti's security police.

For Jitka, Silvio's place quickly became a safe home away from her hotel room. He was fluent in French and English and they could flirt, harmlessly, in two languages. She always became embarrassed at some point because her Italian was inadequate for conversation.

Early in their acquaintanceship, Jitka had learned that Silvio had attended her exhibition of photos from Suakin and had purchased her coffee table book. At one of his weekend soirees— poorly attended—they had discovered one another and spent an hour with her Suakin book, which had thrilled her to the core. This was the book that had brought her parents around to the concept that she could be an artist in a field other than music. And now, it was her book, discovered in this unlikely and remote hinterland that filled her with pride and made her accept Silvio as a man with discriminating taste. If he had been younger, she might have offered herself to him. But as things were, he was a delight, a treasure, a father figure. Silvio, of course, realized all this from the first moment. This child did indeed have—was gifted with—an uncanny ability to capture emotion and intensity in images. He saw at once that she had little interest in dynamics, in speed or even motion. She was not one to photograph the sprinter breaking the tape; rather she looked for the racer concentrating intensely before the race; thinking, perhaps, how to explode off the blocks.

It was a nearly perfect relationship between male and female, because Silvio could easily see himself as the father of this talented girl, and, without ever discussing it, she could easily picture herself as the daughter of a man who would let her find her own way.

Such friendships are rare. Doubly so when recognized.

Silvio's residence was a refuge.

It was at Silvio's that Jitka had encountered Vance Morrisette. *Where to begin about my warrior?* But she had also met forty or fifty other handsome young naval officers at Silvio's and most of them came on a lot harder than

Vance. She had heard propositions in several languages, including some in which the intent was clear, even when the words were not. These, she enjoyed, laughing afterwards as she rode back to her Djibouti guest house or hotel.

But Vance Morrisette was different. He was American and he was a warrior. Two strikes against him from the beginning, but he was good-looking, bordering on handsome, and self-confident—that was immediately obvious to her, but he was also not pushy with her. He was attracted—that much was also immediately clear—but he was not going do anything that was likely to drive her away. He would bear watching. She could remember their first encounter—almost word for word.

"Ah! American."
"Hi."
"*Bon jour.*"
"I don't speak any French."
"It's OK. English is fine."
'My name is Vance."
"Jitka."
"*Jitka?*"
"Jitka." She tried to hide a laugh.
""Jitka is your first name?"
"Yes. First. And only." She laughed aloud. "I never had another. This is my name. Jitka. It is OK with you? My name?"
"Yes. Sure. Fine. Just...I never heard it before. I wasn't sure."
"Sure? Sure of what?" He was off balance and she was amused to see him that way.
He could see that she was playing with him and it was pleasing to be on the receiving end. From her.
"My name, as I mentioned, is Vance, and although it's not as memorable as Jitka, I hope you might remember it. I can tell you that..."
Vance had been visiting Silvio's bar and he had been drinking Mauritian rum, a liquor he had encountered a few years ago, following a life-changing swim in the Indian Ocean. He knew that he was slightly impaired, and his sense of duty told him it was time to stop.
"...that I'm certainly unlikely to forget yours."
"And yours is Vance. I will remember. So?"
"So? What next?" He had to think fast. "So. Why don't we walk outside in Silvio's garden and you can tell me the names for some of his exotic plants.
"We can go," she said, smiling as she took his arm. Passing the glass wall

fronting the garden, Vance saw their reflection in the window, and he was pleased with the way they looked together. It had been over a month since he left South Carolina. Longer than that since he had flirted with a pretty woman.

Outside in the garden, the two found one of the several benches Silvio had positioned in his garden. Vance had been interested to know more about this girl whose background seemed to be very different from women he had encountered in the past.

"I know that you're a photographer."

"Yes. It's true."

"What kind of pictures do you take?"

She laughed. "What kind would you like me to take?" *Playful.*

He was embarrassed by her laughter, thinking he might have put his question in a way that offended her.

"I just meant that...."

"You are asking me if I do the centerfolds for *Playboy*? Maybe for *Hustler*?"

"No, no. Look! I'm sorry that I..."

"I am just pulling your leg, Mister Morrisette. I take pictures of everything." She made a broad gesture with both arms. "Your name. It sounds French. It is? Or no?"

"Yeah, I'm sure it is somewhere back down the line. But I only know about four generations back. And they all came from the east. Upstate in New York. Fleeing the French Revolution. That's all I know. Moved into Utah after the railroads came. Followed the Mormons. But we were never LDS ourselves."

"This is a religious denomination? I am right?"

"That settled in Utah. Yes. But let's go back to your photographs. Didn't I hear you talking with Silvio about a book of photos you published?"

"This is true. He saw my work in London. And he bought my book."

"And he has it here?"

"Yes. He showed me."

"So could we see it? Could I take a look at your work?"

"Yes, of course. If he agrees. We can ask him. I don't see why not."

Conventional stuff. But very pleasant to remember. Several days later when she told him of her plans to visit Somalia she was surprised to see the hardness in his face.

Jitka's original plan was to head for Somalia's north coast town of Boosaaso, bordering the Gulf of Aden. From there, she wanted to consider a cross country route that would take her out onto the very tip of Africa's horn, where she imagined she might find small independent groups of pirates occupying the small villages of the coast. But after talking with many knowledgeable people in Djibouti, she decided to consider heading south from Boosaaso, for Eyl, on the east coast.

Finally, after listening to the girl's half-baked plans, Silvio intervened. He waited to catch her alone.

"We must talk."

"Of course. I am yours."

"I have decided that I will accompany you."

"Pardon?"

"Don't look so surprised. You know that I have a daughter older than you. So I may know things about you that you do not know about yourself."

"And for this, you must accompany me?"

"You need some one who is an adult. Who speaks the language. Who has traveled in the region before. Someone who—unlike yourself—has a legitimate reason to travel there. And this person must be safe for you to travel with. It would be desirable if they were financially independent and could pay their own way."

"Silvio, you know where I want to visit. What possible reason coul...."

"Jitka, you certainly know that I have traveled over much the region that you want to visit. But perhaps you do not know. Remind me to show you some of my monographs written in Somalia. Listen, child. If you search this entire region there is no one better suited to accompany you than myself."

That part, she had to admit, was true.

"Furthermore, no matter how hard you might try to seduce me on this trip, you will not succeed. You must put that out of your mind." This was said with a smile and twinkle and he managed to get a laugh out of the girl, gaining a few seconds for his proposal to sink in. Then he clinched his argument.

"Jitka, if you want us to remain friends, you will not deny me the privilege of accompanying you. I will select a competent driver. You just pay off the man you have hired. I have a dependable driver. And a vehicle. And I will pay for both. On the way I will collect specimens. If it is convenient, perhaps you can photograph some plants for me. My presence will not—for the most part—slow you down to any great degree."

It was easy to convince her, and at some level it was a big comfort to her. He could provide a measure of security that would otherwise have been missing.

All that remained was the details, the nuts and bolts of trip planning. With years of field work behind him, this was really not a problem for Silvio.

Even after learning about Silvio's involvement, Vance still tried to dissuade her, claiming that it was too dangerous and unstable. Silvio's driver, Abshiir, had been encouraging. "I have done, before," he told her with a grin. This was true, but it had been six years earlier and much had happened since than.

"If we lucky, two, three days on road to Boosaaso. I think it will be good trip and not too much danger for you. I know the places for stop on way. Boosaaso big port. At Boosaaso there is airfield and guesthouses for westerners. You can stay. We will need gasoline in containers to be sure of two days." That had been six years ago.

With Silvio and his hand-picked driver accompanying her, Jitka felt better about her proposed venture into Somalia. Her planned route was simplicity itself. They would travel the coast road from Djibouti across the border to Seylac, where paving ended. From there, the coast road was a dirt track, known to be difficult at some times of the year, but considered passable for the next several months. They would continue eastward following the coast to Berbera, on to Boosaaso. This should expose them to several small coastal towns and villages that might support pirate bands. It was common knowledge that the greatest concentration of pirate 'behind-the-scenes" management was operating out of Eyl. This would be the ultimate destination if all went well.

Beyond Boosaaso they would make a decision. Either continue eastward to Cape Guardafui (in Somali, *Ras Caseyr*), looking to meet more pirates, or head south from Boosaaso to Gardho and then cut across eastward to Bender Beyla on the coast of the Indian Ocean. There they were almost certain to encounter pirate bands and the infrastructure supporting them.

The problem was, they had no certain way to assess the degree of danger they would face.

She was still a bit puzzled by Silvio's determination. "I'm going because if I succeed in coming back with several hundred photographs, and even a dozen of them make it to the world's press, it will build my reputation, and I can probably find work in my field for another decade. But why would you want to accompany me, Silvio? That's what I can't understand."

"I'm searching to find the right words, Jitka. Give me a moment."

"I'm risking my neck for fame...and fortune. But you, friend, already have both. Why risk your neck?"

"Perhaps it is for the adventure. Yes, the adventure with a lovely woman. Who is intelligent and interesting. I do not think I would be drawn to this adventure if you were a man. A man who looked like me? With a gray beard? No. Certainly not."

The girl laughed. "But Silvio. You know that when I'm traveling with my camera that I have taken a vow of chastity. I am a nun for the images I take." And she pulled a small, silver cross from inside her sweatshirt, to show him.

"Ah, I am glad that you showed this to me, Jitka. This must stay here. I can lock it away in a safe place until you return. You will not want to take a crucifix into Somalia."

"This little thing could be dangerous? You are joking, surely..."

"Girl, girl, you astonish me. You are not paying attention to the news. You must have heard of the bands they call Al-Shabab."

"Yes, of course, Shabab. The Youth. But they are in the south. No? Mostly in cities. Mogadishu, Merka, the region bordering with Kenya."

"My dear, yes, they are concentrated there. But they are everywhere. And people have been killed for wearing a cross smaller than yours. It is very ugly there. Seriously, that could cost your life."

She slipped the fragile chain over her head and handed it over.

"Then you must keep this for me. And thank you for reminding me of what I should have known. I will have plenty of headscarves to remain covered when we are on the road. But Silvio, listen. Back to my original question. Why have you chosen to make this trip? With me, of course. Because I am so fascinating. And you so Italian. Yes, so you say. But really, why? What will you do?"

"You think, pretty girl, that you are the only person with serious interests? No, I do not think you are so foolish as this. You know what I have done to earn my bread. Where my interests lie."

"The botany. Yes. So explain me what you will do. Every day. If we are not together?"

"Open your map, Jitka, and let's look at the roads between here and Boosaaso."

Within minutes they had Jitka's Michelin map open and were examining the coast road paralleling the Gulf of Aden. Silvio was pointing out the highlands south of Boosaaso and extending west to the town of Ceerigaabo.

"All this region in here is rugged hill country, scrubland with many acacia trees. There are unusual animals. Antelopes that are found nowhere else. And unusual plants. This region below Boosaaso is like an island. Isolated. Once home to incense trees. You know the Frankincense? Myrrh? From the old stories of Greece and Rome, the Bible, of Egypt?"

"Yes. But what happened to these trees? *'Once home to trees,'* you said. What happened to these trees? Of course I know those scents."

"The trees, my dear..."

"I am, you know, from France," said with a tiny pout.

"Yes. Something I am not likely to forget. The trees, my dear girl, were cut to make the charcoal. To sell to Arabs in Yemen and elsewhere. The charcoal. It took away these forests of small trees."

"So what will you study in this region? If they are all vanished?"

"The plants, the small plants. They remain. There will be enough for me to do."

For the next thirty minutes, Jitka listened to the botanical names of plants found in the upland region known as the Warsengeli. He tried, unsuccessfully, to get her to make a commitment to photographing specimens he might not want to carry back, but she laughingly evaded him, and he did not push her.

Two days before they left, Silvio made arrangements for Abshiir to check their vehicle carefully. He was a Somali from one of the northern clans, and he knew the roads well. But he had been working in Djibouti for several years and he practiced a moderate brand of Islam. Silvio had found him dependable in the past and they had covered much of the planned route years ago.

Before departure the Italian professor decided to have a few friends over for dinner. When he mentioned this to Jitka, she seemed interested. "And will you invite the American man who was here before? The one who is former navy?"

"You have forgotten his name?" Silvio laughed. *She is shy about him? This can only mean one thing.*

"I will try to reach him."

That's how, at nine that evening, Jitka and Vance, comfortably fed, could be found sitting at a circular table on the patio outside Silvio's curious abode. Just the two of them. The music coming from inside was by The Eagles, but soon it would probably change to be a local offering whose words neither would know. They were drinking rum and coke, made using sugar cane rum recently brought over from Mauritius. Silvio had a contact near the waterfront and he knew when deliveries from Mauritius were expected.

"How did you get the scar?" Vance asked. Out of a clear, blue sky.

"What scar?"

Pause. "That scar on your ass. C'mon, Jitka."

"It's a long, complex story."

"I've got all night. More if needed." She seemed to be thinking about it.

"Do you want the long version or the short version? Or my deliciously tantalizing lie?"

"Damn. And I thought it was a simple question. Now I can see that nothing, nothing, nothing about you is simple."

"C'est vrai," she laughed.

"OK. I retract the question. I didn't mean to hit a nerve."

"Don't give up so easily, mon ami. Perhaps I was on the edge of revealing what many strong men have nearly died attempting to learn. Perhaps you should persist."

"Thank you, no. I want to live. If it has to do with voodoo, or black arts or ancient Egyptian curses from mummies, I'm just backing out. I want to live."

"And here I was thinking of you as macho. *Le Mec Americain! Quelle dommage!* A story that might have shattered you to your core." Alcohol had made her playful.

"Where will all this lead?" Vance said, tired of the badinage and really willing to forget his question. But Jitka, who rarely drank to intoxication, had broken her own rule, primarily because she found Vance very attractive and also because she was getting ready to leap into the unknown within a few short days and she realized that it really would be very dangerous. Over the borderline, he would be a good memory. Mentally, she was already across.

"A man did this to me. In a bar. But it was an accident."

"The fuck? An accident?

"It was a fight between two stupid, drunken *mecs*. Mecs. Just boys, actually. We were all just kids. In Paris. I happened to be in the middle and I got clipped by a broken bottle. I was cut."

"The hell you say. That's granulation tissue. I know that much. You were gouged."

"It was an accident. The young man was devastated. It bled a lot."

"I bet. But it wasn't stitched up, either,"

"No."

"Why not? If he did it...and it was accidental?"

"He had no money. Nor I. We were students. Lovers. Our parents were angry with us. Both. We were living together. Sometimes we did not eat. There is more. The fight did not stop."

"Any doctor in Paris would have treated you. Stitched it closed."

"Probably. But..."

"Have you ever considered you might...."

"Considered? Get it fixed? Of course. When I was younger and cared about my looks. I did look into it. But I soon learned to live with it. Tell me, Vance, do you find me repulsive?"

"I won't even answer that question."

"Some men find me appealing *because of it*. What is a word in American slang? You believe it? It is a like a...what do you say?... schtick. It is a gimmick. N'est ce pas? Perhaps those men are depraved. Or perverted. But I do not care, because I did not make this world. I simply live here. No, it went untreated and I covered it up as it slowly healed. It took a while for it to fill in. It was a difficult time for me. It was a small lesson about pain. Now, it is nothing. Just me."

"Jitka, I have had several drinks containing rum, and so my wits may be slightly addled, but I think you are the prettiest girl...woman I know. And just this moment I don't give a flying fuck about this conversation, which, admittedly, I initiated, and moreover....ah forget everything I said. Right now I have a compelling need to hold on to you and this music is danceable. So.... will you...."

"But of course." She laid on a fake French accent

Much later he touched it with his lips. Whispering. "Was that a true story you told me? About your scar?"

She smiled but she didn't turn to face him.

"Peut-être."

"English?"

"Maybe."

On the brink of her departure, she had discovered that she was going to miss him.

No one has ever handled me in this way. Like my body is magical.

"Uneducated Sudanese women are unaware of alternatives to circumcision, and 98% of them never see the inside of a school since education of women is not considered a positive value in an Afro-Islamic society. Everything is clearly defined for the Sudanese girl. There are no complicated choices that she has to make. Circumcision is a fact of life, just as tremendous hardship, poverty, scarce water and little food, back-breaking labor, overwhelming heat, dust storms, crippling disease, unalleviated pain and early death are facts of her life. Circumcision happens to everyone. This is the only reality, and she accepts it as everyone accepts it."

Prisoners of Ritual
(An Odyssey into Female Genital Circumcision in Africa)
Hanny Lightfoot-Klein

—42—Return to Boosaaso

Even though his mother ship's crew was returning from this cruise with no major injuries, Abdallah was in a foul mood because of repeated failures to board. He had not been in the boarding party but he had watched with binoculars as the attempts were made. As his vessel moved to another angle, he was infuriated to see that the gangway had not been removed for sea but was still folded up on the port side of the ship.

If that cursed Dinka boat driver had troubled himself to check both sides carefully as he approached from the stern, they would now be headed down to Eyl. Or even—possibly—to Mogadishu.

To the south, the setting sun was reflecting off low clouds overhead and bathing the chalk hills west of Boosaaso with a curious golden glow he could not recall seeing in the past.

The sea was smooth and the weather was mild. He realized that he was angry and he made a conscious attempt to improve his temper before he was back with his family.

He thought about the three wives who would be waiting at home for his return. Of the three, he would have sex tonight with Jaamila, the youngest and prettiest. Every time he performed sex with her, he was aware that he hurt her. Every time, she wept until the pain subsided. It was infuriating. Afterward, he would comfort her a bit, and she would let him hold her until the weeping stopped. She would sometimes tremble in his arms and, in truth, he liked that. Tall and slender, she was of the Darood clan, and the imam advised against marrying her. But he did not forbid it, did not say that it was *haram*. Only that it was not a good idea. Her family had come from the south and she was used to war and violence. The Issaq ways of Puntland would seem strange to her.

But Abdallah had found her shy ways appealing at first, and at sixteen, she was as smooth and beautiful as a camel. He wanted her, and he could afford the *yarad* and even the *dibaad* that her family asked, although—considering her good fortune—it had seemed extortionate. Now, although he still found her beautiful, she failed to satisfy him.

As he turned to watch the wake boiling at the stern, he thought that he needed to impregnate her. She had been in his compound for several months, and yet she was still continuing to bleed. He would see what could be done. She would have to try harder.

The harbor lights at Boosaaso were coming into view as he reflected on the life he was leading as a pirate. Since adopting this way of life, his style of living had changed substantially and by any measure, he was a successful businessman. He now owned the large apartment building facing the waterfront, with four floors and a small rooftop penthouse. Three vehicles.

His men used the first floor for meetings, recreation and equipment storage. There was a radio station there, with antennas on the roof. The third and fourth floors were occupied by his family with the third floor for exclusive use by his three wives. There was room for a fourth, which he intended to consider when he could find a new woman who excited him.

The fourth floor was partly vacant, although it stored old equipment, furniture and carpets that he might eventually sell or discard. The small apartment on the roof was for his private office and personal space. Very few people were allowed there, and when he was away, the stair passage was locked. When he was at sea or on business, the penthouse was locked and the roof was off limits to everyone. And just at the moment, he was at sea.

At the doorway to the wheelhouse, Said stood holding out a small cup of freshly-brewed coffee. He spoke Abdallah's name to get him to turn around and extended the cup.

"Just made," Said added, smiling.

Abdallah took the cup and sipped.

"What? We are out of cardamom?" he said.

"Oh! Someone forgot." Said reached for the cup and turned back to the galley.

"Yallah!" Abdallah said, snorting. He was already beginning to think about Jaamila's young body, and how he would bend her. It was but a moment until Said returned with the coffee and this time, no words were exchanged. The man at the helm was expressionless.

"Wait," Abdallah ordered Said, and turning to the helmsman, Jamal, he asked "Do you want coffee?" The helmsman nodded. *Yes.*

"Bring a cup to Jamal and don't forget the cardamom," he told Said, who slipped away, a second time, abashed. He was still new to this crew and this was only his fifth voyage. He wanted to make a good impression because, as yet, he had only been helping the cook with food and cleaning, and it was his wish to become part of the boarding crews. He was looking forward to handling his own AK-47 again, and perhaps, some day, *Inshallah*, even an RPG. Since the incident with the Mauritians, Abdallah had been displeased with him and he had not handled a weapon. Maybe...and this was a fantasy he indulged...he would be given another opportunity to kill a *gaalo* for daring to resist. But even if not, it would be nice to become wealthy, and even to possess a vehicle. Or a woman.

After the vessel reached its dock in Boosaaso, Abdallah didn't leave until he saw that all weapons were placed ashore, all lines were properly placed, and the ship was secured. An armed guard would be sleeping on board, but, even so, he counted all the weapons on the dock and he would count them again when the RPGs went into locked storage in his building. The AKs were the responsibility of individual men who must keep them in good working order. Rusty weapons were punished with a crippling fine, so he didn't worry too much about AKs; and anyway, they were easily—and cheaply—replaced.

It was dark when Abdallah finally climbed the stairs to his apartments. He visited the bedroom where his three young sons were sleeping. They were seven, five and three. Handsome boys, all, and he was very fond of them. But they were sleeping soundly. He looked at them with warm feelings in his heart and tousled the hair of the youngest, Zaak, who made a contented sound but didn't move.

Then, satisfied that his brood was secure, he continued to the women's apartments where his three wives had separate sleeping rooms. *Awaiting my arrival.*

He had called ahead on his mobile phone to alert his housekeeper, so the women and their servants knew when he was expected home. They knew that he would not want to be fed because he had taken food aboard his vessel. He expected his women to be awake to greet his return from sea.

But Jaamila—they told him—was sleeping. This displeased him. Salome and Yasmeenha, his first wife, on the other hand, were awake and had been anticipating that he might want them. Yasmeenha expected little, in the presence of Salome and Jaamila.

Salome, the younger woman, had decorated her hands and wrists, and as soon as he entered the greeting room, he was aware that she had been squatting over incense burners to perfume her flesh and hair with frankincense.

Abdallah took note of this effort to please him, but for the last several hours he had been thinking about Jaamila and her younger body, and he was not in a mood to be swayed in his intentions.

After exchanging a few words of greeting with Salome, he turned to the servant girl hovering in the doorway and ordered her to wake Jaamila and bring her to his rooftop apartment. The girl left and Salome, disappointed and unhappy, sat down primly on the distant end of the large sofa and studied the patterns on the backs of her hands. Yasmeenha, older and disenchanted with sex from Abdallah, was happy to be, for all intents and purposes, discarded. She offered him food from a tray, but after a few perfunctory exchanges, Abdallah climbed to his lair.

Jaamila appeared in his office-apartment a few minutes later. She appeared to be sleepy, but more than that, she was frightened, sensing his displeasure. She was wearing the light cotton gown in which she had been sleeping, and since the weather was warm, the material revealed much of the body that he found appealing. Immediately, he knew that he made the right decision to have her sent up. But the expression on her face was not one that gave him pleasure.

The room lighting was poor and he told her to come closer so that he could examine her. Her eyes were downcast, and as she approached the arc of light cast by his desk lamp, he could see that her right eye had been blackened.

"Ya, Jaamila," he said, trying not to sound too unpleasant, "Are you not happy to see me at home?"

"Ya, Abdallah. Welcome back. I hope Allah has blessed your voyage."

"I am home safe, wife, as you see," he said, noncommittally, "and for seamen, that is always a blessing. But, Jaamila, what have you done to your eye."

"It is nothing," she said. "It will be gone tomorrow. Nothing."

"But how did it happen?"

When he learned that Jaamila had been involved in an argument with Salome, who was her senior in precedence, and that blows had been exchanged, he was furious. From the wall where it was hanging, he took down the small ceremonial whip used by Somali males as part of the wedding ritual. This device is used on the wedding night to chastise the wife—often symbolically—in order to instill submissiveness in the female.

Now, however, he wanted to sting this girl who had dared to provoke his older wife into striking her. This must not happen again. He lifted his arm and struck Jaamila across the back. Once. Twice. Three times.

With the first blow, the girl gasped and staggered backwards against the wall. Her arms flew up to protect her face and the second blow was higher than he had intended, wrapping around her shoulder. The third blow fell across her buttocks and made her scream.

Good. That's how he should have placed all three blows. But three, he felt, were enough.

Then, when her tears and shuddering had ceased, he would place her on her back on his bed and spread her legs to admit him. At least, this is how he thought it would be. But when he put his arms around the shivering girl, he felt her stiffen, and this angered him even more. He was hoping—had pictured it in his imagination—that she would collapse into him, sobbing perhaps, and beg him to forgive her. But already, in just a few seconds, he was sensing that this was unlikely to happen. Perhaps more blows would be needed before this stubborn child would learn the importance of submission.

This was not the homecoming he had envisioned. Three days ashore and then he intended to be back at sea. This was a season for passenger ships. It would be easy, he knew, to replace Dajaal in his crew. He already had someone else in mind. As for this girl...let her weep. Alone.

Salome was alone in her small apartment and she had smelled of perfume. She had looked at him with longing.

"It has been 18 years since Somalia has had a properly functioning government. Since 2007, 19,000 Somali civilians have been killed and 1.5 million displaced; over 3 million in a population of 8 million need emergency aid.

Terrorism in Somalia
"Ever more atrocious"
The Economist, December 12, 2009

—43—The Hunting Trip

After a failed attempt to board the German liner, the assault team of eight Somalis had returned to their trawler that had been shadowing several miles behind. The Pirellis—each of which had two big Honda outboards attached—were winched back aboard and the disgruntled pirates went below to get food before tumbling into their bunks. They had been on the water for over sixteen hours and some of the men—those three who were over forty—were tired and ready for sleep.

Their leader in this failed attempt, Abdallah, had been quiet and uncommunicative all the way back to their mother ship as the Pirelli faced into light chop from the northeast wind. Everyone in the inflatable boat was wet to the skin by the time they got back aboard the weather-beaten trawler that was their home. By the time their craft was lifted aboard, the breeze had fallen off and their clothes, white with salt, had stiffened against their skin. It was a feeling they had grown used to. Off on the horizon, they could see lights from two other ships, east bound for Bab al Mandeb.

Abdallah was tired and, in addition, he was angry. He didn't even want to investigate the other ships. Unusual for him, the pirate chief had been in second boat which was to board from the starboard stern quarter. The lead boat made a feint at boarding from port side, midships. With Abdallah aboard, the second boat failed to board.

Their attempt today might have been successful if Ali Abdi had been more aggressive. Abdallah blamed himself for taking this man and his brother into their crew. Probably he would not have done so with the recommendation from his brother-in-law who had recommended Ali Abdi, despite the fact that he was from the Saad family. *What was to be expected from doqon farmers? I should have known. These damminin should stay inland, scratching the soil, growing millet, or wheat. Or scratching trees to squeeze out a few drops of frankincense. These damminin certainly don't belong at sea. He threw that hook four times before it caught the rail, and then.... Then that fucking kaffir gaalo simply dropped our hook back over the side. If Ali had kept tension on the line.... And what about his brother at his side? He could easily have killed the man aboard the liner. Pathetic. They are dhagah!*

Actually, Abdallah blamed himself for being weak and indecisive. *This will not happen again,* he vowed. *These two bastards are headed for home as soon as we land.*

Land for the pirates was still several hours away. Their trawler plunked along at a modest nine knots—maybe more with the following wind—and they were headed for the unmarked inlet to the west of Boosaaso. For local seamen it was easy to know when they'd be back in Boosaaso's ample harbor after they picked up the white hills to the east. The chalk bluffs had been eroded into formations that, once seen, were unforgettable. When the wind veered through the north and swung into the northeast, a condition which was relatively uncommon, they would have following seas all the way to the harbor mouth. The good thing about Boosaaso's harbor? Once inside, you were secure. A hundred yards back the creek mouth widened and over the years a series of docks had been built where their trawler might lie up—through almost any weather.

On board the trawler, Abdallah ate his bowl of goat and chickpea stew and cleaned the bowl with a piece of *injera* left from breakfast. In accordance with his long-standing principle as leader he declined to eat anything until all of his men had been fed. This was, he knew, a break with tradition for which he might have been criticized by some, but to him it felt right and he was committed to the practice. Anyway, he had heard that strong *gaalo* leaders followed this practice, but this reason, he could not admit to anyone.

After eating, Abdallah went outside into the trawler's work space and used a plastic bucket to douse himself with salt water. When he had dried off with an expanse of terrycloth, he went below and was asleep in minutes. The towel had smelled of fish.

The trawler crept into the inlet at Boosaaso sometime in the small hours and when Abdallah awoke the morning call to prayer had come and gone. He woke and was not surprised to find that he was still angry with the man—two men actually—who, in his view, were responsible for the previous day's failure to board. But some part of his nature was reluctant to turn his attention to the immediate punishment of the two incompetents he had allowed to join his crew.

The northeast wind was still brisk and the weather was mild. His men were moving on the deck, talking and behaving normally, as if the previous day had not been a colossal failure.

Suddenly, unbidden, a thought popped into his head. He needed a change. He had been working steadily for four months, with only one success. And despite that success, he had continued at sea. It's true that money from his first big payoff at piracy had enabled him to buy an old colonial villa complex at Eyl where his family would have their permanent residence when he quit the sea. And it had given him, among other things, the recently acquired Land Rover that was parked a quarter mile from this dock. But he was still working every day.

Just now, at Boosaaso, he had his family with him, all together in a four-story complex in which his three wives occupied the entire third floor.

Abdallah was proud of his wives, who had borne him six living children. Three were still in Eyl. His first two wives, Yasmeenha and Salome, had three children each; although each of them had lost an infant. His third wife, Jaamila, was the youngest and, not surprising, she was—*had been until recently*—his favorite. She had given him no living children and an early pregnancy had quickly become a painful miscarriage. Jaamila, like his other wives, had been cut, a condition that might have had something to do with the reason she was his favorite, but this was a topic about which he certainly did not wish to speak, nor even allow his thoughts to dwell. Nonetheless, it was clear to the most obtuse observer that Jaamila was his favorite, and having nursed no infants, her small breasts still resembled those of a young girl.

It would be good to be back in his temporary home. But the failure at sea had left him restless and unsatisfied. He knew, instinctively, that he must find a way to deal with Ali Abdi and his worthless brother.

It came to him in a flash. *Hunting! I should go hunting. I need to take my cousins and go hunting.*

Abdallah was Issaq, a member of Somalia's vast Saamaale family whose four clans are all pastoral nomads. Since history has been recorded—even before—they have spent their lives working with animals. Not just worked with animals, but worked with them in a part of the world where everything began. Living, as they do among animals, they are good natural hunters with a feeling for the habits of all wildlife, but in particular with the habits of grazing animals.

Immediately, as the idea formed in his head, Abdallah began to flesh out details. He would take his cousins, Raage and Abdirashiid Ali, who were good shots and good companions. They had chewed *qat* together in the past on countless occasions and they had fished together. They were good fishermen, steady and dependable, and they never complained about weather conditions. He was actually proud to acknowledge them as his cousins and even if they had not been kinsmen, they would have been welcomed as friends and associates.

Outside, on deck, his cousins had finished breakfast and were sipping coffee from calabashes.

'Ya, then, my cousins. Are you interested in hunting with me? We will bring back the good meat animals of Somalia and provide a feast for our shipmates."

It was about six hours later when three dusty, salt encrusted Somali pirates piled into Abdallah's Land Rover and departed from the collection of dwellings that comprised Boosaaso's swelling eastern outskirts. The spanking new Land Rover had been driven up from Kenya by a young Arab in the pay of an Arab merchant. The merchant had become very wealthy by catering to the desires and wishes of pirates who had recently come into possession of quantities of U.S. currency known, colloquially, as *Franklins.*

Two days later, the cousins from the same clan, who were, in truth, remarkably compatible, headed south and east into to the interior. They were all originally from the area bordering the Indian Ocean, north of Eyl, where they maintained their principal residences. Abdallah's women had collected food, including several loaves of bread and nearly half of a goat carcass that had been carefully salted and rubbed down with pepper and other spices. The Land Rover with the three men rolled out of Boosaaso south on the main road leading go Qardho. Four hours later, the sound of aircraft overhead reminded them that they were on the outskirts of that dusty crossroads near the local airstrip.

In Qardho they left the main road, bearing west on dirt tracks where Abdallah relied on his recollections from prior trips. He was taking his cousins to out-of-the-way ruins at Taleex, a little-used spot where there were natural springs of good drinking water. Despite the appeal of this natural resource, the inaccessibility of the spot had prevented the antique wells at Taleex from attracting a permanent population. Even nomadic herders rarely camped or congregated at the site. Its springs made it a veritable mecca for wildlife and Abdallah had killed game at this spot on several occasions in the past. This would be the first occasion on which he would have the opportunity to hunt with an AK-47 with a selector switch permitting automatic fire.

The hunters maneuvered the Land Rover into a narrow *wadi* and covered it loosely with thorn bushes. Fifty yards further down the *wadi* they picked a flat spot that was relatively clear of rocks and made a small fire. The junior man made coffee. He began with the beans that he ground with a stone pestle in a deep cast iron pot; later to be used to cook the lentils that would make part of their supper. Water was poured into an ornate copper kettle with a curved spout, and filtered through a twist of grass. When the brew was poured into each man's small cup, a tiny brass container filled with powdered cardamom was passed around and each man added a pinch to his coffee before taking a sip.

An hour after they had covered the Land Rover their crude encampment had furnished them a meal and each man simply stretched out on the sand and went to sleep. They had all worked for several years as camel boys and were well accustomed to sleeping under the stars. By the time the sun's first direct rays were lighting the dunes, each man was up and moving, and the banked coals had been stirred back to life.

The trip provided a much needed diversion, and the men returned with two small *dikdik*.

"Verily, life is more awful than death; and let no man, though his live heart beat in him like a cannon—let him not hug his life to himself; for, in the predestinated necessities of things, that bounding life of his is not a whit more secure than the life of a man on his death-bed. To-day we inhale the air with expanding lungs, and life runs through us like a thousand Niles; but to-morrow we may collapse in death and all our veins be dry as the brook Kedron in a drought."

From "White Jacket"
Herman Melville

—44—Capture

Jitka thought about that last evening with Vance as the Land Rover jounced along over the coast road. He had been unable to get away from a meeting with the entire UBSA contingent to see his two friends off. *Dommage.* It would have been nice to have a real man kiss her goodbye; wish her success.

The first day they only drove as far as Berbera. Taking it slow. The coast road was scenic, but it was rough and dusty for much of the route. Sometimes, when they were behind heavily laden trucks and passing was dangerous, Silvio would have Abshiir pull to the side and they would take a break to stretch their legs—or relieve their bladders.

Water was a concern and it was not always possible for them to purchase bottled water en route. For this reason, they used bottled water sparingly, sometimes drinking local water that had been heavily chlorinated with the chemical tablets they each carried. They found a hotel in Berbera that was marginal.

From Berbera to Maydh the distance was approximately two hundred miles and, with stops, it was hard for them to average much over thirty-five miles per hour. Seven hours with rest stops. A full day. Depending on conditions they might push on a bit further. They had two small tents.

By seven in the morning of the second day, the sun was already scorching and they had driven fifty miles east of Berbera past the turnoff to the coastal town of Kirin. Their goal was to make it to the town of Xiis by noon so they could find a shady spot and take a nap thorough the peak heat of the day. Then, they planned to continue on until dusk, after which the coast road become too dangerous.

About fifteen miles before they reached Xiis, a rutted track turned off to a small, coastal village. From time to time, terrain permitting, huts could be seen in the distance. As the Land Rover jolted past the turn leading to the village, Jitka had a premonition of the place as a site for small, independent pirates preying on smaller craft; fishing boats, private yachts. In her imagination she could see the waterfront, and a shelving shingle beach, suitable for launching skiffs close to the heavily trafficked lanes of the Gulf of Aden. Back on shore, a few Muslim women, clad head-to-toe in stifling *guntiinos* might be clustered to watch the men leave the beach. The vehicle passed the road without a comment from anyone, but Jitka's imagination was active.

And then, unexpectedly, she remembered a story she had read about a famous American photographer of the Depression Era, Dorothea Lange. One of Lange's best known photographs, *Depression Mother*, almost didn't get taken because the photographer nearly drove past the camp where the mother was located. Lange had passed the camp—so the story went—when some premonition told her to go back. The American had followed her instinct and the result was a photograph that made her name famous. Jitka turned to face Silvio who had his eyes closed in the back seat, but could not possibly have been sleeping.

"I want to go back," she said.

"What? Go back where?"

"That last turnoff. Leading to that village."

"Whatever for? It can't be more than a score of families." Her face told him protest was useless. "But of course. If you wish."

He leaned forward and spoke to the driver.

"What did you see, Jitka, that sparked your interest?"

"It's just a feeling. I can't explain it." She was slightly embarrassed to tell her it was the memory of the experience of a dead American photographer.

Thirty minutes later they were in the small village, where there were, indeed, fishing skiffs on a shelving shingle beach. But if there were pirates in the town, there was no way for the visitors to determine. They rode around the village from one side to the other but they saw nothing that might have indicated sudden prosperity. Or equipment of any type that might have suggested piracy. From the standpoint of advancing her 'pirate agenda' the diversion was a bust.

But one series of photographs may have made the visit worthwhile. At the far east end of the beach, the sea had chiseled into a layered rock formation to carve a series of steps, almost level, extending into the water and several yards beyond. It was Jitka's good fortune to arrive near the place where five Somali women, all fully clad in long skirts—yards of fabric—and blouses with sleeves, had all gone into the sea to bathe together. Waist deep, they were playing and splashing, occasionally submerging to pop up laughing and squealing.

When the jeep approached the women paused to look at the strangers, but when the vehicle did not approach nearer, they quickly ignored it and resumed their frolic. Jitka traded seats with Silvio and used her long lens. She tried to photograph the play in as unobtrusive manner as possible, and as far as she could tell she was successful. After about thirty shots, she felt she had all she could do without getting closer. *It would have been nice*, she thought, *to get in the water with them. These will be keepers*, she was confident.

Maydh was near a place where Silvio had camped in the past and he persuaded her to agree that they could go south into the uplands for most of the remaining day so he could collect specimens. He wanted to head inland to the region around Ceerigaabo. They would be at least halfway to Boosaaso at that point. Since it was his vehicle, and since he had hired the driver, Jitka felt she had to agree, even though her focus was on the coast.

The road inland from Maydh to Ceerigaabo was scenic. It rose above the coastal plain, and the variety of plants was—Jitka had to admit—astonishing considering the harshness of the terrain. She was particularly interested when Silvio pointed the different types of endemic forbs found nowhere else on the planet, including four different species of strongly-scented lavender. He was a natural teacher.

Distant views back toward the coast were wild and spectacular. The rocky slopes had enough green so that their morning took on the aspect of a Sunday picnic. It was easy to forget that they were in a lawless land that was experiencing something akin to undeclared civil war.

"Even with the heat it's still bearable up here," Jitka said. Silvio was kneeling over a clump of *lavendula somaliensis* she had admired and wondering if he ought to take back some roots for his garden in Djibouti.

"You seem to do well in this heat," he said, without looking up.

"Do you want water?"

"No. Thank you, I am nearly done here. Then, if you like, we can go back."

"We could eat our lunch up here if you prefer. Or go back to Ceerigaabo. Maybe we could find cold beer there."

"Speak with Abshiir. You two can decide as you wish. I will only be a few moments more and then we can do as you choose."

When Silvio walked back to the Land Rover, Jitka and Abshiir had opted for Ceerigaabo. There they might expect to find an arbor in the shade, and there Abshiir was confident that he could find cold beer. The road back to the town skirted the edge of Ceerigaabo's airstrip.

They had seen a small passenger jet taking off when they had passed earlier, on the way inland.

The drive back into Ceerigaabo should not have taken more than twenty minutes, but it turned out to be much, much longer. *In fact, life-changing.*

As they rounded a bend in the road and the distant hangars came into view, they were suddenly aware of armed men blocking the road ahead.

Abshiir slowed, then braked to a halt.

"No, no, Abshiir. Don't try to back up or turn around. That is likely to make them shoot at us. And they are not likely to miss with so many weapons. Approach them slowly. Perhaps they just want money."

In the back seat now, Jitka was putting lens caps on her cameras, and stuffing them securely into their carry bags. She was muttering softly to herself. *"Merde, merde, merde."*

"This is not a major route for trucks or buses, Jitka. These men are not likely to be robbers because there is little traffic here for them to rob. They probably came to carry someone to the airfield. Or perhaps to pick up someone arriving. Do not worry yet. Let's see what we can do. Abshiir, you do the talking before we let them find out that I can understand what they are saying. They are likely to be surprised and put off stride by a European who speaks their language."

The vehicle rolled slowly to the men who were standing four abreast with weapons that were trained, menacingly, at the Land Rover.

"Asalaamaleikum," Abshiir mumbled, and the guard replied before ordering them all out of the vehicle.

In Somali, one guard asked where they were headed and what they were doing in the vicinity of the airfield. The others took Jitka and Silvio a few paces away and asked to see their papers. Silvio had paid friends to prepare entry visas with the understanding that even if they were detected as fraudulent it would matter little, since all most border guards wanted was a cash bribe. In this instance, one guard pocketed both passports and when Silvio protested, he was threatened with a blow.

Smiling radiantly, Jitka said something in French that Silvio could not understand, except that it sounded as if she called them "boils on the ass of a great whore," or something very close. So he concluded that they didn't understand French.

All three travelers were placed in the back of the truck with four of their armed captors. It was at once clear to Silvio that the truck had been at the airport to receive an incoming shipment of *qat*, in all probability recently harvested in Yemen. *Qat* degrades quickly with age and consequently time is essential in getting it into the hands of consumers.

Silvio could smell the plant even before they climbed into the back end of the truck, a battered souvenir from the old Soviet Army. Two of the armed men took the keys to Silvio's Land Rover and departed first. As soon as everyone was in the truck, it followed the Land Rover which gradually disappeared from sight.

Up until this point, no one had been struck, and the only violence had been a threat to Silvio. The armed thugs did not realize that Silvio understood their conversation. Periodically he would mutter a few comments to Jitka.

"The stuff in these plastic bags is *qat*. They put those banana peels in the plastic bags to provide moisture. Otherwise, the leaves and twigs dry out and chemicals lose potency."

"Do you think they intend to harm us?"

"No idea at this point. They told Abshiir they were taking us to their leader."

"Where?"

"Boosaaso. Stop talking, for a few minutes. They're watching too close, just now."

She nodded slightly. *Oui. Bien. D'accord!*

Twenty, jolting minutes later they rolled back through dusty Ceerigaabo and Abshiir muttered, glumly, "No beer."

A guard, seated opposite, poked him roughly with the muzzle of an AK and told him to be quiet.

Again, Jitka uttered a string of words in French that Silvio could not understand exactly. Except that it had to do with the guard's parentage, a suggestion that his mother had been a diseased camel, and that his male parentage was uncertain. Fortunately, the other listeners also did not understand.

After they reached the coast road at the town of Maydh, they turned east in the direction of Boosaaso. Silvio put his head between his knees.

"I just remembered that there is a larger airfield at Boosaaso. Don't reply."

Jitka looked at the guards opposite who were watching Silvio closely. She pointed to him and made a crazy sign that the gunmen were unlikely to misunderstand. "He is babbling," she said, knowing they were unlikely to understand her words, but the sign was universal. "The heat. His age. Fear. You ugly baboons. Keep talking, Silvio."

"I think we may be headed for the next town down the line. Before Boosaaso. Halfway. It's just a guess."

She laughed aloud, and repeated the crazy sign. "Watch him, you apes. He could go out of control. I hope we get there soon. I have to pee." This was still little more than an adventure for her, and she still did not recognize how easily, unexpectedly, our threads can snap.

"Don't say anything else that might get them angry," Silvio said looked into space, as if dazed. "We want to get through this. I think we'll be fine."

Fine? Fine? Their plans were totally demolished long before they reached Boosaaso. They were now the prisoners of an armed band of drug-impaired young men; teen-agers of Al-Shabab who were distributing stolen *qat* on the north coast. While the three visitors from Djibouti were riding in the back of the ancient truck, their driver—mildly impaired by *qat*—attempted to pull his vehicle off the road. The vehicle hit a patch of loose sand, dropped off the shoulder of the road onto a sharp rock and blew a front tire causing the truck to overturn.

Jitka struck her head when the truck first tumbled and she was unconscious for the events that followed. She was unconscious and bleeding, but it was clear that she was breathing. Silvio, arms bound, had suffered a dislocated shoulder. His ropes were removed and he was robbed of all his valuables. Abshiir, like Jitka, struck his head and was concussed but he remained conscious. The same happened to two of the Al-Shabab youth guarding them in the truck. Two concussed, two more bruised with minor cuts, but one youth, sixteen, was sitting near the tailgate and had let his leg dangle outside. He was thrown clear, struck a rock with his head, and was killed instantly.

The surviving youth from Al-Shabab were furious. When Abshiir asked for help, one of the enraged youth responded by shooting him several times. The combination of injuries, embarrassment and frustration had made them aggressive toward their captives but they realized that Jitka might be valuable. The old man had fainted from pain and was taken for dead; forgotten. Their leader had gone ahead in Silvio's Land Rover, so the youth, dazed and bleeding, milled aimlessly for several minutes. They were trying to formulate a plan of action when seven armed members of Abdallah's crew in two new Toyota trucks came on them. Pirates versus fundamentalist thieves. Al-Shabab had just hijacked an air shipment of *qat* that had been intended for Abdallah's men and the bags had been scattered.

The new arrivals, armed, older and more experienced in violence, had spotted Silvio's vehicle before they came on the scene of the disabled truck. When they saw the bundles of *qat* on the ground they immediately realized what had happened. They quickly went into action.

"The past few years have seen the arrival in Somalia of 200 to 300 young ethnic Somali men from the U.S., Britain, Canada, Australia, Norway and Sweden, migrants' children returning to their ancestral homeland, according to diplomatic and intelligence sources in East Africa. A Western soldier working in Somalia says these foreign-born Somalis now dominate Al-Shabab. "All their cells are commanded by a foreigner," he says. "All tactical and strategic decisions are taken by foreigners."

"Somalia, Again"
Alex Perry, Nairobi
In: Time, March 1, 2010

—45—Silvio Limps Home

When Al-Shabab's truck transporting the three captives from Djibouti careened off the road, and Silvio had dislocated his shoulder, the old professor passed out from the pain. There are several ways to dislocate one's shoulder and, while they are all painful, they are not all equally difficult to treat. Fortunately, his was an anterior dislocation, very painful, but relatively easy to reduce by those who know how. When Silvio recovered beside the road, he was experiencing intense pain and he couldn't get his arm into a normal position down by his side.

As Abdallah's men arrived, the Somali youth were occupied with getting their truck back onto the road and in recovering *qat* that had been scattered by the tumble. Abshiir's body lay several meters away from the road, face down, with ghastly wounds to his head. It appeared that he had been shot more than once. Silvio shuddered to see his destroyed face; then he crawled over the nearest rise and disappeared from view by the youth who had emptied his pockets and taken his shoes.

Abdallah's men never missed Silvio. They didn't even know he existed.

Gradually, as his head cleared, he began to focus on what had happened. He realized that he was still alive, injured and stripped of his passport, watch, money and several documents that he had felt would help on their ill-fated excursion. They had neglected to take his socks. He was at some distance from the excited youth and hopeful that he might escape.

Every move was painful, but he realized that he had to walk away from this remote spot if he wanted to stay alive.

He used his good arm to hold his bad arm in its dislocated position and began to limp along the gully toward the coast road. The distance, he estimated, would be around three kilometers. Once on the coast road, he might encounter some traffic and there was a possibility that some driver would stop to render assistance.

He thought briefly of Jitka and what her fate might be at the hands of captors, but sharp pain and the problems of staying alive in this hostile place seemed to supercede all other considerations. Hopefully, she had survived the spill. The walk back to the coast road was a painful blur during which he lost feeling in his feet. It took over two hours and he was near collapse.

The first six vehicles that passed him did not stop, or even slow down, a fact that he found astonishing and inconsistent with his perception of Somali behavior. He wondered if it might be a result of the current epidemic of lawlessness, such as that leading to Abshiir's murder.

Thinking about that, and about Jitka's unknown fate, filled him with a desire to remain alive and to return to Djibouti. Somehow, he must make an attempt to help or avenge his friends. When the next westbound truck appeared, he stood in the middle of the road.

The vehicle stopped and the driver cursed at him in Somali.

"You are rude and hateful to someone in need, and Allah is certain to punish you," Silvio replied in the driver's language. It was clear to the driver that the white-haired *gaalo*—who spoke his language—was injured, and could not even climb into the truck's cab without assistance. The driver got out and helped Silvio into the cab.

The truck bounced along the coast road toward Karin—only about eighty kilometers from Berbera. At Berbera Silvio was hopeful that he could find a doctor. At Karin, the driver stopped to gas his vehicle and he told people in the station about the *gaalo* in his cab, describing the position of his arm. As luck would have it, the owner and his adult son had both been soccer players and the father had been a coach. They had both seen dislocated shoulders in the past and they had seen them reduced on the playing field. They approached Silvio and spoke to him though the window.

"Can you get out?," the station owner asked.

"I prefer not to move."

"You should get out," the owner persisted.

"Thank you. But no." He felt as if he would faint.

The owner opened the door and pulled a howling Silvio out by his shirtfront. The position of Silvio's arm and shoulder seemed to confirm what the station owner suspected and he spoke to his son. "We will see. Hold him." His son grabbed the old gentleman from the rear, including his good arm in a bear hug. The father took the bad arm at the wrist and exerted a slow, steady pull that made Silvio yelp from pain. At the same time, the father manipulated the end of the humerus as he maintained the steady traction. The pain was excruciating, and Silvio thought he would pass out, again, but after little more than a minute, the ball popped back into its socket. Relief was immediate. It still hurt, but the pain was lessened substantially. His arm could rest in a more normal position. Some motion was possible.

The station owner listened to his story of the encounter with Al-Shabab and asked several questions concerning the location of the accident and the location of Abshiir's body. He gave Silvio a bottle of water and half of a small loaf of bread.

Two hours later they were in Berbera and Silvio—exhausted and in pain— found a doctor who gave him an analgesic for the pain and found fabric to make a sling. Then the doctor tied the injured arm securely against Silvio's body. There was little else that could be done.

It took two more miserable days for the professor to reach the border with Djibouti. He eventually walked the last two kilometers to the border crossing station, where he told his story to disinterested guards. Finally, an officer listened to his tale, and made a few phone calls. Three hours after reaching the border, Silvio was in the French Military Hospital, doped up with painkillers and with a line started in his good arm. He had lost seven pounds and his feet were swollen so they would not fit in his shoes, brought by his housekeeper. His glasses were gone—lost somewhere in route— along with everything of value he had been carrying. Including the belt in his trousers. His feet were bloody, but the cuts were minor.

Once the word got around to his many friends, people stopped in to see him, but doctors held him for three days, after which he was taken home in a military vehicle.

There was no word of what might have happened to Jitka, and attempts to learn anything from Somali officials were fruitless.

"...economic analysis also explains why Somali pirates typically receive ransom payoffs instead of violent resistance from shipping crews and their owners. It is in everyone's economic interest to negotiate the transactions as quickly and peacefully as possible. Markets operating in a lawless society are more like black markets than free markets, and because the Somali government has lost control of its society, Somali pirates are essentially free to take the law into their own hands. Until Somalia establishes a rule of law and lawful free markets for its citizens, lawless black market piracy will remain profitable."

Captain Hook Meets Adam Smith
Michael Shermer
In: *Skeptic*
Scientific American, October 2009

—46—Jitka Meets Abdallah

Pain. Jitka remembered pain. When she opened her eyes, there was nothing but blackness and she wondered if she had died. For several moments she had no idea where she was or how she might have died, but then the pain in her head returned and she dissolved back into the surrounding darkness.

Sometime later she opened her eyes again and there was some degree of dim light. The pain was less intense but her head still throbbed. As her brain gradually cleared she could see that the light was coming from a crack under the door of her darkened room. The room smelled of dust and musty bedding. A few minutes later she was able to sit up. Crawling to the door she had the idea to look at her watch to see how long she might have been out, but her watch was gone.

Where am I? How did I get here? Where is Silvio? Abshiir? What happened?

Gradually she was able to remember. They were in a truck with armed bandits after being stopped and watching some Somali teen-agers drive off with Silvio's Land Rover. *What had happened?*

Her stomach growled a bit, but food was far from her mind. What had happened? The very last thing she remembered was watching a group of young boys running along the beachfront road. They had passed the boys just before their truck driver shouted something and attempted to pull off onto the shoulder.

Had they stolen her cameras and her box of equipment? If so, her whole idea was now a disaster. She slid over to the wall to get some support for her back and felt her head. There was a tender knot where she had been hit by something solid, and the knot was crossed by a shallow laceration that felt like it was maybe three centimeters long. It hadn't bled much. There was only a small trickle of blood and some sticky hair, but the lump was very tender. What had happened to Silvio? And Abshiir? Her eyes traced the perimeter of the room and there was no sign of another person. She was alone.

She sat for an undetermined time in the darkened room, as the light outside the door grew steadily brighter. Then she could hear voices on the outside and moments later her door opened. Two young Somali males entered. Each had some types of automatic weapon slung over his shoulder and the first man through the door had a coil of rope.

The spoke to her roughly in Somali, and forced her to her feet. She had no idea what they were saying but it seemed imprudent to struggle or offer resistance. It passed her mind that this could be the end game for her, but she did not feel intense fear, because the greater possibility was that her captors would try to extract a ransom for her release. That's what Silvio had stressed.

She was trying to use her intelligence to fight fear, but she knew that it was only a trick to keep it at bay for a time.

The men tied her arms behind her, first with the wrists together and then wrapping the excess rope around her body keep her arms tied against her sides. They had been rough and the ropes were too tight, but she held off complaining immediately because it was unlikely these young men would understand her.

Five minutes later they had taken her onto the roof of the four-story building where a modest penthouse served as a headquarters, office and private living space for Abdallah. The boxy penthouse might have had a spectacular view of Boosaaso's harbor if it had been provided with picture windows; but the only openings in the wall were too small, and too high to do more than admit sunlight from all four sides.

The young men pushed her into the room roughly and said a few words to the man seated behind a large, ornately carved desk. He rose, spoke briefly and motioned them to leave the room. With the door closed, Jitka looked at the man who was apparently their chief, her captor. He appeared to be in his late thirties or early forties, although she knew it could be difficult to estimate the age of Somali men. His hair was curly and close cropped, typical for Somalis, and he was graying at the temples. His beard and mustache was trimmed short in the Arab style. His eyes were piercing and—she thought with a shiver—merciless.

"What language do you speak?" he asked. She was surprised that he spoke in English and she hesitated for a moment, still getting her bearings. "Parlez-vous Francais?"

"English is fine," she answered and was surprised at the sound of her own voice. The fear in it was apparent, even to her.

"How are you called?"

"My name is Jitka."

"What is your occupation?"

For a moment she considered saying *photo-journalist*, but it was never a good idea to be a journalist in an Islamic country. They would already have looked at her photographic equipment.

"Photographer," she said. "I take pictures."

"Who sent you here? To take pictures?"

"I am a free-lance." He was unlikely to understand this term, so she explained. "When I work, I take pictures of people and then sell them to anyone who is interested. Here, I am like a tourist. With a camera."

They were still standing. He motioned her to sit on the bench beside the wall and he pulled a chair from the opposite wall and sat facing her.

"What did you expect to photograph in Somalia? In Boosaaso?"

"I'm not sure how to address you."

"You call me Abdallah. But to my question."

"I came, Mister Abdallah, because the world is interested in the activities of your pirates. People in other countries wish to know more about your seafaring men, what kind of men they are, what led them to this kind of work. And since I had been successful at photographing Africa in the past, I decided to take the chance to visit Somalia. I have spent time in Sudan, and in Egypt in the past."

"What did you photograph in Sudan? Did you photograph in Darfur?"

"No. I spent two weeks in Suakin and I photographed that town and its people."

"I have been in Suakin and it is dead. There is nothing there. It is a dead city."

"Yes, but one with an interesting history and its people and old buildings are fascinating to Europeans. My photos were a success."

"And you wish to do this in Boosaaso? Photograph the town, and its community of ...*burcad badeed*?"

"I do not know these words."

"In English, is maybe ocean robbers. Sea robbers."

"I wish to see if I can capture the truth of what is happening here, Mister...." She suddenly remembered that Silvio had told her that Somalis hated titles and formalities. "Listen, Abdallah, these ropes are very tight and they are cutting off circulation in my hands. Do you think you could loosen them while we're talking?"

"In good time," he said. He turned toward the door and called out a few words in Somali. A couple of minutes later a small boy knocked at the door, then came in and handed Abdallah a funny-looking stick she could not identify.

He tapped the stick in the palm of his left hand, never taking his eyes off Jitka's face. "Earlier, when my men brought you to me, you were unconscious. I look at you very carefully. But before I continue I will explain some things for you." Jitka could feel her stomach muscles tightening.

"I am at the head of one of pirate bands you wish to photograph. I am Somali man, but I have live for time in other countries, including United States, and I have travel in many parts of the world as seaman. Here in Somalia I have three wives. I am master and they obey me. They are, as we say, *baari*. They obey me. For everything."

Jitka was trying to think fast. She did not want to interrupt, or smile, or appear to be inattentive. She tried to keep her face totally blank. But she was trying to think of proper responses.

"When one of my women does not obey me, or fails to respond at my command, I am compelled, by custom, and my own pleasure, to beat her. This is the little whip that I use. Every one of my wives has felt this whip, beginning on our wedding night, and they do not ever forget. Is what I say understandable by you?"

She nodded her head very slightly. *Yes.*

"It is made from hide of rhinoceros. You understand?" She nodded, shuddering.

"So then, since you now—in sense of your word—belong to me, you will understand that you must obey me."

She moved her head again. *Yes.*

"Do not nod your head at me," he said. "Answer."

"Yes." It was the voice of a stranger.

Abdallah walked to the bench where she was sitting and touched her to stand up. He untied and unwrapped the rope from around her body and then removed the loops that were pinching her wrists. She began rubbing them to get circulation to return as he went back to his chair.

"Now," he said, "you must undress your clothes."

She looked at him with an expression of incomprehension, and almost immediately she realized it was a mistake. He sprang from his chair with his tiny whip and struck her five times just above the belt line on her left flank.

It was like an electric shock that did not stop. It was excruciating, and she gasped for breath. Time stopped. She did not see him return to his chair, but when he spoke again, he was seated.

"Perhaps you have never been struck like this before," he said, but it was not a question. More of a musing statement. "Do not resist me again. Or I do it many times. Until you scream very loud."

Heart racing, Jitka began to undress.

"It's happening too fast. Your eyes are open but blind.
Telling yourself this isn't happening, this will not happen.
In another minute this will stop. This will go away."

Rape
Joyce Carol Oates

—47—Ordeal

Jitka was raped. She was raped repeatedly. Violently. Painfully. What
more can be said? It is a violent crime. That is, it's a violent crime in many
countries. In Somalia where there are no laws and no law enforcement and
no rights for women—especially if they are wives—it doesn't appear that
rape is a crime at all. In fact, rape victims sometimes receive the most severe
punishments. Such as...death.

Screaming, she learned, was not a good thing because it angered Abdallah
and he struck her with his little whip until it was hard to breathe. Becoming
rigid was no better, except that he usually responded to rigidity by slapping
her face. His hands were long and slender, and he was a skillful slapper.

By the end of the third day she had lost count of the number of times he
had entered her. She knew she had to think, to use her brain to help her stay
alive. Resisting was futile, reacting was useless. Everything hurt. If her body
was to survive this ordeal, her mind would have to take control.

While Jitka was held by Abdallah she tried everything she could think
of to control her thoughts, to avoid anything that would give offense to
her captor, or that might compromise her chances of remaining alive and
regaining her freedom. It was clear that Abdallah would enjoy playing mind
games with her, and she wanted to keep clear; to avoid any appearance of
cooperating with him; while at the same time she did not wish to appear
overly defiant.

For those first few days she spent most of the daylight hours bound in a
chair in the room Abdallah used as an office. During daylight hours she was
tied in a chair. After sunset and evening prayer she was moved to the bed
and tied, spread-eagled. It was extremely uncomfortable and it took all her
mental effort to avoid screaming as her joints stiffened and muscles cramped.
Because she was dehydrated, she only peed on herself a couple of times. She
had no food for three days. Very little water

Initially, she fought against the pain in her shoulders, hips and wrists by chewing the inside of her cheeks, what her dentist called the *buccal mucosa*. At first, the iron taste of her own blood provided a brief distraction. But on the second day it occurred to her that if she developed some type of infection from the self-inflicted wound, there was no medicine or antibiotic that she could use to fix the damage, and she felt foolish for having made the raw spot in her mouth.

On the third day in the chair she found herself, unaccountably, thinking of Peter Weems.

Peter Weems had been her boyfriend-lover during her last year at Oxford. Once, early in their relationship, she had believed that he had raped her. Now she knew that she had not comprehended the real meaning of rape. When her pain or discomfort was unbearable, she tried, concentrated with every fiber of her being, to remember every detail about Peter Weems. It helped, during endless, lonely, stifling hours.

She had first seen him in the boat sheds by the river when she went down to workout in a hired single. Peter pulled an oar in an eight. She seemed to remember that he rowed for St. Catherine's at the time, and he looked the way an oarsman ought to look. He was tall and rangy, with a pleasant, boyish face something along the Hugh Grant line and he seemed to be popular with his mates.

Later on when she ran into him outside an Oxford bookstore, they both recalled seeing each other on the ramp. *So he remembered me as well*, she had thought. He invited her for a cup of tea, and that was how it started.

Peter was studying architecture. His father was a successful architect specializing in apartment complexes and large commercial developments. Peter was uncertain as to where he wanted to fit in at his father's firm. During the time she knew him, he was considering doing graduate work in Italy, possibly in Milan, where he was making a half-hearted attempt to learn Italian during summer vacations.

Jitka went out with him several times and by the fourth week she decided to sleep with him. It was an easy decision at the time. He had a small flat in a nice part of the city and it had a private entrance. He also owned a sporty little MG that he kept on an Oxford lockup and he had a second lockup in London's East End. Actually, at the time, her girlfriends thought him quite a catch.

Peter was not a bad lover and, from him the girl learned a couple of hitherto unsuspected details about male physiology that she felt confident could be generally applied—when necessary—with reasonable expectation of success. After becoming a couple, they had fun together. His background as well as his education had made him a good conversationalist.

One memorable weekend they drove up to Hadrian's Wall and spent three days exploring remains and historic sites. Jitka took numerous photographs that later went on display in her college library. She sold enough prints to pay for their weekend; over two hundred pounds, but Peter just laughed at her so she used the money to buy equipment.

Another weekend they went down to Greenwich. There were crowds at all the tourist sights, and the Cutty Sark was jammed with visitors. On that occasion Jitka spent several hours photographing the faces of laughing children with a theme of ship details in the background. This collection, too, went on display at her university and ended up in a local gallery.

Her relationship with Peter lasted for the better part of a year, and, on the whole, it was a good experience. When Jitka decided to break it off, she spent considerable time examining her own motives, which she never fully understood. It began when she noticed Peter arranging the magazines on the coffee table in front of the settee in his flat. He stood back to assess the impact and then made a slight adjustment to satisfy some aesthetic sense. The first time Jitka watched him do this, something indefinable pinged in her brain, but she dismissed it and laughed at herself.

A week later, as they were waiting for another couple to join them for dinner, he arranged the magazines again. This time, he replaced one of the more colorful covers on the top of the stack; then lined them up neatly. The alarm bells sounded anew, and Jitka knew at once that their relationship was doomed.

She could never explain it with any precision; not even to herself, but she knew that she did not want a long-term, intimate relationship with a man who arranged the magazines on his coffee table. She didn't even want to go out with a man who entertained thoughts about arranging the mags on his coffee table.

Two weeks later, one month before the end of her last year, she broke it off with Peter. She had decided earlier, but it took her a bit of time to decide how and where and when to do it. But it had to be done; and time was running out. She told him while they were out for a weekend row in a rented punt on the river. She had put on the requisite filmy dress but she drew the line at the big floppy hat.

In retrospect, she wished she had chosen a more public place; perhaps the train stations. Peter apparently never saw it coming. And of course there was no way she could tell him about the reason. *No, there is no one else, Peter. Honestly. It's just that we both have a lot of growing up to do... Oh, Peter, don't look so stricken.* Aaah! It was ghastly, and it took longer than she had wished. Even the moving out took longer than expected. She had more stuff at his place than she had realized.

On the river, as her determination to break off sunk in, Peter wept. Real tears and even some snot. She surprised herself by feeling grateful to him for the tears because somehow they seemed to make it easier for her. At the time she did feel like a nasty bitch, but already she was making travel plans to visit her parents in Paris and the school experience was coming to an end.

In Peter's fantasies of the coming year, he would have had a comfortable place in an Italian city and his smart, gorgeous, talented Anglo-French bird would grace his life and make him the envy of every Italian male. Alas! Not to be.

With her arms bound painfully behind her, her wrists painfully chafed by the coarse, frayed, hand-braided rope, legs wrapped against the chair with several turns of the same rope, bladder about to burst and the taste of blood in her mouth, Jitka tried to think of everything she had ever done while she was with Peter. *Everything.* She tried to remember the location of every mole on his body. The stifling room had an air conditioner, but Abdallah only turned it on while he was there. And the switch must have been somewhere else in the building.

After the third day, they fed her twice daily, once in the morning when she was put in the chair and once after sundown when she went back on the bed. At these brief intervals she was allowed to use a bucket placed beside her bed. Otherwise—no concessions to other calls. After the second day three women came in to move her from one place to the other. Sweating constantly, she was surprised that she rarely had to pee.

The first time two women appeared she entertained the thought that they might be a bit more gentle than Abdallah who handled her roughly, but they quickly disabused her of that notion. They tied her tightly and—despite her complaints —for a time she feared that they would cut off circulation to her hands. Always she was aware that an armed guard might be present outside the door while the women were snatching her around. She never thought seriously about trying to escape because...what...where would she go? They would, she was convinced, kill her without blinking. Although she couldn't understand what the women said in her presence, it was apparent that it was hostile and they viewed her as some type of competition for Abdallah's attention. That, she believed, was almost certain to be true.

Her wrists were chafed raw and they were very sore. She feared infection, but when she mentioned it to Abdallah he had someone come in and apply some unidentified poultice which must have done its job. Although her skin was compromised and her wrists oozed serous fluid—enough to scab over in places—she never developed an infection.

Thirst was a constant torment. With water only twice daily, her urine production was minimal, helped by the fact that she sweated continually in the hot, dry air of the stuffy room. But she was grateful that she wasn't sitting constantly in her own urine.

Each day was a torment, and after the fifth cycle it was hard for her to keep track of individual days. But nothing, nothing compared with the sessions with Abdallah. When he came into the room she kept telling herself, do anything, do anything, just stay alive. Do what it takes to survive. He did not care that he was hurting her. Perhaps it added to his pleasure. It was impossible to tell. She knew, for the first time in her life, that she wanted to live and that she would do whatever necessary to stay alive.

Peter Weems would look pretty good about now, she thought. *Stay alive. Stay alive. Don't resist. Appear neutral. No revulsion. Everything ends in time. Just stay alive. And don't chew your cheeks.*

"...we are failing off the coast of the Horn. As the pirates become more brazen, our Navy, busy building schools and healing goats, appears impotent. We are not protecting the strategic sea lines of communication off the HOA, and this will affect the global economy from the price of shipping insurance premiums to the price of oil. It is also having ill effect on the combat reputation of the U.S. Navy.

"Bring the Navy back to Sea"
Lieutenant David S. Coles, U.S. Navy
In: Proceedings, U.S. Naval Institute, August 2009

—48—What Happened to Jitka?

His assignment in Djibouti was one of the most frustrating periods Vance could ever remember. After Jitka went missing he was beside himself with anger and rage. His assignment for UBSA management was vague; even less well defined than the role assigned to him by his superiors in the Navy. At the Pentagon his superiors had told him that he would be contacted by operatives from Naval Intelligence from time to time for debriefings...but this had not happened. His UBSA bosses had given him no specific assignments. They seemed to want him to tell them what needed to be done. His situation was... bizarre. He was adrift. But all that seemed to matter very little compared to what he was feeling with regard to the French photographer who had disappeared without a trace. *Somewhere in Somalia. I told her not to go. But I never asked her not to go. I never asked.*

For the first three days that the pair was gone, the former SEAL tried to convince himself that in a week or ten days they would be back and she would be showing him her photos. Allow him to count her vertebrae...again.

But then, just under a week after they left, he learned that Silvio had returned with injuries; that their Somali driver had been killed and that Jitka had been captured by some unidentified gang. He immediately found Silvio and was stunned to see his arm in a sling after suffering a shoulder dislocation. The aging professor, usually spry, appeared to have added a few years from their ill-fated ordeal.

"It was a mistake for us to go. I realize that now. I am more to blame than the girl. So the fault rests with me. Perhaps I let her enthusiasm override my better judgment. Forgive me, Vance. I do not sleep for thinking of our child."

Vance was sorry to see him looking so distraught, but he was reluctant to let him off the hook. *It was your fault, you dumb bastard. A generous man and a good friend, but still...that was stupid. I tried to talk Jitka out of going. And you only went because of her..*

"Silvio, where do you think she might be? Who do you think might have captured her?"

"I can show you the exact spot where we were taken. And repeat the details I have already given you. But they took all my maps with the vehicle. She might be anywhere. I do not believe that they will kill her."

Vance quickly produced a new map showing the local roads in Somalia.

Silvio pointed out the road leading southeast from Maydh in the direction of Ceerigabo.

"I asked her if we could make a diversion away from the coast road. It was to visit an area where I had been in the past. Particularly scenic. There are many interesting plants there and there were things I wanted to do. But actually, Vance, it is one of the more scenic spots on the north coast. I wanted her to see it. Selfish of me, to want to please her. I hope you can forgive me."

Vance could see that Silvio was getting choked up and he felt truly sorry for the old man, because it was clear that he had strong feelings for the girl.

"How do you think they picked you out in that relatively remote spot?"

"Vance, I am an old fool. What I think can matter little. But I do believe that the young bandits who assaulted us were in that area to pick up a shipment of *qat*. I would expect that it came over from Yemen. The airfield was in sight from where we were stopped. But, of course, it might have come from Kenya. Unlikely—but not impossible. Judging from the condition of these young men and their vehicle, they may have stolen the shipment. Thieves. Hijackers. They might be anywhere. I would guess they are still somewhere on the north coast, but that is little more than a hunch. Vance, what can we do to find our child?"

"I'm thinking about it, Professor. Every minute."

As the days dragged into weeks, and still no word of Jitka—gone without a trace—Vance's discomfort and unhappiness increased steadily. Silvio was morose, and his house was never lit up on weekends. Jitka's absence left a hole in Vance's life that he had not anticipated. His feelings for the girl were not based on anything she done. He had done it to himself.

Anger and hostility built in him and he had sufficient self-awareness to recognize that he needed help to deal with these feelings but there was no one he could talk to

UBSA had made no demands on him. He was little more than an observer, an advisor whose advice was disregarded. Until the girl was returned, he decided to give up alcohol and to resume a training regimen that was close to what he had practiced as an active SEAL. It was a technique for disciplining and distracting himself, and it was, for the most part, successful.

Nights were difficult for him and when he couldn't sleep, he found some strenuous exercise and practiced it to exhaustion. It was important for him to believe that Jitka was alive, but this inevitably led to considerations of what might be happening to her. Whole weeks passed in a haze of sweat and anger. And then, the calendar showed that she had been missing for a month. It was October and the monsoon season was just beginning.

Days held a semblance of work. Desk work. He tracked reports from the U.S. Navy, NATO and EU, and despite a growing fleet of powerful warships, pirate attacks continued to occur with relentless dependability. It was, as some slimeball once explained to him, exactly like hitting on women in a bar. It was a simple matter of statistics. Playing the percentages.

His appetite disappeared, but he found that the physical exertion helped. During the first month Jitka was gone, he dropped ten pounds, but then he stabilized at the same weight as when he came out of SEAL training. He still saw Silvio once or twice each week, but the old gentleman seemed to have lost the sparkle in his eye.

Vance felt like he was biding his time. Waiting for something to change.

"Where I grew up, death is a constant visitor. A virus, bacteria, a parasite, drought and famine; soldiers, and torturers; could bring it to anyone, any time. Death comes riding on raindrops that turned to floods. It catches the imagination of men in positions of authority who order their subordinates to hunt, torture, and kill people they imagine to be enemies. Death lures many others to take their own lives in order to escape a dismal reality. For many women, because of the perception of lost honor, death comes at the hands of a father, brother, or husband. Death comes to young women giving birth to new life, leaving the new-born orphaned in the hands of strangers.

For those who live in anarchy and civil war, as in the country of my birth, Somalia, death is everywhere."

Infidel
Ayaan Hirsi Ali

—49—Dealing with the Devil; Jitka Chained

One of the things that surprised Jitka about her captivity was how foolish she had been not to consider what captivity might entail. After the first three days she had come to realize that every single aspect of her daily existence, minute by minute, would be difficult, could certainly be the source of pain and might possibly result in death.

For the first three days, Abdallah had kept her bound in a chair or cuffed to the bed in a position that quickly became excruciatingly painful. She complained, then begged, and finally—desperate—she bargained.

Ugh! It was shameful, but her wrists were chafed and sore, not bleeding openly, but oozing serous fluid and she was afraid of a tropical infection that might lead to blood poisoning.

For the first 48 hours she had entertained thoughts of escaping, or possibly of being rescued—but by whom? It was a fantasy. After 72 hours these notions were gone and they did not recur.

After 72 hours—who knows how many hours; perhaps it was longer—it became difficult to recall the events of each day in any kind of chronological sequence, but after three days she persuaded him to take off her handcuffs. To keep her confined and immobilized, he devised a system that would allow some limited freedom of movement within his apartment.

From her bed she was able to move to the bathroom door, although the chain which was attached to her leg iron would not allow her to reach the toilet. She could barely get inside the door, where the bucket she had been using allowed her to come within five feet of the toilet. But the chain wasn't quite long enough. Her complaint made Abdallah laugh.

The chain fastened to her leg iron ran across the room and went out a high window that was above her head. Outside, he had secured the chain to a huge log weighing several hundred pounds. The chain reached from the bed to allow her a degree of privacy behind the bathroom door, but not to the toilet or the sink. She felt that he was trying to break her, as if she was some kind of animal.

Within the range of movement she was permitted there was a single chair where she could sit, and it was possible for her to pace within the small, room; but without the doors open the small two-room complex was essentially airless.

Initially, the heat at midday was stupefying. Every joint complained and her head throbbed much of the time. Her wrists were still chafed and sore but the ankle on her right leg was worse. She had kept a supply of antibiotics in their vehicle, but Abdallah advised her not to ask about it for a second time, and she did not wish to be struck. Her back and flanks were still tender.

Sometime in the middle of the fourth or fifth day, as she lay sweating in her prison bed, Jitka made a decision to stay alive.

I can do this, she thought.

Others have survived, and I can survive, too.

I have some strengths,

And I have resilience.

I must find a way to win him to easier ways.

He comes to me too often,

So I probably appeal to him in some way that his other women do not.

God, please help me, to find a way to get out of this hell.

Surely this cannot be Your plan for me.

I can do this. Just a little help is all I need.

She didn't think of her request as prayer. It was simply an acknowledgement of relative helplessness and a willingness to accept help. She continued like this for a long time. How long, she didn't know. But for a time, she forgot the pains in her ankle and back, and the aches of muscles unused and stiff.

When Abdallah came that evening, she smiled wanly when he sat on the bed and that was enough to make him stare closely.

"Do you want to know why I really came to Somalia?"

"You told me. You came to take pictures with your camera."

202

"But I didn't tell you the kind of pictures I was seeking."

"No."

"I came to photograph Somalia's pirates. Their faces. Their hands. The pirates of the Incense Coast who can climb ropes. The pirates who have captured the imagination of the world. But of whom they know little."

"We are simple seamen, fishermen, camel herders. There is nothing to photograph. We are poor. We work to feed our families and we do not have big homes, expensive automobiles, or wealth."

"But you have interesting lives. You said that you went to hunt the antelopes in the hill country. The wealthiest men in Europe would love to take such a trip. Most of them will never do it. But you have done it."

"That is true."

"And anyway, Abdallah, you are not really poor. This building? Your vehicles? And wives. Your hunting trips."

"You talk too much, woman."

"Can you not see that a photograph of a pirate captain with his antelope taken close to his home, would capture the imagination of European men? Of Americans?"

"What of it? What is that to me? Why do you talk to me of this? Take off the gown. Ugh! I will have Jaamila exchange it tomorrow. You stink."

"Abdallah, may I have my camera tomorrow? I know your men must have it. It would please me, and I, in turn, could try to please you. Will you consider?"

"Lie back, woman."

"Yes." *If I hate myself for this, perhaps I may have to choose not to live, after all.*

She made her voice into a tiny whisper.

"Abdallah?"

"Speak."

"If you let me move freely in the room, I promise I will not try to escape. And I will sing for you. In English and in French. Songs you have never heard." It was the best she could come up with.

He laughed. But she believed he might be thinking about it.

"In Somalia, like many countries across Africa and the Middle East, little girls are made "pure" by having their genitals cut out. There is no other way to describe this procedure, which typically occurs around the age of five. After the child's clitoris and labia are carved out, scraped off, or, in more compassionate areas, merely cut or pricked, the whole area is often sewn up, so that a thick band of tissue forms a chastity belt made of the girl's own scarred flesh. A small hole is carefully situated to permit a thin flow of pee. Only great force can tear the scar tissue wider, for sex."

Infidel
Ayaan Hirsi Ali

—50—Thinking About Survival

A week had passed since Jitka had first seen the inside of her jail. Her jailer had raped her repeatedly every single day except yesterday. Six nights in a row.

Almost every part of her body was giving her pain. He had abraded her deliberately, intentionally, and two days ago when she attempted to use her own saliva, he had slapped her in the face.

Her wrists were still raw and sore from the handcuffs that were old and rusty; and she continually feared they would become infected. He did not keep them on her at night after he devised the leg chain that was secured to her right ankle. That too was causing her skin to become sore and raw, even though she had torn off the corner of a sheet and used it to cushion the chafing.

The leg chain was Abdallah's solution to the problems of keeping her closely confined in the room while still enabling her to use the toilet and to take food. A leg iron secured her right foot above the ankle, It was attached to fifty feet of a heavy steel chain whose far end went out the window and was bolted around a heavy log that would be impossible to lift through the small window. The girl was able to walk to a small table where her food would be placed. For a toilet, there was the bucket, and a cardboard box contained old newspapers and magazines. A second bucket contained water for drinking—and washing.

Abdallah's little apartment actually had a small bathroom, with a western toilet and a sink with running water. A drain in the floor would have enabled her to douse herself if she could have reached it. But the placement of the door on the far wall away from the window meant that chain securing her to the log was too short for her to get to the sink or the toilet. Or the drain. She could get around the door jamb to enter the room, but could not reach either fixture. Thus, the buckets.

After trying for two days to accomplish the impossible she asked Abdallah if the arrangement could be altered to facilitate her.

"I hear your request."

"Will you do it?"

"I will consider it."

"Please."

"Hush, woman. Do not beg me. A Somali woman would never beg."

"I am not a Somali woman."

"This I know. You have not been cut."

This frightened Jitka into silence. She knew that he was a troubled man, often morose and sometimes violent with her. So she did not want to anger him. But she had also guessed that he fancied her above the other women in his compound. *At least, for now.* And she guessed that this would make them hate her.

When he was gone she found her thinking of ways that she could accept his rough, violent thrusts that would be pleasing to him, without making herself feel like a whore. Things she might do. He hurt her more at first than later, because every part of her was rigid and resistant. But as he came to her more and more, she began to understand that at some level she was appealing to him—perhaps it was her helplessness—and she began to consider if she might use that awareness to help her stay alive.

Stay alive. Eat what they bring you. Water is important. Ask him if you can have bottled water. Wait until after you have done or said something that doesn't make him angry.

Her back was stiff and sore from the mattress, even though she had slept on worse in the past. Part of the problem now was related to the stress she was under. She knew she had lost weight so she had begun to think carefully about eating to stay alive and to maintain a degree of resistance to illnesses.

Her breasts, never large to begin with, appeared to have gone down by two sizes.

If I live though this, I may be flat-chested, she thought. *If I can live through it, I wouldn't care if I was flat.*

The nightmare fears were those she did not even want to consider. HIV, AIDS, other venereal diseases, or, *Oh, Mon Dieu, Seigneur! Please, no pregnancy.*

At night, after darkness, she would think of photographic tours she would like to take. About projects for the future. *If there is a future for me. The Camino de Santiago. Pilgrims. Just their faces. Architecture just incidental; in the background. Tell the story with faces. What a coffee table book that might make.*

Unexpectedly, she thought of mythical creatures. Once, while visiting the United States, she had traveled in the south and seen a statue in a garden near Mobile, Alabama. It was a mermaid with two tails, and she had photographed it from several angles. But to get the light she wanted, she would have had to stay all day. It had made her think of Luis Borges and his book about imaginary creatures. Somewhere, around the world these imaginary creatures existed as statues; What a collection that might make. But....

Then, conscious of whatever part was hurting worst, her tears would come and she would see herself—if she survived—ill, confined to a bed, moved somewhere else, tended by others. *Oh, Seigneur!*

What if her captor was killed? Or captured? At least, with Abdallah, she knew a name, his name. And at least he could speak English. She did not know ten words in Somali. And what of Silvio? Abshiir? Abdallah had told her nothing.

Each day someone came in the morning to bring an empty toilet bucket and a fresh pail of water. On leaving they would take away the toilet bucket and the water pail. Water was always in a white bucket and the toilet bucket was always colored; usually green or black. She could find the water pail in the dark.. The white pail, she supposed, was for both washing and drinking, so she was careful not to wash her hands. Then after four or five days, she asked Abdallah if she could have a cup and he had one sent up. Then she could dip water and pour it over her hands, one at a time, into the slop bucket.

Jitka awoke from a fitful sleep to a sound like a cat scratching on a door to be let out. Her parents had always kept a cat while she was growing up. Sometimes, two.

The sound woke her and made her wonder what was happening.

Her nose was stuffed with blood from a nosebleed after Abdallah had slapped her in the face. She had been breathing through her mouth for some undetermined period and her tongue was as dry and raspy as a piece of sandpaper. She realized, with a shock, that the sound she was hearing was her tongue moving slowly across her teeth.

Can this be true? I am making his sound. C'est vrai? She moved her tongue to recreate the sound. *Who could believe this?* It was almost funny. It was something she could never imagine; being wakened by such a curious sound.

I must remember this. In case I ever get out alive I must always remember this as one of the many surprising and unsuspected sounds of which I might be capable. And to fix the sound in her memory, she rubbed her tongue across her teeth several times.

There. Done. *I can remember this.* Now she moistened her tongue and snorted her nose several times to remove dried blood. She would always remember this sound. The sound like a cat scratching against a door. Maybe—like her parents—she would try living with a cat, if the opportunity should arise again.

Horrible. Horrible. To have to live this way. But she was still alive. The pains she felt were almost constant, but she thought, with just a touch of pride, I am still alive. *Still alive. In stifling, reeking hell.*

From outside the apartment, she could hear someone removing the lock from the hasp. Jitka had not been listening or she might have heard the sounds of the footsteps approaching on the roof. The door opened and a Somali woman came in. She was tall and regal in bearing. Young, probably just around early twenties, perhaps, with skin the color of clover honey. Jitka assumed she might be a servant, but the color and cut of the dress she was wearing communicated that she was probably not a servant.

The woman's expression was blank. There was no animosity; there was no friendliness. When she entered the room, Jitka had been standing, moving purposely in a pattern to improve circulation in her legs. She was wearing the same long, loose cotton gown she had worn from the beginning and it had a few blood drops from a nosebleed when Abdallah had slapped her. It was filthy and smelly from several days of wear and sweat and sex.

Jitka could see that the woman was examining her carefully. *Maybe this can be good. Maybe. There's little to lose.* Jitka smiled briefly and pointed to herself. "My name is Jitka. Jitka"

The woman continued looking; full eye contact, but she never smiled.

"*Gaalo,*" she hissed. Jitka had been told this word by Silvio. It meant white, non-muslim. She nodded her head. "Yes. Oui."

"*Abid.*"

This was not a word Jitka knew, so she held up both hands, shook her head—no—and repeated, "Moi....Jitka."

"*Kintirleey. Gaalo.*" Whatever that meant, it was not good.

Jitka looked puzzled and pointed at herself. "I am Jitka."

"Jaamila. " Jaamila was pointing at herself. "Moi." That was a beginning.

"I sit her up.

'I'm going to look inside with this.' I show her the bright metal speculum. 'I look for infection. Okay?'

'Okay.'

She lies back down and spreads her legs. I remove the sheet and pull up her gown.

Her labia are scarred together. The introitus is tiny. Perhaps big enough for one finger. The speculum would never fit. I reach to my side and unwrap a pediatric one. It is much too large. I pull the labia apart and do my best to look inside. I can see green pus. I pull her gown back over her knees and sit back. I'm silent.

What the fuck.

She must have been cut..."

From "Six Months in Sudan,"
(A Young Doctor in a War-Torn Village)
James Maskalyk

—51—A Bit About Jaamila

Jaamila Farah came from and old and distinguished family from the Darood clan living in the north. Abdallah saw her shortly after he had received his first big payout from the ransom of a Saudi crew. She was fifteen. Tall, slender, and her teeth were dazzling. Her hips looked as if they were made to carry babies.

His uncle negotiated the *yarad* with the girl's family. Although Abdallah had a substantial number of camels at his disposal, part of the payments to this girl's family included the transfer of an almost-new Land Rover he had ordered from Kenya, and an undisclosed amount of cash in American currency.

Jaamila, like most Somali girls, had been cut—when she was twelve. The procedure was performed by her grandmother who used a single-edge razor blade she had owned for a decade. The grandmother, impervious to the suffering of others, did a thorough job of performing a classic Pharaonic infibulation. Nothing much was left between Jaamila's legs, and two straws were inserted to maintain an opening for the urethra and the vagina.

Where the girl's clitoris had been located, the grandmother cut away flesh almost to the pubic bone. To seal the opening that she had destroyed, the grandmother used six long acacia thorns and then further lashed them together with a piece of mono-filament fishing line.

Healing took a long time, and was very painful for most of the distance. Jaamila never forgot her grandmother's role and shunned her presence whenever possible.

Jaamila swore that if she should ever have a girl, she would kill the person who tried to do this to her child.

Jaamila's family did not believe that girls needed to be educated and she had never attended a formal classroom. Thus, she was never taught to read; but she was bright and capable, with a natural talent for memorization. She had learned long passages of Somali poetry. At family gatherings she was sometimes called upon to recite, and despite a natural shyness she usually obliged.

When Abdallah's uncle came to her family with an offer, she was not even sure who Abdallah was; but when shown his photograph, she remembered seeing him on several occasions. He was not a bad looking man; tall, as most Somali men are, with a rather stern face. She did not care. Anything to get away from a family dominated by an old woman she had come to hate. At the time of the offer, Abdallah had but two wives in Somalia, but his new wealth had everyone talking and her family knew their slender girl was appealing to men. They drove a hard bargain.

Jaamila had not given a great deal of thought to various aspects of married life, other than the domestic preparation commonly given to all Somali females. Within her own family, her tasks were minimal. She had few close friends among girls and even with those she was not talkative. The space between her legs had little connection with pleasure in her mind and even voiding her bladder was a painful exercise, sometimes taking half-an-hour. Marriage with Abdallah made her recall the prior experience with her grandmother. The reason stemmed from the thoroughness of grandma's infibulation. The girl was essentially sewn shut.

Jaamila's wedding night was unforgettable. In the U.S. Abdallah had abandoned a wife who did not bleed. In this regard, at least, Jaamila met her husband's expectations. Jaamila's wedding night with Abdallah had been unforgettably painful. The girl did, indeed, bleed and Abdallah was able to display the evidence to his waiting audience, mostly members of his Isaaq clan. But he had not endeared himself to Jaamila. She felt about her husband much the same way she felt about her grandmother.

The consequence of that one experience was sufficient to assure that Jaamila would never feel desire for Abdallah, would never be happy to welcome him to her bed, or would be glad to welcome his arrival from a voyage at sea...or a trip into the Warsengeli.

It was not exactly fair to say that she hated Abdallah, or even that she feared him, even though he beat her at times. She was simply indifferent. They were married. It was the custom. He brought food, provided shelter. She prepared and served. It was a life of work and routine. But if she saw him a little or a lot...it was a matter of supreme indifference. She knew, and forced herself to accept, he was the deliverer of pain.

When he came to her, she knew that she had to steel herself. Experience had taught her that the pain he inflicted would not kill her. She could live through it.

Of this response, Abdallah was unaware. Perhaps not so much unaware as just indifferent. And, had he known, it would have been of no consequence.

Jaamila's visits to Jitka established an unspoken bond between them based on shared knowledge and shared suffering. Each pitied the other in different ways, and they had no shared language to discuss their feelings. Jaamila could only show her pity by acts of kindness. Jitka had no such tools in her empty arsenal. All she could do was accept gratefully, although there were occasional tears. In this way, days and weeks, unbearably hot, passed slowly.

Abdallah would be at sea for four or five days. When he returned, he would spend more than half his nights ashore ravishing Jitka.

"When frankincense and myrrh were valued highly, they sustained thriving communities, their towns, ports, ships and camels. The trade also sustained large tracts of woodland in places where all vegetation has a rather tenuous grip on existence. The trees were protected because local people derived wealth and influence from them but ultimately it was the rituals, pleasures and value systems of distant peoples that maintained the incense trade for so many centuries. Now that the trade has become the victim of changing values the question arises—will the goats and fuel needs of impoverished country folk eliminate the rare endemics before the value of these plants and animals has been adequately recognized?"

Island Africa
(The Evolution of Africa's Rare Plants and Animals)
Jonathan Kingdom

—52— Life in Somalia

After weeks of imprisonment, and repeated rapes, Jitka had gone through an entire gamut of responses; initial anger and thoughts of escape, fury and frustration at pain inflicted and rape endured, agony and despair over the possibility of disease—from water, food, infections from open wounds and sores, accumulated filth, bladder or kidney infections, or repeated rape by Abdallah. Finally, she began to consider the strong possibility that she might die *in* the hands of her captor even if it was not *by* his hands.

She had few tears left for weeping and she had decided, firmly, irrevocably, that she wanted to live, and that she would do whatever it took to stay alive. Somehow, this nightmare would end.

It was a searing decision that she made. When Abdallah came to ravage her, she would offer no resistance, she would will her body to relax as much as possible and endure the punishment he inflicted. She was in constant pain and fear, but she had no major injuries. No broken bones or gaping wounds. She had willed herself not to think about Silvio for now. She was hungry all the time, and constant thirst prompted her to drink from the bucket that came daily. *I'm still alive. I'm not sick...yet. Weak, but no recognizable illness.*

She would make an effort to find something they could talk about; some common ground that might interest him, or divert him, even if only for a few moments. She would do what it takes and she would try to find what would work. She was too smart to let this monster triumph over her.

But the night after her decision, he did not come.

The small boy continued to bring her pails containing food two or three times daily. It varied. And he brought water in a pail as well. When he left he carried away the pail that she used for a toilet or for washing. But she was filthy. She could smell herself, and she had never in her life been in such a state. The water bucket was her only source of water, and she had managed to tear a scrap of fabric from the corner of a bedsheet to use as a wash cloth. But it was wasteful of her limited supply of water to attempt to wash thoroughly.

When I'm out of here, she thought, *I am going to spend a week inside a shower. Until I look like a prune.*

Her only garment was a loose fitting white gown something like what Somalis called a *dirha,* much like a long nightgown. It was stained and filthy, but it was all she had. Her original clothing, the things she had been wearing at the time she was captured, were in the corner of the room, thrown carelessly against the wall, but the chain on her ankle would not allow her to travel that far, and it was just as well. How could she have put on the jeans that she once wore under a colorful cotton overskirt? —with a chain on her ankle?

On the second night that Abdallah failed to come she wondered if he had been in some accident. If so, what would become of her? How many people knew she was here? What commands had he given to the boy who was tending her? As if she was livestock? Which in a sense, she was. And what of his wives? Surely they resented her continuing presence, knew when and how often he visited her. They surely must hate her and wish her dead. It was almost enough to break her resolve about willing to live.

It was late in the evening of the second night in which Abdallah had not appeared around his usual time, when she heard the sound of someone working at the outside lock on the door to her room. Abdallah. But the sound was different, this was a different person come to torment her and her pulse began to race as fear of the unknown overcame her. Her plans for swaying Abdallah would go out the window.

The door opened slowly and Jitka was literally holding her breath. The figure who came in the door was tall but slender, wrapped in a colorful *jilbab,* of the type worn outdoors. It was a woman.

Jitka could see her hands and wrists and she was a slender woman, perhaps even thinner than herself. The woman came into the room tentatively, as if entering an enclosure with a caged animal. Jitka was poised, apprehensively on the side the bed, clad in her filthy gown. As the Somali woman took a few tentative steps into the dimly lit room, Jitka was surprised to realize that she

212

was embarrassed to smell this way in front of her female visitor, no matter who she was.

Something in the woman's demeanor, and in the absence of any kind of weapon, told Jitka she need not fear. But this was a response she knew she could not trust.

As the visitor came further into the room, Jitka was able to see her face under the *jilbab* and the woman—a girl actually—was both young and pretty. Now she could be recognized. What was the name? Jaamila.

The woman's eyes were scanning the room, taking in all the elements of Jitka's prison cell and she noted the ankle iron and the chain leading out the window. She could also see the water pail near the bed, the food pail beside the chair and the toilet pail was visible just inside the door to the small bathroom. She walked slowly to the chair near the center of the room and stood behind it as she scanned around the room carefully for a second time. She stood for a long moment just looking at Jitka. Her face had no expression.

Then, as if reaching a difficult decision, the Somali stepped to the front of the chair and sat down, primly, facing Jitka. Still, neither woman spoke. For several long moments they sat facing one another, one chained, one free. Jitka tried to keep any expression from her face, but a hundred emotions were racing through her brain, and she could not prevent tears from welling in her eyes. She did, however, will herself not to brush them away. And *merde, merde, merde,* if one did not leak out of her eye. Still, she did not blink. The other woman seemed not to notice. They sat this way for more than ten long minutes, and Jitka gradually lost all fear of this woman, whose plight, she was beginning to suspect, might not be greatly different from her own. A long time. Tears came, but Jitka finally smiled.

After nearly ten minutes the woman stood, pointed to herself and said some words in Somali that Jitka did not understand. But among the words she said, several times, *Jaamila,* pointing to herself. That was her name. Jaamila.

Jitka understood and shook her head, yes. "I am Jitka. Je suis Jitka. Jitka." The woman nodded and repeated the name.

"Jitka."

Jitka nodded. "Jaamila."

The slow introductions were over.

Jaamila came to within a few paces of were Jitka was sitting on the side the bed. The Somali woman opened the front of her *jilbab* which had velcro tabs at the neck, and dropped the loose fabric off to expose one shoulder. She turned her back to show Jitka the red wheals on her shoulder where she had been hit. Then, once Jitka had seen the marks, she covered again and asked her a question, by nodding her head and speaking in Somali.

"Jitka?"

Jitka pulled down the shoulder her gown and let Jaamila look at her back. Jaamila bent to look closely and then Jitka pulled her gown back. Jaamila shook her head, signifying understanding. Then she resumed her seat and continued looking at Jitka. But now, she was examining the white girl, the *gaalo*—whom she had called *abid*, a term Jitka had never heard— looked at her, from bare feet and raw, chained ankle to filthy gown to dirty hair and nails and animal smell.

Following several minutes of careful study she got up, walked over to Jitka, took her head in both hands and kissed her slowly on the forehead. Something in Jitka's chest seemed as if it would burst, and unexpectedly she uttered an unrecognizable sound that was neither sigh nor groan. Jaamila kissed her again. This time, briefly. Then she turned and left the room without a word.

After the Somali woman had left, Jitka thought about the visit for hours, but she was unable to reach any conclusions about its significance. *But,* she thought, *it would be nice if she came again. She was pretty and she was wearing a good scent.* It would be nice to see a woman from time to time.

The photographer in Jitka had decided immediately that pirate women would be marvelous subjects for a photographic essay. *The women behind the pirates.* As she fell asleep, sweating between stale sheets, for the first time in several days she was thinking about her work.

Jaamila came again, on the afternoon of the following day and she brought a clean gown. After Jitka had changed, Jaamila folded the dirty one, placed it beside the lone chair, and sat down. She was silent. Jitka thanked her in a soft voice, in English and in French and the young Somali nodded as if she had understood, but her face remained expressionless. Jitka hardly knew how to respond, and she wanted to see what the other woman wanted from her. But Jaamila's visits remained a mystery.

That night Abdallah did not visit her and Jitka concluded that he was either at sea or away on a trip of some kind. It was possible he was visiting some of his other wives, but she discounted that idea when Jaamila came again the next day. This time she brought a small iron brazier that Jitka recognized as an incense burner.

Jaamila placed the burner in the middle of the floor, near the chair. She placed a small lump of pale, resinous-looking material in the brazier and lit it with a safety match. The evergreen aroma was immediately identifiable as frankincense.

As the smoke plume from the incense rose, Jaamila began speaking in

Somali, but Jitka could understand nothing. Jaamila pointed to the rising smoke; then lifted the hem of her long gown motioning Jitka to mimic her movements. The young Somali then stepped over the brazier, lifting her hem to encircle the brazier and straddled the plume of rising smoke.

With the hem of her garment back on the floor, the incense smoke was rising up between her legs.

She opened the top of her robe and shook her breast free, loosening the material throat and allowing the incense plume to exit though the top of her dress. She was a chimney, and she shook the material of her dress to distribute the aroma.

Jaamila was smoking herself in incense. The woman closed her eyes and began to chant something in Somali as she bathed in incense smoke.

This process was continued for several minutes as her feet shuffled so that she made several slow revolutions over the brazier. When she finished the last words of the rhythmic chant, she stepped away from the brazier, walked over to where Jitka sat watching and dropped her *abaya* off her left shoulder and bared her arm to Jitka. She said something in Somali, which could only have been 'smell my arm.'

Jitka took her by the wrist and sniffed at her arm from shoulder to elbow. The frankincense seemed to have permeated her skin, giving the impression of an evergreen forest creature. It was pleasant, and Jitka smiled. It was the first honest smile she had made in weeks and the realization made her want to weep.

Jaamila withdrew her arm and pulled the garment back over her shoulder. Then she motioned Jitka to repeat what she had witnessed.

Standing slowly, Jitka stepped over to the brazier as the smoke plume rose steadily.

"Poetic performance in Somalia is not casual or informal, as in might be in Paris cafés or on the street corners of college towns—and it is explicitly competitive. Formal gatherings in the shade of acacia groves often include a panel of hoary elders of literary merit, called *heergeegti*, who serve as judges of the poetry competitions. These may last for weeks as poets rebut one another in a lengthy test of talent and stamina. Winners gain fame and prestige for their clan as well as livestock for themselves; in a country where verbal damage to an enemy may be more wounding than physical harm, counting a poet among one's clan member can be as valuable as an armory of swords."

'A Nation of Bards'
Lark Ellen Gould
in "Saudi Aramco World", August 29, 2009
From the Internet

—53—The Power of Poetry

Abdallah was back from sea after two unsuccessful boarding attempts off the coast of Yemen. His methods for restraining Jitka varied depending on his mood. Several devices for restraint were suspended from the wall of his rooftop retreat, and Jitka could only guess at how some of them might have been employed in the past. For the last week, her ankle restraint allowed her a degree of movement in the apartment. She could still not reach the toilet in the bathroom which had a flush valve. Sometimes, lately, he released her completely until he left her. The second time he did this, she was encouraged to think that he might make this a permanent arrangement. If she could find a way to win him over; if she could ask in a manner that would not make him angry.

She had learned to recognize his mood when he came to her from chewing *qat*, and she knew how to avoid anything that might provoke him while he was still high. Then, his mood could swiftly become cruelly aggressive if she resisted him in any way. He was clearly determined that the girl would not escape from his rooftop penthouse apartment. That would have been embarrassing.

His men knew that he was keeping the girl, but they were reluctant to ask questions. For all they knew, she was living in the women's quarters. But Abdallah was reluctant to put her in proximity to his three wives who were not even close friends with each other. Only Jaamila, the youngest of the three had not shown anger when he had come home with Jitka in bonds. Abdallah had hoped she would be jealous. Jaamila was pretty, and had excited him in the beginning, she was now unruly and wept often. He had given thought to divorcing her. Jaamila had come to him as his third wife, and he had been pleased at the time. But after her first child was miscarried and she was resewn, she became difficult.

This new *gaalo* woman was exciting and different. She had never been cut or sewn, and she was white. This made her different to look at when she was without clothing, and he found it exciting to look at her. Also, he had to admit that she was very pretty. Her breasts were smaller than those of Somali women, but he could overlook that. She was, it had to be acknowledged, not very tall, and he had a fondness for lanky, slender women. But she was well formed and her unfamiliar body type excited him. This was good. She had smooth skin with no blemishes or scars, except for the one on her face.

In the last few weeks she had begun to do things with her hands that no Somali woman had ever done. He would keep her. Also, he had found, she would talk to him and her talk was interesting. But he was clever enough to know that whatever she said, it could not be trusted completely. And he did not like the sound of her name. It sounded harsh.

"Tell me again, *English-French*. Why did you try to come into my country?" he asked her.

"I came to take photographs. As you know....because you damaged my camera."

"I did not damage your camera."

"One of your men damaged it."

"Perhaps we can have it repaired."

"I doubt it. Not around here."

"Why must you oppose me? If I wish it repaired, it will be repaired. Or replaced."

She nodded.

"Why don't you loosen these handcuffs? You can see that my wrists are bleeding and if they become infected, it is possible that I could sicken and die. Then I could examine my own fucking camera."

"Your speech is an offense to Allah. And a Somali woman could not die from such a small wound." He was reaching for his crop as he spoke.

Merde. A Cro-Magnon. What was I thinking to come to this insane place? She knew it was pointless to argue with him. Just agree. Just go along. Hopefully, he would not strike her today.

Last night, after he finally left her, she lay trembling and weeping softly, and wondering if he would let her live. He had been high on something when he came to her. Not high, exactly, but more like spaced out. Like he had been smoking weed. But he was impaired. And he was very rough with her.

After removing the cuffs that had secured her to the bedpost, he threw her down on the bed and pulled off the loose gown she was wearing. Then he spread her legs apart to look at her. When she closed her legs, he turned silently and removed the small whip from the wall. It was like a riding crop and it hurt.

When her hands were restrained, she could not palpate the wheals but some of the most painful places were oozing. Her back was sticking to the sheets. She could tell that it wasn't blood, but, still, she knew the possibility of infection was real.

Abdallah leaned forward and she flinched, involuntarily. He pulled her over roughly and began to strike her with the whip. After ten or twelve, she lost count, and was trying to catch her breath. Her back and buttocks seemed to be on fire. For a moment, she could not even tell that he had stopped.

"We were talking about why you came to my country."

"I came..." She wanted to respond to him. She wanted to assuage his fury. But she could not get her breath. "I came...to...."

Abdallah laughed. "I can beat the words out of you."

"No. Please! Let me....catch...my breath." She was aflame.

"You came with your camera."

"Yes. With my..."

"Camera. To take photographs."

"Yes. Of...."

"Yes?"

"Yes. Of...pirates."

Abdallah burst out laughing. "You said this before. You came to take pictures of me? Of my men? Surely you are mocking me. We are simple men. Taking what we can from a harsh world. Surely you do not want pictures of men like us. We are simple Somalis. We do this because it is all we can do."

"No. The world wants...." It hurt so bad she wanted to scream. *Please. Can't someone give me something?*

"The world wants? The world wants Somalia to go away. But we will never go away. We were here first and we will be here last. We are poets and herders and camel men and seamen. And now...the world calls us pirates."

She was beginning to breathe a bit more normally. It was important to say what he wanted to hear so that he would not hit again. If he hit her again, she did not know if she could bear the pain. This was something to think about. She might have to bear it.

"No. Abdallah. Listen. The world needs to understand you. Who you are." She paused to get her breathing under control. "Who you are. What you are doing. Why you do what you do. They need to know. The world."

"You are a foolish woman."

"No. Perhaps. Yes. Foolish to come here and be captured by you. But in the bigger world outside Somalia I am known as someone who can tell a story with pictures. This is not a boast, Abdallah. I could tell your story to the world."

"I was a camel boy. Then I was a seaman. Now I am called a pirate. In between, I lived in your godless west. I did not like it."

"I can tell any story," she said; but her words sounded pitiful—almost supplicating— and she thought that she had spoken too quickly; should have chosen her words more carefully. *Oh God*, she thought, *If I only had my coffee table book that is languishing, unopened on that shelf in Silvio's house, maybe I could convince this brute. How can a man who looks normal, not bad-looking actually, be so cruel and inhuman?*

"Do you even know what is a camel-boy?" His voice, for the first time in the evening, sounded normal, not high, not aggressive, not threatening or cruel.

If he spreads my legs again, I am going to open them to him, she thought. *I want to stay alive. I want to get back to Djibouti. I want to get back to visit some friends in London. I want to see my parents in Paris. I want to stay alive. Being alive is better than being dead. Getting fucked by a brute is preferable to death. Even...I didn't think I could ever reach this point but...getting AIDS and staying alive is better than death. I want to live. I want to do whatever it takes—please God, help me to persist in this resolution—whatever it takes to stay alive, to see those fucking linnets that were feeding off trees in Silvio's compound.*

A survival strategy was beginning to form in her mind. Not by conscious effort, but subconsciously, and she knew, suddenly, despite the pain, she was beginning to believe that she might live through this ordeal.

"You have been in Paris?" she asked him.

"In Paris, no. In London, yes. And New York."

"You know they have galleries there? Art galleries? Where they exhibit pictures?"

"Of course. Do not insult or anger me."

"But Abdallah, then you must know that they treasure photographs that tell the stories of men, of events, of history, of conflicts, of human activity? You must know this. Am I correct?"

"Continue."

"I came to capture images of you and your men."

"You did not succeed. You wanted to vilify us to the western media."

"No."

"What then?"

"To depict you as you are."

"And how are we?"

"You must answer that yourself. You are as you are. I am not involved. I am but a witness. With my camera."

"We are pirates."

"You are also men. What does Allah say you are?"

"You have no call to speak of Allah."

"And you have no call to deny his involvement in your activities."

"You know that I can punish you whenever you anger me."

"Please, Abdallah. You know that you have hurt me already."

"And may again."

"Please. No."

"Then do not speak of Allah again."

"As you command." She was hunting for a mode of speech that would conciliate him, without giving up her ability to differ. She was still aflame from his lashing and she knew that she did not want to be struck again. Perhaps she had best be silent. But she wanted to push back, just a little. Otherwise....

"Life at sea is the same for all men. We are no different."

"Listen, Abdallah. You travel in small craft. You face great dangers; both from the sea and from those you propose to rob. I make no judgements. My camera makes no judgements, but your work is dangerous, and it is not always successful. In this, it is like many other human endeavors. This is the work of human men. As such, it is of interest to other human men. I make no judgement. I simply try to see."

Abdallah looked at the girl's face and he found it to his liking. There was that dark scar below her right eye, and he found it intriguing that such a pretty female would have a rough scar.

"How did you hurt your face?" he asked.

For a moment the pain was forgotten as she thought, *He is looking at me as a woman. I must try to see him as only a man. Oh, Mon Dieu, please help me now.*

"It's a long story," she began, struggling to invent the best lie of her life.

The first week of Jitka's captivity, was a case study in the complex interactions between men and women, jailers and captives, and abusers and their victims. This overlay, this tissue, this veneer, is complex, and perhaps impossible to capture. Nevertheless, Jitka and Abdallah lived it, and it marked them both. Of the two, Jitka bears the deepest scars. Actually, the *only* scars.

Captivity and imprisonment meant that the space that he had previously reserved for working, sleeping and for chewing *qat* with a few close associates was now preempted for use as a jail cell.

For the first few days he had handcuffed her with her hands behind her back or lashed her into a straight-backed chair. Since the windows to his apartment were barred and the heavy door could be padlocked from outside, it was easy to lock her in for the day.

After her third day, it had been reasonably clear that escape was highly unlikely. Her range of motion increased after the leg chain, but its length prevented her from reaching the flush toilet in the tiny bathroom. With the chain she could just get behind the door to use the bucket that was provided. That was better than the open room. Still, the difficulties made her want to stop eating or drinking.

Over the first several weeks of her confinement, Jitka had two things to occupy her mind during long, lonely, stifling hours. First was her plan to interest Abdallah in her photographs, with a possible outcome of getting out of this hellhole. Once outside, perhaps some other options would suggest themselves. Or, at the very least—and she shuddered to even think of it—perhaps she would be able to jump from the roof. *End this misery.*

The second diversion came from considering possible variants in her growing relationship with Jaamila. Jitka had now concluded that Jaamila, cognizant of Abdallah's schedule, came to visit her every time she was certain her husband would not intrude on them. Jaamila wasn't a friend, perhaps, but she was certainly not an enemy, and the use of the frankincense had seemed to please Abdallah. At any rate, he had not whipped her that night.

More to the point—and this was puzzling to Jitka—he had not questioned her concerning the source of the incense, or any of the paraphernalia. Were they acting in collaboration? Jitka couldn't bring herself to believe that, but it was still unclear what might go on in the orbit of this cruel and bizarre man. She had heard him talking to himself as he cleaned up in the bathroom that was beyond her reach. Then, after listening carefully for several minutes, she concluded that he was reciting poetry.

No! This was too preposterous. Poetry?

After Abdallah left the apartment on that morning, Jitka reflected on his solo recitation. She had never had a particularly strong interest in poetry and, in fact, she had only a passing acquaintance with the poets of her own country. French poetry had never held her, and in any case, her real interest was in the visual poetry of photographs. First she grew up with film, but now she had made, was still making, the transition to digital imaging. It was demanding, and she gave the field her full and undivided attention.

It is, however, difficult to attend university in Great Britain without exposure to a full dose of English poetry, and Jitka had not been spared.

She recalled, in particular, her experience during her third year at Oxford when she had been pursued with some intensity, by a fourth-year youth named Gordon. Gordon Howe.

Gordon had been truly smitten by the girl and she responded to his unfeigned admiration for everything about her, but she was indifferent to him as a lover, as a sweetheart.

Thinking back, it was probably cruel of her to let him court her with such intensity. But at the time there were no other males chasing her and Gordon, from a wealthy family, had a small car, old and quaint-looking, but carefully maintained and smooth-running. An Austin Healy.

He could take her to places she wanted to visit with her camera. Together they visited such sites as Hadrian's Wall, Stonehenge, Bath, Cambridge, and other sites within reasonable range for day trips, or occasional weekend trips.

On their first weekend trip together, the nature of sleeping arrangements was an unspoken question. Eventually, after their evening meal, it simply solved itself. He never asked. She never answered. She climbed into the bed with him. It was, she felt, the least she could do. She was surprised to discover that, despite his age, sophistication and good looks, she was his first.

And somehow, even though she still was not particularly fond of him, his response to her was so overwhelming for him that she was touched with tenderness and she promised herself to be nicer to him. It was sad in a way. She felt so grown up, so mature. A woman—with a boy.

Two weeks later, after Gordon's initiation, when she expressed an interest in photographing canal boats on an English canal, he purchased a large picnic lunch and motored her down to Bath. The term was coming to a close and fruit trees were in bloom all along the roadside. Bath was lovely and they strolled beside the towpath, admiring decorations on the boats, the potted plants, sleeping cats and occasionally a pipe-smoking boat owner who would chat with them for a while. Gordon introduced Jitka to a new British word, the name for a person who walks along the canal, admiring boats and occasionally peeking inside. *Gongoosler*. It made her laugh.

"What it means?" she asked. "No meaning", he said, laughing at her perplexity. "It's just a word."

Later in the day, he retrieved the packed lunch which including a rather expensive bottle of *Chateneauf de Pape* and a delicious array of cold meats; and after they had eaten, he attempted to woo her. Jitka—who at this point felt as if she were a forty-year old Parisienne with a salon, seducing a sixteen-year old boy—was amused; but she was kind. Ah, hubris.

Gordon had a sonnet committed to memory. Shakespeare, no less, and he waited for a moment when conditions were ideal and digestion was well underway. *Mon Dieu*, she thought, *he has worked so hard to do this. Could I be worth so much intensity?*

There were no flowering trees on the slope where they were perched beside the canal. But on the other side, an old, gnarled apple was loaded with white blossoms. *Just a tinge of pink*, she remembered. He began.

"Shall I compare thee to a summer's day?
Thou art more lovely and more temperate.
Rough winds do shake the darling buds of May,
And summer's lease...."

He had worked at this, she could tell, like an actor studying lines. *"Merde, this boy has really spent time on this. Please Seigneur, don't let him be in love with me. Please. It's not fair."*

But Gordon—no mind-reader—was plowing on to the end.

"So long as men can breathe, or eyes can see.
So long lives this.
                    And this gives life to thee."

"I made a copy for you," he had told her, voice thick and almost choking. His sincerity touched her.

Jitka—really a very sweet person—was genuinely moved by Gordon's seriousness, and she decided that she would try to compensate him in a way that would be memorable. And...she did.

They stayed at a small inn in Bath and she found a way to repay for the honest gratitude she felt. The poem stayed with her, and months later, back in *la Belle France*, she decided to commit the poem that Gordon had memorized to recite for her.

Now, years later, miserable, filthy, sweating, sore in most of her body, hungry and churning with a thousand thoughts she could not control, Jitka tried to recall the lines she had once learned. Because of Gordon. Gordon Howe. *Bless you, Gordon.*

Gordon was, of course, in the past, at right at that moment, Jitka Malecek was an uncomfortable prisoner and rape victim at the hands of her captor, pirate emir, Abdallah. She suspected that he was interested in oral poetry and—other than song lyrics— she had but one at her command. *Maybe... ?*

"Shall I compare thee to a summer's day," she said, with as much feeling as she could muster.
"Thou art more lovely...and more temperate.
Rough winds do...."

After the exhausted, desperate girl had finished, she was rewarded, when Abdallah recited a poem of comparable length in Somali. It was totally incomprehensible to her. But she knew she had touched something human in this cruel animal.

Three days later—without a word of explanation, Abdallah removed her bonds. *Oh, Seigneur!* She was free to move around the apartment. She could use the toilet. The basin. It had running water. Oh! The words hadn't mattered. It was all in the rhythm.

She had been his captive just over six weeks. She washed herself three times. Consecutively.

As lawless as Somalia appeared to the outside world, there still existed, in many places, the skeleton of some type of civil government. The governing authority in Boosaaso was a committee of members of the dominant Darood clan, led by a former military man who now served as the harbormaster for the city's busy port. Boosaaso had for many years, been a major shipping center for livestock—cattle, sheep, goats, camels, and a few horses—destined for Yemen, Saudi Arabia or the Emirates.

Faraar Omaar had led the city's governing authority ever since the demise of *Afwayne*, President Siad Barré, in Mogadishu. Faraar was well-respected by clan leaders in the region and he had been forceful in managing the executions of more than a score of criminals convicted of capital crimes in clan deliberations.

Faraar Omaar and Abdallah were on friendly terms and on several occasions they had spent a pleasant afternoon together, chewing *qat*.

Faraar was fully aware of the presence of several gangs of Al-Shabab in the city. They had moved into an abandoned hotel at the city's eastern fringe. It had been built for Saudi investors who expected it to draw tourists to the nearby beach. But the faltering economy of a failing state, coupled with a less than optimum location, meant that it was never fully occupied in the two years required to fail as a business. It was still a new facility when the Shabab gangs arrived and displaced the caretakers. Omaar considered using Boosaaso's meager police force to displace the ruffians, but considering the relative firepower of both sides, he decided to wait and see how bad their presence would prove to be. For the first several months, they concentrated on acting as morality police in local souks and markets. But they soon grew tired of swatting women, many of whom were older than their mothers.

They became aware, as did many others in the city, that Abdallah was keeping a *gaalo* woman on the top floor of his building. It was commonly believed that Abdallah was committing adultery and engaging in all manner of evil deeds with the *gaalo*, and on occasion her cries had been heard by people in nearby buildings. Or so they claimed. After she was taken into Abdallah's custody, she was not seen again. A few people who claimed to have seen her said that she was beautiful, and was possibly a *djinn*.

This, to the youth of Al-Shabab, was an evil that could not be tolerated, even if Abdallah was willing to suffer the flames of hell for all eternity under the spell of this *gaalo* djinn.

Through his contacts at local mosques frequented by Al-Shabab members, Omaar got word that the youth were planning to capture and kill Abdallah's prisoner, and they were carefully plotting a violent assault on his compound. Omaar passed this word on to Abdallah.

The pirate commander pondered for several days, finally coming to the conclusion that an assault on his building would risk the safety of his wives and children, not to mention the other pirates, several of whom, unmarried, occupied parts of the second floor.

Did he want to force a showdown with this crazy Al-Shabab band? Already they had beheaded three Daroods found with crucifixes. They had many automatic weapons. If he faced them there would be losses on his side. If he surprised them in an ambush, more would come. Better to avoid the conflict by removing its cause.

Reluctantly, he decided to spare Jitka's life and return her to Djibouti. There was little need to explain details of the circumstances to her.

Half of his crew were at sea, under the command of One-arm Ali. He would take the second mother ship, a fifty-foot dhow, and transport the girl to Berbera. From there, two of his trusted men would drive her to one of the border crossings into Djibouti.

As an afterthought, he decided that he would return her camera, and allow her free rein to photograph his ship and any of his men during the trip down the coast to Berbera. He smiled to himself as he thought about the cleverness of his plan. If she was as good as she had led him to believe, the world would be able to see for themselves, the faces of Somali seamen who were not intimidated by anything afloat.

One week later, with details complete, Abdallah explained his plan to the astonished girl. She wept silently as she realized he was telling her the truth. She had been his prisoner for a bit over four months.

She owed her life—assuming he told the truth—to....? *Merci, merci!* To Jesus Christ? Gordon Howe? William Shakespeare? Silvio? Peter Weems? Jaamila? *Oh, Seigneur, Seigneur, merci, merci!*

"Left unchallenged, piracy is spiraling out of control, and now threatens the sea-lanes that transport almost half the world's cargo, including one-third of Europe's oil supplies. In addition, many of the proceeds from this modern day piracy may wind up underwriting an extreme Islamist movement. This collective inaction is another example of "the tragedy of the commons," in which decisions to pursue individual self-interest result in a public disaster—not least for the hundreds of sailors held hostage."

Pirates, Then and Now
(How Piracy Was Defeated in the Past and Can Be Again)
Max Boot
Foreign Affairs, July/August 2009

—54—Holidays in the USA

Thanksgiving was over and life was morphing into the dog days leading to Christmas. Melancholy days for an unattached serviceman who was grieving. Dick Emery had arranged with South Carolina to have Vance back in the states. The intention was good, but for Vance, the days hung heavy.

Now December was halfway gone and he was glad to see it go. Two thousand and nine had been a bad year. He could not bear to think that Jitka might be dead, but the alternative was almost as painful. She might be anywhere in Somalia. Or she might have been taken out of the country. Where could he even begin to look? He tried to will himself not to think of her, but that was impossible. Every time he touched his own arm, or his leg, the memory of her magical bones were overwhelming. *No, it was not a shitty year. She made it special.*

He was thinking about Jitka most of the time. About how she had made him feel. She had made him think he was capable of swimming across the Gulf of Aden and kicking the shit out of Yemen. She made him feel....*aah, let's just go with 'very good.'*

He was sitting beside the window of his small apartment in Norfolk where he had holed up over the dead period that occurs around Christmas. To keep from being a rootless male, he had kept a small place near Little Creek, after his split with Rhonda. There was nothing for him here, except that he could use the base facilities to check in with his superiors at the Pentagon. *As if they really give a damn.* He was...lost. Running five or six miles every day. On sandy beaches or trails. Sometimes with a pack of twenty pounds or more. Loneliness was gnawing at him and he had begun mentally undressing young women in public places. Still, he was not on the prowl. Jitka's memory held him in thrall.

Down in Carolina, his bosses at Uncle Bob's were away on holiday; probably somewhere in the Caribbean or else at a ski resort in Colorado. *These bastards have so much money they don't even know what to do with it all.* Again, he was wrong. They did know. And they were actually doing it. *Running, running. Jitka, Jitka. Where are you?*

It was the day after Christmas and, in coastal Virginia, a light rain had just morphed into snow. The temperature was dropping and it was cold enough for snow to stick . But the ground was wet and it wasn't cold enough for a hard freeze, so the light snow was turning to slush.

It will all be gone by tomorrow. But I'll still be here and what the hell am I going to do with myself? He was sitting by the window with a juice tumbler half full of rum and he was thinking about the total disaster he had made of his life.

After he had learned about Jitka's capture while traveling in Somalia, he had been disturbed and agitated far beyond anything he expected. And what about Silvio? What had happened to enable that remarkable gentleman to make it back to Djibouti?

Why did Jitka matter so much to him? Nothing *that* extraordinary had happened between them and he had not expected to feel such a strong attachment to the French girl after so little time. It was hardly as if she was the only girl he had known. *OK. The woman. She only looks like a girl.*

From his window in the apartment, he could see the early evening lights of cars on slushy highways, heading for shopping malls or other errands. It was pleasant not to have work, but the sensation of being alone at the holidays was not pleasing.

But bearable. He was, after all, a SEAL. And SEALs, unlike other men, are hardened against emotional responses. They have conditioned their minds, as well as their bodies, to endure hardships, stresses, pains and difficulties of every sort and to focus instead on the mission, the job, the task to be accomplished.

In the other room, his stereo was offering *Good King Wenceslas* by a group that he recognized as Mannheim Steamroller, and he thought, as he listened to the sound, that he had no idea when the Feast of Stephen took place. *Who the hell was Stephen? I could have used a better education. BYU sucks.*

But, as he had said to himself half a dozen times, it really had been a shitty year. Any way you look at it. He had decided to divorce his wife, and that had been like falling off a log. No problem there. It was better for both of them. No hard feelings. *Well, maybe a few.*

His career with the Navy was not much more encouraging. His years as a SEAL had been great. *But time at the Pentagon? A waste.* His superiors in the Pentagon had refused to take any of his recommendations concerning an appropriate response to piracy. Sometimes they looked at him as if he were insane. After following events closely for three plus years, his solutions were received as if he was either a lunatic or a blithering idiot. Possibly as a consequence, the Navy had given him an assignment that they described as an undercover role to penetrate the upper echelons of a questionable defense contractor. But it was now looking to him as if they had sent him into exile. So three years of effort, on what he hoped might be a career track, had led to an assignment that he could neither understand, nor enjoy.

The year's one bright spot occurred in Djibouti where he had the good fortune to meet a European girl who wanted to photograph Somali's pirates. A European girl? Curious way to describe someone as unique as Jitka. But was she English? Or was she French? *Fuck! Why don't I know that? I slept with her. And don't even know that? I never saw her passport.*

Well, it was *a bit more than that*, Vance. More than just the sleeping part, if that's what you want to call it. You not only slept with her, but you swallowed the subtle poison. And now you will never, never be quite the same. No, SEAL that you are, you will deny this, and even struggle against it. But, when the roll is called up yonder—whatever they do for SEALs—it will all become clear.

Then, of course, came the day where he learned that Jitka had disappeared into Somalia. That she was gone. Disappeared. Feared lost and quite possibly dead. In a lawless land where it was not possible to find her.

Not possible? But I'm a SEAL. We can find anyone. Anywhere. Find 'em and bring 'em out. That's what we're trained to do. And if, on rare occasions, we fail to accomplish our mission, there will be a trail of bodies of those who died in thwarting our mission.

Vance liked Mannheim Steamroller. They were kinda like the TransSiberian Railroad, a great group he saw once when they played D.C. That had been back when he was still married to Rhonda. Not so long ago, but it seemed much longer. He clicked the music off. *Jitka! Jitka!*

The divorce had come through while he was on assignment in Djibouti. Somehow, after all the hassle, receiving the final notification seemed anti-climactic. On the night he learned that the decree had been finalized, he had gone to dinner with Jitka and later they had spent the night at Silvio's place. It would be inaccurate to say that he didn't think of Rhonda, but it would not be accurate to believe that he missed her. Lying beside Jitka he wondered how he had ever come to marry Rhonda in the first place.

He poured another few ounces of rum into his tumbler and picked up the book he had been reading earlier in the day. The book had come earlier in the week and he was about halfway through it. It had been more interesting than he had expected. The book had been a gift from a young naval officer he had known at the Pentagon.

Sheila McKendrick was a Lieutenant, a Naval Academy grad, who appeared to have formed some kind of a crush on him. *OK. Let's not be coy about this.* She had fallen for him, for reasons he did not necessarily understand—or condone. Or encourage. But there it was. *Hot pants?* She was a model of decorum, but it was all out there for anyone to see. He did nothing—*believe me, I did nothing, thought nothing*—to encourage her, but neither did he do anything to hurt her feelings or demean what she was going through. She was, after all, still under thirty and it wasn't clear that she had ever been loved.

Look. Figure it out for yourself. He had been away from the Pentagon for over a year. Almost two. He had not given her his new addresses, and he had lived in several different locations. Yet this young woman had tracked him down. Not to harass him. Or to make demands. She had obtained a mailing address to send him a book. At Christmas. A present. She knew that he was interested in pirates and piracy, and she had found a book to interest him.

Lieutenant McKendrick, USN, had sent him an obscure book written by a Christian missionary, Joshua Himmelhoch. Himmelhoch was a Moravian missionary to China back in the decades preceding America's Civil War, and he carried a message intended to win converts to Jesus in a region of southern China that was plagued with bandits, pirates and criminals of every description.

Where the hell...? Where McKendrick found this old book, tattered and worn, was still a mystery to Vance who could hardly be called a book person. The printer's name seemed to have been deliberately omitted, but the cover page announced the title, "Pirates of South China's Seas and Estuaries," along with the notice that it had been printed in "Center City, Philadelphia," in 1877.

No wonder that the printer had not given any more precise information. The book described the activities of Chinese pirates from the perspective of an American missionary who had been converted to Buddhism by a Chinese prostitute he met—and married—in Canton. Around the 1840's America's young navy was sticking its nose into the affairs of China, along with Britain and other European countries who were trying to gain trade advantages.

Pirates had ravaged the South China Seas for decades, but after powerful ships of the world's armed navies began policing, many pirate organizations moved upriver, into the network of estuaries and the labyrinth of coastal islands that could provide protection to marauders.

Himmelhoch went overseas at age twenty-four, armed with the message of the Lord, but totally lacking in defenses against the wiles of a young woman who was beautiful, intelligent and highly motivated. Perhaps the gentlest interpretation to put on what happened would be to say that Mei Ling knew exactly what she wanted from life, but Joshua Himmelhoch did not.

Since Himmelhoch was the one who wrote the book, we—or in this case, Vance—will only get to hear one side of the story. But that may be adequate, since the author was good at storytelling and his description of river pirates was compelling.

One of the more interesting sections of the books was the part where the youthful missionary, full of the enthusiasm encouraged by his Moravian sponsors, first realized that Buddhism could contain messages worth hearing.

When Vance got the old book he took a quick look, smiled to remember Sheila McKendrick; remembered her with some warmth—*but no lust*—and set it to one side. Then, alone on Christmas day, he had picked it up and begun reading.

Chapter One was just a brief summary of the young man's youth and origins in central Pennslyvania, but in Chapter Two, Himmelhoch had reached China and met the young woman who was going to turn his world upside down. The part that had the greatest impact on Vance was the part where Mei Ling was describing to young Joshua—Vance wondered how they might have been clothed at the time—the meaning of All Souls Festival as practiced in southeastern China.

The Festival honored souls of the departed, a common practice around the world, but the pirates, as described by Mei Ling to Himmelhoch, took a special interest in "orphan ghosts." These were described in Chinese language translated by Himmelhoch.

"There are those who died for reasons that we no longer know. Amongst them are those who died from cruel wounds in battle, those who died from flood and fire and bandits, those who saw their property seized and so took their own lives, married women and young girls seized by force and killed, those who while being punished died unjustly, those who fled from natural calamities and died from illness on the road, those destroyed by wild animals or poisonous snakes, those who died from famine or exposure, those who were caught up in wars and lost their lives, those who killed themselves because of danger, those crushed to death when walls or houses collapsed on them, or those who after their deaths left no sons or grandsons."

Orphan ghosts? Vance read the description of the orphan ghosts three times, and for some reason the words had an appeal for him. *Maybe we're not all that different from Buddhists, or even from those towel-headed Islamic bastards reading their Qurans.* The Chinese spoke of compassion in a way that could appeal to him as a warrior; and all the more since it was purported to reflect the thoughts of violent pirates who sometimes sawed captives in half in order to terrorize other prisoners and compel larger ransoms. *Sawed? Longitudinally?*

This catalogue of evils, as Vance saw it, was far from complete; but even after he had closed the book he went back to read the description of orphan ghosts one more time.

The companionship of a woman would be nice. He thought of trying to locate the Lieutenant and calling to thank her. A phone call couldn't hurt. Could it? But he could hear Jitka's laughter and it was directed at him. *What? A phone call wouldn't hurt anything. Don't you think I should call just to thank her?*

Peut-être. It was as if he could hear the photographer.

Outside, it was beginning to get dark and Vance was debating whether to thaw a TV dinner or slip out and find a place where he could get food. He had wasted much of the afternoon, and had consumed slightly more alcohol than normal to avoid thinking about his next visit to Djibouti with Uncle Bob's. His bosses in South Carolina were expecting him to come up with a plan to draw attention to the role of security contractors in some dramatic way—dramatic, yet positive, that would focus public attention in the same way as the SEAL snipers who rescued the American skipper from pirate hands.

Vance had plenty of ideas, but they all resulted in a lot of dead pirates, and he knew that if he pursued any of these approaches they would all be career-enders as far as the U.S. Navy was concerned. Or make him subject to criminal prosecution. *A rock and a hard place.* Of course, now that he had no dependent, he was always free to resign his commission and try some of his own ideas. *Jitka! Jitka! Jitka!*

He could feel the pressure building. *Jitka!* He was going to do something violent. Hopefully not foolish. But violent, nonetheless.

Just before Christmas, the message from Uncle Bob's had scheduled him to return to Djibouti before the New Year began.

"Nairobi, Kenya—Striking into the heavily patrolled Gulf of Aden, Somali pirates seized a British-flagged chemical tanker on the same day that a ship was taken by brigands in the Indian Ocean, officials said Tuesday.

The double hijacking late Mondays comes a year after an international naval armada began deploying off Somalia to protect shipping. Monday's attacks happened about 1,000 miles apart."

"Somali pirates hijack two ships 'at once' "
The Associated Press
In:USA Today, December 30, 2008

—55—Returning to Djibouti

Silvio had limped back across the border with blistered, bleeding feet and a recently dislocated shoulder. Months later, when she managed to straggle across to the guard station, Jitka's condition was even more pitiable. She had lost just over twenty pounds, roughly fifteen percent of her normal body weight. She was sick with an unidentified systemic infection; she had a yeast infection contracted from her rapist, and she was two months pregnant. This, she suspected and feared, but had not confirmed because weight loss had disrupted her regular periods.

The trip back from Boosaaso had been made primarily in a captured diesel-powered trawler. The trawler, with crew of ten armed pirates—Abdallah included—took her to Berbera. There, Abdallah and five hand-picked subordinates took her to Seylac which was less than twenty-five kilometers from the border crossing into Djibouti. This short leg was also made by sea, in a small dhow.

From the dockside, Abdallah had a hired car pick the girl up. She was unsteady on her legs after the long confinement. Abdallah watched with glasses to see her across and in the hands of Djibouti's border guards. He had arranged to have payoffs made on the Somali side. She crossed easily, but entry was a problem. The exhausted girl was released into the custody of French military personnel after several hours of administrative dithering by Djibouti border guards. Despite delays, the girl was overwhelmed with relief at being on the road to freedom. By early evening she was receiving care in Djibouti's French Naval Hospital, clean, in a clean bed. One of her biggest shocks of the day had been seeing herself in the bathroom mirror.

In early January, Vance Morrisette returned to Djibouti. It was a gloomy trip for him, because he spent a good bit of the flight time thinking about Jitka and what might have happened to her.

Just before he left Virginia on the flight to Dulles, the news had been full of the latest pirate hijacking. Actually, two attacks had been successful at the same time, and even though they occurred a thousand miles apart, they were referred to as the "double hijackings."

This trip, when he reached Djibouti, he was given a room on the floor of a hotel that had been reserved solely for the use of contract personnel from Uncle Bob's.

Early the next morning, Vance visited Dick Emery in his office. Emery's contacts in Djibouti's Security Service had already notified him that the French girl had returned and was in the hospital. He lacked details, but his immediately passed the information on to Vance.

Uncharacteristically, Emery left his desk and gave Vance a comradely hug.

"Welcome back, Commander. I have some wonderful news for you." Vance was stunned to hear.

"Where is she now?" Emery handed him keys to the vehicle.

"French hospital. I won't come with you this time. She won't want to see me."

Vance ran down the steps.

"I'm glad to see you back, Jitka."

"Thank you."

"Very glad."

"Thank you, Vance. Yes. And I—you."

He felt that his face might be cracking apart. Two orderlies entered the room noiselessly, with a gurney, Ignoring Vance, they prepared to move her.

"They are taking me for more tests. I should be back by noon."

"I hope that I can see you again."

"Yes. I, too. To see you."

"I'll be here when you get back."

The two burly orderlies slipped her onto the gurney as if she was weightless, and they were gone—on silent tires.

Vance put his hands over his face. He hardly knew what he was feeling. The only word came to mind was....gratitude.

Thank you! Thank you! Thank you!

She was gone for just over two hours and was clearly exhausted when she returned. He could see she needed to sleep. Nevertheless, they talked for twenty minutes or so and most of what they said hardly need to be repeated here. She told him some of the things that had been done to her, but she couldn't tell everything. He didn't ask any probing questions, only queried her about how she was feeling, if she was getting enough to eat, if she wanted him to do anything. He held her hand as they talked, but that, too, was depressing, because it was limp as a glove and he could see that she was still distressed. Perhaps his presence was somehow making her feel worse. He asked her if he could come tomorrow. She nodded wordlessly... *Yes.*

Walking out on the corridor where a local *Somali--looking* man was buffing the waxed floor, Vance had a momentary urge to take the machine and smash the man, but it was a fleeting impulse. Still, the rage in him was there; he could feel it building. It had been simmering for years, as his Navy, and the navies of the world refused to confront Somali—*and fucking Yemeni*— pirates in the only way that would be likely to succeed.

Recently, his feelings alternated between plain rage and terrifyingly violent rage. What he experienced surprised him because he knew that rage was not good; it blinded one to reason, and when he had been on dangerous missions in the past, no matter what the objectives or the risks, he had always managed to stay collected. He was surprised to feel himself going over some kind of edge where his thoughts were black, murderous, heedless of consequences. This, he knew, was not good. But there it was.

On the following day he was able to obtain a rental vehicle and he headed immediately for Silvio's compound—to compare notes. It was a gamble. He wasn't sure if the professor was even in the country and he was too impatient to call. He wanted to catch him early so he could be at the hospital after she had breakfast.

He was in luck. Silvio was there and the old Italian greeted him with warmth and moist eyes. He had not received the good news and he was elated to learn that Jitka was not only alive, but that she was in Djibouti City. She, of course, believed that he was dead or in captivity, so had not asked to have him contacted.

Then—the bad news for Silvio. She was currently in the hospital where she was being treated for a number of unspecified problems. She had been admitted to the French Naval Hospital so a few strings had to be pulled before both men could see her at the same time.

Silvio's heart sank when he finally got to see her, and he was almost sorry that he had come. In addition to the weight she had lost and the bruises and scars that were still visible, her face was so glum that her sadness was contagious. Vance was not indifferent to her ravaged condition, but it wasn't unexpected and many weeks ago he had decided that if she returned alive, he would cherish her in any condition. This is a difficult decision for anyone to make; even harder to practice. It was a vow he had made to himself.

The first several days of his return passed in a blur and Emery helped by keeping him free of any type of assigned task. His underlying duty to the U.S. Navy—to what could only be described as an undercover investigation of a legitimate American security contractor—had probably been given to him as a means of punishment, to get him out of the way. That possibility had begun to dominate his thinking. Or to sidetrack him from positions where he might have been a possible embarrassment to the Navy...or to DOD.

None of the foreign naval officers he had met in Djibouti had expressed satisfaction with the orders they had been given concerning pirate abatement. Junior officers in the U.S Navy would complain vocally about having their hands tied. Senior officers, more experienced in the requirements of military hierarchies, were reluctant to voice opinions.

The upper echelons of his "employers" in Carolina also expressed displeasure with the extent and scope of their activities. But again, it was the dudes, the cowboys, crackers—ex-grunts wearing khakis and dark sunglasses—who were the most vocal. The suits in offices were more politic and if they complained, it was probably to one another, in private rooms. *Over expensive whiskey.* Vance had already put his cards on the table, but he had failed to make much of an impression.

Although he had held back questioning Jitka about her experience, one question he did ask caused her to pour gasoline on the fire that was already raging in his brain.

"Do you know where they kept you while you were locked up?"

"Yes." Her voice sounded as if it had been shredded. "I was in Boosaaso. One block back from the waterfront road. It was a big apartment. Four stories I believe, and I was held in a rooftop..." Her voice began to give out and tears ran out of both eyes, "...in a rooftop apartment. Like a penthouse. Used as an office. By the pirate leader." She hesitated, and looked at the ceiling.

At that moment if a pirate had been within reach, Vance might have strangled him on the spot. "His name was Abdallah."

Back in his hotel room, Vance pulled his chair to the balcony window and looked out over the city's rooftops at the harbor beyond. Half a dozen warships of the world's navies were visible in the distance, and he knew that every one was surrounded by a defensive perimeter intended to prevent another disaster like the *USS Cole* bombing in Yemen. Heavily-armed patrol craft glided endlessly, on constant watch for any hint of a security breach. There was constant movement in the military anchorage.

Trained as a SEAL leader, Vance knew that a team could probably get ashore undetected at Boosaaso and that within thirty minutes the pirate's lair—occupants included—could be reduced to a pile of body-filled rubble. He was also reasonably certain that—given the proper authorizations—all this could probably take place within 72 hours.

Last year the number of naval ships patrolling the Gulf of Aden—armed with the world's newest and most potent military technology—increased substantially, but their impact on piracy was negligible. On the flight over, Vance had read the latest report that was faxed to him from Uncle Bob's. The report from the piracy reporting center in Kuala Lumpur extolled the fact that the success rate of pirate attacks had declined in the presence of naval warships in the region.

This kind of reporting annoyed Vance. It was true that the success rate had declined. More attacks were being thwarted. But the number of attempts had risen significantly, from 111 in 2008 to 214 in December 2009 when the report was received. So, even though the percentage of successes was down, the total number was up. Forty-seven successful attacks were made in 2009. *That's almost one a week. We're just kidding ourselves with declining success rates.*

The number of attacks was rising steadily, year after year. Now, officials of the struggling, ineffective Somali government was suggesting that pirate bands should be pursued onto their land-based havens. It was an invitation— from one of the planet's least hospitable places.

Returning from the hospital, Vance thought about Jitka's limp hand and feel of each small bone in her fingers. He had felt each one separately. He recalled one of the last nights they spent together when he lay awake, listening to her breathing. He remembered the jut of her hip bone, the delicious feel of her body's curve from hip to waist, and the thin covering of flesh at the iliac crest. That bone lay not more than a quarter inch below the skin. It felt so wonderful to his hand that he had gotten another erection and laughed at himself. She had seemed to him, at that moment, something of a miracle, even as she stirred, as if sensing his touch and his thoughts.

Another time while feeling the bones of her feet and ankles, he had palpated her tibia under its thin tissue of skin.

"You broke this," he said, but it was intended as a question.

"Can you still feel it?" she answered.

"Just a bit. Just barely. What happened?"

"It was years ago. When I first went to school in England. I was riding a bicycle along a canal towpath with some girlfriends, but I was interested in taking photographs of some of the canal boats and the people who live on them. The British have a word for people who do what I was doing."

"So what happened?"

"I was trying to frame a shot while the bike was still moving. I didn't want to seem too nosy."

"And then?"

"Then my bicycle went off the embankment. It was a real cock-up. I battered my camera. The bike was OK."

"And also your leg."

"Yes. Well...."

"Well?"

"Well, perhaps I deserved it. I was being a *gongoosler*. Someone who peeks into canal boats."

The part that was new for Vance was that every time—*every fucking time*—he was with Jitka, he felt happy. Just being with her. Even just in the same room. Even looking like a scarecrow. It was new for him. He couldn't understand it. But he liked it. *Actually, I think I need it.*

What he didn't like was the idea of someone deliberately inflicting pain and torture on this woman. No one should be allowed to get away with that.

The question is, what am I gonna do about it? What if I was CNO and could order any kind of strike that would do the job? One thing for sure. Someone in Boosaaso would feel the pain.

Then the pragmatism began to take over. He started to think about a hypothetical team. About a hypothetical delivery vessel. Hypothetical weapons. A provisional timetable. Contingency plans. The five-paragraph field order. He was, after all, a SEAL.

Slowly, a plan began to form. The orphan ghost of a plan.

"This week America made its most brazen and daring foray into Somalia since the early 1990s, reportedly killing Saleh Ali Nabhan, a Kenyan of Yemeni descent, who had been suspected of an al-Qaeda attack on a hotel in the Kenyan port of Mombasa in 2002.

The American commandos flew in daylight from helicopters from a naval ship off Somalia's coast, attacking Mr. Nabhan and a score of other foreign and Somali fighters as they drove in two lorries across the desert. Mr. Nabhan's body was zipped up with body parts of other fighters and taken to a freezer on the ship for DNA analysis."

"The long arm of America"
Al-Qaeda in Somalia
The Economist, September 19, 2009

—56—Hospital Visits

In Djibouti's French Naval Hospital, Jitka took some consolation from Vance visits, but she was damaged and she could not tell him the things she had done to survive. While she had not begged for her life, she had attempted to propose a bargain with Abdallah that he could not refuse. She was embarrassed by her actions and wished she could have behaved differently. Now, alive, she was seriously considering reneging on every promise she swore to Abdallah to obtain her release. And though she was willing and eager to accept the warmth and protection offered by Vance, she could not reveal everything to him because of the shame she felt.

Vance, long separated from Rhonda, was lonely for another relationship and just waking up to the fact that he was falling—had fallen—in love with Jitka. But Jitka, though she liked Vance and wouldn't have minded keeping him in her life, was not going to expend too much effort on him because she had other goals with higher priority. And right now, her key question was what—if anything—to do with these photos smoldering in her memory cards. Her captor had allowed her to photograph his crews at sea, both on board both the trawler and the dhow. Despite her weakness, she had framed over two hundred images on her voyage back to Seylac. She would have liked to even the score with Abdallah. But how best? To use them? Or destroy them?

It never entered her mind that Vance would like nothing more than to be her avenger.

After Vance's fourth visit to Jitka, he was depressed, angry and—he recognized—prone to hostility. The girl had not improved much and he had stepped outside her room to speak with a doctor who had just looked in on her.

"You are not her husband?" the doctor asked.

"Her brother," Vance lied. "Actually her step brother. Our parents are in France." That part was true. For her, at least.

"She has been in surgery yesterday," the doctor said. He seemed uninterested. "She was pregnant and she would not carry an infant. We found someone from the States to do the procedure. She had been raped, and she was almost hysterical. Now she is calm but very depressed." The doctor walked away scowling. He had refused to perform the D&C for religious reasons.

Can I believe this? Her rapist had impregnated her. Vance had already learned that the expression 'seeing red' was more than a metaphor for anger. It actually happened to him. Like now. No wonder she was sad and depressed. If Vance had known that this doctor had refused to do the procedure and that the girl had asked Silvio to find someone for her, he might have punched the French doctor. Jitka's problems were both physical and mental.

Outside the hospital, he had spent a little time talking to a few sympathetic colleagues from Uncle Bob's, some of whom had met Jitka in the past. He had carefully sounded them out to see if he could detect any vigilante temperaments who might possible be recruited to join him, in some as yet undefined, unauthorized—and probably career-ending—actions that he was contemplating. He had proceeded carefully because he didn't want to solicit anyone to join him and meet with refusal.

In the days spanning Vance's hospital visits to Jitka, his frustration and rage grew by the minute. Several afternoons he dropped in to rant at Dick Emery about work-related issues. It was a transparent form of diversion.

"Tell me straight up, Dick. Do these guys back home have any idea what's going on out here?"

"In what sense, Vance? I'm not tracking with you."

"Do they understand what is going on between the Navy, NATO, and the European Union Naval Forces deployed here?"

"I'm sure they must, Vance. We have some smart people in the front office. You know them all. They've been around the block."

"They know that our command is split?"

"Split? In what sense?"

"Jesus Christ, Dick. Don't you get it, either?"

"Kiss my ass, Vance. We can't all be as smart as you."

"Look, Dick, the Dutch have two ships here. One is attached to the NATO command, same as our navy, the other is connected to EUNAVFOR, the European Union's force."

"So? They're both escorting merchant vessels."

"But the EU has negotiated an arrangement with Kenya. If they apprehend pirates, the captured crew can be handed over to Kenya to be jailed and tried as criminals. But if any NATO ship captures the same pirates, for the same offense, they are simply released. NATO hasn't cut any kind of deal with Kenya. Doesn't this strike you as insane?" Vance was agitated, coming off the edge of his chair. "The EU is running their whole show, and they have a plan. NATO, and the whole goddam United States Navy, who once paid you and me, have got *butkus, nada, fuck all*. Doesn't this seem crazy to you?"

"Sure it does. Like a lot of other things on this fucking planet. If you stopped all the things that are crazy, there wouldn't be much going on, so..."

"Oh, fuck you, my friend. You aren't a lot better tha.."

"Hold on, mister. Hold on and listen up. What do you think happens to the sea monkeys that EUNAV turns over to Kenya? You think they take them jiboneys out to a yardarm somewhere and string 'em up? It just takes 'em a couple weeks longer to get home, that's all."

"Y'know, Dick, I question what you just told me. I don't know for sure. You could be right. But I'm skeptical. I think Kenya has functioning law enforcement, and a working court system. It's not the Hague, but it's a damn sight better than turning them loose."

"I think you may be a bit naive, Vance. No disrespect. But the pirates—many of them—are awash in more cash than they ever had. Some of it can be used to bribe their Kenyan captors. You really think that Kenya gives a flying fuck about the European Union? No. You know better."

The conversation went on in this vein for several more minutes but it was just a continuation of the same stuff; swing and duck, thrust and parry, and both men knew that little would be gained if either man lost his temper.

Emery brought things to a close by the simple expedient of unlocking a cabinet and taking out a bottle of Mauritian rum. "Let's give this a rest and resume it later." *Yeah. Next week or next year.*

"Sure, chief." Vance left after one token drink because he was headed for the hospital.

Half of the contract security types hired by Uncle Bob had gone downhill, from too much booze or beer, or sex, or lack of exercise. They seemed to him to be throwbacks to the declining years of the old west. Probably too slow on the draw to be of much use at the corral gunfight.

In the navy, his Navy, there wasn't a soul he could count on to take the plunge with him into uncharted waters. Not surprising really. Going rogue is a cute expression, so long as it refers to moderate risks—like going without underwear—but when it means fastening to an unknown zip line in total darkness and zooming down to help a friend, it's a whole different matter.

Several things had become clear to him. First, there was no action that he could take—personally—against the pirate gang and pirate leader who had raped Jitka. Second, the distance to Boosaaso was too great for him to attempt anything alone. *Second verse, same as the first.*

Third, if he didn't find some way open for him to get revenge, even at the cost of his career or life, he would never be happy. *Crazy. But there it is.*

Fourth. He was just starting to acknowledge that he was in love with this French girl. It came as a shock when he realized it. *Damn.* Only now, seeing her so hurt, had it become so clear. Even if he could never win her, he still realized that he loved her. It was nothing like with Rhonda. Or any of the others. That was simple lust. This was something different. Different and new.

After his last visit to Jitka, he left the hospital with Silvio, who had been there when he arrived. "Come back to my place and spend the night, my friend. You could probably take a small glass of brandy. I know that you must be very sad. But she will improve. I am sure of it."

That evening, after a quiet dinner with Silvio, the two men moved out on the terrace with their snifters filled with old Italian's choice brandy.

"I am thinking that you love this girl. Am I correct?"

"Yes." It was the first time he had admitted it to anyone other than himself.

"And you would like to kill the man—or men—who raped her."

"Yes."

"And you know they are all Muslims. If you succeeded in killing him—or them—the world would label you as a criminal. Guilty of what your country calls a hate crime.

"If he worked for the Pope it wouldn't matter to me. That has nothing to do with it."

"We might discuss that at another time. When your feelings are not so close to the surface. But you do realize that what I said is true?"

So she has already told Silvio. "Yes."

"I think, my friend, looking at you, that you may be contemplating some rash action."

"What is this, Silvio? Are you some kind of profiler? You can't know what I'm thinking. Or feeling."

"You are a man. I am a man. We both know how men think about these things."

"Or what I'm capable of. But I'm alone on this one, Silvio. There's no one I can talk to about what I would like to do."

"*Au contraire*, Vance. There are many like you who would welcome a chance to strike at and kill pirates. To rid the world of these pests."

'Well, I have yet to...'"

"Unfortunately, many of those most capable of carrying out these wishes also hate Muslim extremists. For a variety of reasons. Many of them valid."

"Yeah, well... they're all hiding."

"They are right here. In Djibouti."

Vance swallowed the last drops from his snifter, placed it on the table and put both hands on the table edge, to look Silvio square in the face.

"Why do you tell me this, Silvio? I have admitted that I would willingly kill the son-of-a-bitch that did this to Jitka. She even told me his name. It's Abdallah. Something like that. A common name."

"And you think that you could find him."

"I know that I could find him. Yesterday, I used Google Earth to visit Boosaaso and I saw the rooftop apartment where this bastard chained Jitka to a bed. He is a pirate commander. Right now, as we speak, our navy could drop a bomb right on top of the desk where he endorses his checks from shipping companies. Goddammit, Silvio, would you tolerate this if you could do something about it?"

"Do not swear, my friend. You do not need to curse so much. This is why we are talking now. So we can perhaps find a way to do something about what disturbs you. I am angry, too. But I have an old man's anger. You have a young man's anger. My hunger for revenge is different from yours. Yours is hot. Mine is as cold as ice. You must bear with me."

Over the next hour, Silvio told Vance about a community of Italians living in Djibouti whose families had once been businessmen or landowners in Somalia. Some of these men were the children or grandchildren of Italians who had been displaced, robbed or in some cases killed by Somalis. Some of these men had criminal or underworld connections and many were connected to former military organizations or to intelligence agencies for various nations.

The youngest and most capable of this group enjoyed some degree of financial independence, either based on their own work or by inheritance. Many were essentially operating as free-lance agents for organized crime, or for government agencies. Even such peaceful groups as UNESCO sometimes needed to hire forceful and competent security agents. The men Silvio described were usually hired through front organizations, layered shells that had been erected around those quintessentially dishonest words, "plausible deniability."

Vance listened to Silvio's description of men whose parents and grandparents had been his friends. He was highly skeptical of the ability of such men to engage in anything resembling a military operation, but he listened respectfully until Silvio seemed to be talked out. By that time, the brandy bottle was half-empty.

One of the more interesting facts of Silvio's descriptions was that most of the young men to whom he referred were multilingual in Italian, French and Somali. With some English. Residents of Djibouti.

"Thank you for sharing all this information with me, Silvio. I really don't know what to make of it, except that I'll think about it for some time and see what conclusions I can draw."

"One more thing to keep in mind, Vance. These younger men, are, for the most part, financially secure. They are physically fit, they despise Islamic fundamentalists, Somali pirates, Somalis in general, and they are frequently inflated by their pride of ancestry. In this regard, they are not so different from the Somalis they detest. The key thing for you to know is that they could probably be engaged in the right crusade—I choose this word deliberately—for very little money. It would not take much. Think on this." Silvio screwed the cap tight on the brandy bottle. "Now, you need to sleep."

The beds in Silvio's place were comfortable, but Vance didn't fall asleep quickly. The room he was given was one he had shared with Jitka. Lying awake in Silvio's tiny guestroom, Vance remembered a conversation in UBSA's Djibouti field office.

Vance had gone in on the day after he arrived from the States. After the perfunctory greeting, his boss had blurted out a question that was puzzling him.

"What the hell is behind this?" he asked, waving a sheet of paper. The message said that Vance was to be advanced fifty thousand U.S. dollars any time he made a request in which he used the expression, "to pull a rabbit out of the hat."

"What the fuck is that supposed to mean?" he asked.

Vance laughed. "It was probably just a joke," he lied. "I can't even remember the conversation." That part was a bigger lie.

"Bullshit," the boss said. "It's not a joke to me. If you come in with that 'white rabbit' line I'll be expected to come up with the cash for you. Or else it could be my ass. It's in writing. I don't get a lot of instructions in writing. As you might guess."

Now, lying alone in a bed full of memories, Vance began replaying his tapes to recall the exact nature of the conversation he had held with the big honcho back in South Carolina.

The thing that had triggered the conversation was the episode of the *Maersk Alabama* that made world news in April, 2009. Somali pirates boarded the American-flagged ship bound for Mombasa, Kenya with a cargo of food aid for Somalia and Uganda. The Somali pirates were foiled by aggressive actions of the crew, but the ship's skipper, Captain Richard Phillips, a graduate of the Massachusetts Maritime Academy, was taken hostage.

Newspapers around the world carried the story of the crew's resistance and the captain's capture for ransom. Coverage intensified after U.S. Navy SEALs parachuted to the scene. They intervened effectively by having trained snipers pick off three pirates. Subsequently, the skipper was recovered safely. He was reunited with his ship and crew in Mombasa. For several days the story of the hijacking, capture of the skipper, his recovery, death of the marauding pirates, and details of the whole drama, played out in the world's media.

The impact of this publicity was not lost by the front office leading Uncle Bob's—as the big boss had made clear.

"You were a SEAL. An officer. Do you think you could ever lead an activity like that as part of UBSA's security organization?"

"Given the right opportunity. Of course."

"But how about creating the opportunity?"

"Are we singing from the same hymnal? The opportunities abound. You know the statistics. This year the boarding attempts are occurring at the rate of about four a week. Better than one every two days. You could use a whole stadium full of snipers, if anyone cared to give a go-ahead to shoot."

"Vance, the reason we pay you more than the Navy did is because we know you can think. We want you to find a way to go out of the box. Those snipers got millions of dollars in publicity for the SEALs. Christ's sake, you were a SEAL. Those SEAL snipers won't have to pay for pussy for the next five years. Just wear the tee-shirt."

"Those shooters were cleared to shoot at the highest levels."

"Vance, don't get testy. It's not productive. We want....we expect you to come up with ways to do these kind of things...to get the kind of press, that SEALs got when they popped those fuckin' sand niggers."

"It's not that easy."

"Goddammit Vance, *make* it that easy. That's why you're here. We want to help you do it. Not get in your way. Think. Be creative. Go out of the box. Spend money. Buy talent. We don't expect you to do everything yourself. Get help when you need it."

"You're sending me to Djibouti, where I can't even carry a sidearm, to accomplish this? Gee. Lucky me."

"Vance, Listen carefully. When you're in Djibouti, if you need money to get something done, all you have to do is go to your mission chief and ask for it. The key phrase will be 'pulling a white rabbit out of a hat.' When you ask for money, and follow up the request with 'pulling a white rabbit out a fucking hat,' you'll get the cash. In American dollars. Immediately. Trust me on this. But don't do it unless you come up with something good."

"Why am I just hearing this now?"

"Shut up and listen. You didn't need to hear it before. And here's the kicker for you. If you spend the fifty grand and do something that comes close to getting the publicity garnered by the *Maersk Alabama*, there will be another fifty grand for you when you get home. We have a line item in the budget for PR."

Lying alone in the bed at Silvio's place, Vance could see the tail end of a full moon through the skylight in the ceiling. It lit the room with a ghostly light and he could sense Jitka's presence, as she was in the past. *And will be again, if I can help it.*

He thought about Silvio's words. About thinking out of the box. People were killing their mortal enemies long before the SEALs were formed. Before the U.S. was even a nation. Silvio had probably hit the nail on the head. There was plenty he could learn from the Italians if he just opened his mind.

When the words formed, he spoke out loud, surprising himself. He was talking to Jitka. *Hang in there, love. I'm working for you. Get better. Come back for me. Come back to me.*

Finally, he fell asleep.

"Nature hath made men so equall, in the faculties of body, and mind; as that though there bee found one man sometimes manifestly stronger in body, or of quicker mind than another; yet when all is reckoned together, the difference between man, and man, is not so considerable, as that one man can thereupon claim to himselfe any benefit, to which another may not pretend as well as he. For as to the strength of body, the weakest has the strength to kill the strongest, either by secret machination, or by confederacy with others, that are in the same danger with himselfe."

> "Leviathan"
> Chapter XIII, Of the Naturall Condition of Mankind,
> as concerning their Felicity, and Misery
> Thomas Hobbes

—57—Silvio's Vengeance

At breakfast, as Silvio's guest, Vance seemed to be calmer than he had been since returning to Djibouti. He had slept soundly after he finally dropped off. As Silvio was pouring a coffee for him he made his decision.

"I would be grateful for any help you can provide, Silvio." The old Italian smiled and hesitated for several moments before replying.

"Good. Then I will make a few phone calls and perhaps you can meet some friends of mine. Maybe even later today. Do you like this bread? It was just baked this morning."

The meeting occurred in what had been one of the old European sections near the waterfront. They went into a dive shop that Vance had visited several times before and where he had spoken to shopkeepers in the past. The shop sold all types of scuba gear, swim fins and diving equipment. They also refilled air tanks, and scheduled occasional trips to popular local dive sites.

Vance was surprised when they passed through the shop and entered a small office in a back room. Three men were in the room. Silvio introduced everyone.

"First names only. We have no need for full names. This is Vance. An American. Vance, this is Anthony, Nikos and Rafael. Anthony owns this shop."

Shaking hands, Vance addressed Anthony. "I have been in your place before. But I can't remember seeing you in the past."

"You have been in several times, Vance. I remember seeing you, but I am not in front often."

The men were sitting in plastic chairs and Anthony came from behind his cluttered desk to join them in a small circle.

"Vance has a problem which could require the help of some capable men."

What the hell am I doing? Vance thought. *I don't know any of these bastards. I don't really know Silvio. These guys could be working for anyone. Russia, MI-5, France, Fuck. Israel. Even China. What am I getting myself into? I know better than this.*

Then the image of Jitka flashed through his mind and he decided to see where this might lead. In recent weeks he had come to believe that his superiors at the Navy had hung him out to dry as a maverick. *Less violent than throwing me under a bus.* UBSA apparently had expectations for him that he was failing to fulfill. He was out of active service with the SEALs where he had really felt competent and capable in the past. The only thing going in his life that made him feel happy was Jitka and she was lying in a hospital bed, with a line in both arms. *Let the chips fall where they may.*

Silvio was still talking to his three friends. Vance had looked them over on entering the room. No body fat on any of them. No paunches. These three were all lean and wiry. Tanned and fit. No hair oil, no after shave. These men were not body builders. There was no way to determine anything about their overall condition and stamina, but superficially there was no reason to suspect they were not fit.

Usually the people that hung around dive shops could be expected to know how to swim. They were all sun-darkened and fit-looking, Mediterranean-style, but Nikos had a nasty scar on his right cheek, running from eye socket to chin. It was obviously meant to disfigure, not to kill, and Vance knew there was a good story behind it. Involving more than two people.

He focussed back on what Silvio was telling the trio.

"Vance is here as an employee of an American security contractor. He is a former military man. Now a civilian employee under contract to the U.S. Department of Defense. His civilian employers want him to take some dramatic action against the Somali pirates. Something that will get them, and their services, into the news. They are willing to bend their own laws and spend money to do it. But their problem is—how to say this?—a certain lack of boldness in decision makers. Dare I call it timidity? So Vance wants to take—as Americans put it—the horns of the bull."

Silvio paused. *Damn,* Vance thought, *Did I actually tell him all this? I don't think so. But he seems to have been reading my mind.*

Nikos leaned forward and touched Vance's arm with one finger. "Tell us, American Vance. Is this accurate? Has he spoken correctly of what you would like to do? Kill some pirates?"

What the hell, Vance thought. *I've come this far. Let's see what happens.*

"Gentlemen, Silvio has stated my intentions in a much clearer fashion than I could have done myself. But let me elaborate."

"One moment," Rafael said as he nudged Nikos. Nikos held up his hand for silence and whistled twice. A clerk from out front came running in, and Nikos made a circling motion with his hand; around the table. The young man opened a wall cabinet to bring out an unopened bottle of *Ouzo* and five tiny glasses. He quickly screwed the cap off the bottle before ducking out of the room. "Go ahead," Nikos said, as he poured each glass full to the brim.

"I want to make a strike against the pirates. Specifically, I want to destroy a pirate den. A particular den. This one is located in Boosaaso. It is the only one for which I am certain of the chief's location. I want to destroy that building and everything in it. My interest is both professional and personal."

Anthony grunted. "Destroy a building?"

"It's a four story building. Five with its rooftop penthouse. Probably built by Europeans a hundred years ago. It should come down easily."

"And who is in this building?"

"Pirates. The pirate commander. Their chief, their emir, and an unknown number of other pirates."

"And their families?"

"Probably. I can't be certain. But that's possibly correct. I hope this will not be a shock to you gentlemen, but I'll be frank. I do not give a rat's ass how many people I kill as long as I get the fucking chief. The leader. If this is a problem with anyone, tell me now." There was no reaction around the table.

"I also want to destroy any of the ships on the waterfront that look as if they might be mother ships for pirate attacks. If I can. This part may be a lot harder. There are a lot of ships in that harbor." This, he knew as he spoke, was pure hubris.

"But they will just buy, or capture, new vessels to use."

"Not the way I want to do it. I want to mine them so they only blow apart after they are crewed and away from the dock. I want to take the crews with them. But first, we focus on the building."

"And you plan to do this....how?"

"This is our first meeting, gents. Don't ask to know everything all at once."

Silvio held up his palm to speak. "We are all friends here, because I am in a position to know these things. We all want the same things. So let us proceed slowly and listen to one another carefully." While he was speaking, he topped off all the small glasses and then raised his as if make a toast. The other four glasses were lifted. "To the death of Somali pirates." Five toasts disappeared down the hatch.

The meeting broke up an hour later with an agreement to meet later that same evening.

On the ride back to what Vance was beginning to consider as Silvio's Motel, the Italian graybeard filled in some of the gaps about his three friends.

"Anthony owns the dive shop. He inherited it from his mother who was a legend in Sicily where she had a reputation as an archaeologist and wreck diver. She came here with her husband after the Second War. Drawn to the Red Sea region because of its antiquity. But her husband died leaving her penniless and pregnant. She moved down to Somalia and worked for an uncle who had a banana plantation in the south. Anthony was born and raised in Somalia. Educated by his mother. They were driven out because they were Catholic. He is kind and loving to all men, but he becomes angry when anyone does something to remind him that they are Muslim and he is not. Vance, you will like him. He swims like a fish. And he can hold his breath for almost two minutes.

"Nikos is half Italian and half Greek. Father is Greek. Mother is Italian. I'm not sure where from. He too, grew up in Africa. Mother died when he was very young. Raised by father who was in importing business. His specialty was grain. At one time he had part interest in a shipping firm that had several ships running between the Black Sea region and Somalia, Kenya, and occasionally Yemen. Like Anthony he, too, was mistreated by Somali Muslims. Somalis killed his father and took his business.

"Nikos has fought them in the past, not usually winning. And he has spent time in their jails. I think he is lucky to be alive. And he knows that. Vance, this man is a bomb, just waiting to explode. But he can fight. And he is completely honest. Same as Anthony. If Nikos says he will do a thing, he will always do it. No matter the consequences for himself."

"Nikos swims?"

"No, Nikos is neither a swimmer nor a diver. But he is a good seaman and he has been in most of the ports around Africa. No mean feat. And he has a marvelous boat. A dhow."

"And Rafael?"

"The best for last. He, too, is of Italian parentage. His mother and father once had businesses in Mogadishu. But they could see a disaster in the making before your Black Hawk went down and they fled to—of all places—Israel. The Israelis let them in and Rafael lived for five years in Israel. I don't know how much he speaks, but he was around fifteen or sixteen at the time so he probably had an Israeli girl friend. In which case he is probably fluent. But he speaks enough English that you can understand him."

"So that makes him best?"

"No. What makes him best is that while in Israel he joined a group of amateur archaeologists who chanced upon two ancient Phoenician shipwrecks. These wrecks, once discovered, attracted professional archaeologists from Europe and the U.S., and Rafael was skillful enough to get himself an job as guide and a kind of informal docent, to investigators from around the world. He knows how to work underwater, he can use most tools, he is very intelligent, and he will not be squeamish about killing Somali pirates."

How did Silvio seem to discern the type of companions Vance was seeking? *Uncanny!* His first reaction to Silvio's friends was positive; much better than he had expected.

A plan was beginning to takes shape. This was the fifth meeting between the group of four conspirators who had agreed to make an assault on the pirate headquarters at Boosaaso.

Vance had been elated to verify that Nikos owned a dhow, with a diesel engine that was used as a dive boat to carry tourists to some of the area's popular sites. It was sixty-five feet long, of a design Vance had never encountered. It had two masts, but the mizzen—if that was what they called it—was also a lateen. It was big enough and comfortable enough to carry tourists for a pleasant day, and its diesel engine let it come and go at will. Nikos had been operating this vessel for years. Nikos agreed to make the vessel available as his contribution, with himself as the skipper.

The real problem had to do with munitions. Vance had estimated that they would require at least four conventional cratering charges to take down the building. Six would be better. As for destroying pirate craft in the water... that he realized, had been more like a pipe dream, impractical with this team, and no access to the type of weapons that would be needed. They would have to focus on the building that was occupied by Abdallah. In addition to the cratering charges, they would need personal weapons, ammunition and grenades of whatever type he could get. He began to make a coded list on a small scrap of paper.

"...case studies reveal that long-term intractable, flourishing piracy is a complex activity that relies on five integral factors; an available population of potential recruits, a secure base of operations, a sophisticated organization, some degree of outside support, and cultural bonds that engender vibrant group solidarity. Activities that interfere with the smooth workings of any of these factors weaken piracy's sustainability."

"What Makes Piracy Work"
Virginia Lunsford (Ph.D., Assoc. Prof of History, USNA)
In: Proceedings, U.S. Naval Institute, December 2008

—58—Details Begin to Mesh

For the next two weeks, Vance was contented to be busy doing things he knew how to do. He was planning the details of an activity that would have the potential to result in his death, mutilation, court martial, or possibly, capture by Somali pirates or Islamic terrorists. *Not just myself.* Along with these very considerable risks, the events he was planning could expose several other individuals to fates equally dire.

On the plus side of this equation, there was Jitka. In her first week in the hospital she had been diagnosed with MRSA, probably contracted there, but it had responded well to newer medications and after a protracted bad spell, she seemed to be on the mend. *But she's still so damn thin. In some places her bones seem like they're ready to poke through her skin.*

She was expected to be out of the hospital in a few days and she was beginning to regain a bit of color. On his last visit, her hair had recently been washed and she smelled so good that he gave serious consideration to climbing into the hospital bed with her.

The arrangements he had made with his three co-conspirators required him to provide the explosives and weaponry, while they would provide the boat, and diving equipment required for a three-man team to hit the beach. Nikos, armed, would remain aboard the dhow on a station at least a mile from the harbor entrance.

If Vance understood anything in this world, it was the essential utility of careful planning and rehearsal. The least screw-up anywhere along the line had the potential to take the whole operation down; with disastrous results.

In some rational corner of his brain, Vance knew the steps he was taking were fundamentally wrong. He knew the quest for revenge was inappropriate. And that no one in either his UBSA or Navy chain of command would approve of the events he was setting in motion. But then his memory shifted back to the way Jitka had looked when he first visited her in the hospital. He could hardly imagine how she must have looked while she was in the hands of Abdallah. Always, he came back to the same place.

Fuck it! I'm going after that bastard!

He had come to like his three companions and he had determined that Rafael and Antonio probably had what it takes to make it as SEALs, at least as far as water skills were concerned. High compliments, indeed, but he had swum for miles with them, and dived off several of Djibouti's challenging reefs. Initially, he had devised several underwater tests, involving equipment swaps and similar acts used to build confidence underwater, but after his second venture with these two, he decided it was foolish to waste energy with worry. These two knew what they were doing. They were both very confident in the water. Nikos, too, appeared to be capable and dependable; a skillful boat handler. The dhow's engine appeared to be clean and well maintained. It had performed well in all of their test runs and swims.

Now, he would need to form some assessment of how confident and capable they would be with weapons, high explosives, and—let's not try to put too good a face on this—killing people. For some it was impossible. For others, it was too easy. Somewhere in the middle there was an approach that Vance could accept. But this, of course, was something that could not be tested.

His role was to find the weaponry they would require and to obtain it, and transfer everything to their dhow without detecting notice. In the past, Vance had become accustomed to making inventories of weapons, munitions, explosives and other items as part of the logistical aspect of team leadership. By this point in his life, list making and list checking had become second nature. *You can't know what gonna run out if you don't know what you took with you.* It was fundamental to his thinking.

The list of wants was comprehensive. *More like a wish list.* It included cratering charges of ammonium nitrate, antipersonnel weapons, primarily claymores and penetrating weapons, like M150 PAMs, designed to punch holes in reinforced concrete. The weapons, he estimated, should easily punch through the hull of a wooden vessel and take out the engine and destroy the boat's utility.

He made a lot of lists, which he would burn after committing to memory. Four men. *We'll all need an appropriate firearm, and spares if something jams, fails, or is damaged by incoming. Four men. Eight suitable weapons. Plus, of course, a sidearm for each. Something with the capability to get the job done.* Glocks would get the job done. Four Glocks. They were reliable. No backups needed. But newer weapons were usually hard to find in places where they were not closely guarded. *Forty-fives? Easier to find on the open market. Should be OK.*

Once we're on the beach. What then?

Vance's vision was to destroy, to destroy utterly, the building where Jitka had been imprisoned and raped. He really did not care if innocent people were inside. He had seen the building as it appeared from space. The white rooftop penthouse was easy to identify. He had grimaced as Jitka told him of some of the things that had been done to her in that small cube on the roof. She couldn't tell him everything and he knew she was leaving things out.

Like the fucking Kaaba. A cube. Almost a cube. I want to see that cocksucker removed from the face of the earth.

When he found himself thinking like this, Vance questioned his own fitness to be a leader. These notions would hardly pass muster at the UBSA, much less at the USNA. *But...fuck it.* He wanted to even the score. He wanted to let someone know that they couldn't get away with these things. That someone cared. That there would be a day of reckoning for those who thought they could be cruel to the helpless.

He tried to imagine the mission after the three swimmers had slipped into the water. What's his name would be left alone in the dhow. *Fuck!* He could never remember that Greek name. *Nikos.* That was it.

Nikos would be alone. Perhaps a mile and a quarter offshore. *Possibly closer.* And even though it would be the dark of the moon, it was very possible that other vessels from Boosaasso might be returning, and that they might challenge him. In any event, we would have left him alone and he might need something capable of addressing hostiles coming at him.

Vance sifted his knowledge of the SEAL armory of efficient weaponry and the thing he came up with was the M136 man-portable anti-armor weapon, a bazooka-like, shoulder fired weapon.. That could punch a hole in anything these rag-heads were likely to be using. *And these sons-a-bitches can make a big hole in anything these fuckin' Somalis are likely to be sailing. Get three. That oughta hold him, while he waits for us.*

I don't see any problems with three of us getting on shore without being detected. Or at least, get to the beach. Coming out of the water might be problematic. We'll pick the dark of the moon, but still, I have no sense for what goes on—on that beach. Even if it is pitch dark. Should we have silencers? It couldn't hurt. But difficult to obtain.

In the weeks after he returned to Djibouti and found Jitka in the hospital, Vance sometimes felt as if he was cracking up. It was, he knew, a combination of tension, anger and frustration, topped off by constant planning and training for the mission.   During this time he was consumed with worry about getting weapons for his intended rogue raid into pirate territory. He needed help from his armorer friend, but he didn't want to expose him to criminal charges down the road. He was also training hard to put himself in top physical condition. He knew that it would require him to be up early, stay up until late and push himself to the limits of endurance. This he was willing to do.

He knew that he was probably ending his career in the US Navy; and it was quite possible that he might be ending his life. But he seemed to be in the grip of forces beyond his control. The Navy had let him down. His putative employer, UBSA, was—as far as he was concerned—useless as a deterrent or a remedy against pirate predation. Jitka seemed to be a changed person. Even his friend, Silvio, seemed somehow altered by his experiences in Somalia. Silvio had never been forthcoming about details of how he had managed to get out of the country after Jitka's capture, and Vance had decided not to push. He had learned from the old professor that their driver had been murdered. The bruising in Silvio's shoulder was still apparent.

His new friends were largely unknowns, and working with them would involve an element of risk. *What the hell.* He knew, in his rational mind, that he was not behaving in a rational manner. But still, running his four miles in the early morning light, he felt that he was doing what he had to do.

At night, exhausted from strenuous training, intense planning and depressing visits to Jitka, he had expected to sleep soundly. But he found himself thinking of the girl for hours before falling asleep. This time, it was different. It surprised him. He thought about her bones.

Jitka was not a thin girl. Technically she was a mesomorph. Before her capture, in a bathing suit she would have stood out on any beach in the world. Now, you could count her ribs. She was all but flat-chested. She had lost weight in captivity; but that weight could be expected to return.

No...this was different. He thought about her bones. About the shape and perfection of her bones. Early in their relationship, he had palpated the old fracture in her tibia, and subsequently he had felt all the bones in her ankles and feet.

Whether she was awake or asleep, something had prompted him to feel for all of her bones, and without any conscious intention he had felt many, *most*, of the bones in her body. Everything that was near the surface. He had cataloged them in his mind so that, he believed, in a dark room full of bodies he could have picked her out of a crowd.

A foolish conceit, of course, and he realized it. Still, he had continued, feeling and cataloging her collar bones, humerus, scapulae, the vertebrae all the way to her coccyx. It was unbelievable to him, how good she felt to his hands, and he felt foolish to have lived so long before finding out about the magic in a woman's bones. But then, when he thought about it carefully, no one he had ever known before had bones that seemed to him as beautiful or as compelling as Jitka's.

Thinking about the jut of her hip when she lay on her side, or her rib cage when she arched her back, could arouse him. This was a new sensation for him, and it was a puzzling as it was magical.

One of the more curious aspects of his marvelous discovery was that Jitka never remarked on what he was doing, or why he was doing it. Sometime she might be awake as he was quietly feeling the bones of her arm and hand, from acromion process to finger tips. Slowly, gently, thoroughly. *Surely she must wonder what the hell I'm doing. Or why I'm doing it.* But the expression on her face was one of bemused tolerance. *No, it's more than that. It's as if she's blissed out.*

How to describe the expression on her face as he felt the bones of her pelvis, then shifted to her femur at the hip, moved about three inches at a time to her knee, and then slowed down as he hit bone near the surface; her tibia? She had a quiet smile, amused detachment. Did it feel good? He wasn't trying to arouse her. He was trying to catalog her. He was trying to *possess* her. And she seemed to understand. She never spoke, never tried to break the spell. At her ankles he had to slow down and change position to palpate her foot thoroughly.

Lying alone in his bed in the transient BOQ in Djibouti, he realized, of a sudden, that what he felt for Jitka was unique in his experience. He would have protected her had it been in his power. Now, he wanted to avenge her. He wanted to punish her captor. Her captors. There were more than one.

For the next weeks he intensified his training regimen and he insisted that his three new companions were with him for most of the time. He wanted to see them when they were exhausted, to form some opinion about their ability to carry on when they were at the limit of their endurance.

Considering that they were not active military personnel, he was surprised at their abilities. Nikos excepted, in the water they performed with confidence, both on the surface in open water swims, and underwater. They had all racked up plenty of hours underwater, and they were more familiar with some of the local forms of stinging corals than he was.

Running, they tired quicker than he would have preferred, but the problem was in their legs, not their wind. Anyway, as he figured it, they wouldn't have to go more than mile or two—at most. Both ways. Hopefully, if they planned carefully, they would just need to move inland from the waterfront for a couple of blocks to the target. The date for the next new moon was marked on his calendar with a post-it note. Ever cautious, he did not want to circle the date for someone to find.

"Resolution 1838 "calls upon all states interested in the security of maritime activities to take part actively in the fight against piracy on the high seas off the coast of Somalia, in particular by deploying naval vessels and military aircraft." The French-drafted text urges states with naval vessels and military aircraft operating on the high seas and airspace off the Somali coast "to use the necessary means, in conformity with international law...for the repression of acts of piracy."

It again "condemns and deplores all acts of piracy and armed robbery at sea against vessels off the coast of Somalia." France's UN Ambassador Jean-Maurice Ripert immediately welcomed the unanimous adoption of the text, saying it sends "a clear signal to the pirates. It states very clearly that you can use force against the pirates."

New Somalia piracy resolution adopted at UN
October 7, 2008
(from the Internet; Google.com)

—59—Plans, and Coincidences

When you think about it for a moment, everything that happens in your life is a coincidence. Actually, in everyone else's life at well. Every event is coincident with many other events. We just don't know—or care—about most of them. For example...

Last year, Silvio DiPaolo had a female visitor at his compound, a Swedish academic he had known years before, both in Italy and in Somalia. Annika Anders was an archaeologist who had specialized in East Africa's prehistory, and in particular, she was interested in the prehistory of the Horn of Africa.

In the years following World War II, it was possible for Europeans with resources to travel with some security in Somalia and a youthful Annika had uncovered the tools of ancient humans at several locations in Italian Somalia. In particular, she had found cores, scrapers, and a variety of flaked tools at half a dozen locations in the vicinity of the Webi Shebeli north of Mogadishu. That had been years ago, back in the 70's. Now, among the community of specialists she inhabited, she was considered an authority.

At the end of her long career as an academic, she was taking a final cruise with a group of friends. They were traveling in a small Norwegian-flagged cruise ship, bound for Cambodia with planned stops at places of archaeological interest in route. The planned stop at Djibouti was primarily for fuel and provisioning.

When Silvio first knew Annika, she was making herself into an authority on the Doian Culture in southern Somalia. The name was taken from the Somali word, *doi,* meaning a particular orange sand in which certain stone tools were found. Annika was the second in charge of a European team that included Germans and Danes as well as Norwegians and Italians. Silvio, the botanist, joined three Italian archaeologists from his university, based solely on his ability with the spoken and written language.

He and Annika were both young, intelligent, married, and isolated from their spouses in a place that was hot, dusty, backward and—at least marginally—dangerous. Need more? Annika eyes were—still are—cornflower blue.

After one season in the field, Annika went home with boxes filled with rocks that had been hammered into crude tools and she tried to put Silvio out of her mind. Silvio went back to Italy with few boxes and less weighty specimens, but he did not try to put Annika out of his mind. But decades passed, spouses died, careers flourished and distance was maintained. Such things happen.

Silvio knew that Annika had, over subsequent years, made numerous trips back to Somalia and other sites in East Africa. During those visits, she had never tried to contact him again. He learned—from searching the Internet for East African archaeology and reading papers she wrote—that she had been particularly interested in locating cave art, or rock art linked to the cultures she had investigated.

Now, after the passage of a lifetime, she had contacted him again, and they had arranged to meet for lunch during her brief stop.

The coincidence, unknown to anyone on the planet, present company excepted, was that the youth who waited on their outside table had, until age fourteen, been a camel boy in the mountains of northwest Somalia, south of Hargeysa. Raised by Sunni parents, he had been taught that idol worship was an offense to Allah and would be severely punished for eternity in a hellish afterlife. Once, during a sandstorm, he had crawled between the parallel faces of a huge block that had split in an ancient geologic past. On both faces there were incised figures of men with weapons pursuing small antelope, resembling *Beira.* The boy had taken a rock and spent several hours pecking away all traces of these figures. Annika would have wept just to have a glance at these figures. The young boy had believed that he was pleasing Allah. It was a meaningless coincidence, better off unknown. *Hardly worth mentioning.* Except that it illustrates, in a way, the total disconnect between peoples and cultures that.... But, pardon me, You already understand this. It was...a coincidence.

Sometimes coincidences are meaningless and insignificant. Other times, they make all the difference, life or death, rich or poor, success or failure. We just never know.

Vance had been training for weeks. He had managed to get his hands on six M150 PAM devices. It was as easy as pulling a rabbit out of a hat. The acronym stands for Penetration Augmented Munitions, a kind of shaped charge used to blast through armor or reinforced concrete. He might have obtained more of them but they weigh about thirty-five pounds each and he didn't think his team could run up the beach with more than two apiece. Vance needed six.

The coincidence in this case? Inexplicably, Vance's armorer friend had recently discovered an inventory error in which signed records showed that he was responsible for eight fewer than he actually had on hand. He checked several times. He had eight more than his records showed. When Vance let him know, obliquely, that he could use six, to his amazement he was told that he would have to take eight. *Figure the odds on this. OK. I'll take 'em.* Two could always be abandoned at sea. *Hey, they don't float.*

The team practiced several times, over their weeks of preparation and it was ugly at first, gradually improving until Vance was satisfied that they had a good shot at success. Initially they had flagged after running for a hundred yards in sand; but they improved rapidly.

Weapons were relatively easy to find in that part of the world; none easier than the ubiquitous AK-47, dependable, reliable, relatively cheap. It was easy to find ammunition, too, even though it sometimes meant doing business with Yemeni smugglers

During this entire time, Vance worked and moved like a sleepwalker. He knew he was breaking the rules; that he would eventually have to pay a substantial penalty. But all he could think of was Jitka's whispered description of the place where she had been held. He had easily found the target building on Google Earth and he printed a copy and confirmed it with the girl.

At night he dreamed of her. Sometimes he woke at night, feeling the sharp shin bone of his own leg and trying to recall the feel of the healed fracture in her tibia. Some nights he had trouble getting back to sleep, but he told himself this was an indication that he wasn't pushing himself hard enough. The next day he would drive himself harder.

Vance made arrangements with his armorer pal to "borrow" a Radio Firing Device. The RFD he asked for was an older version of the Mk 186, the unit he had been trained on and with which he was familiar. There were newer versions in the hands of SEAL Teams within the last two years, but the older units, still capable of getting the job done, were still around and Vance had no trouble in getting the unit off the base and delivered onto the dhow.

Things were coming together much more smoothly than he had imagined and he warned himself against hubris. This was one of his biggest fears; that if he failed in the mission he envisioned, it would be because of his inattention to every detail. Check, double check, then check again. Once that proverbial stuff hits the fan, it's too late for more checking.

So what, exactly, was the mission he was planning? His plan was to kill the pirate leader and anyone else in the building he occupied. Vance knew what the building looked like, and he knew what Abdallah looked like. Any males past puberty in that building were fair game in his mind. Women and children would not be killed intentionally, certainly not if it could be avoided, but it was his intention to destroy the building, the pirate's den, if it was at all possible. He believed that it would be possible with proper positioning of six PAM's. He had paid careful attention to the structure of buildings in Djibouti that were approximately the same size as Jitka's prison. The strongest of them were of reinforced concrete and he was reasonably sure that six charges would do the job. Some of these buildings under five stories were even made of mud brick. Jitka's building, he was reasonably certain from available images, would be of concrete.

If he could have made this assault with one of his old SEAL teams it would have been much more straightforward. A Snatch-and-Grab type operation. But he had no interest in taking a prisoner—or prisoners. He knew what he was planning was professional suicide, possibly even actual suicide—unintentional, true—but still, it seemed to him that this mission was something he was compelled to do. What was surprising to him was the intensity with which his three new companions were just as eager to participate in this raid.

Silvio gave him the back stories, about how they had lost relatives and livelihoods as a consequence of religious fundamentalists, gangs or pirates; not this same group being targetted, but his new companions were indifferent. The targets were pirates and they were Somalis. Vance had shown them photos of Abdallah and his men using photos taken from Jitka's camera. But they had not recognized any specific individuals.

Weapons? He would have preferred to be carrying some of the newer Heckler & Koch MP5 weapons when his three-man team went ashore. But these were in demand and the inventory was highly visible. Unlike the PAM munitions, the MP5s were too risky to let off base. Too much at stake. On the other hand, AK47s were a dime a dozen in Djibouti, and that's what it came down to; money.

The days flashed by. On one of his nightly visits to Jitka she broke down and told him about the random way Abdallah occasionally beat her just to make her submissive. Vance's throat tightened as he listened to her talk. He was carefully re-mapping the bones in her left ankle and foot. "If I had been there," he whispered, "it would never have happened. Not like that." After he spoke he noticed that she was trying to smile but her lips were cracked.

"You're smiling? You don't think I could have stopped him?"

"*Pas de tout*, not so." she said, pointing to her water glass. "But your words reminded me of something that I learned as a schoolgirl, long ago, in France."

"Tell it." He held the glass so she could take a sip from the straw.

" Back when France was still known as Gaul, the north was invaded by Francs. They had a king whose name Clovis. He was a brave warrior. Clovis was a pagan, but he married a girl named Clotilde who happened to be a Christian. Clotilde tried to convert Clovis, but you know how that goes.

"One day Clovis was in a battle where he and his men were getting the worst of it. Am I boring you Vance?"

It was the most she had talked at one time since he had been back. While she was talking he had slipped his hand under the sheet and was feeling— very gently— her rib cage and sternum. He smiled. "Keep going."

"Clovis feared he would lose. So he looked up and asked Clotilde's God to help him. He promised that if he won, he would become a Christian."

"Was I looking as if I was bored? I'm just happy to be here with you."

She answered by letting her hand rest on his arm.

"So. So." She seemed to be momentarily distracted, but after a brief pause she continued. "Clovis won his battle, and when he returned to his home, he kept his promise. Together with Clotilde he went to be instructed in his catechism by Remi, the Bishop of Reims. When he was told how Christ was flogged before being nailed to the cross he was first moved, and then angered. Clovis said 'Ah! If I had been there, those things would not have happened in that way.' This is what you just said to me. That you would be my champion. You made me remember that story. It was so sweet. You touched my heart. But I am talking too much. May I..." And she nodded for the water, again. *God, she is still so thin.* He had looked away. He had felt naked.

Now, securing the weapons for his planned raid inside the cramped space below deck on the dhow, Vance was remembering this visit, the feel of her bony ribs, her smile. He had kissed her dry, cracked lips when he left.

The weeks since his return had passed for him like a blur. It was dreamlike—as if he was sleepwalking. He expected that she would have been out of the hospital by now, but she was still occupying a bed and she looked so unhappy, he began to understand, for the first time in his life, the meaning of "a broken heart."

Sometimes he felt as if he had a cinder block in his own chest. Usually his response to this feeling was to go out and run on the local roads for three or four miles, pushing himself to exhaustion.

One afternoon, after he had been back about two weeks, she told him, weeping, about the D&C. She had struggled with the decision even though she was certain that she could never carry or bear a child by Abdallah. After she made her agonizing choice, she learned that two French surgeons who were competent to perform this operation had refused. Two months, a good heartbeat, and she was healthy enough, or soon would be. She had been reluctant to tell Vance she was pregnant, but needing help, she appealed to Silvio. Vance held her hand and listened. He didn't tell her that he already knew what had happened.

The professor would have brought a doctor from Italy to perform the abortion, but he spoke to several of his contacts on the American base and found a U.S. Navy surgeon who looked into the case and agreed to do the procedure. Medically, everything went smoothly, but emotionally it was a train wreck for everyone who knew Jitka and what she had endured.

Back in his room, Vance had resisted the urge to take a drink, because he was pretty sure that if he started, it might be hard to stop.

Over and over he calculated and recalculated a timeline for the various contingencies he felt they could face in Somalia.

The plan was for Nikos to remain aboard the dhow, armed and prepared to destroy any Somalis who approached for any conceivable reason. Vance and the other two conspirators would swim ashore. Single tanks with scuba in case of an emergency need, but they would not use their tanks going in. Swim fins. Off the beach in about eight or ten feet of water they would pick a spot where everything would be left together on the bottom. A small float would lead them back to their cache for the return swim to the boat.

Once on the beach, they would slip on Somali clothes provided by Rafael and carried ashore in a waterproof bag. AKs would be slung under the baggy wraps in maneuvers they had practiced repeatedly. The PAMs and the borrowed RFD would be trotted across the sand beach and onto the unpaved street leading to the beachfront road. From there, it should be easy to find Abdallah's building. They would probably have to shoot their way in and from here it could become unpredictable. He estimated he could place and arm six devices in effective locations in under fifteen minutes. Rafael and Anthony would have to provide cover for him. They had made several scenarios and practiced repeatedly. Vance wanted to believe he could make it work, but the more they practiced, the less certain he became. He took heart from the confidence his companions seemed to have in his ability to pull this off.

During the week leading up to the raid, when he visited Jitka, Vance realized that he wanted to live with her. He wanted it more than he had ever wanted anything else, and he realized that he would be willing to give up almost everything to do it. *Almost? Almost everything? How consuming can that be?* The "almost" was inserted because even as intense as his feelings were, his intelligence told him that attitudes and emotions change. And though he might be willing to turn his life upside down today, and mean it, and actually do it, he knew, with his brain and not his heart, that such feelings were unlikely to last a lifetime, and that a time might come when he might change and come to regret some of the choices he had made.

Still...he had made up his mind. He was going down the coast of Somalia, *Inshallah, you bastards, and take out the building where Abdallah has his headquarters.* Hopefully, if he was lucky, he would take out Abdallah and some members of his pirate crew in the process. It would be an insignificant event with regard to curbing piracy, but it might give a few pirates pause. Conceivably it might embolden....

Aah! Bullshit. Why do I let myself imagine that this could possibly make a difference. I'm doing this for myself. As some kind of a psychological gesture to Jitka, to my feelings about her, and for her; and as a turning point in my life, which up the this point, somewhere in the middle, has been pretty much "straight arrow."

If he could persuade Jitka to marry him—or just to live with him—perhaps he could take her to the American West, and she could find material to capture her photographic interests. Would she love him? *Could she love me?* Maybe it didn't really matter if she could enjoy being with him, and doing some things together. *Anything.* He did, however, want her to allow him to love her, to touch and handle and absorb all the parts of her.

Would he ever tell her about the acts he was contemplating; that hopefully he would be able to pull off? *Probably not.* Barring something unforeseen—blood would certainly be shed on this escapade, and he would bear the sole responsibility. Highly likely that some of it would be innocent. *Fortunes of war. It's the price we have to pay. We can't let these considerations paralyze us into inaction. Innocents die everyday in traffic accidents. Who gets the blame for that?*

The days were counting down to the new moon. Four more to go. He was satisfied that the three-man team would make it to the beach. They would tow the PAMs on a float. Not much would show above the water line. And they could tow it right up to the beach. Abandon it there when they crossed the narrow strand. It looked, from several angles to be less than fifty yards. Then the unpaved sand street inland, and then they would cross the beach road quickly, each man with an AK on his shoulder and lugging two PAMs apiece. They had practiced this maneuver, and he felt confident they would do it well enough. Of course, if they were facing hostile fire it would be a whole new ball-game. But that seemed a remote possibility. No one would be expecting them. He would place the PAMs and they would detonate them from the dhow. He would make all the connections himself. The uncertainty had to do with the level of activity that might be expected on a Somali beach on a moonless night. It was, he was beginning to acknowledge, a long shot.

They would time things to be on the beach on the darkest night of the year, between two and three in the morning. Based on his examination of photographs taken from space, he was reasonably certain that they could go ashore within a hundred yards or so of the targeted building.

Under different circumstances, Vance might have seen what was coming, even though it was a Top Secret military operation. He was trained to read the tea leaves and his Pentagon days had introduced him to many of the top brass currently at Djibouti, and on duty elsewhere in the theater. But he had been distracted, first by the situation with Jitka, and then by his plans to seek revenge on the men who had captured her and the man who had raped her. He had little contact with movers and shakers from whom he might have divined a few clues.

As Al Qaeda strengthened its position in Yemen, key players from several locations moved into that country to establish a network of strongholds in the northwest. One of the most powerful of these players was Ahmed Sheik Khama, a Saudi with personal ties to Osama dating from the decade before 9-11.

British intelligence had tipped off the U.S. that Khama had drifted into Yemen and that he had been assigned to make contact with Somali pirates in bases bordering the Gulf of Aden in an effort to intensify attacks on shipping. The idea was—as best the Brits were able to predict Al Qaeda's plans—to tie up the naval warships of crusader nations, and force them to spend time and money trying to combat pirate raids that were, essentially, unstoppable.

Khama had been on the "kill or capture" list for years, but he had been elusive. When the British informed their U.S. counterparts that Khama had scheduled a meeting with pirate leaders in Boosaaso, top brass in the region sought permission to take off the gloves and go after him. The Al Qaeda chief was expected to fly into Somalia at the same time that Vance had planned to go ashore and create mayhem. It's funny how things work out.

The dhow carrying Vance and his three co-conspirators left its dock space on the day before their intended raid. Considering that their whole program had something of a rag-tag "Our Gang" flavor, they were as well prepared as any reasonable *impromptu* commander could expect. And they had everything they would need to carry out their plan. Almost everything.

They just had no way to know that a much greater effort was progressing in parallel with their own, aimed at the same target, at the building where Abdallah had invited five pirate commanders from coastal cities of Maydh, Laasgoray, Qandala, Caluula and Bareeda. All of these men, together with several of their deputies, had shown up for the meeting, which was expected to provide Saudi financial support for new electronic equipment. They were all staying on one floor of Abdallah's building.

Originally, military and security personnel had contemplated something of a snatch-and-grab mission, but that was always problematical, and when they learned that it was to be more of a group meeting, heavily attended by pirate leaders, the plans were changed to an attack to cut the head off a serpent.

The dhow with Vance and his companions was proceeding almost due east, directly down the Somali Coast within an hour of the planned staging point for their assault. Lacking a radar, they had no way to know that a three-ship naval assault force was moving out of shipping lanes to the north, in a direction perpendicular to their own course. And that the two tracks were within an hour of visual range. One major difference was that the missile frigate could track the rogue dhow with heartbreaking ease. Since they were on courses that might possibly intersect, the dhow was considered as a potential hostile. As such, it was tracked and targeted.

When Nikos estimated they were about two hours from landfall, he noticed that Vance seemed tired. "Sleep, Navy. You can nap for one hour and I will call you." Rafael was already snoring. Vance closed his eyes and was asleep in minutes. He dreamed he was with Jitka at Silvio's place.

Silvio's new vehicle was a Mitsubishi. When Vance saw it, he laughed.
"What is funny about Silvio's car?" Jitka asked.
"I can't tell you," he replied.
" You are a naughty boy," she said. "It's not nice to keep secrets. Perhaps I should keep a...."
"OK. OK. But do you know what Mitsubishi means? The words?"
"Of course not. But you will tell me?"
"It means 'three diamonds.' Mitsu means three; bishi means diamonds. I learned that from a Japanese-American girl I once knew in San Diego."

Now, Jitka laughed. "And you will tell me the rest of this story?" And she made a small move to let him know it would be well if he told her. In his dream he and Jitka were scantily clad.

"OK. OK. If you're gonna play hardball. I happened to get a glance at part of her anatomy where she had that Mitsubishi emblem tattooed. I was curious about what it meant. But also I was exhausted and just about asleep on my feet. We had covered a lot of miles that day, and we were carrying a bit of weight. I wasn't gonna be awake much longer."

"And...? So....?"

"She told me it meant three diamonds. And then, I asked her if she owned one, or if she had worked for the company. She told me, it was a sign for her. That she was like the car. Three diamonds. I must have looked puzzled, because she said, 'This is like your instruction manual for how to drive me." I was still slow to get it. After a pause she gave me a smile—she knew I was dead on my feet—and said 'It will come to you when you wake up. My three diamonds.' "

"Vance, you have been a bad boy in your Navy life."

"No, not really."

"Ah, *dommage*. I was hoping so."

"OK. OK. I'll try to be bad."

This was the dream he had, but it wasn't a dream he would remember.

No one aboard the dhow heard the missile coming. The explosion detonated all eight of the M-150 PAM devices so the explosion was impressive and the dhow was utterly destroyed. Anthony was blown apart and died instantly. Nikos, burned everywhere, was thrown naked into the water some distance from the boat but, although he had numerous broken bones, he was still alive. Actually, technically, he drowned. The third man, Raphael,...who knows what happened? Nothing. No traces, no hints. Just gone. Vance like Nikos was hurled into the sea some distance from the explosion. He was alive in the water for some moments. It was confusing. He was aware from the shattered condition of his body, that his injuries were not survivable and that he would die in moments. Still, there was no pain. *This should be excruciating, therefore I am in shock.* He tried to focus his mind. *These are the last thoughts I will have before I am dead.* It seemed important to make them count. Not to waste an instant. *Jitka. Jitka. I hope you will remember me and that you will think well of me. Jitka.* He tried to recall the way her bones felt, and he tried not to think of what had happened to his own body.

And then. Then. Then. Oh, fuck. He was being squeezed and things were starting to hurt. Everything was water. There was a fleeting memory of the knobby bones in Jitka's knees. The iron taste of blood. Like rust. Darkness. Then the dark, salt sea closed around him and all his tapes ceased playing. Done. *An orphan ghost?*

Officers aboard the missile frigate were surprised by the explosion of the dhow and they concluded, correctly, that she had been carrying explosives. Their plans to conduct a 'snatch and grab' operation on the building were called off at the last moment. A Hellfire missile dropped right onto the rooftop office where Jitka had been tormented. It demolished the entire building where Abdallah had planned his meeting, and it killed everyone inside. The Al Qaeda representative from Yemen was killed along with four of his aides. Abdallah was killed as were six of his crew. His three wives and six children were killed when the building collapsed. Everything Vance had intended came to pass, but the circumstances were considerably different. Twenty-six fatalities in all. Six of them were children. The American youth from Minneapolis had gone to chew qat with boys on the beach near where Vance had planned to come ashore. Said Haad escaped the attack and decided he might give up piracy. He began planning to return to Mogadishu with the youth from Al-Shabab.

Lt. Commander Morrisette, USN, had considered many possible contingencies, but the one that happened had not been on his list.

In the days and weeks that followed, Vance's superiors in the Pentagon branch of Naval Intelligence were hard pressed to learn what had happened to him. The fact that he was operating as if he had left the Navy made it difficult for them to conduct an investigation overtly. Like Vance, they had been, in the same sense, hoist on their own petard.

Management at UBSA was mystified by his disappearance. They had been unaware of his involvement with Nikos and his pals. Vance had, by direction from headquarters, always operated with a great deal of autonomy, and he only checked in with his mission chief, every three or four days. Initially, Dick Emery took some grief about the fifty grand, but eventually he was cleared of suspicion. In any case, he had a signed receipt.

The families of Nikos, Rafael and Anthony were not aware of their activities with Vance, and they were used to all of their menfolk being away from home for several days at a time. But after the third day of absence, when the dhow did not reappear at its regular dock space, family members began to worry. Silvio was the only person who had a good idea of what might have happened, and there was no one with whom he wanted to share his suspicions.

Jitka, of course, knew nothing. And after Vance failed to visit her for two straight days, she asked Silvio if he had seen him. This was painful for the old Italian who had come to think of the girl as a daughter, and he was uncomfortable as he lied to her. She wept over his abrupt disappearance. It was one more grief to bear.

UBSA had to file a missing persons report with local authorities in Djibouti, and of course the appropriate agencies in French and US. Military establishments had to be filled in with everything that was known.

When brass at the Pentagon attempted to get NCIS involved, they found that the circumstances of the case had placed Vance is a legal no-man's land, which had not been sufficiently well thought out.

The investigation proceeded very slowly—almost ponderously—because Vance had not left any clues behind. Even the post-it note on the calendar had little information to reveal.

The SEALs who had helped him—in ways both legal and illegal—were not implicated in any way. The armorer never got his RFD back, but it was an older unit and he turned in some broken parts and got salvage credit. No repercussions. Everyone had done a good job of covering tracks, and it was difficult for investigators to determine who among Vance's contacts was worth interrogating.

Within a week, they had linked Vance's disappearance to the vanished dhow, and the three Djiboutis. Theories abounded. When the facts at Djibouti were matched to details of events offshore from the successful naval raid at Boosaaso it was reasonable to make some connections. But details of this whole disappearing act still remains something of a mystery.

Vance has been presumed dead by his employers in Carolina. The Navy has had some difficulty in deciding how to handle his apparent demise and as a result a few new rules have been written. Fortunately he left no widow, no children, no parents and no heirs. His estranged sister received an American flag which she donated to an American Legion post, along with a photograph of him in uniform. His immediate superiors have breathed many collective sighs of relief at their good fortune with this one.

Jitka left the hospital three days after the death of Vance and his team. Silvio insisted that she stay with him in his compound for a week before she returned to Europe. He was gnawed by guilt at lying to her about Vance, and he tried to compensate by pampering her. This, of course, she found annoying. But it was hard to criticize. He treated her with such tenderness. They talked about Vance every day. She had inquired at the office for Uncle Bob's where she knew that Vance worked sometimes, but they had no information, and they seemed to think that she might have some ideas.

She had been a position that many women never experience. Vance was the third man to fall seriously in love with her. Unlike the other two, he had never told her, but she knew it from the way he touched her. She also knew that he was, unlike the others, a man that she could love. And perhaps would love. *Maybe I already do. I miss him.* No one had ever handled her like that. He had taken possession of her body. The others who had loved her would probably have been better husbands. Vance was a warrior. He was trained for war and she thought he was probably good at it. She had some problems with his career choice, but there was no question that he was a real man, and he had made Jitka understand how someone could love you without physical sex or words.

"The imprudence of our thoughts recoils upon our heads. Who toys with the sword shall perish by the sword. This astounding adventure, of which the most astounding part is that it is true, comes on us as an unavoidable consequence. Something of the sort had to happen. You repeat this to yourself while you marvel that such a thing could happen in the year of grace before last. But it has happened—and there is no disputing its logic."

> Lord Jim
> (from Chapter Thirty-six)
> Joseph Conrad

—60—Let's Call It Irony

The U.S. Navy finally used a technique that had been advocated by Lt. Commander Vance Morrisette. Only...sometimes things don't work out the way we would like. Vance had begun to harbor a secret vision of some kind of life with Jitka in it. Maybe it was marriage and maybe it was something else. He wasn't sure if this girl would marry him, but he was reasonably certain that she would live with him for some period of time. He wanted to get her out into the west. He wanted to get her into Utah. And Arizona. New Mexico. He wanted to get her into a land with beautiful scenery and beautiful faces.

He had no idea that things would turn out so very differently.

He knew that he was planning to break all the rules, but if the outcome had been, for the most part, *good*, he figured that the brass might cut him some slack. *But what if everything turns to shit?*

It happened that way, we know, but Vance just never anticipated *how* it might happen. On discarded scraps of paper with notes on possible contingencies, the big one was never on the list. Sad.

Vance had been in the Navy for sixteen years and he had once planned on going the distance—for retirement. Truth, to tell, it wasn't out of the question that he might have retired with a star, but, now, that was whiskey under the bridge.

He had been confident that he would still be employable with civilian security firms, but none of those jobs had been especially appealing to him. He didn't protest the assignment with UBSA because he felt it might give him a taste of civilian employment without interrupting his navy career track.

271

After he met Jitka—as a divorced man—childless, and warping toward his fifth decade, he began to think about the second half of his life.

When NCIS began to look into his disappearance, they immediately discovered that he had been one of a handful of SEAL officers to successfully complete Marine Sniper training at Twenty-Nine Palms. Soon after he was assigned to the Pentagon and began tracking pirate activities, he wrote a memo to his superiors titled "Lessons from Deer Hunters." The memo reminded his bosses that deer hunters often succeeded by using scoped rifles and shooting from high positions where they could see for long distances. Vance reminded his readers that Somali pirates frequently did not have large arsenals of weapons and that sometimes the attackers might have only one or two RPGs, the weapons that caused the most concern prior to actual boarding. A trained sniper positioned high about the attacking craft could expect to kill the man holding the RPG and possibly dissuade his mates from picking it up. For assurance, two snipers, linked by headsets could expect to take out two RPG holders simultaneously.

Vance's memo did not get a positive response and he became temporarily discouraged when one senior officer described it as "off-the-wall." Later, in the affair of the *Maersk Alabama*, the success was clearly linked to the employment of trained snipers. The shooters had successfully recovered the skipper, unharmed, after his capture by pirates. But somehow, to Vance's dismay, no one saw that snipers might also have played a proactive role by preventing a boarding from ever taking place.

Investigators learned that he had made a proposal for an experiment to be tried with a small team, to determine what degree of success could be obtained in repelling boarding attempts, without initiating the use of RPGs. The evidence indicated that Vance had been considered as something of a maverick by a few of his superiors and that he was given a one-off assignment to get him out of people's hair.

Talks with his cohort, or with men who had been assigned to his service with active SEAL units, did not corroborate these opinions.

When Vance disappeared, his absence did not leave a large gap in anyone's life. His parents had died in Utah years before. He had been estranged from his sister for some years and she did not even know where he was living in the states. His former wife was already living with another man who owned a tavern in Baltimore. Vance had friends in many places around the world. And men who had served with him, or under him, had only good things to say about him. But he had lived for much of his life as a warrior and he died as one. At least—one might say—in the warrior mode.

Investigators who rummaged through his personal belongings found an article from the Internet dating from September 2008. It was titled "Life in Somalia's pirate town," and it was written by BBC Africa analyst, Mary Harper. The opening paragraphs had been marked with a highlighter.

"Whenever word comes out that pirates have taken yet another ship in the Somali region of Puntland, extraordinary things start to happen. There is a great rush to the port of Eyl where most of the hijacked vessels are kept by the well-armed pirate gangs. People put on ties and smart clothes. They arrive in land cruisers with their laptops, one saying he is the pirates' accountant, another that he is their chief negotiator.

With yet more foreign vessels seized off the coast of Somalia this week, it could be said that hijackings in the region have become epidemic. Insurance premiums for ships sailing through he busy Gulf of Aden have increased tenfold over the past year because of the pirates, most of whom come from the semi-autonomous regions of Puntland.

In Eyl, there is a lot of money to be made, and everybody is anxious for a cut."

A photograph of a pirate skiff was circled with a note. *Discuss w/ Jitka.* Of five pirates in the skiff, one was holding an RPG. His profile was outlined with the highlighter and cross hairs were centered on his chest.

"....no single (terrorist) attack would be likely to have wide-ranging economic consequences (for all their plundering, pirates cause at most $16 B in losses a year—in an industry that handled upward of $7 trillion worth of goods in 2005). Perhaps most important, while jihadists would presumably aim for the destruction of the maritime economy, pirates depend on it for their livelihood."

> From: "The Maritime Dimension of International Security;
> Terrorism, Piracy, and Challenges for the United States,"
> Peter Chalk, Rand Corporation
> (reprinted in Atlantic, September 2008)

Epilogue

The Navy's investigation into Vance's absence and presumed death could never make a final, conclusive determination. Investigators closest to the details could tie him to several individuals in Djibouti, who went missing at the same time. They also had a boat that disappeared with them. They had a report about an explosion aboard a dhow matching all the characteristics of the missing craft in Djibouti. They could piece together several plausible explanations. But nothing was certain. It was still a mystery.

It's curious that Vance's death was connected with the outcome he was seeking, the destruction of Abdallah, his gang and his lair. It is ironic, too, that the commander was killed after the Navy finally employed the technique he had advocated for dealing with vessels behaving suspiciously. Hoist on his own petard, as military men might say.

Back in Washington, where his records were securely locked away in consequence of his unorthodox assignment, nothing has been removed and a special file contains the incomplete conclusions reached by NCIS.

How about Jitka? Jitka had no idea of the dreams that were in Vance's head. She knew that she wanted to continue to make a name for herself as a photographer, but her ambition had nothing to do with fame or wealth. She wanted to be acknowledged by other photographers, and by the public in general, for her ability to stop people in the their tracks and let them see what she had seen. She had the soul and ambition of an artist, although she might not have put it in exactly that way.

For the girl, everything changed after her months of imprisonment in the hands of her sadistic rapist-captor. She might have survived that experience with far less emotional damage if Abdallah had not impregnated her.

The abortion was a searing experience for a girl raised as a Catholic. Strictly speaking, she scarcely considered herself a good Catholic, or even a good Christian, but her vaccination into a certain morality had taken, and it had been harsh to decide to destroy life within her own body. It had been harsh, too, to be repelled by a life that was in her. Harsher to realize that it might be impossible for her to love a child that had grown in her body, stemming from the horror of the circumstances.

Jitka went back to Paris for several weeks and stayed with her parents. But they were showing their age, with problems of their own and they were unable to provide what she needed. It wasn't that they didn't love her. But you can't give what you don't have. She suspected, correctly, that no one would ever touch her, handle her, in the same way as Vance. Ever.

She needs love of the kind that includes some sex, but which is bigger and less selfish than just raw physicality. She needs the kind of relationship in which a person is attracted to her, and wants, wants, wants more than anything for her to let them love her. Some people need to *be* loved. Some just need *to* love. Some are flowers. Some are gardeners. It really that simple.

Both kinds are out there. It's not imaginary. But it isn't always easy to find. And with the passage of time it gets harder each year we age. Still....

The sad part of the story is that this was the kind of relationship that Vance was capable of providing. Looking back, she now sees that she gave her body to Vance, because it was clear how badly he wanted her.

Imprisonment, beatings, rape, abortion followed by the loss of a man who she knew was in love with her, and who she might allow to love her; even possibly come to love him in return; it was a full plate of unhappy. And it shows in her face. She looks sad. But on Jitka, sad is still beautiful. In the initial weeks following Vance's disappearance, the only man to allowed to appreciate Jitka's beauty was Silvio.

Jitka has returned to Paris and is living with her parents for a time. Next year she is planning to visit the U.S. for an extended stay and her first destination will be Phoenix. She intends to travel alone.

Silvio? No one ever linked Silvio to the events in the Gulf of Aden. He was contacted briefly as one of Vance's acquaintances. Nothing was learned.

He watched the sad-faced girl who spent a lot of time alone in her room, or wandering in his garden, taking close ups of his collection of East African succulents. She would put them on his computer, and play with them for hours—on photo shop. She wanted to do black and white but Silvio insisted on color. He stuck his nose into cropping, enlarging. At dinner they talked several times about collaboration on a book about succulents. *Or forbs.*

She didn't laugh much for weeks following her release from the hospital. And Silvio, gnawed by guilt and complicity, debated if he should tell her what he knew. If...and when.

Silvio was savvy enough to know that someone, somewhere, would be conducting an investigation, and he knew that it would not be wise to be drawn into it, in any capacity. He decided that—while he might want to tell Jitka at some time in the future—he would wait at least two years before telling her the facts he knew. Once he made that decision, things were easier for him.

Did the destruction of an old, five-story, Arab-style apartment complex with office spaces on the first floor have any impact on piracy? Not really. Abdallah's building was destroyed, true, and so was Abdallah, his principal lieutenants and his wives and children. These were, from the Navy's perspective, simply collateral damage. The target was the Yemeni chief with direct ties to bin Laden. Other pirate bands operating out of Boosaaso moved quickly to fill the spaces left by the deaths in Boosaaso. Actually, for many Somalis it created some significant job opportunities.

In subsequent years of a new administration, it is unclear how the U.S. response to piracy off the Horn of Africa is likely to change. To date, the response by the UN appears to have been totally ineffective, and no nation has appeared willing to provoke an international response by employing a proactive approach to pirate suppression. Based on evidence available to the public, it appears that shippers and insurers are treating piracy as part of the cost of doing business. Something resembling the protection rackets that thrive in many of the world's largest cities.

Piracy in the 21st Century is not just alive; it is thriving. There are risks, but the rewards are sometimes great.

Oh! One final thing. That little Somali-American bastard from Minneapolis flew back to the U.S. and is living at home with his family. Hopefully, some day he'll get what's coming to him.

Late news:
In March 2010, private security guards aboard a Panamanian-flagged, Saudi-owned ship repelled a pirate attack by shooting up a skiff and killing a Somali pirate. A Spanish warship arrived on the scene, arrested the surviving pirates, sank the mother ship and transferred the body and survivors to an unidentified nation.

According to the Associated Press report: Legal experts said there is no consensus on who is responsible for investigating the incident.

"This will be scrutinized very closely," said Arvinder Sambei, a legal consultant for the United Nation's anti-piracy program.

"There's always been concern about these (private security) companies," Sambei says. "Who are they responsible to? The bottom line is somebody has been killed and someone has to give an accounting for that."

A BRIEF GLOSSARY OF FOREIGN WORDS, U.S. MILITARY ACRONYMS, ETC.

Since much of the action in this story takes place in East Africa, many of the words encountered are in African languages. Since it would be inconvenient to explain every term where it is encountered, it seemed reasonable to rely on context to provide a general idea for the term employed. Where this fails the Glossary should help. All words are Somali unless otherwise noted. Acronyms—many in common use—are in English, but may not be familiar to every reader.

Abaya, Veil, a long black dress, cloak like, worn by Muslim women in Arabia and many parts of Africa

Abid, Slave

AC, Air Conditioner

Afwayne, Big mouth, the Somali name for former president, Siad Barré

Alhamdulillah, *Arabic*, Formal part of response, "Fine" to query, "How are you?"

Al-Shabab, or Shabaab, *Arabic*, The youth. An armed, Islamist militia comprised largely of rootless young men who control most of southern Somalia and parts of the rest of the country. These youth, influenced by Al Qaeda, promote the return to Sharia law

Angello, a kind of Somali pancake, buttered and sugared, like French toast

Asalaamaleikum, *Arabic*. Peace be unto you. A formal greeting

ASW, U.S. mil. Anti-Submarine Warfare

Baari, A pious slave, said of women. Women who are *baari* are totally subservient to their husbands. They become well-trained work animals, tolerating everything.

Beira, *(Dorcotragus megalotis)* One of several small, handsome antelopes found in Horn of Africa. The Beira occupy the mountainous region just inland from Somalia's northern coast along the Gulf of Aden, in the region known as Warsengeli

Bismillah, *Arabic,* In the name of Allah

BOQ, U.S. mil., Bachelor Officer Quarters

CJTF-HOA, U.S. mil., Combined Joint Task Force-Horn of Africa, The military response to terrorism and piracy in the Near East, joining the military forces of the U.S. NATO allies and members of the European Union.

COSCO, China Overseas Shipping Corporation

CPO, U.S. mil., Chief Petty Officer

Dallill, Loss of face, an embarrassment or property destruction as an offense resulting in the payment of damages or blood money

Dammin, Damminin, Dunce, dunces

Dayr, Rainy season. Somalia has two rainy seasons. Gu and dayr. Dayr is the second rainy season, lasting from October to December.

Dhagah, Stone

Dibaad, Bride wealth. A portion of the bride's wealth that is returned to the groom's family to be awarded to the new couple as a wedding gift. In effect, the bride is purchased by the groom's family, but part of that price comes back to the wedded couple. Think of it as 'kickback."

Dikdik, *(Madoqua piacentini)* A small graceful antelope, native to the Horn of Africa, whose range extends along Somalia's south-east coast.

Dil, Homicide, as an offence resulting in the payment of damages

Dirha, A long, flowing Somali dress.

Diya, Blood Wealth, A term related cross-tribal offences from murder to loss of property, which can only be resolved by the transfer of wealth.

Djinn, Sometimes djinni, or jinni. A spirit that can take human or animal form with supernatural powers over normal humans

DOD, U.S. mil., Department of Defense

Doqon, Dumb, dumb as a date palm, dumb as a post

EU NAVFOR, U.S. mil., European Union—Naval Forces, the group assigned to the Indian Ocean region.

Flechette, One dictionary definion for this term: A steel missile or dart dropped from an airplane, used in World War I. From the French word, *fleche*, Arrow.

Gaalo, Infidel, usually translated as white unbeliever, also *kufr*.

Goon, Wounding, as an offense resulting in the payment of damages

Guban, Harsh land, scrub land

Guntiino, A woman's large, loose-fitting garment

Hadith, *Arabic*, Ahadith, plural, Documented teachings or actions of prophet Mohammed (xyzzyx) which were not contained in the Quran, but were verified by family members or close companions of the Prophet and are part of the tradition.

Halal, *Arabic*, permitted under Islamic law

Haram, *Arabic*, forbidden under Islamic law

Haud, South. In the dialect of Somalia's north, this designation refers to the extensive grassy plains in the central and western portions of Somalia abutting and extending into Ethiopia's Ogaden region. The area of good grazing land has been fought over by Somalia and Ethiopia for more than a century

Heer, An assembly of males and females of the same clan or sub-clan grouping who pay to belong and agree to abide by the common decisions of the group. It is, by tradition, one of the most important political institutions in Somalia. The groups may include several thousand members. Males over fifteen can speak and vote, but women can do neither

Hidjab, Hijab, A female covering. Usually zippered

HOA, U.S. mil., abbreviation for Horn of Africa

Innaa Lillaahi wa innaa Illaahi raaji'uun, *Arabic*, From Allah we come and to Allah we return

Inshallah, *Arabic* If Allah wills it

JCS, U.S. mil., abbreviation for Joint Chiefs of Staff

IMB, acronym for International Maritime Bureau, an organization that collects data relative to pirate attacks, and other activities of interest to the maritime community.

JDAM U.S. mil., acronym for Joint Direct Attack Munition. This device is a tailkit designed to fit an existing inventory of bombs from all services, which makes the bombs steerable as controlled by on-board guidance systems. Existing weapons have greater range, accuracy and penetrating power. Basically, this device converts a conventional, free-falling bomb into a precision-guided, "smart" weapon.

Jellaba, *Arabic* Also djellabah, a loose-fitting, hooded gown or robe worn by men. Popular in North Africa and other parts of Africa.

Jiilaal, the first season of the Somali year, December to March, the hot, dry, dusty season that is the year's harshest for Somali nomads.

Jilbab, a Somali covering for a woman's neck and head, large, bulky, up to nine yards of cloth

Kaffir, Arabic, from *kafir*, "infidel," or "unbeliever." The Arabic verb *kafara* mean "to deny."

<u>Kintirleey,</u> She with the clitoris, a term used to describe girls who have not been infibulated—female circumcision; and suturing. From kintir, the anatomical part.

<u>Kiristaan,</u> Christian

<u>LDS,</u> Church of Jesus Christ of Latter Day Saints, commonly known as Mormons.

<u>Ma'alim,</u> Teacher

<u>Magalo,</u> The city, (i.e megalopolis)

<u>Marsa, Mersa,</u> *Arabic,* harbor, port

<u>MashAllah,</u> *Arabic,* If Allah wills it

<u>Mina', Mînaî,</u> *Arabic,* port

<u>MSF,</u> *French,* Medicins Sans Frontieres, Doctors Without Borders

<u>PAM,</u> U.S. mil., acronym for Penetration Augmented Munitions, an explosive penetration weapon of the type sometimes called "shaped charge."

<u>PAO,</u> U.S. mil., Public Affairs Officer.

<u>Perim,</u> *Arabic,* A small, waterless, volcanic island in the Strait of Mandeb (Bab el Mandeb) about 90 miles west of Aden. Its area is about five square miles. Once in the hands of France it later was managed by the British, who from 1857 to 1936 used it as a coaling station and a site for a lighthouse. Today it belongs to Yemen. In Joseph Conrad's novel, *Lord Jim,* the ship *Patna* was on a course for *Perim* on her journey to the Red Sea when the misadventure began.

<u>Qat,</u> A narcotic leaf of a small tree; widely chewed in East Africa and Yemen to induce euphoria. Also Qaat, Khat and other variant spellings. Widely grown in Yemen.

<u>Sharia,</u> Islamic law, based on injunctions contained in the Quran and subsequent interpretations established in Islamic traditions.

<u>UAV</u>, U.S. mil., Unmanned Aerial Vehicle; a military drone.

<u>Warsengeli</u>, The mountainous highlands region on the north coast of the Horn of Africa, in the neighborhood of the port city of Boosaaso.

<u>WHO</u>, World Health Organization.

<u>Yarad</u>, Bride-wealth, the amount paid by the groom's family to the bride's family. A substantial portion of the wealth, which may be mostly in the form of livestock, is ritually returned to the groom's family and often constitutes a wedding present to the new couple

<u>Xyzzyx</u>. This is not a word, but rather a symbol used here exclusively. In Arabic typography, a complex character, a contraction perhaps comparable to the ampersand, is used in writing. In the language of Islam, it is common to repeat a formula every time the Prophet's name is mentioned. ('May God exalt his mention and protect him from imperfection). In written documents this is cumbersome and space consuming, so Arab typography has created a character that has no equivalent outside that language. Typographically, it takes the same space as a single character. When you encounter *Xyzzyx*, the formula may be inserted. Hopefully, this contraction will not earn a fatwa.